PARA BELLUM

(ARK ROYAL, BOOK XIII)

CHRISTOPHER G. NUTTALL

ISBN: 9781792772351

Cover by Justin Adams
http://www.variastudios.com/

http://www.chrishanger.net
http://chrishanger.wordpress.com/
http://www.facebook.com/ChristopherGNuttall

All Comments Welcome!

DEAR READERS

I must apologise for the long delay between this book being announced as a forthcoming project and its appearance. However, as I'm sure you'll agree, I have a good excuse.

As you may know, if you follow my blog, my health began to deteriorate in November 2017 and, after a brief period when I thought the problem was behind me, started to collapse again in April 2018. The doctors tried several possible approaches before discovering, thanks to a private MRI/CT scan my wife insisted I take, that I had lymphoma. Chemotherapy was prescribed. This may just have been in time to save my life. I collapsed when I went for the first set of treatments, allowing the doctors to realise that I *also* had a nasty chest infection.

I ended up spending three weeks in the hospital, having antibiotics fed into my system and my lung drained of fluid. This was not a pleasant experience and I found myself being moved between the haematology ward and the high-dependency care unit, depending on my exact condition. Eventually, they gave me the first treatment in two sections and—after my health started to improve—allowed me to go home. I was not, however, in a good condition for some time afterwards. The side effects made it hard to eat, at first, and then I caught a cold because my immune system had been badly weakened by the treatments. It was some time before I was able to muster the energy to finish this book.

Obviously, I hope to regain full health once the treatments have been finished. I have a backlog of story ideas I want to write, including the start of a new *The Empire's Corps* arc and a couple of completely new universes that need developing. (I spent a lot of time thinking of ideas while lying in that hospital bed.) If you want to pray for me, please do.

I hope to finish the *Invincible* trilogy sooner rather than later, too, but I cannot guarantee anything. Please bear with me.

Thank you,
Christopher G. Nuttall
Edinburgh, 2018

DEDICATION

To the doctors and nurses of the Western General Hospital,
who took very good care of me and
probably saved my life, as well as this book.
Thank you.
CGN

CONTENTS

PROLOGUE I

From: Admiral Kathy Lauder, UK BIOPREP
To: Admiral Sir John Naiser, First Space Lord
Classification: Top Secret, Eyes-Only FSL

John.

MY OFFICIAL CONCLUSIONS ARE in the report forwarded to your office, which you can read at your leisure. My unofficial conclusion is that I'm bloody terrified. Bioweapons have been a constant threat since every kid with a modified chemistry set could start brewing up something nasty in his parents' basement, and we saw a whole string of nasty outbreaks during the Age of Unrest, but this is an order of magnitude more dangerous than anything we've seen. The concept of a virus that could pass from one species to another was the stuff of low-budget fiction, until now. A sentient alien virus, capable of infecting humans as easily as the common cold, must be reckoned a serious threat. We may find it very difficult to defend ourselves.

We can and we will take precautions. The virus does not appear to cope well with ultraviolet light, allowing us to ensure it doesn't spread through the air. We have had some success with experimental counter-viral treatments, when those treatments are carried out within a few short hours of infection. We can be fairly sure of catching an infected person within a few hours, through the use of a simple blood test. However, once the virus starts to infect the body's organs and builds control structures, we have been unable to do more than slow it down. Euthanasia may be the only logical response, particularly once the virus reaches the brain. It isn't clear—yet—if the virus is capable of masquerading as the infected person, but I think we have to assume that it can and it will. Our people may be subverted and turned against us. It is vitally important that we perform regular blood tests within all sensitive installations.

Worse, there is no reason to assume that the infections will be limited only to humanity—and our alien allies. We believe the virus can spread into animals too, presenting us with a unique threat. The prospect of dogs—or smaller animals, like rats—being used to carry the virus into human settlements cannot be overlooked. In the event of a major outbreak on Earth, Admiral, we must assume our own ecosystem will be turned against us. The absolute worst case scenario suggests that the virus can even infect our entire ecology. It is vitally important that we *don't* let the virus gain a foothold on Earth. If necessary, we will need to destroy any infection with nuclear weapons.

My team has not, as yet, been able to put together a coherent scenario for the virus's evolution. However, given its aggressive nature and ability to cross the species barrier, it seems likely that the virus is not remotely natural. Someone *designed* it, Admiral; someone designed it as a weapon. I don't know if the creators unleashed it as a final shot at enemies they couldn't defeat by any normal means, or if it broke loose and destroyed its own creators before starting to ravage the rest of the galaxy, but I don't believe it's natural. It's just too effective a killing machine. If we can find its creators, we may be able to convince them to stop their virus before it destroys us and every other known sentient race. If not...

Of course, some people might consider that whistling in the dark.

PROLOGUE II

IT WAS VERY QUIET IN THE UNDERGROUND CHAMBER.

President Aleksandr Sergeyevich Nekrasov lifted his head from the report and looked at the other two men—and one woman—sitting at the table. Their faces were carefully blank, the result of a lifetime spent struggling for power and security. None of them dared betray their thoughts too openly. The slightest hint of weakness might prove disastrous. It might cost them their lives. And yet, Aleksandr could tell they were scared. They were the most powerful people in Russia, but were they powerful enough to stand against the latest interstellar menace? He had a feeling that they were about to find out.

He spoke, with heavy irony. "Your comments, gentlemen?"

Admiral Svetlana Zadornov smiled, humourlessly. "We made a serious mistake, Mr. President."

Aleksandr studied her for a long moment, knowing that she was almost certainly the most ambitious—and dangerous—person in the room. Women in Russia were expected to marry and have at least four children by the time they reached their mid-twenties, not go into the navy and fight their way up the ladder to flag rank. Svetlana had faced a whole string of challenges, from lecherous instructors to alien battleships, and she'd overcome them all. She was good. She *had* to be good. The only thing keeping her from being an even greater threat was her sex…and that might not matter, if she laid the groundwork properly. She was a national hero as well as a naval star.

He cocked his eyebrow. "How so?"

Svetlana had no patience for political bullshit. "We assumed that we were dealing with another alien race, one akin to the Tadpoles or the Foxes. We believed that we could make contact—covert contact—and manipulate events to our advantage. Instead, we have betrayed the human race to an… to an alien virus. We must assume that *Dezhnev* was taken and her crew… assimilated. The Great Powers will be furious."

"If they find out," Director Igor Ivanovich Zaitsev said, smoothly. The FSB Director leaned forward, his cold eyes moving from face to face. "The ship's captain had orders to destroy his vessel rather than let her fall into enemy hands, did he not?"

"Yes," Svetlana said. "But we have no guarantee he was able to carry out those orders. He might have been lured into talks, while the virus steadily overcame his crew. There's no sense, from the British reports, that our vaccinations will be enough to stop the virus in its tracks. The ship might well have been taken with datacores intact."

"And if the virus can take control of the crew, they'll happily unlock the datacores for their new masters," General Stepan Viktorovich Dyakov rumbled. "They'll be turned into willing traitors."

"Yes, General," Svetlana said. "*Dezhnev* did not carry a full database, a sensible precaution when the ship intended to make contact with an unknown alien race, but she still carried enough information to make life very difficult. The virus, assuming it took the ship intact, now knows the layout of human space."

Aleksandr kept his face impassive, somehow. The Solar Treaty—rewritten after the Tadpoles had taught humanity that it wasn't alone in the universe—had made it clear that *no* new alien races were to learn *anything* of the human sphere's inner workings until contact had been established and humanity was sure it wasn't about to be attacked again. A hostile alien race would have to spend a great deal of time surveying the tramlines before they found the ones that led to the more densely-populated worlds—and Earth itself. Humanity could use that time to set up defensive lines and prepare for war. But if the virus had captured an intact navigational datacore, the virus would already know where to attack. His bid to break Russia free of its shackles might have led to disaster for the entire human race.

He wanted to shout his fury and frustration to the stars. The other Great Powers had never forgiven, let alone forgotten, how Aleksandr's predecessor had tried to use bioweapons on the Tadpoles during peace negotiations. Russia had seen no choice—it was the only way to recover their principal colony and its population—but it had been a disastrous failure. Nothing had been said publicly, there had been no angry denunciations of Russia… yet, trade and investment had almost dried up. The country had been badly weakened. It had practically had to mortgage its future to remain a Great Power. Aleksandr was all too aware that keeping up with the latest military technology was costing his country dearly. And yet, they *had* to keep up. The rising powers would not hesitate to displace Russia if they thought they could get away with it.

The Indians already tried to displace the British, Aleksandr thought. *And the British were in a far stronger position than ourselves.*

He looked down at the report for a long moment, trying not to think about the people on the streets outside. They'd made huge sacrifices, they'd allowed the state to dictate to them…and yet, they were trapped in an austere nightmare. Mother Russia could feed her children—*that* was no longer a problem, thanks to modern technology—but they had little in the way of luxury or hope. Aleksandr knew there were grumblers, people complaining that their lives were drab and empty. The FSB had it under control, he'd been assured, but he knew better than to take that for granted. Life in Russia was steadily becoming worse. How long would it be until Moscow exploded into revolution, once again?

Svetlana cleared her throat. "There is nothing to be gained from recriminations," she said, dryly. "We have to decide how to proceed."

How generous, Aleksandr thought. Svetlana was sneakily making it clear that *she* wasn't going to call their attention to the fact that *she* was the one who'd argued against sending a covert contact team—and, in doing so, was quietly rubbing their noses in it. *And how do you intend to use this to unseat me?*

"We have to assume the worst," Svetlana continued. "The virus knows that we intended to betray our fellow humans. It may seek to use that against us. If it truly understands human psychology, it will see it as a gamble worth taking. It can certainly present enough proof to overcome doubt and suspicion from the other Great Powers."

"Great," Zaitsev said, sarcastically.

"Therefore, we need to take action," Svetlana said. "We have to act before it can take advantage of its newfound knowledge. And I know how we should proceed."

CHAPTER ONE

THE CHAMBER, CAPTAIN SIR STEPHEN SHIELDS thought as he faced his judges, had cost the Royal Navy a great deal of money. No expense had been spared in a bid to make it clear that justice *would* be done, from the magnificent wooden boxes for the judges to the smaller chair and table for himself and his lawyer. He couldn't help thinking that the giant painting of the king hanging from the far wall was worth a few million pounds. The entire courtroom had probably cost as much as a cruiser. He wondered, rather sardonically, how they intended to explain the expense during the next audit. The Royal Navy had been having problems funding the latest generation of ships even before *Invincible* had stumbled across a whole new threat.

He kept his face as impassive as possible, despite a growing headache, as his judges hurled question after question at him. It was hard, so hard, to keep from snapping at them as they asked the same question time and time again, sometimes rephrasing the words in a bid to catch him out. They weren't interested in the truth, he felt. The five flag officers facing him were more interested in politics than the threat facing the entire human race. He wondered, sourly, just who'd smoothed their path through the navy. His family had enemies. They'd have worked overtime to make sure that *their* people were in place to push for a court-martial.

"No, sir," he said, in response to a particularly irritating question. "I feel that my ship and crew performed adequately."

An admiral leaned forward. "Captain, some of our analysts believe that you didn't make enough of an attempt at opening communications," he said. "What do you say to that?"

Some of our analysts, Stephen thought. *The ones who give the answers they know their masters want?*

He braced himself. "As you can see from my records, *Admiral*, we did attempt to open communications. However, we came under enemy fire. Further attempts at opening communications were unsuccessful—and, when we realised what we were facing, we understood why. There is little hope of opening a dialogue when someone simply *won't* talk to you."

"But you should have tried," the Admiral said.

Stephen felt his temper start to snap. He ignored the warning nudge from his lawyer. "With all due respect, Admiral, firing on someone is *also* a form of communication. The aliens—the virus—wanted us dead."

Another admiral chuckled. "He's got you there, Fred."

The first admiral glowered. "Captain Shields, you used classified technology to make your escape. In doing so, you revealed its existence to the enemy. How do you justify *that*?"

Stephen felt a hot flash of anger. They'd been over *that* three times already. He was tempted to suggest they simply refer to the written record, but he knew they wouldn't listen. They wanted to hear it from the horse's mouth. Again.

"*Invincible* needed to return home safely, carrying her cargo of precious knowledge," Stephen said, flatly. "We had lost contact with the Russians and we had no way to be *sure* that any previous messages would reach Falkirk, let alone Earth. Accordingly, I saw no option but to deploy every weapon in our arsenal to ensure that my ship made it safely through the tramline and escaped."

He allowed his voice to harden. "I understand the importance of keeping secret weapons secret until they are actually used, Admiral, but we had

2

no choice. I had to do everything in my power to maximise our chances of escape. Deploying classified technology was, in my judgement, the only thing to do. What would you do in my place?"

There was a long silence. Stephen waited, wondering what the admiral would say? He'd bet half his salary that his questioners had never commanded starships, even during peacetime. No, they'd stayed home and nitpicked from the comfort of their armchairs...he shook his head in exasperation. He knew that, sometimes, officers made mistakes. But they rarely had anything like enough time to think of the perfect solution.

The chairman cleared his throat. "I believe we've gone as far as we can for the day," he said, making a show of checking his watch. "Captain Shields, thank you for your time. You'll have our decision by the end of the week."

Unless you want to call me back for some worthless questioning, Stephen thought. *You've heard everything I can tell you—twice, perhaps—and you still want to waste my time.*

He kept that thought off his face. "Thank you, Mr. Chairman," he said. It was hard not to allow sarcasm to slip into his voice. "I am at your disposal."

His lawyer walked next to him as they headed for the hatch. "They're unsure how to proceed," he muttered. "As long as they're asking questions, they don't have to make any decisions."

"No wonder they're not on command decks," Stephen muttered back. A starship captain had to make a decision and stick to it, even if that meant putting his neck on the line, not waffle endlessly until his ship was blown into dust and plasma. "Seriously, what's our chances?"

The lawyer said nothing until they walked through the hatch and into the corridor. "I'd say sixty-forty they recommend that all charges be dropped," he said. "There's no moment of egregious misconduct from you, Captain, and without that they'll have some problems justifying putting you in front of a court-martial board. I think they'll be happier *not* trying to try a national hero."

Stephen shrugged. One half of the country had considered him a hero when he and his ship had returned, bringing warning of a new interstellar war; the other half had seen him as a villain, the bearer of bad news. *That half would believe—they'd* want *to believe—that Stephen had fucked up First Contact so badly that a multispecies alien confederation had declared war on Earth. And, because of his family connections, his fate wouldn't be decided by the navy. Parliament would become involved. The final decision wouldn't be based on anything he'd actually* done, *but on what was politically acceptable.*

And my superiors will throw me under the shuttlecraft, he thought, sourly. The First Space Lord had signalled his support, but Stephen had no illusions. If the politicians wanted him punished, he'd be punished. *Perhaps I should have gone into law instead, or sought an easy seat in Parliament.*

He shook his head. He loved the navy. He loved command. And the situation was *not* hopeless. His family's enemies would have to find a figleaf of justification before they could hang him—perhaps literally—and, so far, no such justification had materialised. He had to keep fighting if he wanted to return to his ship. *Invincible* was currently being repaired, under his XO's command. He was damned if he was just letting go of command after how hard he'd had to work to get it.

A young midshipwoman ran up and saluted. "Captain Shields?"

Stephen returned her salute. "Yes?"

"Sir, a car has arrived for you," the midshipwoman said. "It's waiting at the main gate."

Stephen dismissed his lawyer and hurried down the stairs to the main gate. A large black limousine, with tinted windows, was waiting for him. A uniformed chauffeur stepped out of the front door as Stephen approached, saluted him, and opened the rear door. Stephen was not remotely surprised to see his brother sitting in the vehicle. It was the sort of thing his brother would do.

"Duncan," he said, stiffly. "What are you doing here?"

"Get in," Duncan said. "We don't have much time."

Stephen hesitated, then climbed into the limousine. The chauffeur closed the door behind him. Silence fell, abruptly. Duncan gestured to a seat; Stephen looked around, noting the silent maid lingering at the back of the vehicle, then sat down. The vehicle hummed into life a moment later. There was barely any sense of motion.

"Our latest car," Duncan said. He sounded as if he'd built the limo himself. "What do you think?"

Stephen snorted. "How much of the family fortune did you waste on this...this white elephant?"

"I assure you that this vehicle isn't *useless*," Duncan said. "We have a minibar, a small portable cooker, desks and chairs and, of course, secure links to the datanet. I can conduct my business while travelling around the country."

"You could also get from one end of the country to the other in less than an hour," Stephen pointed out, although he knew it was a waste of time. Duncan had always believed an aristocrat had to *look* wealthy as well as be wealthy. The family name *demanded* a show of conspicuous consumption. Stephen had never believed that, but then he'd gone into the navy, where efficiency was prized over everything else. "I assume you have a reason for meeting me?"

Duncan smiled. "Do I need a reason to speak to my little brother?"

"You never said a word to me at school," Stephen said. "Ever."

"You know as well as I do that older kids are not supposed to talk to the younger kids," Duncan said. That was unfortunately true. "I'm sure I said a word or two to you during the holidays. And did I not speak to you after we *both* left school?"

Stephen shrugged. "And now?"

Duncan met his eyes. "The Leader of the Opposition has been trying to figure out a way to use your court-martial to bring down the government," he said. "However, it doesn't look as though you gave them enough rope to hang the Prime Minister. I doubt a vote of no confidence could be passed right now."

"That's something," Stephen said. He'd always disliked politics, even though he'd been brought up in an aristocratic family. The navy life was far simpler. "What now?"

"They'll try and find some kind of face-saving solution, I suppose," Duncan said. "They staked too much on you. Now, they need to find a way to let you go without making it look as though they were tormenting you for fun and games. I imagine they'll redefine the whole courtroom session as a fact-finding mission."

"They certainly found a great many facts," Stephen said, dryly. "When can I go back to my ship?"

"When they figure out a way to save face." Duncan shrugged. "We're not going to hammer them too hard over the issue—the government's majority is too thin—but they won't take that for granted. They'll assume we'll take full advantage of their mistake."

"Perhaps you should," Stephen said. "*Really* try and put the boot in."

"We wouldn't be able to do enough damage to matter," Duncan said. "And we don't want a political catfight right now. The country is unsettled enough."

He tapped a switch. The tinted windows became transparent. Stephen frowned as he realised where they were. The limo was crossing Admiralty Bridge, heading towards Whitehall, driving past a steady stream of protesters. Many of them were carrying signs, protesting against the new war. He sucked in his breath, sharply. They were walking so closely together that the virus would have a field day, if one of the protesters was infected. They'd all be infected soon enough.

"I thought large gatherings were going to be banned," he said, as he spotted a handful of policemen. They were watching the crowd, but making no attempt to break it up. "What happened?"

Duncan gave him a sharp look. "Political realities," he said, curtly. He tapped the switch again. The windows darkened. "Shutting down the schools is one thing, but shutting down everything else is quite another. And there's no reason to believe the virus has reached Earth."

Stephen gritted his teeth. There had been a number of starships at Wensleydale that hadn't known to take extensive precautions against biological contamination, even though they were dealing with a previously-unknown alien race. And some of those ships had disappeared. It was tempting to believe that their crews had managed to hit the self-destruct before they'd been overwhelmed, but he didn't dare believe it. Planetary defence networks had orders to destroy the ships on sight, yet...it would be easy to sneak a shuttle down to the surface and begin the infection. Earth might already have been infected.

"Those idiots are going to get themselves killed," he snarled. "And they'll get a lot of innocent people killed with them."

"Perhaps," Duncan said. "But they also don't want war."

Stephen laughed, harshly. "Do you suppose the universe *cares* what they want?"

"No," Duncan said. He sounded as though he understood. "But they do have good reasons for *wanting* it."

"I know," Stephen said.

He shook his head. He understood, too. Of course he understood. Twenty years ago, the First Interstellar War had brought the human race to the brink of defeat. The Tadpoles had bombarded Earth, killing millions of humans and destroying the work of hundreds of years. And then Britain had skirmished with India, shortly before the *Second* Interstellar War had pitted humanity and its enemies-turned-allies against a pair of alien races that had made common cause and set out to conquer the galaxy together. The human race had seen too much change in the past few years, too many reminders that the universe was red in tooth and claw. He was uneasily aware that Britain—and the remainder of the Great Powers—had lost so much that *something* was going to break. And now...

And now, we have a whole new war, against an extremely dangerous and deadly race, he thought. *I'd vote against it too if I thought it would make a difference.*

"We're switching to a full war footing now, aren't we?" Stephen met his brother's eyes, hoping to see confirmation. "Aren't we?"

"We are," Stephen confirmed. "The Opposition's grown-ups realise that the threat exists, even though their backbenchers want to use the crisis to demand concessions. We're preparing for war at breakneck speed."

Stephen nodded, relieved. The Royal Navy had been taken unawares by the new threat, but a great many lessons had been learnt during the First Interstellar War. *This* time, procedures were in place to call up the reserves, draw weapons and spare parts from stockpiles that had been extensively built up during peacetime and prepare to go on the offensive. Starships were probably already being dispatched to Falkirk, the point of contact, in hopes of blunting an alien offensive before it could reach the more populated parts of the human sphere. He was fairly sure the Admiralty was already considering ways to go on the offensive. No one ever won a war by sitting still and waiting to be hit.

But we have no idea of just how much territory they control, he reminded himself. *They might be expecting us to launch an offensive; hell, they may intend to destroy the invasion fleet and then follow up with a full-scale offensive of their own.*

"There is a cost, of course," Duncan added. "Do you know how many people are reservists?"

"No," Stephen said.

"There's always been a push to favour reservists when it comes to selecting candidates for a job," Duncan said. "The family industries have done their part. But if the reservists are called up to go to war, there's going to be a problem replacing them. Losing one reservist isn't a bad thing, but losing *all* of them at once...there is no way replacements for everyone can be invited to apply, be interviewed and accepted before the losses start to bite."

He shook his head. "And that problem is affecting the entire country," he said. "I dare say it's going to get worse before it gets better."

"Probably," Stephen said. "But think how much worse it will be if we lose."

"I know that," Duncan snapped. "But how many people don't grasp the sheer scale of the threat? There were all sorts of problems during the Second Interstellar War. They'll be worse here."

"Probably," Stephen said, again. Civilians didn't understand the realities of interstellar warfare. A threat might be a few hundred light-years away, but that didn't mean it couldn't touch Earth. "I can't wait to go back to space."

"I don't blame you," Duncan told him. There was an oddly wistful tone in his voice. "I wish I could go to space too."

The limo came to a halt. Stephen looked up as the door opened, revealing the chauffeur and a darkening sky. He glanced at his watch as Duncan rose and climbed out of the vehicle. It was seven o'clock. And yet, it was strikingly quiet. He frowned as he followed his brother onto the streets. London was a city that never slept. Normally, the streets would be filled with tourists making their way to the theatres or the city's vast selection of cafes and restaurants. There was nowhere else in the entire world that had so many diversions for the educated palate. And yet, the city was quiet. Even the hum of traffic was dulled.

"The club's still open," Duncan said. "I thought I'd treat you to dinner."

Stephen glowered at his retreating back. "And the rest of the city?"

"Martial law has been declared," Duncan reminded him. "The city is shutting down for the night."

Good, Stephen thought. He snorted, rudely, as they walked past the bowing doorman and headed up the stairs. Naturally, the aristocracy had ensured that *their* spaces were spared the attention of the law. *But the population will not be pleased.*

He shook his head as they passed a cluster of UV lights. The public would not be pleased, if they realised what was happening. There was nothing to be gained by shutting down the city's nightlife to prevent infection if a handful of select clubs were allowed to remain open. And yet, it would help keep the population alive, if the virus reached Earth...

...And that, as far as he was concerned, was all that mattered.

CHAPTER TWO

SHE WAS NOT, *PRECISELY*, A PRISONER.

Captain (Marines) Alice Campbell lay on her back in the hospital ward, as naked as the day she was born. Her hands and feet were secured with thin metal straps, strong enough to hold an enhanced human, while cold light blazed down at all hours of the day. It wasn't quite as bad as the dreaded Conduct After Capture course—no one was hitting her, or threatening to rape her—but it was still unpleasant. There were few luxuries in the room and none of them made up for being trapped. She was uneasily aware that she was losing muscle tone with every day that passed on her back.

She looked up at the holographic images playing over her head and scowled. The doctors probably thought they were being kind and sensitive, when they'd refused her access to any news channels, but she found it frustrating. She wanted to know what was going on, damn it! No one had been very informative since she'd been taken from *Invincible*, save for a nurse who'd told her she'd been moved to a highly-classified military base. Alice guessed she was on an asteroid. No one in their right mind would conduct biological warfare research on a planetary surface.

Probably some distance from the rest of the system, she thought, as she switched off the holograms. There was only so much *Doctor Who* one could stand before one started to go mad. *And probably quite close to the sun, for convenient disposal of any accidents.*

She sighed, inwardly. She was no expert on biological warfare, but her training had included simulations of operations in regions infected by genetically-engineered—and effectively incurable—diseases. The briefing officers had made it clear that the only defence against biological weapons involved engineering the disease themselves, then using the disease to create a vaccine. Alice had asked, after the briefing, if there was any difference between biological warfare defence research and biological *warfare* research. The briefing officer had hesitated to answer, then admitted—finally—that there was very little difference between the two. One had to play with fire in order to keep *others* from playing with fire.

A door opened. It was practically silent, but she'd been lying in the chamber long enough to become intimately familiar with every one of its sounds. She turned her head to see a figure, covered from head to toe, walking towards her. The doctors *never* entered the room without protective garments, even though she was constantly bathed in ultraviolet light. They were too scared of infection to show her their faces. She could barely see their eyes through their masks.

They have to be bloody uncomfortable, she thought, nastily. *She'd* tried to fight in protective suits, back during basic training, and it had been hot and sweaty. They'd also made easy targets. Hiding from enemy fire was hard enough when one *wasn't* wearing a heavy suit. *But they're right to be scared.*

"Alice," the doctor said. "Can you hear me?"

"I can't hear anything," Alice said, dryly. "Not a single word."

She knew she should cooperate, but she was growing sick of lying on her back. She was used to a complete lack of privacy—prudes didn't join the Royal Marines—but the isolation was getting to her. She wanted to *talk* to someone, someone she actually *liked*. She'd even chat with her sister if it meant being able to talk to someone who wasn't a doctor.

"That's good to hear," the doctor said, her sarcasm washing off him like water off a duck's back. "Are you ready to proceed?"

Alice looked up, interested. The doctors had promised a cure for the alien virus trying to take over her body, yet since she'd arrived at the asteroid base they'd been more interested in taking samples than actually curing her. She supposed her body was a living reservoir of alien virus, and she couldn't really blame the doctors for wanting as many samples as possible, but she wanted it *gone*. The aliens had infested her system. She wanted her body to be *hers* again.

And if the virus manages to adapt to their treatments, she thought, *it will take me over anyway.*

She shuddered at the thought. She wasn't scared of conventional threats. She knew she could handle anything any *human* opponent could mete out. They could hurt her, they could kill her, but they couldn't break her. But the alien virus didn't care about how mentally strong she was. Given time, it would worm its way into her brain and take over. There was no hope of resistance. It scared her more than she cared to admit.

The doctor leaned forward. "Are you alright? Your heartbeat just spiked."

"Bad thoughts, doctor," Alice said. "What are we going to do today?"

"We believe we can sweep the virus out of your system," the doctor said. "However, I must warn you that there is a high risk of death..."

Alice laughed, despite herself. "You *do* know what I do for a living?"

The doctor sounded irked. "I'm required to explain what is about to happen," he said. "A few years ago, a process of cellular rejuvenation was developed that—in theory—promised a form of immortality. Tests appeared promising, but experiments on living humans were universally disastrous. I'll spare you the medical technobabble, Alice. All you really need to know is that the process both rejuvenated and killed the body's cells. The operation was a success..."

"But the patient died," Alice finished. "Why do you think it will work on me?"

"It won't rejuvenate you," the doctor said. "What it *will* do, we think, is kill the alien cells. They are so profoundly different from yours that they can be taken out without risking your health."

"You think," Alice said. "What if you're wrong?"

"Then you die on the operating table," the doctor said, flatly. "If you need time to think about it…"

Alice shook her head. None of the other treatments had worked. The best she could hope for was remaining in the isolation ward, with constant treatments to keep the infection under tight control. The slightest mistake—or the virus successfully adapting to new circumstances—would end her life, once and for all. It was worth any risk to get rid of the virus. Besides, if she died, at least she'd be free. The thought of seeing her mother and grandparents again was tempting. She'd always believed there was *something* after death.

"Now, please," she said. "I see no reason to delay."

"They'll start setting up the equipment now," the doctor said. He walked around her slowly, studying her naked body. "Have you been feeling any differently recently?"

"Not really," Alice said. There were so many sensors placed against her skin that the doctors would know if there had been any changes. They were probably more aware of her body than she was. "Just the regular hot and cold flashes."

"The virus is a tricky customer and no mistake," the doctor said. "But we have made a start on understanding it."

"I hope so," Alice said. "Do you have a vaccine yet?"

"No," the doctor told her. "But we live in hope."

He sat by the side of her bed and chatted to her about nothing until the orderlies entered the room. Alice was almost grateful for his company, even though he had nothing useful to say. The doctors were under orders not to talk about current affairs…Alice *hoped* that meant that nothing had happened since *Invincible* had escaped the alien system. Her imagination provided too many dangerous scenarios. There could be a full-scale war going on right now, with hundreds of alien ships pouring into the human sphere, or the aliens could be mounting a stealth assault. She had no way to know.

We know how to detect the infected, she told herself. *And there's no way any ships will be allowed to land on Earth without being checked first.*

14

She felt the jerk as the orderlies detached the bed from the wall and pushed it towards the door. Alice looked up, interested, as they passed into the corridor, but it was as bare and bland as the average military base. There were no paintings on the walls, nothing that might make the setting a little more comfortable. The bed moved down the corridor, passed through a pair of airlocks and entered an operations theatre. A large machine, covered with glowing lights and computer displays, squatted in the centre of the chamber. It took Alice a moment to realise that they were going to put her inside the machine.

"Your heartbeat is picking up again," the doctor said. "Are you alright?"

"Yes," Alice snapped. She took a deep breath, controlling her fears. She'd been through worse. She'd been through a *lot* worse. "What's...what's going to happen?"

"You're going inside the machine," the doctor told her. "You'll hear a buzzing sound, but you shouldn't feel anything. And then we'll take you out once the process is completed."

Dead or alive, Alice thought, morbidly.

She felt her body start to tense as the orderlies carefully inserted the bed into the machine and pushed her inside. Alice had never been particularly claustrophobic—and her training had cured her of what little she'd had—but she still felt nervous as the hatch closed behind her head. She was lying in a long metal tube that resembled a coffin...she told herself, sharply, to stop worrying. If the process worked, she could return to duty; if the process failed...well, she hoped the platoon would say something nice about her during the funeral. And then they'd get drunk at the wake and swap lies about her. She hoped they'd be good lies.

I wasn't a failure, she thought, as she waited. *They wouldn't have promoted me if I'd failed.*

"We're about to begin," a voice said. It was loud enough to make her jump. "Are you ready?"

"Yes," Alice said. She calmed herself, again. "I'm ready."

"You shouldn't feel anything," the voice told her. "If you do, please let us know."

"Yes, sir," Alice said, tiredly. "Get on with it."

There was a long pause, then she felt the machine start to vibrate. The buzzing started a second later, sending chills down her spine. It felt as if she was trapped inside a wood chipper. It was hard to escape the sense that she was about to be tossed down the chute to her doom, even though she knew better. Her body started to quiver a moment later. It felt as though she was standing under a very hot sun. No, it felt as though she was sunburnt... under the skin. The buzzing grew louder. She gritted her teeth and tried to force herself to relax, somehow. Her skin started to crawl. It felt as though a hundred fingers were drifting over her bare skin...

A stab of pain shot through her. For an insane moment, she thought she'd been stabbed everywhere, that a knife had stabbed her...her mind spun as she struggled to make sense of her feelings. She'd been stabbed...no, she hadn't been stabbed. Fire burned along her veins, tearing at her sanity... she told herself, firmly, that the alien cells were burning up. Her emotions were completely out of control, flashes of rage followed by quivering fear and burning arousal. She felt her arms and legs jerk, despite the restraints. It felt as though she was convulsing, as if death was not far away.

She thought she saw, just for a moment, her father standing in front of her. She felt a hot flash of anger before realising that it was just a hallucination. She had no interest in seeing the old man again, not after he'd murdered his wife, Alice's mother. Maybe she had committed adultery. That was no excuse for murder, for forcing Alice and her sister to grow up with their grandparents and a succession of boarding schools. Her lips twitched. They'd asked if she really thought she could cope with military training. After boarding school, military training had been a snap. She certainly hadn't been one of those tough guys who'd cried when they realised they were sleeping away from home for the first time in their lives.

They didn't go to boarding school, she thought. For all the grumbling about military rations, the Royal Marines had better food than the boarding schools. Less unpleasant disciplinarians, too. The sergeants had been bastards, but they hadn't been *bastards. They'd have learnt better if they had.*

There was a hot stab of pain, stabbing right into her brain. Alice screamed, helplessly. She thought she heard someone trying to talk to her, but it was impossible to make out the words over her own screaming. She was on fire. Her entire body was burning. She screamed and screamed until the world went black...

...And she woke up in a different room.

She took a shuddering breath, swallowing hard as her body tried to retch. There was nothing in her stomach to throw up, she thought. She tested her restraints—she was still tied to the bed—and then lifted her head. Her skin looked normal, even though she was *sure* she should be nothing more than ashes. She didn't even look burnt. Her body felt...it took her a moment to realise that she felt normal.

"Good morning," a voice said. A man wearing a doctor's uniform peered down at her. "How are you feeling?"

Alice blinked at him. He wasn't wearing a protective suit. "Am I... am I safe?"

"We believe so," the doctor said. He looked to be in his late forties, old enough to be her father. His nametag read VENN. "How are you feeling?"

"Hungry," Alice said, after a moment. "Am I cured?"

"We killed the alien biological material in you," Venn told her. "You've been asleep for several days, Alice. We wanted to be sure it wouldn't grow back."

"And it didn't," Alice said. "Right?"

Venn smiled. "Right."

Alice tried to lift a hand. "Can I get up now?"

"If you like," the doctor said. He carefully undid the restraints, one by one. "I wouldn't push yourself too far though, Alice. You've been through hell."

"Hell was basic training," Alice said, dryly. She sat upright, looking down at herself. Her arms and legs felt uncomfortably flabby, unsurprisingly. She hadn't had any real exercise in weeks. "Is there anything to eat?"

"It's on the way," Venn said. "Alice, there are some things you need to know."

Alice swung her legs over the side of the bed and stood, gingerly. Stabs of pain flared up her legs, reminding her that she hadn't been allowed to *walk* for weeks. She cursed under her breath. It was going to take months to get back into condition, if the Royal Marines hadn't already given her a medical discharge. They certainly wouldn't let her take command of a company until she was back up to speed. She silently promised herself a long program of heavy-duty exercise, whatever else she had to do. She'd been the first woman to receive a commando badge. She was damned if she was just giving up.

"First, the virus did make one permanent change to your system," Venn said. "Your scent has changed in a manner we don't quite understand. We *think* it's a marker that you were infected, a marker that other infected would be able to sense, but we don't know for sure. We also can't find a way to fix it. The aliens may always consider you one of them."

"That's something I may be able to use," Alice said, slowly. She sniffed her palm, experimentally. "I can't smell anything, though."

Venn nodded. "Most humans wouldn't be able to smell it," he said. "A dog, however...be careful around dogs. They're training dogs to sniff for infected now. You'll give them a false positive."

"Ouch," Alice said. "Anything else?"

"You've had quite an uncomfortable set of days," Venn told her. "You were lucky to be sedated. Now...you're going to be passing water at an accelerated rate until you finish passing the alien material out of your system and..."

Alice met his eyes. "When can I leave?"

"We would prefer to keep you under observation for several days," Venn said. "After that, if there's no sign of a relapse, we can release you. I don't know where the military will want you to go, afterwards. They may wish to keep a close eye on you."

"Probably," Alice said. She *had* been infected, after all. It was unlikely she'd be allowed to return to Earth. "I want to return to active duty."

"That's a matter for higher authority," Venn said. "I can certify that we have killed the alien biological matter in your blood, Alice, but I can't clear you for active duty."

Alice rubbed her forehead. No, Venn *couldn't* clear her. God knew she was in no state to return to active duty. She had to get back into shape, then endure interviews with the shrinks until they cleared her...if they ever did. They'd be worried about tiny fragments of alien biological matter hiding within her body. The virus might just be biding its time, waiting for her to leave isolation before it started to take over her body again. And yet... she could think of a dozen simple precautions. Surely, she wouldn't *have* to spend the rest of her life in isolation.

"I'll see what my superiors say," she said, as the door opened. An orderly entered, carrying a tray of food and drink. "And I will return to duty."

"I hope so," Venn said. "You've been very lucky, Alice. Everyone else we studied is too far gone to help. The alien virus left its mark on you, but them? They're never going to be free."

Alice shivered.

CHAPTER THREE

"WELL," FLIGHT LIEUTENANT MONICA SMITH SAID as they stood on the balcony and looked down at the starfighters on HMS *Invincible's* landing deck, "they don't *look* particularly photogenic."

Wing Commander Richard Redbird resisted—barely—the urge to make a rude gesture in her general direction. "Just because they don't *look* good doesn't mean they're *not* good," he said. "And just because you can't stand in front of them with your hair streaming in the wind doesn't mean you can't fly them."

Monica smirked. "I *did* get asked to model in front of the Tornadoes," she reminded him, mischievously. She struck a dramatic pose, pushing out her breasts. "My photo was on everyone's wall."

Richard rolled his eyes at her. Monica *had* been asked to pose in front of the aerospace fighters, although it had been by a PR guy with a slight lack of common sense. Richard found it hard to believe that any prospective starfighter pilots would be attracted to the navy by a pretty blonde girl standing in front of a spacecraft, even though he *did* have to admit that starfighter pilots were often lacking in common sense too. Their survival rates were so low that senior officers made allowances for them.

"I think you were replaced the moment some hot babe in her underwear came along," he said, finally. "And how many seconds do you think *that* took?"

He ignored her snort of irritation and turned his attention back to the starfighters. The Hawks didn't *look* like much, he had to admit. They certainly didn't look as *deadly* as the Tornadoes. They looked more like worker bees from a shipyard than jet fighters. But they were configured for operations in space, while the Tornadoes had been designed to operate in planetary atmospheres as well as deep space. The concept was cool, he admitted freely, but the technology was not quite up to the task. The Tornadoes lacked the manoeuvrability of craft designed to operate solely in space, while they were larger than aircraft designed to operate within a planetary atmosphere. Richard knew, all too well, that the high loss rate amongst *Invincible's* pilots during their encounter with the alien virus owed much to their outmatched starfighters. The aliens had kicked their ass.

It could have been worse, he told himself. *But if we'd been flying genuine starfighters...*

He allowed himself a smile as he studied the Hawks. They had come out of a multinational design project, something that had worried defence commenters back when the project had been announced, but Richard hadn't heard any complaints from their pilots. And there *would* have been complaints, if the craft hadn't lived up to their promise. The multinational nature of the project was an advantage, even if it was a blow to national pride. Being able to fly off American and French carriers might be useful. No, it *would* be useful. They were going to war, again.

Monica caught his eye. "You got your speech prepped for the maggots?"

"I know what I'm going to tell them, yes," Richard said. He'd lost nearly all of his surviving pilots as the Royal Navy distributed their experience through the fleet. He was lucky he'd been able to keep Monica. There had been times when he'd thought the carrier's flight wing would consist of him and a collection of newly-graduated pilots and reservists. "Are you ready to slot them into your squadron?"

Monica gave him a sweet smile. "They'll be kicking ass and taking names by the end of the day."

"Make sure of it," Richard said, dryly. He watched the ground crew move the Hawk into the launch tubes. "We'll be deploying soon."

Monica perked up. "You heard something?"

"Nothing official, not yet, but the repairs are almost completed," Richard said. "Do you think they're going to let an assault carrier sit around doing nothing when there's a war on?"

"I've already got ten pounds on us leading the assault into enemy lines," Monica said. "Do you want to place a bet?"

Richard shook his head, firmly. Gambling had always been a problem on Royal Navy vessels, although senior officers tended to turn a blind eye as long as the stakes weren't too high. They were also supposed to set a good example by *not* gambling themselves, at least not in public. Richard had no difficulty following *that* rule. He'd learnt the hard way that his luck didn't cover gambling.

"We'll just have to wait and see," Monica said. "They'll give us *some* time to get used to our new fighters before we go to war, right?"

"If they realise there might be a problem," Richard said. The maggots—the new graduates—wouldn't be a problem. They'd flown Hawks in the simulators, if they hadn't actually taken them into deep space. The reservists, on the other hand, might need more time to brush up their skills. "We may be doing our training as we travel to our next target."

He closed his eyes for a long moment. *Invincible* was an *assault* carrier. She wasn't designed to sit around defending a fixed target. No, she was designed to go on the offensive. Richard had no doubt they'd be heading back to Alien-1 as soon as the ship was cleared to depart. And then...he shook his head. He had no qualms about shooting enemy pilots, but he'd never contemplated facing enemy pilots who were nothing more than puppets for an alien virus. God alone knew how many unknown races had been woven together into a viral empire. Did the virus's victims *know* they were enslaved?

It doesn't matter, he told himself, firmly. *You have to kill them or they will very definitely kill you.*

His wristcom bleeped. It was time to meet the new pilots.

"Come on," he said. "It's time."

Richard couldn't help feeling a flicker of relief as he walked through the airlock into Pilot Country. It had been strange over the past few weeks, with him and Monica rattling around like peas in a pod; *Invincible* had felt almost like a ghost ship. It was a relief to finally have some new pilots and starfighters, even though the lack of experienced personnel meant that he was going to have to take more and more on himself until the reservists were up to speed. He'd already shovelled more of his work onto Monica than was good for him. If the XO had noticed and made a fuss...

He put the thought aside as he strode into the briefing compartment, Monica right behind him. The pilots hastily put their eReaders, datapads and newspapers away and snapped to attention. Richard surveyed them for a long moment, easily separating the reservists from the newly-graduated. The latter looked too eager to be true. They hadn't realised, not yet, just how poor their odds of survival were. The reservists, on the other hand, understood all too well.

"At ease," Richard ordered. "Welcome onboard HMS *Invincible*."

He waited for the pilots to relax, then leaned forward. "I won't give you any bullshit, not while you're under my command. Whatever you've heard through the grapevine or seen on the news, rest assured that the situation is worse. We're going up against an enemy that can take over our very bodies, if it can get a grip on us. Thankfully"—he allowed himself a cold smile— "they can't get to you in your cockpits. They'll be trying to kill you instead.

"We don't pretend to understand their thinking. There were times when they pushed the offensive against us, regardless of casualties, and times when they simply ignored us as long as we didn't engage them directly. Given their nature, intelligence believes that we can expect to see suicide attacks as well as more...*conventional* tactics. They are so alien, ladies and gentlemen, that their behaviour may be completely unpredictable. Even the Tadpoles, as weird as they are, use understandable tactics. These guys do not."

He smiled, thinly. "They also use a mixture of spacecraft and weapons that range from the primitive to the frighteningly advanced. Their best starfighters appear to be slightly better than ours, their worst are nothing more than target practice. Again, we don't understand why they haven't upgraded or simply junked their older craft. It's tempting to believe that they're incapable of operating shipyards, and the starships we saw were all captured in battle, but that might be just whistling in the dark. There's no reason to believe they *cannot* build and operate a shipyard if they feel the need. And they *will* feel the need.

"I expect each and every one of you to review the records from Alien-1. See if you spot any patterns, anything that might have been missed. Bear in mind that those records have been used to build simulator programs. What you see in the records is what you will be facing in the simulators."

Richard took a long breath. "Are there any questions?"

"Yes, sir," a newly-graduated pilot said. He didn't look old enough to shave. "Why are reservists being pushed ahead of active-duty pilots?"

Monica snorted. Richard shot her a warning look.

"Ideally, there would be a cadre of experienced pilots on this ship and the reservists—and new pilots like yourself—would be slotted into place below them," Richard said, with a patience he didn't feel. "By the time a place…ah…*opened up* for promotion, you would know what you are doing. Instead, we have two experienced pilots and sixty newcomers who are either inexperienced or haven't sat in a cockpit for years. The reservists are going ahead because they know their ass from their elbow. Alright?"

The newcomer flushed and sat down rather quickly. Richard concealed his amusement with an effort. He'd thought his high standing during basic training would translate into a higher position on his first ship too, although he hadn't managed to put his foot in his mouth *quite* so badly. And his superiors had been *very* experienced. He felt a flicker of envy. He'd sell his soul for a dozen experienced officers who could take the younger ones in hand.

"We will be spending the next few days in the simulators," he told them. "All of us. When we're not eating or sleeping, we will be in the simulators. We're going to go through everything before I let you take your starfighters out for a test flight—and fight. And *then* we're going to drill and drill and drill until you can do everything in your sleep. By the time we encounter the enemy, I want to be ready."

He made a show of looking at his wristcom and checking the time. "We'll start drilling in ten minutes," he said. "Go take a piss, if you need one, or just head straight to the simulators. I want you all in your cockpits and ready to go. Anyone who *isn't* ready to depart will be in deep shit. Squadron commanders, remain behind; everyone else, dismissed."

The briefing compartment emptied rapidly. Richard watched them go, wondering which of the pilots would become aces, which ones would cause him trouble and which ones wouldn't survive their first encounter with the enemy. The reservists, at least, should be *slightly* more mature than the newly-graduated pilots. They'd have served on ships before returning to civilian life. He took a breath and turned to his new officers. If only they weren't almost as green as their new subordinates.

"We'll be spending a lot of time together over the next few days," he said, studying the small group. "I hope you're ready to do your duty."

"I was called away from a comfortable armchair, sir," Flight Lieutenant Gabby Rancher said, tartly. She was a slight woman, but her cold eyes suggested she wasn't someone who could be messed with. "I hope this is not going to be a long deployment."

Richard raised his eyebrows. "What were you doing back home?"

"Running a store, if you must know," Gabby said. "It will all collapse without me."

"I can't make any promises," Richard said. "It may be a very long deployment indeed."

"They always are," Flight Lieutenant Hamster Aberdeen said. He was muscular enough to pass for a Royal Marine—and bulky enough that Richard couldn't help wondering how he'd fit into a starfighter cockpit. "Personally, I'm quite looking forward to it. Not being able to talk to my ex-wife is quite a pleasant thought."

Monica leaned forward. "However did you get a name like *Hamster*?"

"My parents were sadists," Aberdeen said. "*They* thought that a shitty name would force me to learn how to defend myself. I haven't spoken to them in years."

"My condolences," Richard said. "Are you ready to take command of a squadron?"

"I'm going to give it the old college try," Aberdeen assured him. "You do realise, though, that my only experience of squadron command lasted thirty minutes? Outside simulations, I mean."

Richard nodded. He'd read the man's record very carefully. Aberdeen had assumed command of his squadron after his CO had been killed, keeping the formation together until it could return to the carrier. Technically, Aberdeen should have *stayed* in command—it was practically tradition—but the CAG had put someone else in command instead. Richard had gone through the files with a fine-toothed comb, trying to see if there was any *reason* for the effective demotion, only to discover that nothing had been written down. Perhaps the CAG had a senior pilot who had more squadron experience.

It would still have been a slap in the face for Aberdeen, Richard thought. *And it might have been why he left the navy the following year.*

"You still have more experience than most of the newcomers," he said, out loud. "And you'll have a chance to get much more."

He looked at Flight Lieutenant Regina Freehold. "And you? Are you ready?"

"I am as ready as I will ever be," Regina said. She had an odd accent, one Richard couldn't place. He made a note to reread her file. "But I have never commanded men in combat before."

"There's a first time for everything," Monica said. "You just have to pretend you know what you're doing until...until it's actually true."

"We'll *all* be in the simulators," Richard said. "I'm not expecting wonders, but I *am* expecting you to set a good example."

He glanced at his wristcom. "We have five minutes," he said. "Dismissed. We'll have a more formal chat later."

Monica grinned at him as the reservists left the room. "It could be worse," she said. "We could have nothing *but* maggots."

Richard groaned. "Someone's been watching *Stellar Star XVI* too many times."

"It was very educational when I was a teenager," Monica said. "And it helped me decide what I wanted to do with my life."

"I don't want to know," Richard said. He held up a hand to ward off any further disclosures. "I really do not want to know."

Monica shrugged. "More seriously, the maggots have nothing to unlearn. They have all the skills they need to get the experience that will keep them alive. The reservists...well, they have something to unlearn. Hopefully, we can iron out all the bugs in their training before they actually take their craft into space. The simulator is a great place to make mistakes."

"I know," Richard said. Simulated disasters weren't *real*, even if the instructors had chewed him out for mistakes that would—in real life—have killed him. "But we have to pretend that it *is* real."

"So no letting them fly along a trench and blasting a torpedo into a concealed air vent," Monica said. She looked thoughtful, just for a second. "You know, we could have done that with the Tornadoes."

"If we didn't mind being blown out of the air," Richard said. He took a long breath. "You'd better get going. We have two minutes."

"A girl is always fashionably late," Monica said. She leaned closer. He could feel her breath on his face. "Do you regret saying *no*?"

Richard swallowed, hard. Monica had tried to seduce him, the night they'd returned to Earth. He'd turned her down, even though he'd been tempted. Very tempted. Monica was beautiful and fit and...Parts of his body had been telling him what a fool he'd been for weeks. And yet...she was his subordinate. He couldn't sleep with her or they'd both be cashiered.

"No," he lied. "I have a job to do. And so do you."

Monica shrugged and walked through the hatch. Richard carefully averted his eyes as he sat back and surveyed the empty room. Sixty newcomers, almost all strangers...they'd remain strangers too, at least until they saw the elephant. Richard had no illusions. Too many of the men and women under his command would die in the first engagement. He wondered, morbidly, which one would be the first to die. The man who looked as if he'd stepped off a recruiting poster? The pretty brunette? The young man who seemed to be desperately in need of a growth spurt? Or would it be one of the reservists?

He shook his head as he stood and walked out of the room. There was no point in getting close to any of them, not yet. Perhaps not ever. He hated to lose people under his command, but he knew he would. There was no way to avoid it. No matter what he did, no matter how hard he forced them to train, some of his pilots were going to die. The aliens would blow them out of space, killing them instantly. Only a handful of pilots had managed to eject while under enemy fire.

But I'll do everything in my power to keep them alive, he promised himself. *And bring them back home safely.*

And yet he knew, all too well, that it was a promise he couldn't keep.

CHAPTER FOUR

"THE FIRST SPACE LORD WILL SEE YOU NOW, CAPTAIN."

Stephen rose and followed the midshipwoman through the door and into a large office. It was surprisingly bare for a room designed more for show than substance, although a large painting of HMS *Warspite* blowing a hole in an Indian carrier was mounted on the far wall, allowing the First Space Lord to turn and see his greatest triumph. A single desk sat in the middle of the room, flanked by a handful of chairs. Admiral Sir John Naiser himself was seated behind the desk. He looked up expectantly as Stephen was shown into the room.

"Captain Shields," he said. "Please, take a seat."

"Sir," Stephen said.

He sat down and waited, keeping his face under tight control. Admiral Sir John Naiser was a *legend*. He'd flown starfighters, hunted renegade humans, discovered a whole new alien race and served in the brief Anglo-Indian War before commanding the task force that had put an end to the Second Interstellar War. They'd met before, of course, but Stephen's admiration was undiminished. Admiral Sir John Naiser's life read like a storybook. Only Theodore Smith could be said to stand above Sir John in the Royal Navy's pantheon of heroes.

And Admiral Smith died in combat, like Nelson, Stephen thought. *We never got to see him grow old.*

31

"The Board of Inquiry has finished its deliberations," Sir John said. "After much careful consideration—and study of the evidence, of course—they have decided that your actions, based on what you knew at the time, were completely justified. Some of them feel that you acted a little rashly at times, but—given that you had an urgent need to both gather intelligence and rescue your missing crewmen—the others overrode them. Accordingly, there will be no court-martial and you may return to your ship."

Stephen let out a breath he hadn't realised he'd been holding. The Board of Inquiry had made the decision it had been told to make by its political superiors. And that meant...what? Had someone decided there wasn't enough evidence to make the charges stick if Stephen went before a court-martial? Or had Duncan and his allies made a string of backroom deals to ensure that Stephen wouldn't be charged? It made Stephen's blood boil to think that someone might have escaped justice because he had friends in high places, even though he had *family* in high places. If he were to be cleared of all charges, he would have been preferred to be cleared of all charges for the right reasons.

You should be grateful, he told himself, severely. *A court-martial would look bad on your record even if you were cleared of all charges.*

"Thank you, sir," he said, finally. "It was...it was a concern."

Sir John's lips twitched. "I'm sure it *was*, Captain," he said. "Unfortunately, there are other...*issues* involved. I assume you've been following the news?"

"Yes, sir," Stephen said. The news, and Duncan's private briefings. "I'm not exactly flavour of the month, am I?"

"No, Captain," Sir John said. "There are people—too *many* people—who blame you for the virus. No *sensible* person could reasonably blame you for its mere existence, but you know what they say about crowds. They're only half as smart as the stupidest person in them. I believe it would be a good idea to get you and your crew out of the solar system—out of sight and mind—for a few months, just to let things cool off a little."

"I see," Stephen said, irked. Commander Daniel Newcomb had told him that *Invincible's* crew hadn't been allowed down to the surface, but he hadn't realised it was more than just an ill-judged attempt to prevent infection. "Where do you want us to go?"

Sir John smiled, humourlessly. "Alien-1."

He keyed a hidden control, activating a holographic starchart. A hundred stars appeared in front of them, each one surrounded by a halo of smaller icons representing British—and human—military installations and deployments. Stephen leaned forward, studying it with interest. A sizable number of icons were orbiting Falkirk, while other—darker—icons were positioned near Alien-1. He sucked in his breath as alerts flashed up on the display, reminding them that some elements were hours or days out of date. Some of the icons on the display might already have been destroyed. The aliens could have begun their advance already.

If they're coming, Stephen thought. He shook his head. He was morbidly sure the virus was coming, if only to expand into a whole new selection of host bodies. Humans, Tadpoles, Foxes, Cows, Vesy…not to mention all the animals and planetary biospheres. *No, it will be coming. The only question is when they'll be coming.*

"Right now, we have established a multinational blocking force at Falkirk, under the command of Admiral Jimmy Weisskopf," Sir John said. "He's a good man—I served with him during the Second Interstellar War. The Chinese were irritated that an American got command of the joint fleet, but the Russians—for some reason—refused to back them and their protests got nowhere. That's something we may have to watch, but"—he gave a thin-lipped smile—"it should remain well above your pay grade.

"What we don't have, Captain, is any accurate intelligence on our foe. We know the location of one of their bases, but we don't know anything else about them. How much territory do they actually control? How many starships do they command? How aggressive are they actually going to be? Frankly, I'm astonished they haven't launched a major attack already."

"So am I, sir," Stephen said.

Sir John nodded, shortly. "Getting that intelligence will be your job, Captain," he said, lifting his eyes to the chart. "Your ship—and a small flotilla under your command—will be tasked with probing alien space and covertly gathering as much intelligence as possible. Ideally, we would like you to remain undetected...but we would also like you to capture an alien ship for analysis. *That*, I'm afraid, will not be conducive to remaining undetected."

Stephen nodded, slowly. The First Space Lord was right. If they jumped an alien ship at the edge of an inhabited star system, they *might* be able to capture and dissect it before alien reinforcements arrived...but it was unlikely they could keep the alien from screaming for help before it was too late. The virus would be alert to *Invincible's* presence and do everything in its power to stop the assault carrier from making her escape. He would have to give the matter some thought.

"We'll think of something," he said.

"I hope so," Sir John told him. "You won't have any valid timescale for the mission. I can't put any sort of time limit on your deployment. However, if they do mount an offensive into our space, your orders will switch from sneaking around to doing as much damage as possible to the enemy's rear. Do everything in your power to hamper their thrust into our space. Take out supply dumps, smash cloudscoops, etc..."

Until we get hunted down and destroyed, Stephen thought. He had few illusions. The virus wasn't likely to let him raise havoc indefinitely. *It will send everything it has after us...which will ease the pressure on Earth.*

"We won't let you down, sir," he said.

"I have no doubt of it," Sir John said. He picked up a white envelope and passed it to Stephen. "Your formal orders, Captain, to take command of Task Force Drake. You'll note that you have two survey ships—HMS *Magellan* and HMS *Raleigh*—as well as two destroyers and four support freighters. You also—and this is the bit where you're going to have to be diplomatic—have a Russian ship under your command. *Yuriy Ivanov* is, apparently, a cruiser."

Stephen lifted his eyebrows. "A cruiser?"

"More like a small *battlecruiser*, according to our long-range sensors," Sir John told him. "The Russians haven't said very much about her, save for the barest handful of details, but we've been able to establish that she's quite large for a cruiser. I think she might have been an experiment that was not a complete success, but they'd done too much work on her to simply scrap the hull and start again. I think they probably class her as expendable."

He shrugged. "In any case, the Russians have insisted on deploying her to look for *Dezhnev.*"

Stephen winced. *Dezhnev* had vanished, sometime during the mission to Alien-1. No one had been able to establish what had happened to the Russian destroyer, although there were no shortage of theories. The virus might have caught a sniff of *Dezhnev* at some point, tracked her down and jumped her. She'd been so far from *Invincible*, watching the alien system from what had been supposed to be a safe distance, that her sudden destruction had gone unnoticed. Or…she might have been captured. The only thing anyone knew for sure was that *Dezhnev* had never returned to the human sphere.

Unless the virus took the ship intact and sent it creeping through the tramlines, Stephen thought, grimly. *How much did it manage to recover from the ship's datacores?*

It wasn't a pleasant thought. *Dezhnev* and her crew hadn't *known* about the virus. They might not have realised they needed to take extreme precautions to keep their crew safe from infection. And if they had been captured and infected, they'd be sharing everything they knew with the virus soon enough. And then…

They may know everything about human space, Stephen thought. *We have to find out what happened to that ship.*

"The Russians do have a point, sir," he said, slowly. "We do need to know what happened to *Dezhnev.*"

"Yes, but right now our priority lies in gathering intelligence," Sir John said. "The Russians have agreed to serve under your command, Captain, but keep an eye on them. There's something about the whole business that bothers me."

"Yes, sir," Stephen said. "Do you have any other orders?"

"You have standing orders to attempt to make peaceful contact if, and only if, it won't endanger your ship," Sir John said. "There are...*politicians*... who believe we should at least *try* to make peaceful contact. I don't think we can hope to co-exist with the virus, at least until we develop a vaccine, but hope springs eternal in the minds of the deluded. If you see a chance to try, Captain, take it. If not...well, there's plenty of leeway in your orders. I will understand."

"Yes, sir," Stephen said, feeling his heart sink. "Why haven't they attacked us already?"

"A good question," Sir John said. "And the same question has been asked already, countless times, by a number of politicians. We saw enough ships on active duty to give them a real punch, if they wanted to shove us away from Alien-1. The pacifist side of the aisle believes that the virus responded to our presence, but isn't particularly aggressive. If we leave it alone, it will leave us alone."

"Sir, it's absorbed at least two alien races," Stephen said. "We have good reason to believe that it is *very* aggressive."

"Yes," Sir John said. "And that makes me think that they're preparing to hit us."

Stephen nodded, slowly. No military force in human history could launch a major operation without a great deal of planning and preparation, particularly when caught by surprise. The Royal Navy—and every other military force in the human sphere—maintained a Quick Reaction Force, to deal with any unexpected problems, but it took time to gear up the remainder of the military for war. The virus might be taking the time to lay the logistical framework for a push into human space before actually launching the invasion. God knew the Royal Navy would have the same problem if the situation was reversed.

But Alien-1 has to be quite important to them, he thought. *At the very least, they should try to secure the systems between Alien-1 and Falkirk.*

"They'll have to blast their way through Falkirk," Stephen mused. "Unless they have some drive system we've never heard of..."

"There is the jump drive," Sir John said. "Incredibly expensive and quite dangerous, but they could use it...if they have it."

"Yes, sir," Stephen said. "And they *might* have it."

He sighed. The jump drive had been humanity's best shot at escaping the tyranny of the tramlines, but—so far—no one had managed to slim the system down enough to cram it into a single starship. Even a battleship or a fleet carrier couldn't carry a jump drive without stripping everything else out of the hull. There *was* a framework that could be used to jump a fleet from one star to the next—it had been used, famously, to end the last war—but it was grossly inefficient. It was also a sitting duck.

"We're relying on you to find out, Captain," Sir John said. He nodded to the envelope in Stephen's hand. "Your travel orders have been cut, Captain. A shuttle has been assigned to you at Northolt, which will fly you directly to *Invincible*. Ideally, I'll want your squadron assembled and you on your way by the end of the week. The Russian ship will join you when you depart."

"Yes, sir," Stephen said, crisply. He'd only brought a small carryall down to Earth when he'd left the ship. There was nothing he couldn't replace, if he had to head straight back to *Invincible*. "I won't let you down."

"Collect a car from downstairs," Sir John ordered. "And good luck."

And don't go talking to anyone else along the way, Stephen added, silently. It was rare for the First Space Lord to take such interest in a mere captain's travel arrangements. Normally, one of his officers would take care of it. But Stephen was a political football. His family connections had embroiled him in politics from a very early age. He doubted the First Space Lord liked *that*. *Better to get me off the planet as quickly as possible.*

"Thank you, sir," he said. He stood and saluted. "I'll be back."

The First Space Lord's staff were nothing if not efficient. A car was waiting for him as soon as he reached the door, with a junior officer at the wheel. The Royal Navy had never been particularly enamoured of the concept of self-driving cars, fearing the dangers of what would happen when—if—hackers managed to break into the control network. It had never happened, but the network *had* been shut down deliberately during the Battle of Earth.

Afterwards, Stephen had heard that demand for human-driven cars had skyrocketed. Too many people had been trapped, away from their homes, when their cars had simply pulled to the side and shut down.

They shouldn't have depended on a computer to do the driving, Stephen thought, as he clambered into the backseat. *They were lucky it wasn't a great deal worse.*

Rain was pelting down over London, splashing off the car's windows, but there was still a small army of protesters outside the secure zone. Stephen watched them for a long moment, wondering if they really thought they'd accomplish anything. It only took one side to start a war and, so far, the virus had been very aggressive. Stephen had even heard scenarios that suggested the virus had sent the generation ship to Wensleydale in hopes of securing a foothold on the colony world, although that would have required precognition. The generation ship had been launched hundreds of years ago and Wensleydale had only been settled for five. But then, it probably didn't matter. The virus didn't need a whole new host population to breed.

We might have to start killing entire planets, Stephen thought. *If it really can take over a whole biosphere, we're done.*

He leaned back in his seat as the car slipped onto the motorway and accelerated towards Northholt. The streets were clear, with surprisingly little traffic. Wartime preparations were starting to bite, he guessed. He'd caught snatches of a debate in parliament about evacuating the children to the countryside, in hopes of avoiding the chaos of the First Interstellar War, but so far nothing seemed to have been decided. Stephen himself was in two minds about it. The cities *would* be priority targets, if the virus took the high orbitals, yet scattering the population randomly would tear families apart for years. But if Earth was attacked again, it would be the least of their problems...

"We'll be at Northholt in twenty minutes, sir," the driver said. "Is there anything I can do for you?"

"No, thank you," Stephen said.

He opened his orders and read them, twice. There weren't any surprises, although there was an order to cooperate with the Russians as much as possible. He read the section twice, then guessed that someone was trying to patch up the Great Power alliance that had dominated the world for nearly a hundred years. Stephen suspected that *that* particular genie had well and truly escaped the bottle—there were quite a few lesser powers making their bid for great power status—yet he didn't blame the Foreign Office for trying. An alliance with the four other Great Powers might have involved a great deal of holding one's nose while turning a blind eye to the less savoury aspects of one's allies, but it *had* been relatively predictable. A world where there were more than five superpowers would be far less understandable.

And more likely to go crashing down into war, Stephen thought. The Solar Treaty forbade acts of aggression within the solar system, but—with more nations deploying warships and space-based weapons—the treaty was starting to fray. *And who knows what will happen then?*

CHAPTER FIVE

ALICE DROPPED TO THE DECK, braced herself, then started to perform a series of push-ups. Her body started to ache at once, ache in a manner that reminded her of her first days in the CCF, back when she hadn't been anything like as fit. She cursed under her breath and forced herself to keep going, reminding herself—in the words of her instructors—that pain was weakness leaving the body. And yet, she felt dreadfully unfit. It was all she could do to stumble through a pathetic fifty push-ups. She had the nasty feeling that it would take her a very long time indeed to qualify for active service.

"I'm not giving up," she muttered, as she sank to the hard metal deck. Her body was covered in sweat. "I'm not giving up."

"That's good to hear," a new voice said. "Captain Campbell?"

Alice looked up, sharply. A middle-aged man was standing there, wearing a grey suit he somehow managed to make look like a uniform. She rolled over and stood, wondering precisely how she'd managed to miss him entering the gym. She was supposed to be aware of her surroundings at all times, damn it. Her eyes flickered over her visitor, catching the tell-tale signs of a military career. She would bet half her paycheck that he was a marine himself. He wasn't even looking at her chest.

Not that there's much to see, she thought, ruefully. Her sister had inherited their mother's chest. *Years of constant training will do that to you.*

"Yes," she said, carefully. "And you are?"

"Colonel Watson," the man said. He held out a hand, which she shook automatically. "It's a pleasure to make your acquaintance."

Alice eyed him, warily. "Are you sure it shouldn't be *Doctor* Watson?"

Watson smiled. "Ah, you've caught me out. I'm also a practicing psychologist in my other life. I got a bit of shell in me, you see, and I didn't want to leave the marines."

"I see," Alice said. She didn't relax. She could run rings around a civilian psychologist, someone who knew less about the military life than she did about the civilian, but someone with genuine experience would be harder to fool. Not that she wanted to *fool* Doctor Watson, of course. She just wanted him to clear her for active duty. "Why didn't you study actual *medicine*?"

Watson showed no offense at her sally. "A battlefield medic would have to keep up with the rest of the company," he reminded her. "And that, alas, is beyond me."

He cocked his head. "I've taken the liberty of organising coffee and biscuits in the next room," he added. "Will you join me for a snack?"

"I've been on weirder dates," Alice said, more to see how he would react to her words than anything else. He showed no visible reaction. "Why not?"

She grabbed a towel off the rack and rubbed herself down as she followed Watson into the next compartment. It was nothing more than a small sitting room, with a table made of faux-wood and a pair of comfortable armchairs. A tray of imported biscuits sat on the table, next to a pot of coffee, a jug of milk and two empty mugs. Alice felt her mouth begin to water as she saw the biscuits. She hadn't tasted *proper* food since she'd been infected. The asteroid staff did their best, but they couldn't disguise the origins of their food. Their meat and vegetables were as fake as the wooden table in front of her.

"Take a seat," Watson said. He poured them both mugs of coffee, then sat down facing her. "This discussion is to be strictly informal."

Alice winced. "I take it that means that the records will *only* be watched by a few hundred people?"

"More a case of us both speaking freely, without regard to rank," Watson said. He didn't bother to deny that the conversation would be recorded. Alice wouldn't have believed him if he had. There was little privacy on a military base. "I read your application to return to active duty with great interest."

Alice nodded. "I'm wasting away here," she said, flexing her arms. They *felt* weak, even though a civilian would have thought her strikingly muscular. She'd worked hard to build up her strength. "And there's nothing useful I can do for you. Not here."

"It certainly seems so," Watson agreed. He took a sip of his coffee. "It's been a week since you had the operation. The medics inform me that no trace of the alien virus remains in your blood."

"They seem pretty certain," Alice said, although she was fairly sure that the reports included a great deal of CYA. They wouldn't be *entirely* sure that all traces of the virus were gone unless they vaporised her entire body. She had a feeling the medics wanted to dissect her after she died, just to see if the virus had found a hidey-hole somewhere within her flesh and blood. The thought was terrifying. "And I haven't had any odd…sensations since the operation."

"Indeed," Watson said. He nodded to the biscuit tray. "Eat something, please?"

Alice took a chocolate chip cookie and bit into it. The biscuit tasted heavenly. Someone had used a fraction of their mass allowance on biscuits… she had to smile at the thought. It wasn't the first time someone had chosen to bring along a luxury, something to remind them of home, rather than something more practical. She supposed she should be grateful. Food from Earth could be quite expensive in the asteroids. She didn't think that any of the Belters were making cookies.

They probably will, one day, she thought. *They're quite determined to limit their dependence on Earth.*

"I've read every one of your statements," Watson said. "And I've read each and every report on your progress, from the day you applied to join the Royal Marines until…well, yesterday."

"I'm sure they made fascinating reading," Alice said. She took a sip of her coffee and smiled at the taste. Watson was *definitely* an experienced officer. "What did you learn?"

Watson met her eyes. "Why did you choose the Royal Marines? You had to know there was a good chance you'd be rejected out of hand."

"For being a woman," Alice said, curtly. The Royal Marines—and the other front-line combat units—were supposed to be men-only. There were rumours of spec-ops units composed entirely of women, but Alice had never heard anything to suggest that those rumours had any grounding in reality. *She* would certainly have been invited to join if there was any truth in the rumours. "I wanted a challenge."

"And you got one," Watson said. "Didn't you?"

Alice nodded. The recruiters had told her that the instructors wouldn't make any allowances for her. Alice had accepted it—it wasn't as if the enemy would go easy on her either—but she hadn't really understood until she'd reported for training. They'd pushed her hard, practically *daring* her to complain about her treatment; she'd gritted her teeth and forced herself onwards, never allowing herself to show a moment of weakness. She'd come too close to disaster when she'd twisted her ankle, she admitted privately; she really should have taken that injury to the medics. But she'd kept going...

She hadn't graduated in the top ten. But she'd graduated.

"You don't give up," Watson said. "Sergeant Woodman said as much, in his report. He figured you could be killed, but not actually *beaten*. He was rather impressed with you."

"I always thought he hated me," Alice said. Woodman had been a bully. Or so she'd thought. Military instructors needed to act like bullies without crossing the line into actual bullying. "What else did he say?"

"Suffice it to say that he figured you were an asset we shouldn't waste," Watson said. "But"—he took another biscuit and held it up—"you are not in a good state right now."

"I can get back into shape," Alice said, feeling her chances of returning to active duty slipping away. "Marines have suffered much worse than me and returned to service…"

"Yes, they have," Watson agreed. "But your condition is unique."

"I wasn't the only one to be infected," Alice said.

"No, but you are the only one to be *freed*," Watson said. "There's a school of thought that argues that we should keep you under constant observation."

"I don't think they'd learn anything useful," Alice said, tartly.

"You're also not in a good state, physically speaking," Watson said. "Right now, I would not clear you for active service. You could not keep up with the platoon."

"I'm trying to get back into shape," Alice told him.

"Yes," Watson said. "You don't give up."

He took a bite of his biscuit. "There's also the possibility that you were… *influenced*…by the alien virus while it infested your body. A number of people believe you to be a security risk. They want you either locked up in a secure holding facility or—at the very least—discharged from the military."

Alice tensed. She'd heard horror stories of captured soldiers being conditioned and returned to their fellows as unwitting spies. It hadn't happened in decades, as far as anyone knew, but it was still horrific. She wasn't sure she could withstand an attack on her mind. She'd been trained to resist everything from drugs to direct brain stimulation, but her instructors had made it clear that everyone broke eventually. They hadn't said it directly, yet Alice had no difficulty reading between the lines. If they were captured and subjected to such treatment, they had to try to kill themselves before they were twisted out of all recognition.

"I have been tested extensively," she said. "And the tests found nothing."

"They know that," Watson said. "But they also know we're dealing with something *alien*."

"And you don't know its limits," Alice said. She took a breath. How would she *know* she wasn't under alien control? She thought her thoughts were her own, but what if she was wrong? How would she *know*? "Is there any way to be sure?"

"Not that we have been able to determine," Watson said. "You see the problem, I'm sure?"

"You want to keep me locked up," Alice said. She thought for a long moment. It wouldn't be *that* hard to escape the asteroid, now she was no longer strapped to a bed. She could run...and yet, the urge to run might be an alien command. How could she tell the difference between her thoughts and alien commands? She would never *know* if she was in control of her own body. "Damn it."

"Not quite," Watson said. "The issue was debated quite hotly. Some people argued that you should be kept locked up, as you put it. Others pointed out that we had no evidence that could be used to detain you. You're not a traitor or a criminal, merely the...victim...of an unprecedented alien threat. You are no longer infected and keeping you here would be a legal nightmare."

"I thought the government could hold whoever it pleased," Alice said. "Or am I wrong?"

She knew she wasn't. She'd read her history books. The emergency powers granted to the government after the Morningside Incident, which had brought the Troubles out into the open, had never been truly relaxed. If the government wanted to hold her without charge, it could do so with minimal oversight...all the more so, she admitted sourly, as it wouldn't be *that* hard to build a case for keeping her confined. It wasn't as if she was being held in Colchester or another high security prison. The asteroid was more comfortable than the barracks onboard ship.

"No," Watson said. "But the government *does* require a valid *reason* to detain you."

"But it has one," Alice said. She took a breath. "Get to the point."

Watson smiled. "You cannot return to active service," he said, bluntly. "You're not in fighting trim, Alice, and there's a question mark over your mental health. On the other hand, you *are* one of the few people who have

46

encountered the new alien threat and survived. Your knowledge may be quite useful."

"Everything I know is in my reports," Alice said, dryly. She'd spent quite a bit of time writing down everything she could remember, from the interior of the alien hulk to the sensation of being infected. "I held nothing back."

"You have two choices," Watson said. "First, you can remain here. You will be studied, of course, but otherwise it will be a reasonably comfortable existence. Given time, the doctors will find a way to confirm that you are no longer a threat and release you. You can then reapply for active service, as I'm sure you won't waste your time here."

"No, sir," Alice said.

"Second, you can return to *Invincible* as a consultant. You will..."

Alice choked. "A *consultant*?"

"You will be consulted on the alien threat," Watson said. "And you can spend the time in transit getting back into shape. Again, you will be watched and monitored constantly, but at least you'll be making a valuable contribution."

Alice winced. She'd had a friend who'd been shunted over to the Attorney General's Corps with those precise words. Perhaps he was making a valuable contribution, wherever he'd ended up, but he hadn't joined the military to be a backroom bureaucrat. He'd wanted to join the infantry and test himself against Britain's enemies. The idea of making a valuable contribution was little more than consolation for the simple fact that one had been shifted out of the combat arms. And now *she* had been shunted out too.

"You won't be part of the Royal Marine contingent," Watson said, confirming her worst fears. "But you *will* be able to train with them. I can have orders cut for you to be tested and, if you pass, to be allowed to join the marines again. However, your CO may have his doubts about someone who was touched by the aliens. You might be wise not to push."

"I know," Alice said.

She looked down at her hands for a long moment. She didn't *want* to stay on the asteroid, even if she wasn't being held in tight confinement.

She wanted to get stuck into the enemy before it was too late. She had no doubt there would be war. She'd felt the virus from the inside. She knew how aggressive it was, how quickly it had adapted itself to a whole new biochemistry. Coexistence was not an option.

And yet, if she returned to *Invincible*, what would she be?

Not a marine, not really. She couldn't reclaim the uniform until she returned to active duty or chose to transfer sideways into the support arms. She wasn't sure she could stand it, even though—as an experienced offi-cer—she'd have a far better handle on what the combat arms needed than someone who'd never seen the elephant. Perhaps it was her duty. And yet, after everything she'd done, she didn't want to end up a useless REMF…

"I'll just have to qualify for active service," she said. She looked up and met his eyes. "I'll return to *Invincible*."

"Very good," Watson said. He finished his coffee and poured himself a second mug. "I'll arrange transport tomorrow, after you complete a final battery of tests. Once done, I suggest you get a good night's sleep. I imagine there will be quite a few questions when you return to the ship."

"Probably," Alice said. "Unless they don't want to come too close to me for fear of being infected…"

She allowed her voice to trail away. Was there a danger? She didn't know. Her environment would be closely monitored. *She* would be monitored too. If the virus started to take her over—again—the ship's doctors would know long before she became contagious and take precautions. *Invincible* was the sole ship that had encountered the aliens. The crew knew, all too well, the dangers of letting the virus get a foothold amongst them. Alice would be surprised if the ship wasn't constantly flooded with UV lights.

Which will make it impossible for the virus to spread, she thought. *And if the crew are in combat suits, or even sealed shipsuits, they should be safe from harm.*

"You may experience some isolation, yes," Watson said. "And there will be some…ah…precautions taken, just in case you do become a threat. But otherwise…you will be free to spend your time doing everything you need to do to reapply for active service."

If they trust me enough, Alice thought. Major Henry Parkinson might refuse to recertify her, even if she passed all the tests. He'd be in an awkward position, for sure. *He won't be entirely certain he can trust me. He'll look at me and wonder if an alien is looking back.*

"I understand," she said, firmly. "I won't change my mind. I'll go straight to *Invincible*."

"Tomorrow," Watson corrected. He stood. "I wish you the best of luck, Alice, whatever you decide to do in the future. You can change your mind up to the point you actually climb aboard the shuttle. After that…you're stuck."

Alice shrugged. It wasn't as if she'd been able to choose her duty assignments. She went where she was sent. She'd spent a few months on embassy duty, which had been boring, and a few months guarding bases in the Security Zone, which had been anything but. Returning to *Invincible* was better than remaining in a prison, no matter how comfortable it was. She would have a chance to…

Her lips twisted into a wry smile. She'd have a chance to make a valuable contribution.

And I might have a chance to hurt the aliens, she thought. *And that would be worth almost anything.*

CHAPTER SIX

"WE'RE COMING UP ON *INVINCIBLE* NOW, SIR," Crewman Jones said. "Do you want to watch from the cockpit?"

Stephen looked up from his datapad. He'd thought he was keeping abreast of his paperwork—and Commander Newcomb had taken as much of the burden on himself as possible—but there were times when he wondered if the sole purpose of the Royal Navy was to churn out paperwork and drive its commanding officers insane. The flight had been spent skimming countless reports, from updates on production figures to the latest set of speculations about the alien virus and its motives. Stephen had been mildly relieved to see that very few of the navy's analysts believed that the virus was friendly, or that it could be appeased in some way, but their scenarios were universally depressing. Humanity could lose the war without firing a shot.

"Yes, thank you," he said.

He stood and walked into the cockpit, taking the co-pilot's seat. Crewman Jones took the pilot's seat and tapped a handful of controls, adjusting their course and speed as they approached the Hamilton Shipyards. The defences would be on a hair-trigger, watching for signs of alien attack. Stephen knew there were hundreds of ways to die in space, most of them involving nothing more than one's own stupidity in the face of the cold equations, but dying because there was a mix-up with the IFF signals would be amongst the worst ways to go. Military technology had advanced radically since the day a caveman had figured out that he could use a club to bash his enemy's head into mush, but it was still impossible to totally eliminate the risk of friendly fire. A blue-on-blue would be utterly disastrous.

"They've checked our IFF," Jones said. "We are clear to enter the shipyard."

Stephen leaned forward, spotting a handful of lights in the distance. The Hamilton Shipyards looked oddly disorganised, at least to civilian eyes. A handful of space stations, a cluster of spider-like construction slips scattered around seemingly at random, dozens of industrial nodes, working overtime to keep the fleet supplied...he smiled, realising that the Royal Navy was definitely taking the threat seriously. The yard was working at full capacity.

"They've moved your ship out of her berth," Jones said. "We'll be docking in two minutes."

"Noted," Stephen said.

The shuttle steered towards a cluster of lights at the edge of the shipyard. Stephen watched, feeling his heart begin to pound in his chest, as *Invincible* took on shape and form. She was a long dark shape, flanked by two starfighter launch and landing tubes; she looked smooth, with a sleekness to her form that older designs lacked. His experienced eye picked out the sensor blisters and weapons mounts on her hull, yet they didn't seem to weaken her appearance. *Invincible* looked deadly. Her designers had gone to some lengths to make her look striking.

Because the Tadpoles taught us that starships could be elegant as well as functional, Stephen thought. Most human starships were blocky, ugly shapes. Even civilian craft were designed more for function than appearance. The Tadpoles, on the other hand, had turned their starships into works of art. *And the navy wants to impress the people who pay the bills.*

He scowled at the thought. The Navy League had been pressing for more fleet carriers and battleships for the last ten years, pointing out that Britain had to keep up with the aliens as well as the other Great Powers, but there was no denying that the navy was *expensive*. It wasn't difficult to see why factions in parliament wanted to reroute some of the navy's budget to more popular, vote-grabbing areas like health or education. And yet, the navy was Britain's shield. If it fell, the nation fell with it.

"*Invincible* is ordering us to land in the main shuttlebay," Jones said. "Is that acceptable?"

"Quite acceptable," Stephen said.

He watched, feeling a sense of pride, as the shuttle glided towards the shuttlebay. To hell with his brother and his political games. *Invincible* was where Stephen belonged. He'd take his ship back into harm's way, putting his body between his nation and war's desolation. He smiled as the shuttle landed neatly on the deck, alarms bleeping as the shuttlebay hatch slowly closed. It wouldn't take long to pressurise the deck. And then...

"Nice landing," he said, standing. "Will you be returning to Earth?"

"I have orders to take this craft to the shipyard hub," Jones said. "I'll probably be transporting other people back to Earth."

Stephen walked into the rear of the shuttle and picked up his carryall. The First Space Lord's staff had packed his bag, then rushed it to Northholt before the shuttle departed. Stephen wasn't sure how he felt about *that*, even though he appreciated the thought. They'd wasted a great deal of effort that could have been better spent elsewhere. It wasn't as though Stephen couldn't draw whatever he needed from the ship or the shipyard's stores.

They really wanted me off-planet as quickly as possible, he thought, as he slung his carryall over his shoulder and headed to the hatch. *The politics must be growing dangerous.*

He checked the telltales—the deck was pressurised now—and opened the hatch. The air smelt—unmistakably—of a shipyard. Commander Daniel Newcomb and the remainder of Stephen's senior officers were waiting for him, their faces calm and composed. Stephen was relieved he hadn't lost anyone, even though the Admiralty had been threatening to poach some of his officers for months. He didn't really have time to break in a new officer as well as sneak into alien-controlled space. But then, his crew *were* the only ones with experience fighting the alien threat. It made sense for the navy to spread that experience as widely as possible.

Putting the thought aside, he faced Commander Newcomb. "Commander. Permission to come aboard?"

"Granted," Newcomb said. He saluted, smartly. "Welcome back, Captain."

"Thank you," Stephen said. "I assume command."

"I stand relieved," Commander Newcomb said. There was a hint of irritation in his voice, so carefully hidden that only someone who knew him very well would be able to hear it. He'd been *Invincible's* effective CO for the last few weeks. Now, he was just the XO again. "I have a handful of reports for your attention."

Stephen nodded. He didn't really blame Newcomb for being irritated. But then, Stephen also happened to know that Newcomb was on the short list for promotion to command rank when a slot opened up. His experience over the last few weeks would only help him. It was unlikely the navy would deprive him of a chance to shine.

He returned his officers' salutes, then dismissed them with a nod. "Walk with me, Commander," he said. "What's our status?"

Newcomb strode beside him as they passed through the airlock and headed down the corridor towards the intership car. "Our armour is at full integrity and our damaged weapons and their mountings have been replaced," he said. "There were some weaknesses in the ablative armour that were exposed by the engagement, so the construction crews took the liberty of installing some extra layers. It's all detailed in the reports I sent you."

He paused, inviting Stephen to comment, then continued. "The downside is that a third of our crew has been reassigned to other ships, to be replaced by a collection of newly-graduated crewmen and recalled reservists. They have no experience whatsoever of serving on a ship like ours. Fortunately, I managed to keep most of the crew chiefs and experienced crewmen, so the rough edges are being smoothed out even as we speak. That said…"

Stephen felt his heart sink. It wouldn't be the first time he'd commanded an inexperienced crew—*Invincible* was the first of her class, ensuring that her first cruise had largely been spent identifying and removing problems that hadn't been predicted by her designers—but he was taking his ship into a warzone. He promised himself, silently, that he'd work the crew hard. They could not be allowed to slip into complacency with a powerful alien threat lurking on the other side of the tramlines.

Newcomb looked grim. "Our greatest weakness lies in our starfighter arm, sir. We have only *two* experienced pilots, plus the CAG. The remainder are all either new or reservists."

"Darn." Stephen had to struggle to keep his voice mild. "Are they being trained?"

"Yes, sir," Newcomb said. "They've spent practically every waking hour in the simulators. I believe that Commander Redbird is quite determined to ensure that they're ready to go into battle."

"Let us hope they will be," Stephen said. Simulators had their place, but they simply couldn't substitute for *real* combat. There were always surprises when humanity went up against an alien foe. "I take it there's no point in asking for our old pilots back?"

"They were scattered across the navy, sir," Newcomb said. "I'd be surprised if we even got *one* back."

Stephen shook his head in disbelief as they stepped into the intership car. He understood the logic of spreading the experienced pilots as far as possible, but still…he was taking his ship into a goddamned warzone! He needed experienced pilots, not enthusiastic newcomers and grumbling reservists. At least the latter would have had *some* experience. He just hoped it had been *real* experience.

The hatch opened. He stepped onto the bridge and looked around. As always, it took his breath away. The bridge had been designed to be photogenic as well as functional. His command chair sat in the centre, surrounded by holographic displays; the other consoles were neatly arranged in a formation that suggested his ship was plunging onwards into the unknown. It was completely pointless—the bridge could look like anything—but he had to admit it looked good. He just hoped that the aesthetics helped convince the public to support the navy, instead of convincing them that the admirals were wasting money on fripperies. It was sheer luck that the Royal Navy had avoided a repeat of the American Space Force One scandal.

"Captain on the bridge," Newcomb said.

"As you were," Stephen said. *Invincible* was moored within the Hamilton Shipyards, one of the most heavily-defended locations outside Earth's Halo, but every station was fully manned and the carrier was ready to go to war at a moment's notice. Everyone knew the virus could already have sneaked a fleet through the tramlines and into Sol. "Status report?"

"The ship is currently on low-level alert," Lieutenant Sonia Michelle said. The helmswoman sounded nervous. She'd been left in command when the remainder of the officers went to greet their captain. "Drives and weapons can be brought online at a moment's notice, sir; starfighters can be deployed within five to ten minutes. Two-thirds of our crew are currently onboard or performing EVAs. The remainder are on Hamilton Seven, but can be recalled within forty minutes."

"Good," Stephen said. Hamilton Seven wasn't Sin City, let alone Earth, but it had enough distractions to be a popular shore leave destination for crewmen who weren't allowed to travel too far from their ships. "Please inform Commander Redbird that I need to speak to him immediately."

"Yes, sir."

"Commander Newcomb, you have the bridge," Stephen said. "We'll discuss our deployment orders later."

"Yes, sir," Newcomb said. "I have the bridge."

• • •

Richard had to swallow hard as he clambered out of the simulator and staggered to the cold metal deck. Being yanked out of a VR sim had always been unpleasant, although—thankfully—the Royal Navy's simulators didn't involve direct brain simulation. The boffins kept promising a neural link that allowed a pilot to control his starfighter through thought alone, but so far nothing *practical* had come out of the labs. Richard was almost relieved. The idea of having his mind linked to a starfighter was terrifying.

Although it would speed up reaction time, he thought. Starfighter pilots had very good reflexes—the ones who didn't ended up dead, if they didn't wash out of the training centre—but even they had their limits. *If we could react with the speed of thought...*

"The Captain wants to see you," Lieutenant-Commander Rebecca Wycliffe said. The CAG held out a pill. "Do you need this?"

"Probably not," Richard grunted. Rebecca was his senior officer, even though he had control over the carrier's fighter wing. He didn't want to show weakness in front of her. "Will you continue monitoring the exercise?"

"Of course," Rebecca said. "They're doing better."

"They could hardly be doing worse," Richard grumbled. "But I suppose they're learning."

He shook his head in disbelief. It was amazing just how many things the pilots had to unlearn. He wasn't sure which set was worse. The newly-graduated were all spit and polish and basic mistakes, while the reservists had forgotten what little military protocol they knew. They were lucky they were starfighter pilots. Anywhere else, there wouldn't have been anything like so many allowances made for them. He had a feeling that at least two of his reservists would have ended up in front of a court-martial within the week.

"Yes, they are," Rebecca said. "Give them some time."

Richard nodded, then headed for the hatch on wobbly legs. He wondered, morbidly, if he was growing old. Perhaps it was time to seek a transfer to command rank. It wasn't as if a starfighter pilot hadn't made the jump before. The First Space Lord himself had been a starfighter pilot. He sighed as he forced himself to stand up straight. No, he wouldn't apply for command rank. He was a starfighter pilot and he'd die a starfighter pilot.

Unless they find a medical excuse to discharge me, he thought, sourly. *They'll say I'm getting too old to fly a starfighter.*

He sighed, again. He wasn't *that* old. But being a starfighter pilot was a young man's game, one an older man couldn't play. Experience didn't always beat youth when experience had slower reflexes and more awareness of risks…he put the thought aside as he reached the Captain's Ready Room. Pulling himself upright, he pushed the buzzer and waited. The hatch slid open a moment later. Captain Shields was seated behind his desk.

"Captain," Richard said, saluting.

"Take a seat," Captain Shields ordered. He waited until Richard had sat down, then continued. "How are the starfighters?"

Richard took a moment to gather his thoughts. He'd been too busy over the last week to actually write any reports, although Captain Shields was sensible enough to realise that report-writing wasn't anything like as important as getting his starfighters and their pilots ready for battle. Aristocratic brat or not, the Captain had a surprising amount of common sense. Richard couldn't help finding that a relief.

"The starfighters themselves are in top-notch condition," Richard said. "I've watched the ground crews take the craft to pieces, then put them back together. Overall, we can deploy our entire roster of Hawks and Tornados, although it should be noted that we don't have enough pilots to fly *both* sets of craft at once. I don't know why we've been asked to keep the Tornados."

"We may have a use for them," Captain Shields said. He didn't sound too pleased. The Tornadoes had been a nice idea, but somewhat impractical. "Storing them isn't too difficult."

Richard had his doubts—the hangar space could be used for additional Hawks—but he suspected there was no point in arguing. "The pilots are the current weak link, sir," he said, instead. "We've been running them through endless drills, and they are getting better, but frankly I think we'd be looking at a couple of months before the squadrons would be certified for operations if we weren't going to war. Right now, unit cohesion is very poor."

Captain Shields frowned. "A discipline problem?"

"Not in the sense you mean, Captain," Richard said. "Normally, we would slot a couple of new pilots into a squadron, which would allow them to be absorbed without trouble. Their more experienced comrades would have no trouble showing them the ropes. Here, though, we simply don't have coherent squadrons. We're having to build unit cohesion up from scratch and it's slow going. Everyone is a stranger to everyone else. I'd hate to have to mix-and-match the pilots if we have to reconstruct the squadrons on the fly."

He leaned forward, trying to project as much confidence as possible. "We should be able to overcome the problems, sir," he added. "But it will take time."

"I hope you'll have enough time," Captain Shields said. "Between you and me, Commander, we're expected to depart by the end of the week. The time spent in transit *should* give you more opportunities to train, but...I expect you to do your best."

"Yes, sir," Richard said. "We *will* overcome our problems. We just need... a little more time."

"Ask me for anything but time," Captain Shields quoted. "Are your Squadron Commanders up to the task?"

"Flight Lieutenant Smith is the sole officer I was able to keep, so I have no worries about her," Richard said. "The other three are reservists, with limited experience. Unfortunately, their subordinates have picked up on that. Mistakes have been made...thankfully, all the deaths were in the simulators. They're learning as we go along."

Captain Shields frowned. "Should I be begging for more experienced officers?"

Richard winced. The practical side of his mind insisted that *yes*, Captain Shields should ask for more officers. But he also knew that the reservists would see it as a demotion. Hell, it would *be* a demotion. And they weren't doing *that* badly...

"Give them two more weeks," he said. "If they don't shape up, we can beg for more officers."

"We'll have to do it at Falkirk," Captain Shields said. "I..."

His intercom bleeped. "Go ahead."

"Captain, HMS *Magellan* has arrived," Commander Newcomb said. "Her commander would like to speak to you."

"Understood," Captain Shields said. "Patch him through to me."

He looked at Richard. "Do the best you can," he said. "And inform me if you need help."

"Yes, sir," Richard said. "You'll be the first to know."

CHAPTER SEVEN

"LADIES AND GENTLEMEN, WE HAVE DOCKED with HMS *Invincible*," the shuttle pilot called. "All aboard who's going aboard."

Alice gritted her teeth, wondering why Watson—or whoever had made her travel arrangements—had stuck her with *this* particular pilot. Perhaps it was a test of her patience—or her endurance. After enduring a blatant come-on that didn't so much test the limits as drive a battleship through them, she rather thought she could have been excused for breaking the young idiot's neck. It *had* been a long time since she'd gone to bed with anyone, she had to admit, but did he really think she'd like the idea of spending the flight in his arms? The pilot was revolting. No wonder he was assigned to an isolated base. The real question was why he hadn't been dishonourably discharged long ago.

She stood and picked up her single carryall, ignoring the way the pilot's eyes roamed over her body. It wasn't as if there was much to see. She'd traded her uniform for a bland shipsuit, but it revealed little of her curves. Hell, it showed more of her muscles than anything else. She might have been weakened, after spending several weeks lying on her back, but she was still strong enough to take him out with a single punch. And yet...his presence might be a test. Watson was probably still watching her.

"You missed a chance to get what only I can provide," the pilot called, as she started to open the hatch. "I can take you to heaven and then..."

"So can my hand," Alice called back. "And it doesn't talk back to me either."

She stepped through the airlock before the pilot could respond, feeling the gravity quiver slightly as the assault carrier's gravity field took over. The corridor was empty, save for a single man. Major Henry Parkinson stood there, in full uniform, his hands crossed over his chest. Alice kept her face as expressionless as she could while she closed the hatch, allowing the pilot to depart. She hadn't expected a welcoming band, but she had expected more than just her superior officer.

"Major," she said. Her mouth was suddenly dry. "Permission to come aboard."

"Granted," Parkinson said. His eyes never left her face. "Alice, I…"

He moved with blinding speed. Alice barely had time to realise she was under attack before his fist cracked into her jaw. She stumbled backwards, more shocked than hurt. He'd pulled that punch. He could have laid her out on the deck if he wanted and she knew it. And yet, a month before, she would have seen the punch coming and dodged it. She'd fallen further than she cared to admit. She rubbed her jaw, trying to keep her face expressionless. Parkinson knew she'd fallen too, now.

"You have a *long* way to go," Parkinson rumbled.

"Yes, sir," Alice said. There was no point in trying to deny it. "But I will catch up."

"That's good to hear," Parkinson said. "You're on detached duty. You have been assigned a cabin in the lower levels. You may make use of the facilities in Marine Country, if they are not required for other purposes, but otherwise you are not to consider yourself a marine unless I recall you to duty. Your men are no longer under your command. Do you understand me?"

"Yes, sir," Alice said. "Apparently, I'm a *consultant* now. Whatever that means."

"It means you get paid a great deal of money to be absolutely useless," Parkinson said. He grinned, suddenly. "You can watch our exercises and tell us what we're doing wrong."

Not allowing me to take part, Alice thought, although she knew it wasn't entirely fair. She doubted she could pass the entry tests right now, let alone the qualifying exams. *Or perhaps not taking the enemy seriously.*

She shook her head. Major Parkinson was well aware of the threat. He'd seen men under his command fall to the new threat. He'd probably read all the reports too. He wouldn't let the virus get a foothold without a fight. She had no doubt of it. Parkinson was smart as well as tough. And she didn't blame him for being wary of her.

"I'll be sure to nitpick," she said. If Parkinson wanted her to watch and comment, she'd watch and comment. "When are we starting?"

"We may find something else for you to do," Parkinson added, without answering her question. "Coming?"

He turned and strode down the corridor. Alice hefted her carryall and followed, resisting the urge to rub her aching jaw. She'd have to find someone to spar with, someone who would give her a challenge without effortlessly overpowering her every time. She tried to recall the roster in hopes of finding someone who taught martial arts, but no one came to mind. The *really* skilled martial artists tended to remain on Earth.

Invincible felt different, although it took her a few moments to put her finger on why. The atmosphere smelt like a shipyard, rather than a starship that had been on active duty for the past nine months. *That* had to be a little frustrating for the ship's crew, she guessed. Their ship smelt as if it had come off the slips yesterday. That would change, as *Invincible* headed back into deep space; they'd just have to endure it until then. The lights felt a little brighter too. She suspected they'd worked UV projectors into the light panels. The air was probably cleaner than it had been in weeks.

And we'll all be constantly exposed to UV light, she thought. *Does that have any ill-effects?*

She dismissed the thought as Parkinson stopped outside a hatch and pressed his finger against the scanner. The hatch hissed open, revealing a mid-sized cabin. It was no larger than the bedroom she'd had at her grandmother's house, but—compared to her accommodation in Marine

Country—it was luxury incarnate. The private bathroom alone was pure heaven. She opened her mouth to protest, but Parkinson was already striding inside. She hoped he'd understand she hadn't chosen the cabin for herself.

He should know it, she told herself. *Whoever assigned it to me didn't realise I'd prefer somewhere smaller.*

"You will remain here, when you are not training or otherwise engaged," Parkinson said, firmly. "You have access to enough entertainment to keep you occupied for years. If you go outside without permission, you will be in deep shit."

"Oh," Alice said. She was a prisoner then, no matter what Parkinson claimed. "And what sort of shit will I land in?"

"The sort that gets you thrown into the brig for the remainder of the voyage," Parkinson said, sharply. His face softened as he turned to face her. "Look, Alice, things are not what they were. It was all I could do to get you this cabin instead of a reserved room in the brig. Don't be foolish, okay?"

"Yes, sir," Alice said. She looked down at the medical bracelet on her hand. By now, the little tattletale had probably established a live feed to the ship's computers and was feeding data to the medical staff. "I won't be foolish."

Parkinson smiled. "There are MREs under the bed," he added. "Feel free to eat, if you wish, or sleep. I'll be back soon."

He turned and walked out of the cabin. The hatch closed behind him. Alice tried to open it, in a spirit of slight experimentation with the rules, and was unsurprised to discover that it wouldn't open for her. There *were* ways to get the door open—and she knew several different tricks she could try—but they'd all damage the system beyond repair. It would mark her out as a...

Alien spy, I suppose, she thought, as she started to search the small compartment. *Or someone who can't follow orders.*

She wasn't surprised when, five minutes after she began her search, she'd discovered no less than seven optical and audio pickups concealed within the room itself. There would be more, she was sure, including a handful too tiny to be seen with the naked eye and completely beyond detection without specialised equipment. She was tempted to remove the bugs she *had* found, but that would just have upset her minders. Instead, she opened the drawer under the bed and removed a single MRE. Parkinson had crammed nearly thirty into the tiny compartment. It made her wonder, as she opened the packet and triggered the heating element, just how long he was expecting her to remain in the cabin. She'd get cabin fever soon enough.

But at least I'm on a ship, she thought, as she felt the deck quiver beneath her feet. The main drives were powering up, one by one. *And I'll be on my way back into alien space before too long.*

The MRE started to steam. She removed the heating element with the ease of long practice, tossed it into a bin and opened the remaining packets. The army's curry and rice bore little resemblance to the curries her grandmother had made, once upon a time, but they were edible and filling. Her grandmother had been a bit of a rebel, in her own way. There had been a time when making ethnic food caused people to regard you with suspicion. She wondered, idly, how the army had ever gotten away with serving curry-in-a-bag.

Probably because no one dared say the army was anything but ultra-patriotic, she thought, wryly. *And most of the people outside the army probably never knew anyway.*

She poured her dinner onto a plate, then sat down and started to eat. Parkinson *would* be back—or *someone* would be back. She wanted to be ready for them. And then...she silently catalogued all the things she could do with the equipment in Marine Country. Hours of exercise—supervised or not—would set her on the road to recovery. And then, she just needed to find a sparring partner...

And hope I can convince Parkinson to trust me before it's too late, she reminded herself. *If he doesn't trust me, I'll never get a chance to return to active duty.*

• • •

Captain Katy Shaw was older than Stephen had anticipated, even though he'd read her file with considerable attention. The Royal Navy normally transferred its officers to a different ship when they were promoted, but Survey was a law unto itself. Katy Shaw had served on HMS *Magellan* ever since she'd been a young midshipwoman, moving steadily up the ranks until she'd finally stepped into the command chair. Stephen didn't think that denying an officer a chance to transfer was a good idea, but he had to admit that Katy presumably knew her command from top to bottom. Besides, she was a born survey officer. It was unlikely she could take command of a military ship.

She was a tall woman, with red hair that was steadily going grey. Stephen couldn't help being reminded of his second governess, a formidable woman who hadn't put up with any nonsense from Stephen or his brother. Katy Shaw's record was formidable too. Her ship had opened up new tramlines, located dozens of habitable worlds and—before she took command—stumbled across the Foxes and Cows. *Magellan* had been lucky to escape without being detected and destroyed. Stephen had read that report very carefully too.

"Captain," he said. "Welcome onboard HMS *Invincible*."

"Thank you, Captain," Katy said. "Please, call me Katy."

"Stephen," Stephen said. Technically, she had more time in grade than he did, but the Royal Navy insisted that warship captains had automatic seniority over non-warship captains. It was a sensible precaution, he'd always felt, but one that always put noses out of joint. "It's a pleasure to meet you."

"Thank you," Katy said. A steward brought them both tea, then withdrew as silently as he'd come. "Although I cannot say I like the sound of the mission."

"We have to know just how much territory our enemy controls," Stephen said. "And your ship was designed for stealthy operations."

Katy didn't look pleased. *Magellan* and her sisters were designed to be incredibly stealthy in the hopes that they'd be able to locate any potential threats and slip away without making contact. Their cloaking devices and

ECM nodes were as capable as anything mounted by a warship. But survey officers were more interested in opening up new areas of space for exploration than spying on enemy planets. They were, at heart, more civilian than military.

"I understand that we have been drafted for the duration of the conflict," she said, finally. "I have already taken the liberty of offloading non-essential crew members. However...I should warn you that there *will* be protests."

Stephen had to smile. "Tell them to stand in line."

Katy shrugged. "I'm sure they will," she said. "We were preparing to depart on a two-year mission when you returned home."

"You'll still be exploring unexplored space," Stephen said. "Or doesn't it count if someone else got there first?"

"It still counts," Katy said. She leaned back in her chair. "What do you want from us, Captain?"

"We'll be probing the stars around Alien-1 in the hopes of determining how much space the virus controls," Stephen said. "Your specific orders are to accompany *Invincible* and use your specialised equipment in support of the mission. In the event of us making contact with the enemy, you and your crews will take the lead in a bid to establish lines of communication with the virus. I've been told that your communication crews are trained in thousands of ways to communicate."

"Yes," Katy said. "We have quite a few ways to open communications. But the system has never really been tested."

Stephen nodded. The Tadpoles had been the ones to figure out how to speak to humanity, not the other way around. The Vesy had been forced to learn Russian, then English; the Foxes and the Cows had copied a captured Tadpole database. Survey Command might be very proud of its First Contact package, but it had never been *used*. There was no way to be sure how a completely unknown alien race would react.

They might think we're being dreadfully rude, he thought, with a flicker of amusement. *Or they might be completely bemused by something we consider to be as clear as water.*

"We may have a chance to test it, then," he said, although he was certain that trying to open communications would be a waste of time. "If we encounter hostility, *Magellan* and *Raleigh* are to retreat at once while *Invincible* and the other gunslingers hold the line. Should you lose touch with us, beat feet back to Falkirk and report to Admiral Weisskopf. He can send a message down the flicker network for further orders."

Katy nodded. "It sounds simple enough," she said. "And workable."

"The devil is in the details, of course," Stephen said, dryly.

"Always," Katy agreed. "Some of my crew believe you muffed the first attempt at opening contact. What would you say to that?"

"They fired on us," Stephen said. "And opening fire is *also* a way of opening communications. It says *die, you bastards*."

He looked down at his desk for a long moment. He'd spent enough time in the upper crust to *know* that ambassadors and translators *always* worked hard to clarify messages and make allowances for mistakes. It was hard enough to avoid accidental mistranslations and insults when both parties were *human*, even if they didn't speak the same language. Aliens were...well, *alien*. It was impossible to be sure they'd meant to give offence. A smart diplomat left as much room as possible for manoeuvring around potential insults.

But opening fire? Without provocation? Stephen couldn't believe that indicated anything but naked hostility. Humanity wouldn't fire on an unknown alien ship unless it presented a clear and present danger, yet... it would be easy, so easy, to believe that the aliens *did* pose a threat. It was one of the nightmare scenarios he'd studied during his time at the Luna Academy. A human ship, believing itself to be in danger, firing on a hyper-advanced alien starship...

...And, the next thing they knew, the aliens made the sun go nova.

"We know our duty," Katy said, breaking into his thoughts. "And we won't let you down."

Stephen nodded. No one reached command rank, even in survey, without a degree of hard common sense. Katy might bemoan the failure to open communications, she might try to open communications if she got a chance, but she understood the dangers. Her ship wouldn't be risked unless there was a very real chance of ending the war. And Stephen wouldn't blame her for trying.

"Thank you," he said. He leaned forward. The next question had to be asked, even though it was a technical breach of etiquette. "Do you know Captain Hashing?"

"He's a good man," Katy said, calmly. If the breach of etiquette bothered her, she didn't show it. "Worked his way up through the ranks like me, although he was always more interested in gas giants than Earth-compatible worlds. He had—still has, for all I know—a theory that we'd be abandoning planetside habitats forever, once our tech reached the point it could keep us alive in space indefinitely. The future generations of humanity would grow up in habitats orbiting gas giants, or sailing between the stars in immense ships. I believe he was considering retirement when the news hit."

Her lips quirked. "He's quite a rich man, thanks to some nifty investments with his share of the reward money. He was talking about establishing his own colony in orbit around Jupiter or Saturn. He's certainly rich enough to do it when he retires."

Stephen frowned. "But he'll do his job?"

"Yes," Katy said, flatly. "He'll do his job."

CHAPTER EIGHT

"CAPTAIN," COMMANDER NEWCOMB SAID. "All systems check out A-OK. Your starship is fully at your command."

Stephen leaned back in his command chair. It had been a long week, with barely any time to catch some rest between inspecting his ship from top to bottom and stowing away as many supplies as she could carry in each and every nook and cranny, but they were finally ready to depart. And they'd met the First Space Lord's deadline. His little flotilla would have no trouble reaching Falkirk on time.

Which makes a pleasant change, he thought, as he checked the displays one last time. *Our shakedown cruise was nowhere near as uneventful.*

"Communications, inform System Command that we are departing on schedule," he ordered, calmly. "Helm, take us out as planned."

"Aye, Captain."

Stephen smiled, feeling a flicker of anticipation as the drives grew louder. There would be no more micromanaging once his ship crossed the tramline, no more contradictory orders that were cancelled bare seconds after he'd read them...no, they'd be cut off from Earth and he would be in sole command. Going into enemy space would be dangerous—he had no illusions about *that*—but he'd also be isolated from his superiors. He would *definitely* be in sole command.

"We're underway, Captain," Lieutenant Sonia Michelle said. The helms-woman kept her eyes on her console. "We'll be crossing the shipyard bound-aries in two minutes and we'll be crossing the tramline in three hours, seventeen minutes."

"The remainder of the task force have fallen in behind us," Lieutenant Alison Adams added, shortly. "They're keeping pace, as planned."

"Good," Stephen said. "Communications, please extend my compliments to the other commanding officers and inform them that I'm inviting them to a dinner, to be held once we've crossed the tramline. Once they acknowl-edge, forward the details to the galley."

"Aye, sir," Lieutenant Thomas Morse said.

Stephen nodded and turned his attention back to the display. Sol was teeming with activity, from warships and freighters heading to the front to asteroid miners buzzing about like angry bees. The solar system hadn't been so active since the *last* interstellar war, even though the massive colo-nisation program had been underway for years. Hundreds of thousands of people were leaving the planet each month, heading for their new homes on a distant colony world. Stephen had seen the incentives being offered to the colonists. He just hoped they'd have the sense to realise that life on an untamed world would be nothing to write home about.

He pushed the thought aside as he checked his inbox. There was noth-ing new, save for a single update from the family's private news service. Stephen glanced at the header, decided it wasn't immediately important and put it aside for later consideration. He'd feared that their orders would be changed on short notice, but it seemed as though they were going to be allowed to proceed as planned. *That* was a minor miracle in its own right.

The Admiralty has just over three hours to send us some new orders, Stephen reminded himself, grimly. There had been some talk about *Invincible* escort-ing a convoy to Falkirk, but the convoy organisers had kept falling behind until the Admiralty had dropped the plan. *But once we cross the tramline, we're free.*

He studied his console thoughtfully, noting that the starship's drives and life support were functioning well within acceptable parameters. He would have been surprised if they weren't—they'd ironed out all the bugs during their shakedown cruise—but it was better for any problems to manifest within the solar system, rather than in an alien star system. Being rescued—and towed back to the shipyard—would be embarrassing, yet it would be preferable to being caught by a fleet of alien ships. Stephen knew what fate awaited *Invincible*'s crew if they were captured. He'd already determined to blow up the ship rather than see her fall into enemy hands.

"Cruising speed achieved, Captain," Sonia said. "We'll be crossing the tramline in three hours."

Stephen had to smile. One thing the civilians never realised was that space was *big*, unimaginably big. *Invincible* might be one of the fastest things in space, certainly when compared to the giant fleet carriers, but even she took time to get from place to place. He didn't really begrudge the time, even though part of him wanted to cross the tramline before his superiors could send him new orders. The gulf between the shipyard—and Earth—and the tramline was a buffer between humanity and an invading fleet. He dreaded to think what would happen if the Royal Navy ran into an enemy that wasn't bound by the tyranny of the tramlines. They could jump into orbit and lay waste to Earth before the defenders could react.

And it might be theoretically possible, Stephen thought, grimly. He'd read papers suggesting that there *were* ways to fold space that didn't require more power than the entire Royal Navy generated in a year. *Someone more advanced than us might be able to do it and then...*

He pushed the thought aside and concentrated on the reports. Nothing seemed to be going wrong, yet. He eyed his console suspiciously—in his experience, something *always* went wrong when a starship left the shipyard—and then forced himself to relax. They'd just have to deal with any problems as they cropped up. He had a good ship and a good crew. He didn't need to worry himself to death.

Not yet, anyway, he thought. *We'll be facing the aliens soon enough.*

Time passed, slowly. Stephen watched and waited, feeling a flicker of relief as they reached the tramline and made transit. The display blanked, just long enough to worry him, then started to fill up with icons. Terra Nova's endless civil war hadn't put a stop to activity in deep space, well beyond the reach of any of the factions. There was going to be a political headache, the analysts said, when Terra Nova evolved a government that controlled the entire planet. Legally, that government would have jurisdiction over the entire system; practically, the off-planet governments and corporations and independent settlers wouldn't recognise the government's authority. And some of them were loaded for bear. Stephen suspected that the planetary government would always be at a major disadvantage. They simply couldn't afford to build a fleet capable of imposing their authority without making their plan blindingly obvious.

"Captain," Morse said. "The other commanding officers have informed us that they will be attending the dinner party."

Surprise, surprise, Stephen thought. It would be a rare officer who'd *decline* such an invitation, unless there were *extreme* extenuating circumstances. *But I do have to talk to them before we reach the front.*

He stood. "Commander Newcomb, you have the bridge," he said. "I'll be in my Ready Room."

"Aye, Captain," Newcomb said. "I have the bridge."

Stephen kept a wary eye on the live feed from the bridge while he worked in his Ready Room, although he wasn't really expecting trouble. The miners-turned-pirates who infested parts of the system weren't likely to pick a fight with either of the destroyers, let alone the whole flotilla. It said something about the general lack of law and order in the Terra Nova system that space pirates actually existed. Anywhere else, they'd be cut off from their supply bases and hunted down like dogs. He suspected it was just a matter of time before the spacers crafted their own government, with the power to impose law and destroy pirate gangs. There was nothing *romantic* about space pirates.

He worked until late afternoon, then changed into his dress uniform and made his way down to the Flag Mess. He'd been tempted to tear the compartment out and replace it with something more useful, when he'd seen it for the first time, but he had to admit it did have its uses. And yet, the compartment was really too luxurious for his peace of mind. It looked as if it belonged on a luxury liner, not a warship heading to the front.

The designers probably wanted to suck up to the admirals, he thought, as he waited for his guests. *They wouldn't be happy unless they had the finest accommodation on the ship.*

His lips twitched at the thought. He'd seen the old tin-cans that the Royal Navy had built during the first expansion into space. They'd been little more than glorified rockets, lacking everything from artificial gravity to starfighters. The crews had endured horrific living conditions, their lives more at risk from their own ships than enemy action. Stephen wondered, idly, what those men would have made of *Invincible*. They'd probably take one look and wonder if they were hallucinating. Stephen's ship was ridiculously luxurious compared to the tin-cans.

The hatch opened. Stephen straightened up. "Captain Brisling," he said, as a middle-aged dark-skinned woman stepped into the compartment. "It's good to see you again."

"And you," Captain Samra Brisling said. "You seem to have done well for yourself."

Stephen nodded, then greeted the other commanding officers. Captain Vandal Hashing was older than he'd expected, even though Katy Shaw had told Stephen that Hashing was on the verge of retirement. Captain Jonathon Linguine looked ridiculously *young* to be a destroyer captain, particularly as he had no aristocratic connections that Stephen had been able to uncover. But then, his file had made it clear that he was an above-average officer, with a string of commendations to his name. He would make battleship command in five years or burn out early.

"Captain," Captain Pavel Kaminov said. The Russian's voice was strongly accented, somewhat to Stephen's surprise. English was *everyone's* second language these days. You couldn't be a spacer unless you spoke perfect English. "Thank you for your invitation."

"You're welcome," Stephen said, shaking Kaminov's hand. "We're glad to have you along."

He studied Kaminov for a long moment. The Russian was tall and thin, his face strikingly pale. It was hard to make even a guess at his age. Kaminov's file stated that he was in his late forties, but MI6 hadn't been able to confirm any of the details. Stephen wasn't too surprised. The Great Powers rarely shared *complete* files with anyone. He just hoped the Russians hadn't exaggerated Kaminov's combat experience. *That* might cause all sorts of problems.

"Please, be seated," he said. He waved a hand at the table. "We're quite informal here."

"That's a relief," Katy Shaw said, as she sat. "I've never been quite sure which fork I should use for soup."

Stephen smiled at the weak joke. "We won't be able to enjoy fresh ingredients for long, so get it while you can," he said. "My chef worked overtime to prepare this delicious repast."

He motioned for Kaminov to sit next to him as the steward brought in the first course, a clear chicken soup. The Russian seemed oddly amused by the whole affair, although he ate without hesitation. Stephen guessed he hadn't spent much time with foreigners. The Russians hadn't participated in many of the multinational fleet exercises that had been carried out between the wars. Their self-imposed isolation had cost them dearly.

Conversation flowed around the dinner table as the various captains chatted freely. Stephen listened, occasionally inserting a comment or question, as Katy and Hashing talked about survey work beyond the rim of explored space. They made it sound like a wonderful adventure, even though Stephen knew that their crews would be thoroughly bored of each new planet by the time the survey team moved to the next star system. But then, it couldn't be helped. The survey team needed to be *sure* the planet didn't have any unpleasant surprises before the first colony mission arrived.

And some planets have been quite inhospitable, he reminded himself. *They turned out to be nothing more than poisonous snakes in the grass.*

He met Kaminov's eyes. "I was wondering why your government saw fit to assign your ship to this mission," he said. "They were not very forth-coming to us."

"We lost a destroyer to the enemy aliens," Kaminov rumbled, after a moment. "The government wants to know what happened to her."

Stephen nodded, slowly. There had been no sign of *Dezhnev* since she'd vanished in Alien-1. He didn't blame the Russians for wanting to know what had happened to her, although he had a private suspicion that they'd never know. *Dezhnev* could have slipped too close to an alien starship and been blown into atoms, or suffered a catastrophic life support failure that had killed her entire crew. Stephen doubted that any such failure would have killed the crew *instantly*, but in a hostile star system the Russians wouldn't dare signal for help. They might have suffocated long before they could be rescued.

"We also want to know as much as possible about the new aliens," Kaminov added, after a moment. "Gathering intelligence is not my preferred role, Captain, but I wasn't given a choice."

"Orders are orders," Linguine said. The young man sipped his wine, thoughtfully. "What will you do if you locate her?"

Kaminov made a motion that *might* have been a shrug. "It depends. If we can recover her, I have orders to try. If not, I have orders to destroy her. But if she was captured, we are unlikely to see her."

"True," Stephen agreed, slowly. Any captured alien ships would *not* be added to the line of battle. They'd be taken to a secret location and carefully disassembled, piece by piece, until the boffins worked out what made them tick. It was hard to believe that the virus wouldn't do the same, even though its psychology was thoroughly inhuman. The virus would certainly want to dissect the ship's datacores for actionable intelligence. "Did her CO have orders to destroy his datacores if the ship came under fire?"

"He did," Kaminov confirmed. "But we cannot tell if he carried out his orders."

Assuming his ship was actually captured, Stephen thought. *But we have to assume the worst.*

"We shouldn't have any trouble with our mission," Samra said. "As long as we are careful, we should remain undetected."

"I'm sure that's what *Dezhnev* thought," Linguine commented. "The alien sensor grids might be far better than ours."

"Or they may have devoted more effort to covering Alien-1 than we devoted to covering Earth," Stephen pointed out. "Their economy might be more geared to war production than ours."

"If they really are a single entity, they might not care about comforts," Hashing said. "They might be able to devote a great deal more of their GNP to the military than anyone else."

Stephen winced at the thought. He knew, all too well, just how much money was funnelled into the Royal Navy each year. It was hard to blame the politicians who wanted to redirect some of the money elsewhere, even though he *knew* Britain *had* to keep up with the other Great Powers. But if the virus didn't have to worry about such matters, it could construct a far larger navy without risking political upheaval or civil unrest. And if it could out-produce its new enemies…

"They might also not take the war seriously," Katy said. "If they don't see us as a real threat…"

"Every living thing wants to survive," Kaminov said.

"I don't think *politicians* want to survive," Linguine said.

Samra snorted. "Politicians are isolated from the consequences of their decisions," she said, dryly. "That ensures that they develop an unrealistic view of the world. The virus, on the other hand, presumably knows *everything* about its surroundings. It won't assume that we will leave it in peace."

"It's already shown that its aggressive—and hostile," Stephen agreed. "And yes, it wants to survive."

"But how are we going to beat it?" Hashing took a sip of his wine. "We have no vaccine, we have no way of freeing countless innocents from its grip. This is a hostage crisis on an unprecedented scale."

"We wipe it out," Kaminov said. "We destroy its ships, we smash its asteroid habitats, we burn its planets to dust and ash. And when we're done, we keep the entire system under a very close watch. If it moves again, we destroy it."

Hashing glared. "You're talking about genocide."

"Spare me your false morality," Kaminov said. "Your country deported millions of fourth-generation citizens, many of whom went to their deaths. And they were *human*. The virus is very definitely *not*."

He leaned forward. "This virus poses a terrifying threat. If it gets loose on Earth, countless millions will die—or be robbed of their freedom. There is no such thing as an immoral tactic when confronted with such a foe. It is them—the virus, really—or us."

"If we do as you wish, we will be wiping out at least two alien races, neither of whom have done anything wrong beyond being infected," Hashing said, sharply. "They didn't make a *choice* to fight us..."

"It doesn't matter," Kaminov said. He lowered his voice. "What would you have us do? Treat the virus with kid gloves until it broke free and exterminated us? I understand your point, Captain, but the survival of humanity and our allies is at stake. We have *got* to put ourselves first."

"We can contain the virus," Samra said.

"Are you *sure*?" Kaminov gave her a sharp look. "What if you're wrong?"

"The decision isn't in our hands," Stephen said. "Our job is to scout out the alien homeworlds."

"And then prepare to destroy them," Kaminov said. "We cannot allow the virus to exist."

Hashing snorted. "And how would we be sure of getting every last fragment of it?"

"We couldn't," Kaminov said. "But we have to try."

Stephen winced, inwardly. He hated to admit it, but Kaminov had a point. The virus could not be allowed to exist. And yet, destroying the virus meant destroying untold billions of innocent aliens, aliens who had been hosts from birth to death. They didn't deserve to die.

It's going to be a long mission, he thought.

CHAPTER NINE

ALICE FELT NAKED.

She crawled through the Jefferies Tube, feeling as if she was being watched. The hunters were after her. She paused outside a hatch and checked the telltales, then keyed the switch to open it. The hatch slid open, revealing an empty tube. Gritting her teeth, she pulled herself through the hatch and listened carefully. There was no sign of any pursuit.

Which means nothing, she reminded herself, as she looked up and down the tube. *They'll be moving as quietly as possible.*

She forced herself to keep moving, despite the sweat pouring down her back. It stung to admit it, but—in hindsight—she wondered if agreeing to play the quarry had been a bright idea. The marines would find it easier to catch her than someone in better shape, even if she *did* know the ship like the back of her hand. It was a far cry from the Escape and Evasion courses she'd passed during basic training. But then, the marines were undermanned. Better to let them chase her than a crewman who wouldn't know how to hide.

A sound echoed down the tubes. She tensed, listening carefully. Someone following her? She'd done everything in her power to evade detection, but she knew from experience just how far sound could travel in an enclosed space. She thought she heard someone coming up the tubes, someone who wanted to catch her...turning to the right, she opened a hatch and scrambled out into the corridor. A pair of passing crewmen gave her an odd look, but ignored her. They'd have been told not to pay any attention to the marine version of hide and seek.

But the marines will be after me in a few moments, Alice thought. *Someone* would have noticed the hatch being opened…and it wouldn't take them long to realise that *Alice* was the only person who could have opened the hatch. *I have to move.*

She forced herself to think as she hurried down the corridor. Unless she missed her guess, the marines would be guarding the hatches that led further into the ship. They wouldn't want her to slip past them and hide. She glanced at her wristcom, calculatingly. If she managed to stay ahead of them for another two hours, she'd win. But she doubted she could keep ahead of them. They had a rough idea of where she was now and…

Footsteps, she thought, as the sound reached her ears. *They're coming.*

Her hand dropped to the stunner at her belt. She could fight, if she wished…it would certainly make the game a little more exciting. But she didn't think she could stun them all before it was too late. Parkinson would have a number of sharp things to say to his men if they were stunned, yet… it wouldn't make any difference to her. She considered jumping back into the tubes, then dismissed the thought. They'd have blocked off the exits by now, unless they'd slipped badly since she'd been infected. Instead, she ducked into a storage room and looked around. The walls were lined with spacesuits. A thought struck her as the hatch hissed closed behind her. If she got *into* one of the spacesuits and remained very still…

Alice grinned as she hastily took one of the suits and pulled it over her shipsuit. The hunters might not think to check the storage room at first, not when they *knew* there was no way out. They wouldn't expect her to trap herself, would they? If she was lucky, she could make that work against them. She finished donning the spacesuit, then leaned against the bulkhead and waited. They *would* check the storage room, sooner or later. She just hoped they couldn't see her eyes.

The hatch hissed open, five minutes later. Alice cursed under her breath. That was quicker than she'd expected. Perhaps they'd narrowed her location down more than she'd thought. It made sense, she supposed. They might have had checkpoints all along the corridor. If they knew she hadn't gone in either direction, she practically *had* to be in the storage room...

I should have kept the stunner within reach, she thought, as two marines entered the compartment and looked around. They moved with a calm professionalism that made her smile, even though she was starting to wonder if she'd ever be able to rejoin their ranks. *I could have stunned them both and walked out of the compartment.*

Alice tensed as the marines poked and prodded around the compartment, making sure she wasn't hiding behind the spacesuits or the boxes of supplies. Would they think she might be hiding *in* the spacesuits? They stopped after a long moment, muttering to each other so quietly that Alice couldn't make out the words, then headed out the hatch. Alice almost started giggling. Parkinson was *not* going to be pleased with the two marines when the time came to review the exercise. Bundled up in a spacesuit, Alice would have been an easy target...if they'd seen her. And they hadn't thought to check...

Unless they're waiting outside, she thought. *They might be waiting for me to show them where I'm hiding.*

She considered it for a long moment, then dismissed the thought. They'd been told, time and time again, not to be *clever*. If they'd known where she was, they should have grabbed her immediately. Instead...she wondered, wryly, just what Parkinson was thinking. If he had a rough idea of where she was, he might order the marines to make a more careful search of the entire section. She considered, briefly, simply staying where she was, then dismissed the idea. The next set of searchers might be a little more careful.

Smiling, she clambered out of the spacesuit and headed for the hatch, unhooking the stunner from her belt. The hatch hissed open, revealing a pair of marines standing with their backs to her. They spun around, their hands grabbing for weapons, too late. Alice stunned them both and watched as they fell to the deck. Parkinson was going to kill them. Her lips twitched at the thought. No, he wouldn't kill them, but he'd give them the ass-chewing of the millennium. She checked one of the bodies until she found the terminals, then used the marine's fingerprint to unlock the device. Parkinson's orders popped up on the screen. He seemed to think she'd somehow made it into the next section.

The marine's headset bleeped. "Higgins, report."

Alice hesitated. She'd seen countless movies where the good guys were able to impersonate the bad guys and convince their superiors that nothing was wrong, but it didn't work so well in real life. She simply didn't *sound* like a male marine. And yet, Parkinson would *know* that something was wrong. Higgins hadn't responded. And that meant…

She put the terminal down on the deck—the marines would probably be able to track it—and hurried down to the section hatch, careful not to go too close. Parkinson would dispatch some of his men to check on the fallen marines…and, if she was lucky, they'd be sent from the force guarding the hatch. She smiled as she heard footsteps running towards her. The marines were on their way. She pressed herself into a sideroom, clutching the stunner in one hand. If Parkinson outguessed her, she'd have bare seconds to take them down before they got her. But the marines ran past…she gave them a few moments to get out of hearing range, then hurried down the corridor herself. The hatch looked unguarded…

There'll be guards on the far side, she reminded herself. *Parkinson won't leave the hatch completely empty.*

She keyed the switch, opening the hatch. Three men stood on the far side, their weapons raised and pointed at her. Alice froze, hastily evaluating the situation. Perhaps if she jumped them…she shook her head, inwardly. She'd never been able to best a male marine in a no-holds-barred fight, let alone three of them. She would do some damage, but they'd bring her down and…

One of the marines jabbed his rifle at her. "Bang. You're dead."

"Alas, woe is me," Alice said. The marine wasn't one of the men who'd served under her direct command. That was a relief, although she knew it was meaningless. "Contact the Major and tell him that the exercise is over."

"I already know," Parkinson said, appearing from a side hatch. "How did you evade my sweep?"

Alice smirked. "I was *inside* one of the hanging spacesuits," she said. "They didn't think to check."

Parkinson looked pained. "I'll...*discuss* it with them when they wake up," he said. "Congrats on staying ahead of us for so long."

"Thank you, sir," Alice said. "What now?"

"Return to your cabin," Parkinson said. "We'll talk about the exercise later."

Alice nodded stiffly—she knew better than to argue in front of the men—and headed off to her cabin. Her body ached, even though she'd been exercising heavily ever since *Invincible* had left the Sol System far behind. She gritted her teeth, promising herself that she wasn't going to give up. She'd been through too much to transfer to the rear or simply accept a medical discharge. She *would* be a marine again.

Her cabin felt uncomfortably large as she stepped inside. It might be small, compared to a middle-class hotel on Earth, but it was still larger than the barracks. She looked at her terminal for a moment, half-expecting to see the post-exercise report already waiting for her, then sighed and stepped into the washroom. A shower, a rest...and then she could go back for more exercise. She was *not* going to give up.

At least I stayed ahead of them for a few hours, she thought, as she turned on the water. *I'd like to see a civilian do that.*

. . .

Richard smiled to himself as his starfighter twisted in space, reversing course in the blink of an eye. The three enemy starfighters didn't realise what he was doing until it was already too late, allowing him a chance to fire into their blind spots. Two starfighters vanished from the display before their pilots even realised they were under attack. The third threw himself into a series of evasive manoeuvres that were somewhat less random than they should have been. Richard calmly lined up the shot, then blew the pilot out of space. A squawk of outrage echoed over the communications link.

"You're dead," Richard said, cheerfully. "All *three* of you are dead."

He took a moment to survey the situation. The simulated mission had been simple enough. One side had to attack the convoy, the other had to defend…it was a shame, really, that the defenders had allowed themselves to be drawn out of formation. They'd killed seven of the attackers, but the attackers had devastated the convoy. Seven freighters had been destroyed, with three more heavily damaged. The defenders might have killed more ships, but the attackers had won on points.

And this was just a simulation, he thought. *What will happen when we face a real enemy?*

"The exercise is now terminated," he said. The display faded away into a grey mist. "All pilots, get a shower and a snack, then report to the briefing room."

He opened the simulator and clambered out, feeling his legs threatening to collapse beneath him. Honestly! There was no *reason* to house the simulators in mock starfighter cockpits, was there? He leaned against the simulator until he was sure he could walk properly, then headed for the hatch. Behind him, the other pods were cracking open. The pilots were probably already assessing their performance. Richard wondered how many of them would realise just how poorly they'd actually *done*.

Too much inexperience combined with a lack of command talent, Richard thought, as he showered and changed into a fresh uniform. *They're going to have to be broken of that problem. Quickly.*

He sighed as he made his way to the briefing room. To be fair, the stats *had* been improving over the past week. The pilots were learning from their experiences. But Richard was all too aware that experience simply wasn't the same as reality. The aliens would present them with all sort of surprises, surprises that were completely unpredictable. Who knew how his pilots would cope with the unknown?

Monica entered a moment later, looking clean and tidy. "My pilots did their job," she said, as she sat at the back. "You can't say otherwise."

"No," Richard agreed. Monica knew what she was doing. It was a shame the reservists had so much they needed to relearn. "They did very well."

The room slowly filled with pilots. Richard resisted the urge to make sarcastic comments about pilots who would be late to their own funerals. They should have learnt how to shower at the academy, surely. He waited until the compartment was full, then slapped the table hard enough to make everyone jump. The pilots stopped chattering and stared at him in surprise.

"That exercise was a failure," Richard said, sharply. His voice echoed in the silent compartment. "And *why* was it a failure?"

He waited, just to see if someone would try to answer, then went on. "The mission objective was to get the convoy from Alpha to Beta without losing a single ship. What happened? Seven out of ten ships were destroyed! And *why* were they destroyed? They were destroyed because their escorting starfighters were more concerned with scoring kills than covering the convoy they were meant to be escorting! Do you know what would have happened if the engagement had been *real*?

"For want of a nail..."—he shook his head in annoyance, remembering how his instructors had forced him to study the whole poem—"a kingdom was lost, eventually. What would have happened if that convoy had failed to reach its destination? We might have lost a base, which would have led to the loss of a star system, which might have cost us the war itself...all because a pack of starfighter pilots couldn't be bothered to carry out their actual mission."

His gaze swept the room. He understood, better than he cared to admit, the urge to score kills. Every pilot wanted to paint a golden ace on their cockpit, to signify that they had killed over five enemy starfighters; every pilot wanted to be known as a brave and skilled flyer. He understood, but the mission came first. There was no room for mavericks in the compartment. The starfighter pilots *had* to follow orders.

"I understand how you feel," he said, quietly. "But the mission comes first."

Richard took a long breath. "We have two weeks to reach Falkirk, then we'll be heading into enemy territory. By then, I want all of our weaknesses smoothed out. I want each and every one of you to put the mission first. And if you don't"—he let his words hang in the air for a second—"you will be traded for a more experienced pilot from one of the fleet carriers."

Which may be a little harsh, he thought, keeping his face under tight control. *And it might nip your careers in the bud.*

He took a long breath. "Get some food, then report back to the simulators. We're going to be going through the exercise again. Dismissed."

"I think they took your words to heart," Monica said, once they were alone. "But they also think they have to rack up kills."

"Not when they're charged with escorting a convoy," Richard muttered. "*Stellar Star and the Starfighter Pilots* has a lot to answer for."

"I think *Battle of Earth* and *Ark Royal* might have been more of an influence," Monica said, dryly. "No one *really* takes *Stellar Star and the Starfighter Pilots* seriously."

Richard shrugged. *Battle of Earth* and *Ark Royal* were hugely patriotic movies, written and produced by scriptwriters who were more interested in spectacle and propaganda than realism. Richard had never met Theodore Smith, but he *had* met Admiral Fitzwilliam and the actor who'd played him hadn't looked anything like the former First Space Lord. It was a minor miracle they'd produced a realistic *Ark Royal*. Richard would have expected them to present a starship out of a futuristic fantasy. The producers had probably boosted Royal Navy recruitment for generations to come.

"It doesn't matter," he said, dismissing the movies and their producers. What they knew about life in the navy could be written on the back of a second-class postage stamp, with room left over. "What matters is carrying out the mission."

"I know," Monica said. "And they know it too. They're just..."

"Inexperienced," Richard said. He ground his teeth in frustration. "And young."

Monica pointed a finger at him. "You're in your late twenties," she said. "You're not *that* much older than them. And I'm only a couple of years younger than you. Give them time."

"We don't *have* time," Richard said. "What happens if we get attacked tomorrow?"

He looked at the bulkhead, visualising the empty system on the far side. The virus could have sneaked ships down the tramlines easily, if it wished. They might be attacked at any moment. Richard didn't blame the captain for feeling paranoid, even though he'd heard—and squelched—some grumbling from his pilots. The virus had every reason to try to attack enemy fleets before they reached Falkirk.

"Then we fight bravely," Monica said. The calm confidence in her voice was almost reassuring. "They won't let you down."

"I hope not," Richard said. He turned away from her, heading towards the desk. "But right now I'm more concerned with them letting themselves down."

"They'll do better in the real world," Monica assured him. "Didn't we?"

Richard gave her a sharp look, but said nothing.

CHAPTER TEN

STEPHEN HAD TAKEN THE PRECAUTION, as the fleet approached the Falkirk Tramline, of sounding the alert and bringing his crew to battlestations. There had been no suggestion that Falkirk had actually been attacked, let alone occupied, but he was feeling paranoid. The virus could easily have subverted a handful of crewmen, then steadily spread through the multinational force despite the best precautions human ingenuity could devise. Stephen *hoped* he was merely being paranoid. If the virus had overwhelmed the multinational fleet, humanity was probably doomed.

"Jump completed, Captain," Sonia said.

"Transmit our IFF to System Command," Stephen ordered. "Tactical?"

"The sensors are coming back online now," Lieutenant-Commander David Arthur reported, calmly. "Long-range sensors suggest that the system hasn't been attacked."

Stephen frowned as the display started to fill with icons. Six months ago, Falkirk hadn't been considered anything more than a refuelling post for starships *en route* to Wensleydale. It had a gas giant and a handful of rocky airless worlds, but little else to attract spacefaring powers when there were plenty of more habitable worlds. Britain had laid claim to the system more to secure the trade links to Wensleydale than anything else. Now, it had been turned into a formidable military base. Nine fleet carriers, twelve battleships, and over a hundred smaller ships held station near the tramline, while a handful of space stations orbited the gas giant and mining craft buzzed around the asteroids. The defenders were already working on building up a small industrial base. It would never match a major colony, but it would reduce shipping costs…

"Captain, we're picking up a challenge," Morse said. "They're demanding that we repeat our IFF."

Stephen's eyes narrowed. There hadn't been *time* for *Invincible's* arrival to have been noticed, let alone her IFF signal reach Admiral Weisskopf. A new icon flickered to life on the display, a Japanese destroyer sitting near the tramline. Stephen relaxed, slightly. The Japanese ship might have orders to recheck every ship entering the system.

"Repeat the signal," he ordered. "And request permission to rendezvous with the main fleet."

"Aye, Captain," Morse said. There was a long pause. "They've cleared us to proceed, sir."

Stephen nodded. "Helm, set course to rendezvous with Admiral Weisskopf."

"Aye, sir."

Newcomb glanced at him. "Do you think we'll be haggling over whoever owns this system in the next few years?"

"Probably," Stephen said. Britain might have claimed the system, but the other human—and alien—powers had provided a great deal of investment. When—if—the viral crisis ended, there was going to be an argument over who should *actually* have jurisdiction. "We might end up cutting a deal with the other Great Powers."

He put the thought aside as *Invincible* and her flotilla glided towards the Multinational Fleet's position. Up close, it was even more impressive than he'd realised. The Tadpoles and the Foxes had both sent contingents to join their human allies, fearing the consequences if the virus managed to infect human space. Stephen had read papers suggesting the virus would have no trouble infecting every alien race known to mankind, as long as they were carbon-based. So far, no one had encountered a race that *wasn't* carbon-based. Humanity's allies had excellent reasons for wanting to make a stand so far from their homeworlds.

"Captain," Morse said. "Admiral Weisskopf sends his compliments and invites you to join him onboard USS *Texas*."

"Please inform the admiral that I will be delighted," Stephen said. "Have my shuttle prepared for departure."

"Aye, Captain."

"We're settling into position now," Sonia said. "The fleet doesn't seem to want us to come too close."

"Very good," Stephen said. He wasn't too surprised. *Invincible* had had infected humans onboard. Admiral Weisskopf had good reason to be concerned. "Inform Admiral Weisskopf that I'm on my way."

He passed the bridge to Newcomb, then changed into his dress uniform and walked directly to his shuttle. The pilot disengaged from *Invincible* with commendable speed and took the shuttle straight towards *Texas*, disregarding the remainder of the fleet. Stephen looked forward with interest as the American battleship came into view. *Texas* was larger than her British counterparts, although Stephen wasn't so sure that her extra weapons and armour gave her an edge. It looked as if she'd have problems bringing all of her weapons to bear on a single target.

And she's a bigger target too, he thought. He could see some advantages to the design. The Americans could rotate their ship, allowing each plasma gun a chance to fire and then recharge while maintaining a consistent bombardment. They could presumably *overcharge* their plasma cannons, if they were rotating their ship. They'd run the risk of accidentally overloading the plasma containment chambers, but they'd presumably hardwired some safeguards into the system. *She would be a tricky customer in a fight.*

"Captain, we're being ordered to dock at the upper airlock, rather than land in their shuttlebay," the pilot said. "We'll be docked in two minutes."

"Understood," Stephen said. Hopefully, docking at an airlock meant a certain lack of formality. And yet…he had a feeling that the Americans were feeling paranoid. If the shuttle was carrying a nuke, it would do a great deal *less* damage if it detonated outside the battleship's hull. They wouldn't let him land in the shuttlebay unless they were *entirely* sure of his *bona fides*. "Dock as soon as you can."

He took a long breath as the shuttle docked with the giant battleship. The gravity field flickered a moment later, growing stronger momentarily before the shuttle's generator automatically shut down. Stephen stood and headed for the hatch, silently cursing whoever had designed his dress uniform under his breath. It felt uncomfortable when he needed to feel relaxed.

A pair of United States Marines in dress uniform stood at the far side of the hatch, behind a biohazard barrier. "Sir," the leader said. "We need to do a blood test."

Stephen nodded, holding out his hand for the scanner. It bleeped a moment later, signalling that he was clean. The marines relaxed visibly— if Stephen had been infected, their odds of survival would have been very low—and motioned him through the barrier and into an inner hatch. A young ensign was waiting for him. She looked so young that she made Stephen feel old.

"Welcome onboard, Captain," she said. "Admiral Weisskopf is waiting for you."

Stephen looked around with interest as she led him through a maze of corridors. The American ship wasn't *that* different to its British counterparts, not on the inside. It would have been hard to tell it *was* an American ship if the American flag hadn't been displayed everywhere. Otherwise, it felt just like a British ship. But that wasn't really a surprise. A great many components had been standardised, even before the First Interstellar War. The battleship would have her secrets, of course, just like *Invincible*, but...

He pushed the thought aside as the ensign opened a hatch. "Admiral Weisskopf, sir," she said. "Captain Shields, HMS *Invincible*."

Stephen stepped past her and into the cabin. Admiral Weisskopf was a short muscular man with skin so dark that Stephen found it hard to look him in the eye. He saluted as the hatch hissed closed behind him. Admiral

Weisskopf looked back at him with equal interest. The last time they'd met, *Invincible* had been returning to Earth. Now...

"Take a seat," Admiral Weisskopf said. He had a thick Texan accent that Stephen found a little hard to follow. "I take it you didn't get put in front of a court-martial after all."

"It was a close-run thing," Stephen said. He sat down, resting his hands on his lap. "Luckily, I followed proper procedure. They had no grounds to charge me with anything."

"And so they've sent you and your ship back here," Admiral Weisskopf said. His face twisted in displeasure. "I am not happy at the thought of poking the hornet's nest."

Stephen met his eyes. "Wouldn't you prefer to know what's coming at you?"

"I have destroyers in the systems between us and Alien-1," Admiral Weisskopf said, "although they may miss the signs of a major enemy offensive. I'm feeling rather exposed out here."

"I know, sir," Stephen said. "My orders are to attempt to remain undetected..."

"Which may prove difficult," Admiral Weisskopf said, cutting him off. "If it was up to me, *Captain*, you and your little flotilla would join the MNF and stand in defence of the tramline chain to Earth."

He snorted, rudely. "But it's not up to me, is it?"

Stephen said nothing. He understood Admiral Weisskopf's concerns. But, at the same time, he also understood the importance of finding out what was coming towards the human sphere before it actually arrived. They knew almost nothing about their new foe, nothing they could use to calculate just how strong the virus actually was. *Invincible's* mission might be their only hope of peering through the fog of war before it was too late. Every analyst agreed that it was only a matter of time before the offensive began.

"Of course not," Admiral Weisskopf said. "Good luck, Captain. Try not to stir up a swarm of angry hornets."

"Yes, sir," Stephen said. "What is the current situation?"

Admiral Weisskopf frowned. "So far, there's been no trace of anything sneaking down the tramline chain from Alien-1. Which proves nothing, of course. We've seeded the whole system with scansats, but as long as the bastards are careful they can get a whole fleet into attack position without being detected. You know how badly fucked we'd be if they did get control of this system. They'd be able to attack us from four different angles."

"Yes, sir," Stephen said. He didn't *think* the virus would want to leave such a powerful fleet in its rear, but they'd seen more than enough evidence to confirm that the virus simply didn't *think* like humans. Hell, if cut off from its supply lines, Admiral Weisskopf's fleet would simply wither on the vine. "And Wensleydale?"

"The quarantine has not been broken, as far as we can tell," Admiral Weisskopf said. "None of the captured—and presumed infected—starships have been located. We assume they're attempting to infect our worlds, but so far they haven't shown themselves. Nor have we spotted the missing Russian ship. We're assuming the worst."

He looked up at Stephen. "Understand this, Captain. My priority is maintaining control of this system and keeping the bastards out. I have strict orders *not* to go haring after you if you run into trouble. Your ships will be on their own. I *cannot* leave my post, Captain, and I cannot draw down my defences to assist you. Be absolutely clear on that. I cannot provide any assistance once you've crossed the tramline."

Stephen nodded, unsurprised. "I understand, Admiral," he said. "We planned on the assumption that we'd be alone."

"Good thinking," Admiral Weisskopf grunted. "Just make absolutely sure that you don't get spotted. I really *don't* want them to come boiling out of the tramline with blood in their eyes."

"Yes, sir," Stephen said.

He didn't take the Admiral's words personally. Admiral Weisskopf had every reason to be concerned. Falkirk was heavily defended, but no defence was perfect. The virus could easily deploy a blocking force to pin Admiral Weisskopf down, then dispatch the rest of its fleet into the human sphere.

And then...Stephen couldn't help feeling pity for the American. He was the only man who could lose the war in an afternoon.

There are other defence lines closer to Earth, Stephen thought. *But the aliens could come at us from a hundred different directions.*

Admiral Weisskopf smiled. "Now that's over, Captain," he said, "I hope you'll have time to join my staff and I for dinner."

"It would be my pleasure," Stephen said. "But afterwards, I will have to return to my ship."

"Of course," Admiral Weisskopf said. "And you'll be leaving tomorrow?"

Stephen nodded. "We have orders to move fast," he said. "And there's no hope of shore leave here."

"Tell me about it," Admiral Weisskopf said, as he lead the way to the Officers Mess. "It'll be years before there's anything more exciting than cloud-skimming in this system."

"Yes, sir," Stephen said, with the private thought it wouldn't be long before the NAAFI and its counterparts started to set up shop within the system. And they'd be followed by far less scrupulous organisations. "There's nothing else to do here."

Dinner was surprisingly spicy, Stephen discovered, although he found himself enjoying it more than he'd expected. Admiral Weisskopf explained that his cook was Mexican, someone who had joined the USN to escape the chaos that gripped the Mexican Protectorates on a regular basis. Stephen had to admit he'd never eaten anything like it, even in London's handful of curry houses. He was tempted to suggest that the cook open a restaurant in London, although it was possible he wouldn't be granted a licence. The city's authorities were suspicious of anything that smacked of ethnic food.

Which is stupid, Stephen thought. The Troubles had left scars in their wake. He couldn't help wondering just how much Britain had lost in the chaos. *It isn't as if we ever went to war with Mexico.*

He took a sip of his beer and surveyed the table. The Americans seemed to be considerably less formal than their British counterparts, with junior officers enjoying a freedom to speak that would probably have landed their counterparts in hot water. They didn't seem to care so much about the dinner arrangements, either. There hadn't been any set courses, just an invitation for the diners to help themselves. Stephen was pretty sure the Americans would be more formal if diplomats or senior officers were involved, but he found their attitude rather relaxing. It was nice not to have to worry about the proper way to hold a fork.

"You'll be able to check in with the destroyers on the near side of Alien-1," Admiral Weisskopf said, once the meal was finished. "After that, you're on your own."

"Yes, sir," Stephen said. "I knew the job was dangerous when I took it."

"More dangerous than you might think," Admiral Weisskopf warned. "Watch your back."

"Yes, sir," Stephen said.

He was in a pensive mood as the shuttle disengaged from *Texas* and headed back to *Invincible*. He'd read Admiral Weisskopf's orders. He wasn't surprised that Admiral Weisskopf was unwilling to detach ships from the MNF to go to *Invincible's* aid. His orders gave him very little leeway. He was to hold Falkirk and, if that proved impossible, he was to withdraw down the tramline chain. He was not to go gallivanting off on missions that might make it harder for him to carry out his orders.

"Captain, we'll dock in two minutes," the pilot said. "Do you have any specific orders?"

"Just dock at the forward airlock," Stephen ordered. He keyed his wrist-com. "Commander Newcomb, meet me in my Ready Room in forty minutes."

He sighed as he sat back and studied the MNF. It looked alert, but no fleet could remain on alert indefinitely. And yet, Admiral Weisskopf had been right. An attack could come at any moment, catching the defenders by surprise. The MNF would be constantly rotating its positions, with some units at battlestations while others remained at a lower state of readiness. They had no choice. They couldn't keep their crews at alert indefinitely without burning them out.

A low rumble echoed through the shuttle—the gravity field flickered again—as the craft docked with *Invincible*. Stephen rose and walked through the airlock, thinking hard. There didn't seem to be any reason to make any changes to the original plan, save perhaps for the presence of scouting destroyers in the systems between Falkirk and Alien-1. He could send messages with them, allowing him to keep his own destroyers in reserve. It wasn't ideal—the flicker network had spoilt them—but it was the best he could do. Admiral Weisskopf would need their records from Alien-1 before they pushed into unexplored space.

Commander Newcomb met Stephen in his Ready Room. "How was it?"

"We're going to be on our own, as we anticipated," Stephen said, and shortly outlined what had happened during the meeting. "The MNF isn't allowed to leave Falkirk."

"It makes sense, sir," Newcomb said. "Falkirk is a bottleneck system."

"Unless the virus has its own version of the jump drive," Stephen said. The virus might not be deterred by the immense cost of building and using the drive. "They could leapfrog around the MNF and strike at Earth."

"They'd still need to get control of the tramlines," Newcomb pointed out. "I don't believe they could produce an indefinite supply of jump cages."

Stephen shrugged. They knew so *little* about their enemy. The virus might have no qualms about wasting vast amounts of resources; hell, the resources it would expend on building jump drive cages might be a tiny fraction of its overall resources. He cursed under his breath. MI6 could make reasonably accurate guesses at how many ships the Great Powers might be able and willing to build—and semi-accurate guesses about the alien powers—but the virus was a complete blank. The idea of an entire star system being converted into a war machine was terrifying. Even during the darkest days of the First Interstellar War, humanity hadn't embraced collectivism. There was no way the Great Powers would agree to unite as one. But the virus? It *was* a single entity.

It must have some way of splitting up and recombining, Stephen thought. *I wonder if we could turn it against itself...*

He put the thought aside for later consideration and sighed. "Commander, ready the ship for departure as planned," he said. "I have to write my final reports to the Admiralty, then get some rest."

"Yes, sir," Newcomb said. "I'll take care of it personally."

CHAPTER ELEVEN

"JUMP COMPLETED, CAPTAIN," SONIA SAID. Her voice was hushed. "The remainder of the flotilla has followed us through."

"Cloaking device engaged," Lieutenant-Commander David Arthur said. "I've established laser links to the flotilla."

Which doesn't mean that we're not being watched by unseen eyes, Stephen thought. *Our cloaking device would have flickered on transit.*

He watched as the tactical display slowly filled with icons. The dwarf star system had been unnamed when *Invincible* had passed through the first time; someone, probably one of Admiral Weisskopf's stellar cartographers, had named the system Grumpy. Stephen wasn't sure how he'd managed to get away with it, although he did have to admit that Grumpy was largely useless as anything more than a transit system. The next system was much more interesting—and useful. But the wrangling over who had the first claim had been terminated by the discovery of Alien-1 on the far side.

"Helm, take us to Tramline Two," he ordered. "But keep us in stealth at all times."

"Aye, sir," Sonia said.

Stephen smiled, despite the situation. She was practically whispering, even though the odds of the aliens overhearing her were nil. Stephen had always found that more than a little amusing. It was, perhaps, a legacy of the days when the Royal Navy had deployed submarines, rather than starships; the days when a single cough, at the wrong time, could bring an enemy fleet down on their heads. But now...his crew could sing and dance to their heart's content and no one would hear them. Sound simply didn't travel through a vacuum.

In space, no one can hear you scream, he thought, with a flicker of amusement. He'd watched the latest set of *Alien* remakes as a child, although they were less amusing now that they were facing an enemy that *did* turn humans into hosts. *Or be able to tell if there's something seriously wrong with you.*

He pushed the thought out of his mind as *Invincible* continued her slow transit across the system. Her active sensors were stepped down—active sensor pulses would have drawn watching eyes like flies to shit—but her passive sensors were picking up nothing. Not, he reminded himself, that that proved the flotilla was alone. Standard doctrine insisted that every star system should be picketed, if the ships were available. He would have been astonished if the virus *hadn't* deployed a small fleet of watching eyes. The Royal Navy had done the same. There was only one known line of contact between the human race and its new enemy. It *had* to be picketed.

Unless they're so alien their doctrine makes no sense to us, he thought. It was hard to believe—the Tadpoles and Foxes might have been alien, but their doctrine was understandable—and yet, the virus was unlike any foe humanity had ever faced. *They might be letting us slip through the door so they can slam it closed behind us.*

He scowled. It didn't seem likely, unless the virus had some sort of sensor system that was light years ahead of anything the Royal Navy possessed. *That* didn't seem likely either—the virus hadn't been able to track *Invincible* while she was in stealth—but it was impossible to be sure. The enemy ships *might* have something up their sleeve, something the Royal Navy's boffins hadn't even imagined, let alone turned into workable hardware. He gritted his teeth, reminding himself—again—that the virus hadn't shown them anything too advanced. The uncertainty would be more harmful than their weapons. He'd be questioning his own judgement for weeks and months to come, simply because he wasn't sure what he was facing.

Most surprises happen because someone misunderstood what they saw, he thought. He'd had that drilled into his head, time and time again, at the Academy. *But when facing aliens, surprises happen because their technology is more advanced or went down a different path than our own...*

The sensor console *pinged*. "Captain," Lieutenant Alison Adams said. "We may have a contact."

Stephen tensed. "A contact?"

"Yes, Captain," Alison said. "I'm picking up an energy flux, twelve light-seconds from our outer engagement envelope."

"Show me," Stephen ordered.

He leaned forward as a blurry icon appeared in front of him. The enemy contact—if it was an enemy contact—was slowly closing on the flotilla. It was out of immediate weapons range—unless, again, it had a super-advanced weapons system Stephen had never heard of—but it wouldn't be long until it entered missile range. And then...he studied the flicker for a long moment, as if staring would allow him to divine the contact's power curves. A lone destroyer wouldn't stand a chance against his ships, but a brief exchange of fire would bring any *other* ships in the system down on his head like a ton of bricks. Hell, he wasn't even sure it *was* a contact. Sensor ghosts were far from unknown when the cloaking system was engaged.

"Check with the other ships," he ordered. "See if they're picking it up too."

"The datanet says no," Alison reported. "But sir, that proves nothing."

"I know," Stephen said. *Invincible* was the only ship picking up the sensor contact, but they might simply have gotten lucky. A tiny flicker in an enemy cloaking device might be enough to let one ship detect them, if it was in the right place at the right time. And now...the icon was right in front of him. "Tell them to keep their eyes open."

His mind raced. If the contact was real, he needed to evade it before jumping through the next tramline. He didn't dare have an enemy ship shadow them right up to the jump point, giving the bastards a chance to set up an ambush on the far side. But if the contact wasn't real, if he was jumping at shadows…he shook his head. He had to assume the contact was real. He didn't dare do anything else.

"Bring the ship to battlestations," he ordered. Alarms howled through the mighty ship. He couldn't launch fighters—not without revealing his exact position—but he could prepare for combat. "Helm, alter course. Take us away from the contact."

"Aye, sir," Sonia said.

Stephen watched the contact for a long moment, trying to guess what the enemy commander was thinking. Did he know he'd stumbled on an entire flotilla? Or did he think he'd detected a single starship? The survey ships were supposed to be *good* at concealing their presence—no one wanted to accidentally start a war with a completely unknown alien race—but their crews included a number of civilians. Stephen found it easy to imagine a screw-up had given the aliens a chance to detect the survey vessels, although his sensors hadn't detected anything alarming. Or…had the Russians had a little accident? Or…Stephen dismissed the thought. There was no point in worrying about it now. Besides, they might simply have gotten very unlucky. He'd altered course as soon as he'd left Falkirk, but there was only a limited number of vectors his ship could have followed as it approached the tramline.

For all we know, this system could be seeded with stealthed scansats, he thought. The virus hadn't shown any inclination to push out towards Falkirk, but it hadn't known there was a prospective threat on the far side of the tramlines. *They've certainly had enough time to secure the system and deploy early-warning scansats.*

"Course altered, Captain," Sonia said. "The remainder of the flotilla is following us."

Stephen nodded, considering his options. If the aliens had locked onto one of the smaller ships, they should *follow* that ship…he briefly considered ordering *Invincible* to alter course again, then put the thought aside. They had no idea what they were facing. He studied the blurred image for a moment, wondering if he dared make a guess. But there simply wasn't enough data. They could be facing anything from a destroyer to a battleship.

Or something even larger, Stephen thought. *They might have started to build superdreadnaughts of their own.*

He smiled. The boffins insisted that there were limits to the size of military starships, but civilian ships didn't have such problems. He'd seen the plans for giant colonist-carriers that made fleet carriers look tiny. They'd struck him as excessive, even though the government was determined to move as many people off Earth and out of the Sol System as possible. The smaller colonist-carriers could still move fifty thousand colonists in a single voyage. But it was unlikely the aliens had pointed a colonist-carrier in his direction.

Or maybe not, he reminded himself. *They sent a sublight colony ship to infect our worlds.*

"Captain, the contact is keeping pace with us," Alison said. "It's holding position."

Commander Newcomb's face popped up in Stephen's display. "Captain, if it's holding position, it's probably a sensor ghost."

Stephen frowned. Newcomb was right—even the most able crew in the Royal Navy would have difficulty holding a *precise* position, relative to their target—but he didn't dare take it for granted. Were they wasting their time? Or were they being shadowed by an alien starship? There was no way he could simply resume course for the tramline without knowing, yet…he didn't want to reveal their position either. The mission would fail before it had truly begun.

"Helm, increase speed," he ordered. "Let them try and keep pace with us."

"Aye, Captain," Alison said.

Stephen felt the tension grew stronger as the drives started to hum. The carrier had an impressive—and classified—top speed, but everyone knew that there was a good chance that increasing speed would also increase their chances of being detected. There was no way the cloaking device could hide *everything.* A single power fluctuation would be enough to give the enemy a solid lock on *Invincible's* hull. And then…the enemy ship, if indeed it *was* an enemy ship, was still out of missile range, but it would have plenty of opportunity to whistle up reinforcements. Or simply close to attack range and open fire.

I could scatter the flotilla, with orders to link up again by the tramline, Stephen thought. *And then see who was shadowed...*

He dismissed the thought with a flicker of irritation. There was too great a chance of the ships being picked off, one by one. Or a lone ship being overwhelmed and forced to surrender. No, no one would surrender in *this* war. There would be no POW camps for human captives, merely infection and the complete loss of freedom and individuality. He had strict orders to blow his ship to dust rather than let his crew be taken alive. And, if worse came to worst, he'd do it too.

"She's still maintaining course and speed," Alison said. "Captain, I think we're dealing with a ghost."

Stephen nodded, slowly. It was certainly starting to *look* as if they were panicking over nothing. And yet, there was that quiet nagging doubt. He didn't dare relax—or resume course towards the tramline—until he *knew*. But how *could* he know?

"Prepare to reverse course, maximum power," he ordered. "Take us straight towards the unknown contact."

Sonia sounded nervous. "Aye, Captain."

Stephen didn't really blame her. If there *was* an enemy ship shadowing them, he was about to betray his ship's location...and close the range so sharply that *Invincible* might find herself impaled on the enemy's weapons. He had no qualms about taking on a destroyer, or even a cruiser, but a battleship might be beyond their ability to handle. A close-range engagement would be disastrous. And yet, he saw no choice. He *had* to know what he was facing.

"Contact the other ships," he added. "The survey ships are to stand off and watch, then return to Falkirk if there's something we can't handle. The remaining ships are to shadow us."

"Aye, Captain," Lieutenant Thomas Morse said.

Stephen took a breath. "Reverse course, *now!*"

He felt a shudder running through his ship as she spun on her axis, then bolted towards the enemy contact. There was a very real risk in carrying out the manoeuvre, even though he knew his ship could handle it. *Invincible* had been designed for speed and agility as well as firepower and survivability. And yet...he allowed himself a flicker of relief as Sonia completed the manoeuvre successfully. Breaking his ship's back would probably have earned him a court-martial even if the ship *hadn't* been destroyed by a prowling enemy battleship.

"Sir, the contact is still holding position," Alison reported. "I think she's definitely a sensor ghost."

Either that, or her captain has the reactions of a cat, Stephen thought. It didn't seem too likely. He doubted the finest crew in the Royal Navy could keep their ship under such tight control. A starfighter might be able to manage it. But a starfighter couldn't cloak. *She's a sensor ghost.*

"Resume course towards the tramline," he ordered, after a long moment. "And spread out the flotilla a little. I want to know if there are any other sensor contacts within range."

"Aye, Captain."

"Commander Newcomb, have the engineering crews examine the cloaking device," he added, slowly. "As best as they can while the device is functional. We cannot waste too much of our time chasing ghosts."

"Aye, Captain."

Stephen sat back in his chair, cursing under his breath. The little diversion had taken far too much of their time. The Admiralty would understand—he hoped—that the mission couldn't operate on a tight timescale, but the civilian government might feel differently. No, it *would* feel differently. Someone without experience in space operations might not realise that Stephen hadn't been able to simply ignore the sensor ghost. The simple fact that *Invincible* had been the only ship to *see* the ghost didn't prove anything.

Although it was indicative, Stephen thought. He couldn't keep the scowl off his face. *And someone will certainly make that point, back home.*

His console chimed. "Captain," Newcomb said. "The engineers ran a set of standard diagnostics. They found nothing. They'd like permission to deactivate the cloak long enough to carry out a set of more advanced checks."

Stephen cursed under his breath. It was the same old problem. There was no way to be completely *sure* that the system was deserted. If it was, fine; if it wasn't, deactivating the cloak might well give their location away. He could order the flotilla to head into interstellar space on a dogleg course that would keep them well away from any prospective watching eyes—although, again, there was no way to be *sure*—and deactivate the cloak when they were light-hours from the tramline, but...they had to reach Alien-1. God alone knew what that virus was doing over there.

They could be preparing to attack, he thought. *Or their fleet might already be on the way.*

"Denied," he said, a little harshly. "We have to continue towards our destination."

"Yes, sir," Newcomb said. His voice was flat, a clear sign that he disapproved. "I'll ask them to continue running the standard diagnostics."

"Do so," Stephen ordered. He didn't really blame Newcomb for disapproving. The last thing they needed was to waste time chasing *more* sensor ghosts around the system. "And then come to the bridge to assume command."

"Aye, sir."

Stephen closed the connection and leaned back in his chair, feeling the tension slowly fade into nothingness. His crew had done well, he thought, but they'd been facing nothing more substantial than an electronic sensor ghost. Absently, he tapped his console, bringing up the automated readiness reports. The experienced officers had done their work well—and thank God he'd been able to keep most of his bridge crew—but the newcomers were still having problems. He sighed in irritation. They'd just have to keep running drills until everyone was thoroughly sick of them.

And when we reach Alien-1, we'll be tested properly, he thought. *And we'll suffer a worse fate than being shouted at by our supervisors if we fail.*

His lips quirked into a thin smile. As a junior officer, he'd resented the endless series of drills; as a senior officer, he understood their value. Hard training, easy mission; easy training, hard mission. He just hoped the drills weren't misleading. He'd read too many horror stories from the First Interstellar War where the captains and crews had done everything right, as far as they'd known, and still had the shit kicked out of them. Their training hadn't prepared them for an alien foe with advanced technology and a willingness to use it.

Commander Newcomb stepped onto the bridge. "Captain?"

"We'll be crossing the tramline in seventeen hours," Stephen said, standing. "And then we have one more system to cross before we reach Alien-1. Wake me just before we reach the tramline or if we encounter any more sensor contacts."

"Aye, sir," Newcomb said.

"You have the bridge," Stephen said. "I'll be in my ready room."

He turned and strode into his ready room. He'd take a short nap, then start writing a brief report on the sensor ghost. The boffins would need to be informed, although he'd have to make sure the Admiralty knew to watch their attempts to *fix* the problem carefully. He'd heard stories about how the Tadpoles had managed to sneak through sensor grids; they'd realised, somehow, that the grids were programmed to ignore transient contacts that didn't appear solid. The recriminations had been savage.

It seemed like a good idea at the time, he reminded himself. No one had seen any point in tracking down random contacts. *But that is true of everything, isn't it?*

CHAPTER TWELVE

"THERE'S NO SIGN OF ANY ENEMY CONTACTS within the system," Alison said. "I can't even detect a settlement on the planet's surface."

Stephen frowned. The alien system—unnamed, thanks to the political wrangling—was a decent piece of real estate. A habitable planet, three gas giants and a large asteroid field...he could see why the Russians were insisting that *they* had a solid claim to the system, even though it was right next to Alien-1. He couldn't imagine any *human* power leaving the system undeveloped. The Tadpoles or Foxes would certainly settle the system for themselves if *they* had the inside track. But the virus seemed to have left the system completely alone.

Unless it has already infected the planet's biosphere, he thought, morbidly. *It might not see any value in landing colonists...*

He shook his head. It made no sense. The virus was a spacefaring power. It *needed* to set up industrial nodes and shipyards, if nothing else. Stephen was prepared to accept that the virus might not want—or need—a conventional economy, one geared towards supporting a capitalist system, but surely it needed to build up its fleet. It made no sense whatsoever. But... he reminded himself, once again, that the virus was alien. They didn't dare assume that it thought like humans.

"Take us to the tramline, dogleg course," he ordered. There had been no more sensor contacts, but he was still wary. "And prepare to enter Alien-1."

He forced himself to wait—and read the reports from his department heads—as the small flotilla headed towards the tramline. If nothing else, the sensor ghost had concentrated quite a few minds. His departments were performing with a much greater level of efficiency, at least in the simulators. It was a shame his crew couldn't carry out any live-fire exercises, but they would be far too revealing. Stephen wouldn't have cared to bet that the aliens weren't keeping an eye on the unnamed system. It was a single transit away from one of their core systems.

Unless they have so many core systems they can afford to lose one, Stephen thought, morbidly. There was no way to know *just* how far the virus had spread over the last few thousand years. A hundred worlds like Alien-1 would be able to produce and support a war machine that would grind Earth—and her alien allies—into powder. *That's what we're here to find out.*

"Captain," Morse said. "The Russians are requesting permission to hop through the tramline first."

Stephen hesitated. He'd intended to send one of the destroyers through first, just to make sure the other side was clear. He didn't like to admit it, but the tiny destroyers were expendable. And yet...he scowled, studying the Russian ship on the display. He'd done his best to befriend his Russian counterpart, but the man had kept his distance. Stephen wasn't sure if Kaminov had his own agenda, or if he was worried about running afoul of his political commissioner...he shook his head. There was no way to know. But if the Russians wanted the dubious honour of jumping through the tramline first...

"Inform them that they may take the lead," Stephen said. "And remind them not to hesitate if they run into trouble."

He forced himself to wait as the tramline slowly came into view. The odds of the enemy mounting a successful ambush were very low—every spacer knew that, beyond a shadow of a doubt—but if the enemy *had* managed to track the flotilla they might *just* get a fleet into place to open fire as soon as *Invincible* crossed the tramlines. Her sensors down, her cloaking device fluctuating...she'd be naked and vulnerable. But the enemy would have to get very lucky to succeed. Stephen had studied interstellar war extensively and he knew that only a handful of ambushes had ever been pulled off successfully. Even the most skilful crews would need a great deal of luck to succeed.

"Captain," Sonia said. "We're in position."

"Very good," Stephen ordered. Sweat prickled down his back. "Order the Russians to proceed."

He forced himself to watch, as dispassionately as possible, as *Yuriy Ivanov* slowly moved towards the tramline and vanished. A timer popped up on the display as soon as her icon flashed out of existence, counting the seconds until her planned return. Stephen braced himself, wondering just what the Russian ship had encountered. If she *had* run into a trap...he cursed under his breath. If the Russians didn't return, he'd have no choice, but to back off and find another jump point. The Russians would have to fend for themselves.

And they might just be infected, he thought. The doctors seemed confident that it would take hours for the virus to infect a ship's crew, but Stephen didn't dare take that for granted. If the virus was more aggressive than they'd realised, if it could take over a body in less than ten minutes, the Russian ship might become an enemy before his crew had a chance to get suspicious. *The virus has changed everything.*

An alert sounded as *Yuriy Ivanov* flashed back into the alien system. A datalink opened a moment later, the records being automatically shunted into a sealed computer system. The Royal Navy was all too aware of the dangers of being hacked, even though the Russians would have to be mad to try something during wartime. But if the ship was no longer friendly... Stephen gritted his teeth until they started to hurt. There were just too many unknowns.

"Local space on the far side of the tramline appears to be clear," Alison said. The analyst decks were already studying the records. "However, there is definitely a great deal of industrial activity within the system."

We already knew that, Stephen thought, ungraciously. *They have nearly as much industry within this system as we do orbiting Earth.*

He studied the records for a long moment, knowing the decision to jump—or not to jump—was his and his alone. It looked safe, yet there was the constant nagging doubt. There could be an entire fleet on the far side of the tramline, just waiting for them. The Russians hadn't sprung an ambush, but that meant nothing. *Yuriy Ivanov* wasn't a prize compared to *Invincible.*

"Prepare to jump," he ordered. "The destroyers will take the lead. We'll jump after them, with the survey ships following. *Yuriy Ivanov* can bring up the rear."

He half-expected the Russians to argue, but they said nothing as the flotilla shook itself into formation, then headed towards the tramline. Stephen felt his heart start to race, despite the near-certainty of remaining undetected as they entered the enemy system. If they were wrong, they were in deep trouble...

"Jump in ten seconds," Sonia said. "Five...four..."

The universe seemed to darken, just for a second. Stephen sucked in his breath as the display blanked, then hastily started to reboot. A sun—an enemy sun—appeared in from of him, followed by a handful of planets and energy sources. There was no sign of any enemy spacecraft near the tramline, but there were hundreds of tiny ships making their way to and from the giant asteroid field. It looked as if the system's industrial activity had increased markedly over the last six months. Stephen couldn't help finding that an ominous sign.

"The remainder of the flotilla has made transit," Alison reported.

"They're asking for orders," Morse added. "Captain?"

"Order them to hold position, for the moment," Stephen said. More and more data was flowing into the display, none of it reassuring. There were limits to what they could find out with passive sensors, but—for the moment—it didn't seem to matter. "We need to pick up as much as we can from here before we head further into the system."

"Aye, sir," Morse said.

"I'm picking up a small squadron of starships," Alison said, sharply. "Warbook calls them five heavy cruisers and a fleet carrier."

Stephen tensed. "Heading towards us?"

"Not precisely," Alison said. "I'd say they were heading towards the tramline."

"Falkirk can handle them, if they're going there," Commander Newcomb said. "Unless they're building up a greater fleet."

Stephen nodded, tersely. It certainly *looked* as though the aliens weren't heading towards his ships, although it was impossible to be sure. And yet… Newcomb was right. Five heavy cruisers and a carrier would be smashed into atoms if they tried to punch their way into Falkirk. What were they doing? Setting up tripwires? Or drilling themselves? Perhaps they needed to exercise their crews too…

"They're reducing speed," Alison said. She frowned. "Captain, I think there's an enemy installation here"—an icon flashed up on the display—"but I can't tell for sure."

"Deploy two stealthed drones," Stephen ordered. He didn't want to take the flotilla any closer to the enemy ships than strictly necessary. "And let me know the moment they detect anything."

"Aye, Captain."

Stephen knew, as his ships drifted away from the tramline, that he should get some rest. But he couldn't force himself to leave his bridge as more and more information flowed into the datanet. It was rapidly becoming clear that they'd underestimated the system's industrial potential. He was starting to wonder if Alien-1 alone possessed more industrial nodes than the entire Human Sphere. It was possible, he supposed, even though he'd grown used to thinking of Sol as the most heavily-industrialised system in known space. The desperate push to match the Tadpoles—and support the growing colonisation effort—had paid off in spades. But it was starting to look as though it hadn't paid off *enough*.

Alison swore, quietly. "Captain, the probes just got a clear look at the alien installation," she said. Her voice was very quiet. "It's a fleet base, larger than Nelson or Nimitz. There's an entire fleet there."

Stephen leaned forward. "Show me."

The display updated, again. Stephen resisted the urge to swear too as the alien fleet snapped into view. Hundreds of ships, spearheaded by a dozen battleships and twenty fleet carriers...it was a force, he thought, that could do immense damage to Falkirk. Or Sol, if it managed to punch its way through the interior defence lines. And who knew what would happen then?

"That's a lot of ships," Commander Newcomb said, quietly.

"They might be hoping to intercept our ships, rather than set off to invade the Human Sphere," Lieutenant-Commander David Arthur said. "If they expect *us* to invade..."

"They might be caught out of position if we did," Newcomb snapped. "No, that's an invasion force."

"It certainly looks that way," Stephen agreed. "Communications, raise *Daring*. She is to return to Falkirk immediately, carrying a warning. The defenders have to know what might be coming in their direction."

"Aye, sir," Morse said.

Stephen studied the display for a long moment, trying to determine if there was any way *Invincible* could take the offensive. She carried mass drivers as well as more conventional—and modern—weapons, but there were just too many alien ships for his crews to guarantee hitting anything. The alien ships might have stepped down their drives, but they hadn't powered down *all* of their sensor systems. It was clear they weren't entirely unprotected. A mass driver attack might do nothing more than alert them to *Invincible's* presence.

"And order the remainder of the flotilla to proceed to survey the system, remaining under cloak at all times," he added. "And then we have to decide how to proceed."

"Aye, sir."

. . .

Alice had known, beyond a shadow of a doubt, when *Invincible* had crossed the tramline into Alien-1. She'd felt it, of course, but she'd also felt...*something* nagging at the back of her mind from the moment the jump had been completed. Space seemed to *hum* with the virus's presence, a call she had to fight to ignore. And yet, it didn't seem to be aimed at her. She honestly wasn't sure if she was imagining it or if it was a form of telepathy. The virus didn't appear to be telepathic, as far as she could tell, but...it was impossible to be sure. She hoped she *was* imagining it. There was no way to win against a telepathic opponent.

Unless you act so swiftly that the opponent has no time to read your mind, she thought, sourly. *But you have to start by realising that your opponent is telepathic.*

She dismissed the thought in irritation and turned her attention back to the display. The captain and his officers seemed to believe that she would have an insight into how the virus was deploying its forces, but in truth she couldn't think of anything the analysts hadn't already come up with for themselves. The virus was definitely preparing for war, although it seemed to be moving on its own schedule. There was something terrifying about the sheer lack of concern it seemed to be showing about the prospect of being attacked *first*. Was it a sign that the virus hadn't been attacked before—that it had always been the aggressor—or that Alien-1 and its installations were heavily protected? How many starships—and weapons platforms—did the virus have? Could it guarantee the safety of its installations even if it sent over two hundred ships into human space?

Probably, Alice thought. *Or perhaps it just doesn't care.*

It wasn't something that sat well with her, even though she'd sensed the virus's true nature from the moment she'd been infected. She'd been taught to value the men under her command, she'd been taught not to spend them lightly...but the virus simply didn't care about individuals. It wasn't *precisely* a hive mind, yet...it wouldn't blanch at throwing hundreds of thousands of bodies into the fire if it meant ultimate victory. The bodies were meaningless. She didn't think that the virus could afford to spend battleships and fleet carriers *quite* so freely—it took nearly fifteen months to build a battleship and at least two more months to shake the ship into fighting trim. Unless the virus already had so many battleships that it could afford to spend them like water...

She dismissed the thought as more data flowed into the network. It was starting to look as though her first guess had been right. Alien-1 and the other planets within the system were heavily defended. The virus might not be taking a big risk after all. And that meant...trouble. She idly calculated just how many ships the virus might have, then dismissed the thought. There was no way to be sure. The only thing she knew for certain was that Alien-1 wasn't alone. There had to be other systems under the virus's control. The constant stream of ships heading in and out of the other tramlines proved it.

And it won't be long before they go on the offensive, she thought. *And that will be extremely bad news for Falkirk.*

• • •

"Well?"

Captain Pavel Kaminov kept his face under tight control as he turned to face the wretched *zampolit*. He was a patriot, willing to lay down his life in defence of Mother Russia, but he couldn't help finding the political commissioner to be a headache. If there was one thing he envied his British counterparts, it was the lack of a government watchdog peering over their shoulders at all times. He wouldn't have minded so much if the man had had a gram of common sense—or at least experience serving on a starship—but his lack of either was so obvious that there was no point in trying to hide his true nature. It was just...irritating.

"We have not yet located *Dezhnev*," he said, coolly. There was no point in trying to lie. The *zampolit* had agents all over the ship. "She may have been destroyed."

"They would have taken her intact," the *zampolit* insisted. "She would be a valuable prize."

"A prize with a commanding officer who had orders to destroy her, rather than let her fall into enemy hands," Pavel said. It was an argument they'd had many times before. He'd insisted that *Dezhnev's* CO would have destroyed her, if he'd thought he'd lose his ship, but the asshole was right. There was a good chance that *Dezhnev* had been captured intact, her data-banks ransacked and her crew infected. "So far, we haven't seen her."

The *zampolit* looked thoroughly displeased. Pavel did his best to ignore him. If an alien ship had fallen into *his* hands, he'd have made sure it wasn't held anywhere *obvious*. He'd have transferred it to an installation on the far side of the solar system and carefully dissected it, piece by piece. The British had done that years ago, when they'd captured a Tadpole starship. There was nothing to be gained by leaving a captured alien ship in orbit. Who knew? The original owners might want it back.

We do want her back, Pavel thought. *But we also want to know what the bastards learnt from her.*

"So," the *zampolit* said. His face twisted, as if he'd bitten into something sour. "What now?"

"We do as we're told," Pavel said. His ship had orders to survey the gas giants, carrying out a tactical survey for the day when humanity went on the offensive. It galled him to follow foreign orders, but he hadn't been given a choice. His sealed orders only came into effect if he located *Dezhnev*. "And we keep our eyes open for our missing ship."

And hope for the best, he added, in the privacy of his own mind. *Because if she has been captured, we're unlikely ever to be able to see her again.*

CHAPTER THIRTEEN

"WELL," STEPHEN SAID, addressing the holographic commanding officers. "It seems we have a decision to make."

He took a sip of his tea as he studied the display. A week of carefully probing Alien-1 had yielded a wealth of data, none of it reassuring. A sizable fleet near the alien base, clearly preparing for deployment; secondary fleets orbiting the major worlds, ready to defend them against all threats; a network of orbital weapons and sensor platforms that seemed to have tripled in size since their last visit to the system...Alien-1, alone, could mount a sustained offensive against the Human Sphere. He dreaded to think about the odds if there were two or three more alien worlds with similar industrial and military potential.

"We have already informed Falkirk of the alien fleet," he continued. He tapped a control, bringing up an in-system display. "We now need to decide how to proceed. Tramline Two or Tramline Three?"

"Tramline Two," Captain Hashing said. "The vast majority of alien traffic has come through that tramline."

Captain Kaminov nodded in agreement. "It seems likely that any major alien worlds will be on the far side of that chain," he agreed. "The other system appears to have attracted far less interest."

Stephen wasn't inclined to disagree, although he knew it was important to survey both tramlines. There was no way to be *sure* that Tramline Three was useless. Indeed, if it *was* a dead end, there was no logical reason for *any* traffic to be passing through the tramline. It was possible, he supposed, that the virus *did* see a reason...he shook his head. The only way to know what was on the far side was to go and look.

Which raises an obvious question, he thought. *Do we detach one of the survey ships to examine the system or do we keep the flotilla together?*

It was a tricky problem. On one hand, sending a single ship to survey Tramline Three would speed up the process; on the other, if the ship ran into trouble, Stephen would never know what had killed it. And yet...

"I'm going to detach *Raleigh*," he said, after a moment. "Captain Hashing, your orders are to cross Tramline Three and survey the far side. If you encounter other tramlines, you have permission to make up to two jumps into enemy space before returning to Alien-1. We will attempt to link up with you at the RV point"—he'd taken care to designate it before sending his ships prowling through the enemy star system—"but if you don't make contact with us within a week head straight back to Falkirk. Make sure they know what happened before you do anything else."

"Understood," Captain Hashing said. He sounded pleased, even though everyone agreed that Tramline Three wasn't particularly important. Independent command made up for a lot of things. "I'll make sure to leave a stealthed buoy behind before heading back to Falkirk."

"Good thinking," Stephen said. "We'll do the same, if we get there first."

He studied the star chart for a long moment. "And the remainder of us will head through Tramline Two," he added. "As before, we will proceed under maximum stealth. Does anyone have a problem with it?"

"Not unless we run into another sensor ghost," Captain Jonathon Linguine said. The destroyer captain sounded oddly amused. "We couldn't take the risk of assuming that it *is* a ghost, not here."

"And end up making bloody fools of ourselves," Captain Shaw added.

Stephen felt a flicker of annoyance. They'd checked and rechecked the cloaking device, but they'd found nothing wrong. The engineers hadn't been too worried, pointing out that the device could simply have reflected a power fluctuation from *Invincible* herself, yet Stephen knew that Linguine was right. They didn't dare assume that any further sensor contacts were nothing more than sensor ghosts. It would be too dangerous.

"We did what we had to do," he said, flatly. He made a show of checking his wristcom. "We will pass through the tramlines in twenty hours from now, unless anyone has any objections."

He waited, but there were none.

"Very well," he said. "Good luck to us all."

He cancelled the conversation with a tap of his finger, then sat back in his chair. It was easy to pretend confidence, but he knew better than to let himself become overconfident. They hadn't had the chance to explore Tramline Two—or Tramline Three—during their last visit to the system. There was definitely no way to know what was lurking on the far side; it could be anything from a transit system to a minor—or major—colony world. He would just have to wait and see.

If I'd wanted to probe the unknown, I'd have gone into the survey service, he thought, wryly. He had considered it, years ago, but his family's military tradition had forbidden it. The fighting arms were the only suitable place for a second son. *But now, the military has to take the lead.*

His doorbell chimed. "Come."

Commander Newcomb stepped into the room. "Captain," he said. "I have the latest reports from the stealth drones. The analysts are predicting that the alien fleet will make its move in two weeks at most."

"But they have no way to be sure," Stephen said. He'd had his tactical staff looking for a way to break through the alien defences and cripple their fleet, but—so far—every idea they'd come up with had been a guaranteed failure. *Invincible* would be destroyed, for nothing. "The fleet could be leaving in an hour—or a year—and we would never know until we saw it go."

"Yes, sir," Commander Newcomb said. "We simply don't know."

Stephen sighed. There was no point in sending another ship back to Falkirk. Admiral Weisskopf could hardly put himself any *more* on alert. A fleet that size would certainly be detected as it passed through the tramlines...Stephen hoped. And it hadn't grown larger over the past couple of days. He sighed again as he tapped his console, bringing up the report. The analysts seemed to have done nothing more than combining a handful of reasonable estimates with outright guessing. There was no way Stephen could place any credence in their report.

"They don't seem to have any support arm," he mused. "No fleet train to back them up."

"Yet," Commander Newcomb said. "They *are* mustering freighters around Alien-1."

"True," Stephen agreed. He stood. "And that makes it all the more important that we head directly to Tramline Two. We need to know what is waiting for us."

"Yes, sir," Commander Newcomb said.

• • •

"You're late," Wing Commander Richard Redbird said, as he stepped into the observation blister. "Was there a *reason* you didn't show up to the simulations?"

Flying Officer Samra Alibis started. "Sir, I..."

Richard looked her up and down. Samra was so young that he couldn't help thinking that she should be tucked up in bed, not flying a starfighter. He was tempted to wonder if she'd lied about her age to join the navy, although the navy performed background checks on each and every prospective recruit before allowing them to take the oath and shipping them off for basic training. Samra couldn't have had an easy time of it, he noted. Her tinted skin was clear proof that she had immigrants in the family tree. Someone would probably have given her a very hard time indeed.

"You are late," Richard said, allowing his voice to harden. "Do you have an excuse?"

"I was just looking at the stars," Samra said. "Commander, I..."

Richard gave her a sharp look. "The next time the alarms howl, young lady, it might be real," he said. "Will you be distracted again?"

"No, sir," Samra said. She stood. "I was just..."

"Report to your Squadron Leader after the simulations are completed," Richard ordered, curtly. Monica would give Samra a sharp lecture—and enough push-ups to leave her arms aching for hours—but otherwise...she wouldn't suffer too badly. Her fellow pilots would remind her about her mistake time and time again, until something else happened and they forgot about it. "And I do not expect to see you distracted again."

He sat down, motioning for her to sit beside him. "What distracted you?"

Samra stood next to him, but didn't sit. "I was just...sir, the simulations aren't real."

"Be glad of it," Richard said, dryly. He looked up at her. "How many times did you get blown away over the last two weeks?"

Samra's dark skin darkened further. "Too many times."

"Correct," Richard said. "The simulations are designed to put you through your paces, *without* actually causing any harm. You need to train now to make life easier when you fly into combat."

"But it isn't *real*," Samra repeated. "Sir...it feels like we're playing games."

Richard felt a flicker of sympathy, mingled with annoyance. He'd felt the same way too, back before he'd seen the elephant for the first time. The simulators were as close to real as the Royal Navy could do, but...they weren't real. The edge he felt when he went into combat was lacking. And an inexperienced pilot wouldn't realise, at least at first, that it wasn't a bad thing. He could try all sorts of things in the simulators that would probably get him killed if he tried them in the real world.

"We're preparing for war," he said, flatly. "We might be jumped tomorrow, Samra, and if we are...we will discover just how well we've prepared to actually fight."

He grinned at her, just for a moment. "I understand how you feel," he said, checking his wristcom. They still had five hours before the ship jumped through the enemy tramline and headed into unexplored space. "But you know what? You'll learn better the moment you go into war. Believe me, you'll learn better."

If you survive, he added, silently. Simulations or no simulations, a pilot had a very good chance of dying on his first mission. It took five or six *real* missions before the odds started to improve. And then...who knew? Richard knew better than to think he was invincible, even though he'd flown more combat missions than he cared to count. A single plasma bolt—or railgun pellet—could still blow him to atoms in a flash. *I could die on the next mission too.*

"Yes, sir," Samra said. She didn't sound as though she believed him. "I..."

"Then go to the simulators and practice," Richard ordered. "You need to know what you're doing."

Samra hesitated, then saluted. "Aye, sir," she said. "I'll go there now."

And face the wrath of Monica, Richard thought, as Samra left the compartment. *Monica won't be happy at only taking ten pilots into combat.*

He sat back and peered out at the stars. Samra was right. The stars *were* distracting, even though they were barely moving. It was hard to believe that each of the spots of light was a giant ball of flaming gas in its own right, let alone that most of them had planets and asteroids—and maybe even intelligent life—of their own. A number of stars were effectively disconnected from the tramline network. Who knew what was lurking there?

We may never find out, Richard thought. The virus—and its last set of victims—had built an STL colony ship, but humanity had never tried to turn the detailed plans put together by space enthusiasts into reality. *Unless we do find a way to escape the tramlines completely.*

He studied the stars for a long moment, then rose and headed back to his duty station. There was too much work to do, including a short disciplinary note he needed to write. Samra probably wouldn't get into any real trouble, although she wouldn't feel that way. Monica was likely to have her cleaning the decks if she wasn't lucky. But if it happened again, Richard would have to take official notice of it.

We're losing our edge, he reflected, morbidly. His pilots needed to fly outside the ship, but that wasn't going to happen. *Let us just hope that we are ready for our first real encounter with the enemy. If we're not...*

He put the thought aside. Whatever happened would happen. And all he could do was try to be ready for it.

. . .

"Captain," Sonia said. "We are ready to jump."

Stephen nodded. Tramline Two looked normal, a simple line of gravitational force stretching from Alien-1 to an unknown destination—*Alien-2*, he silently termed it—but his sensors could pick up a handful of ships making transit further down the tramline. The tramline wasn't just busy, it was overloaded. And yet...he reminded himself, sharply, that he had orders to try to take an alien ship intact if possible. He might have an opportunity to do just that.

"Order the Russians to make the first jump," Stephen said. The Russians had demanded the honour, again. He wondered, absently, if they hoped to lay claim to more systems, although it would never stand up in court. "And stand ready..."

He watched the Russian ship vanish, only to reappear five minutes later. She didn't seem to have run into any trouble. Stephen studied the data as it popped up in front of him, frowning as he realised that Alien-2 was nothing more than a transit system. A white dwarf was unlikely to have any planets of its own, although it might well have two or more tramlines. It would certainly be more useful than a groundhog might assume, at first glance. He had a feeling they were about to find out.

"Take us through," he ordered. He felt his heartbeat start to pick up again. "Now."

The universe darkened, again. Stephen tensed, watching grimly as the display blanked and hastily started to reboot itself. The star—a lone wanderer through space—appeared in front of him, but no other icons followed it. Stephen leaned forward, watching and waiting. It was nearly ten minutes before the sensors picked up the other tramline, heading further into the unknown. The handful of alien ships they'd seen crossing the tramline seemed to have vanished.

They're probably somewhere along a least-time course to the next tramline, Stephen thought, grimly. The aliens had no need to hide within a system they'd presumably used for generations. *And we might not be able to see them until we get a great deal closer.*

"Long-range sensors are not picking up any trace of settlements within the system," Alison reported. The sensor officer sounded grim, almost frustrated. "I can't even detect any asteroids or comets."

"They've probably fallen into the sun," Sonia commented. "That's a very old star."

Stephen was inclined to agree. It wasn't uncommon for small human groups to set up hidden colonies orbiting other useless stars, but it didn't look as though the virus was inclined to do the same. Besides, Sonia was right. There was no real estate within the system to convert into a habitat. The system's only real value lay in its tramlines.

He leaned back in his chair. "Helm, take us on a dogleg towards the second tramline," he ordered. It didn't seem as though there was any point in spending more time surveying Alien-2. "Sensors, keep a sharp eye out for alien contacts."

"Aye, Captain."

Commander Newcomb's face appeared in the display. "This system *is* something of a relief."

Stephen nodded. He'd feared encountering another Alien-1, or something bigger. He was morbidly certain that there was *something* on the far side of the next tramline, but...they hadn't encountered it *yet.* He smiled at the thought, then turned his attention to the display. It was definitely starting to look as through the system was completely empty.

"We'll proceed through the second tramline as quickly as possible," he said. The sense that they had to hurry was pressing, even though he knew they couldn't speed matters up much further. "I think..."

An alarm sounded. "Captain, I'm picking up a lone alien ship," Alison said. "She's heading towards Tramline One. Warbook calls her a light carrier."

Stephen learned forward. A light carrier...a *lone* light carrier. *Invincible* and her consorts could take her, perhaps even *capture* her. The risk of trying to board was significant, but...the analysts had predicted, perhaps with more hope than common sense, that the virus wouldn't hit the self-destruct. The prospect of infecting the boarding party could hardly be overlooked. Who knew? The boarders might discover that they'd been caught in a Trojan Horse.

But we know the danger, Stephen thought. His crew had direct experience with the virus. They knew to be careful. *And this is a chance we cannot allow to slip by.*

He evaluated the situation as quickly as possible. If the light carrier managed to get off an alert, *Invincible* would be hunted by the alien fleet. But it would take time for the aliens to mobilise and start beating the bushes for the human ships. Assuming they had other ships in Alien-2, it would still take hours for them to mobilise. And if they didn't, there was a prospect of taking the light carrier intact without the aliens ever knowing what had happened to her. He could hardly overlook the possibilities. Who knew if they'd ever get another such opportunity?

"Helm, take us on an intercept course," he ordered. The alien ship wouldn't know what was closing in on them until it was too late. It certainly didn't look as though she was running constant scans for trouble. "Commander Newcomb, prepare to launch starfighters and marine assault shuttles. We're taking that ship."

Newcomb grinned. "Yes, sir!"

CHAPTER FOURTEEN

WELL, RICHARD THOUGHT. *You wanted to fly into combat, didn't you?*

He braced himself as the catapult hurled his starfighter out into the interplanetary wasteland surrounding the dull white star. Powered down, the Hawk would be an easy target if anyone spotted her...assuming, of course, that they *did* spot her. Richard had tried to detect a powered-down Hawk on a ballistic trajectory during the time he'd spent on Earth and discovered, to his amusement, that it wasn't easy. Even active sensors would have trouble tracking the starfighters as they made their way towards their target.

And that will change, the moment we bring up our drives, he thought, as the starfighter's computer checked and rechecked the laser links to the other starfighters. *Invincible* had put five of her six squadrons into space, reserving only one for fighter defence. *They'll see us coming and take steps.*

He wondered, vaguely, just how the virus was reacting to the war. The Royal Navy generally kept at least one squadron of starfighters on one-minute launch alert during wartime, even though it put a great deal of wear and tear on the equipment. Every captain's worst nightmare was having his starfighters trapped inside the hull while his ship was systematically blasted to debris, something that had happened during the First Interstellar

War. Richard knew the other Great Powers agreed, but did the virus? They were so deep within alien space that the virus might feel completely secure.

But we're not that far within alien space, he reminded himself. *It wouldn't be hard to slip an attack force into Alien-2 if there was anything worth attacking.*

He smiled at the thought, then studied the live feed from *Invincible's* passive sensors. The alien carrier looked to have been purpose-built, rather than a converted freighter; he rather suspected that meant that she'd be a tougher customer than the Royal Navy's small fleet of carrier-conversions. It was rare for a light carrier to be built from scratch, at least in the Human Sphere. The Royal Navy hadn't seen any value in building them until there was a sudden demand for starfighter platforms and, by then, it had been too late to do anything other than start converting freighters. But even afterwards, the Royal Navy had rejected plans to build newer light carriers. The shipyards were needed to replenish the losses from two interstellar wars.

The alien carrier was running a light sensor sweep, one that *should* pick up the starfighters as they approached. Richard idly speculated on precisely how close they'd get before the aliens registered their presence, although he knew better than to take anything for granted. It depended on just how alert the sensor crews were…and there was no way to know just how alert the virus's infected hosts would be. They might see something that would force them to take a closer look or they might miss the incoming starfighters completely. Richard had hoped for the best, but planned for the worst. If the aliens managed to launch their starfighters before his ships could power up and close the range, his inexperienced pilots would be thrust into their first real engagement at knife-range. It was one of the reasons he'd insisted on deploying almost all of his starfighters. They'd have numbers, if nothing else.

His HUD washed red, suddenly. "Shit," he swore. "They have us!"

He keyed his console, flash-waking the starfighter's drive. The enemy carrier had locked on, at extreme range. Richard would have been impressed if the bastards hadn't managed to detect them at precisely the wrong moment, too close to back off and too far away to sit on top of their launch tubes and blast anything that came out. Red icons flashed across the display as enemy starfighters poured into space, rotating round to engage the human starfighters. Richard sucked in his breath. *That* was an astonishingly quick reaction time.

"All ships, follow me in," he ordered, tersely. "Fire at will. I say again, fire at will."

"Which one of them is Will?" Flying Officer Stamford asked. "The first one…"

Richard rolled his eyes. "Crack witticisms when you're telling lies about plasma bolts that missed you by millimetres," he said, coldly. "In combat, I expect you to focus."

The alien ships fell into a formation that looked vaguely familiar, the alien version—he assumed—of the starfighter swarm. It seemed completely random, as if the aliens couldn't be bothered holding anything that looked like an orderly formation, but he knew better. An orderly formation might look good during the Festival of Britain, yet—in actual combat—would be nothing more than suicide. A pilot who flew a predictable formation was a dead pilot. Everyone knew it. Richard watched the aliens for a long moment, noting that their craft seemed to be slightly more manoeuvrable than their human counterparts, and then boosted his craft forward. It was time to make war.

"They're firing on us," another pilot said. She sounded deeply shocked. "Don't we get the first shot?"

"Return fire," Richard ordered, ignoring the question. Simulators *definitely* had their limits. "Hit the bastards!"

An alien fighter lunged at him, firing a steady stream of plasma bolts. *They* didn't seem to care about the risk of overheating their plasma chambers and blowing themselves to hell, Richard noted absently. If the briefings were accurate—and he didn't doubt them—the virus saw its pilots and other host bodies as completely expendable. They'd regard losing them with the same lack of concern Richard would show for a lock of hair or a toenail clipping. He couldn't understand how anyone could think that way, but the virus wasn't human. It simply didn't *think* like a human.

He blew the alien fighter away with a single shot, then yanked his starfighter to one side as another alien pilot targeted him. There was something odd about the way it flew, something he couldn't put his finger on, but it hardly mattered. He twisted his ship through a series of evasive manoeuvres while Monica lined up the shot, then blew his pursuer away. Richard wondered if the aliens had forgotten that starfighter operations were meant to be a team effort. They'd hardly be the first starfighter pilots to see the contest as one-on-one, rather than operating as a team. Human pilots did it all the time.

And it costs us, when we run into someone who hasn't forgotten, he thought, as he picked off another alien fighter. *We have to remain focused.*

He avoided a third fighter, then pulled back to survey the overall situation. He'd lost four fighters to enemy fire, but overall his greater numbers had told. The aliens had fought bravely and well, yet they were steadily being worn down. They would probably have retreated, if they'd had anywhere to go. It was possible that they were trying to delay the humans long enough for help to arrive, but Richard doubted it. *Invincible's* jammers were supposed to be blocking all signals that might have called for help. And yet... he glanced at the in-system display. The white dwarf looked useless, but the aliens might have scattered a handful of scansats throughout the system anyway. They might have spotted the engagement already.

And then they'll call reinforcements, Richard thought. *But where will they come from?*

"Watch your ass," Monica said. "They're trying to kill you."

"I saw them coming a mile off," Richard said. The last of the alien fighters were closing in rapidly, firing as they came. He doubted they'd actually *hit* anything until they got a great deal closer, but...they didn't seem to care. If they valued themselves as little as the analysts thought, they might simply feel that the risk was worthwhile. "You watch *my* back."

He picked off one of the alien fighters—Monica killed the other one— and led the rest of the squadron towards the alien carrier. Up close, it was larger than he'd thought, studded with plasma guns and sensor blisters that allowed it to put a terrifying amount of point defence fire into space. Richard allowed himself a moment of relief that his pilots weren't trying to take out a *bigger* target, then studied the alien carrier thoughtfully. It looked almost *human*, strikingly crude rather than the melted-hull designs favoured by the Tadpoles. The virus didn't seem to have any sense of aesthetics. Even the old *Ark Royal*, a ship that had looked like a brick with a handful of protrusions, had been more elegant than the alien ship.

"Take out their plasma guns," he ordered, as he swept down to the alien hull. "And *don't* give them a clear shot at you."

The aliens kept firing, even as Richard started to pick off their weapons and sensor blisters. The alien ship was trying to pick up speed, but it looked as though her acceleration curves were quite low. Richard studied it thoughtfully, wondering why a purpose-built light carrier wasn't considerably faster. A human-designed light carrier *would* be fast enough to keep up with the destroyers and frigates that would escort her from place to place. Even one of the carrier-conversions would be faster on its feet.

They're alien, he reminded himself. *For all we know, we're the first multistar species they've encountered.*

He dismissed the thought as he picked off another pair of plasma guns. The aliens were still firing, desperately. He was tempted to put a hail of plasma bolts through their drives, even though it was a considerable risk. Captain Shields would not be impressed if he accidentally blew the alien carrier into dust, not when he wanted to take the starship intact. Richard doubted it was possible, but the captain felt differently. He didn't envy the marines who would actually have to land on the alien ship and take control.

And we can't even force them to surrender, he thought. *We can't even talk to the bastards.*

The last alien plasma gun vanished in a shower of sparks, quenched by the icy cold of interplanetary space. Richard nodded to himself, noting that the estimates of how many starfighters the alien ship could carry had been reasonably accurate, then led his pilots away from their target. It was up to the marines now.

"Seven pilots gone," Monica said, quietly. Her voice was very grim. "It could have been worse."

"I know," Richard said. He'd done his best to avoid getting to know the new pilots, at least until they'd survived their first encounter with the enemy, but it looked as though he was never going to get to know some of them. "No beacons?"

"It doesn't look that way," Monica said. "I don't think any of them had a chance to eject."

Richard nodded, curtly. It was rare for pilots to be able to eject into space, even though they'd trained extensively to trigger the ejection system if their craft was hit. Normally, they'd be dead within a second. But he'd hoped...he dismissed the thought with a bitter shrug. There was no point in worrying about it, not now. They'd hold a wake, once the carrier had broken contact with any alien reinforcements that happened to arrive, and then...forget about them. Richard had watched too many pilots die to allow himself to feel anything more than mild grief and guilt.

"All ships, return to the barn," he ordered. The pilots would need time to recuperate while their commanders hastily reorganised their squadrons. "You did well, all of you."

He ignored the handful of bitter remarks with the ease of long practice. He'd told them, over and over again, that the odds of surviving their first missions were quite low, but they hadn't believed him. Of *course* they hadn't believed him. They'd known they were invincible. *Richard* had known he was invincible when *he'd* been a young pilot. But now, they'd watched seven of their comrades die in—Richard glanced at the starfighter's timer—less than five minutes. They were shocked, suddenly feeling their own mortality. It would take time for them to get over it.

They'll make it, he thought. *I did, didn't I?*

• • •

"Captain," Commander Newcomb said. "The starfighters report that they have swept the alien hull clear of plasma guns."

Stephen nodded. "Send in the marines," he ordered. "Now."

. . .

Alice couldn't help feeling like supercargo as she sat at the back of the marine assault shuttle and watched the platoon prepare for the assault. *She* should be in command, *she* should be leading the assault into enemy territory, but Major Parkinson had made it clear that she was to remain at the back and provide *advice* to Sergeant Bert Radcliffe and his men. It made her think of the intelligence officer she'd taken on a HALO jump, two years ago. Had the man felt just as useless as she did now? She supposed she should be grateful that no one had suggested that she tie herself to one of the marines. At least they knew *she* knew what she was doing.

She took a long breath, then accessed the live feed from the shuttle's sensors as it glided towards the alien craft. The alien ship was strikingly ugly, although it didn't look as alien as some of the other ships she'd seen. She'd studied the desperate attempt to capture an alien battlecruiser during the First Interstellar War and she'd been struck by just how lucky the marines had been. They'd gone blind into an alien ship and come out alive, bringing the ship with them. They'd certainly deserved their prize money. She wondered, absently, just how much money she'd get if they managed to bring *this* alien ship home intact. Enough to ensure that she'd be comfortable for the rest of her life?

Don't be stupid, she told herself, dryly. *You'd be bored stiff within a week if you had to live in the lap of luxury.*

Her lips quirked at the thought as the alien ship came closer. It was trying to run, but there was no way a carrier—even a small one—could outrun the assault shuttles over such a short distance. Major Parkinson was sending messages, inviting the aliens to surrender, even though Alice had told him it was a waste of time. The virus wasn't interested in talking to its human enemies—or anyone, really. It was more concerned with infecting or killing as many of them as possible. The only guarantee that the aliens wouldn't hit the self-destruct as soon as the marines boarded was that they'd want a chance to infect the marines.

Infect more marines, Alice thought. *They already got me.*

She pushed the thought out of her mind as the assault shuttle grounded on the alien ship, the hatch popping open a second later. The lead elements were heading out before the hatch was fully open, the first two carrying weapons while their successors carried the breaching equipment between them. Alice stayed at the rear, one hand holding her rifle as she followed the last of the marines onto the hull. She kept her eyes firmly fixed on the metal hull, feeling it quiver under her feet. The last thing she wanted was to be distracted by the stars.

A light flared as the breaching equipment went to work, cutting into the alien hull. Metal bubbled and started to boil, allowing the lead marines to hack their way further into the alien ship while the others hastily established a small tent to keep the atmosphere from leaking out into space. Alice frowned to herself, feeling her skin crawl as the nanoprobes started to test the alien atmosphere. As expected, it was lousy with the virus. Anyone who took an unprotected breath would wind up infected.

"Bastards," Corporal Glen Hammersmith observed. "We don't dare take off the suits. We'd be in quarantine for a week."

"We may be in quarantine anyway," Parkinson said. "We have to be careful."

"It could be worse," Alice said, more tartly than she'd meant. "You could be in hospital for a month instead."

"Yeah," Corporal Student said. "That would be bad."

Worse than bad, Alice thought. *It would be the end of your career, as surely as it ended mine.*

She watched the lead marines open the makeshift hatch, then jump into the alien ship. Their reports echoed back a moment later, informing her that the ship appeared to have been designed for aliens substantially larger than humans. Alice allowed herself a moment of relief as she dropped through the hatch herself, feeling the alien gravity field grabbing at her as her feet touched the deck. It was stronger than she'd expected, but her suit had no trouble compensating. It made her wonder if the aliens would be stronger than the average human. People had been speculating for years that humans who grew up on heavy-worlds would be stronger too, but—so far—no habitable heavy-world had been discovered. Instead...

Alice turned her head from side to side. The corridor was almost normal—she was disappointed that they hadn't managed to drop right into the alien bridge—but there was something about it that was subtly *wrong*. She felt her skin itch as the suit reported higher and higher concentrations of the virus, pushing against her armour. It was flowing through the air, passing a warning to the aliens lurking further into the ship. Alice was *sure* of it, on a level she couldn't explain. She knew it.

They know we're here, she thought, although she suspected the aliens had known the boarding party had been hacking into the hull from the moment they'd started. Their hull-mounted sensors would have picked up the breach. *And they'll be readying a counterattack.*

"Jesus," Corporal Hammersmith said. He sounded shocked. "What the hell is that?"

Alice turned, saw the horror...and froze.

CHAPTER FIFTEEN

FOR A MOMENT, ALICE'S MIND REFUSED TO ACCEPT what she was seeing. The alien was...very alien. It was...a collection of foamy bubbles, gliding towards them; it was...she couldn't help thinking of an octopus, one that had just climbed out of a soapy bath. It seemed to shine with a golden light, yet...she blinked in surprise as the alien hefted a weapon, only to be fired upon by the marines. The bullets sank into the foam and vanished.

"Plasma fire," Sergeant Radcliffe snapped. "Now!"

Hammersmith lifted his plasma gun and fired, blasting the alien into a shower of bubbles, drenching the marines in golden liquid. Alice cursed as her suit screamed an alert—the liquid was concentrated virus—and drew her own plasma gun as three more aliens oozed towards them. Her mind raced, even as she blew the lead alien into another shower of liquid. Was she looking at the virus's natural form? Or was it something they'd made to make it easier to infect their targets? The suits seemed to be capable of handling the liquid, ensuring it wouldn't infect the marines, but...she felt it dripping down her spine. She had to remind herself, sharply, that the suit was still intact.

And yet, I'm responding to the liquid's presence, she thought. She was sure she was imagining it, yet it was impossible to dismiss. *What is it doing to me?*

She pushed the thought aside as the marines started to hurry down the corridor, looking for access points. Nanoprobes zoomed ahead of them, picking out concentrations of aliens before they were wiped out by the virus. They'd underestimated the aliens, Alice thought morbidly. The nanoprobes should have been untouchable, but they were being picked off one by one. Their mere presence was disturbing the air. She made a mental note to propose that the *next* boarding party carried UV lights as well as their standard equipment. It might deprive the aliens of some of their tricks.

"In here," Stewart said. "I've found a computer node."

"Get it hooked up and try to hack it," Radcliffe ordered. "The rest of you, stay with me."

Alice fell into position behind the platoon as they made their way through a series of barricades. The aliens didn't seem to have prepared for a boarding party, but they made up for it by throwing themselves at the marines as soon as they saw them. The blobs—as Hammersmith termed them—were the worst, but the other aliens weren't much better. They appeared out of nowhere, firing madly, and threw themselves at the marines. Alice had faced suicidal humans before, back in the Security Zone, but this was far worse. The aliens seemed to be insane.

They're infected, she reminded herself, as she put a bullet through a tall alien's face. It seemed to keep coming until she blew it's arms and legs into bloody chunks too, at which point it sagged onto the deck and died. She felt as if she was in a zombie movie. *They can't help themselves.*

"The hackers are going to work," Hammersmith reported. "But they're saying it may take some time."

Alice nodded. There was no way the alien computer network would be immediately compatible with the human-designed system. She'd been assured that the combination of translation and adaptation software would be enough to allow the hackers to punch their way into the alien system, but it would take time—and no one, not even the most overconfident spook, had been able to tell her how long it would take. The marines had planned on the assumption that the hackers would *never* be able to get into the alien system. Alice hoped, as Parkinson directed his men towards the alien engineering compartment, that they wouldn't need the hackers. They didn't dare count on them.

The engagement became more and more nightmarish as the marines fought their way towards the bridge. The ship itself seemed to be alive and lashing out at its tormentors, alternatively bathing them in concentrated virus or fiddling with the gravity in hopes of slowing them down. The blobs kept appearing out of nowhere, one landing on top of a marine and cracking through his armour with lethal force. He didn't live long enough to be infected. Alice hoped his body could be recovered, although she had her doubts. The marines had orders not to take any bodies back to *Invincible*, but merely burn them in place. She hated the thought of *not* taking her comrade back home...yet she understood the logic. A dead body could still infect its former comrades.

Radcliffe led the charge onto the alien bridge, firing rapidly into the alien positions. It was the strangest place Alice had ever seen, reminding her more of a bathhouse than a starship's control centre. Blobs sat on top of consoles, reaching for weapons as the marines entered; they were blown away in seconds, leaving the marines alone. A moment later, the lights failed completely. Alice felt...*something*...clutch at her heart before Hammersmith made contact. The hackers had finally managed to get into the alien ship's control network and shut it down. Or, at least, shut *some* of it down. There were parts of it, he reported, that seemed immune to tampering.

"Then we have to sweep the remainder of the ship," Parkinson said. "And take them all out before they can do something stupid."

Alice nodded. "And then the boffins can go to work," she said. She eyed the remains of one of the blobs, feeling ice at the back of her spine. Water—or concentrated virus—was dripping from the ceiling. "Let them see what they make of the alien ship."

. . .

"The marines report that they have swept the ship from one end to the other," Commander Newcomb reported. "If there are any aliens left alive, they're very well hidden."

Stephen let out a breath he hadn't realised he'd been holding. The odds of success had been low, very low, but they'd succeeded. He made a mental note to ensure that the marines were given medals for their success, if *Invincible* made it back home. They'd also have a fair claim to a considerable amount of prize money. Even if they managed to pull next to nothing out of the alien databanks—and he knew the odds of success there were poor too, no matter what the hackers claimed—the insight into alien technology would make the risk of trying to capture the ship worthwhile. They'd scored a great victory.

"Shut her down completely," he ordered, "and then prepare to tow her into deep space."

"Aye, Captain."

Stephen looked at Alison. "Is there any sign that other alien ships are on their way?"

"No, Captain," Alison said. "The sensors are clear."

Which doesn't mean they can't be sneaking up on us in cloak, Stephen thought. *We have to be careful.*

He studied the console for a long moment, then smiled to himself. "We'll get her well away from here, then we'll start inspecting her hull," he said. "And then we'll see what we see."

"Aye, sir," Newcomb said.

"And pass on a message from me to the starfighters *and* the marines," Stephen added. "Well done."

"Aye, sir."

Stephen forced himself to sit back and relax as *Austere* and *Yuriy Ivanov* prepared to take the alien ship under tow. They *had* scored a great victory, although it would be meaningless if they failed to get the data back to Earth. And, while his ship and crew had performed well, he had no illusions about *just* how badly they'd damaged the alien ability to make war. A lone light carrier wouldn't materially affect the balance of power between humanity and the virus. The immense fleet they'd seen in Alien-1 wouldn't be delayed by the loss of a single carrier. Their victory here might be their last.

But the crew doesn't need to know that, not now, Stephen told himself. *There will be time for considering the implications later.*

"Captain," Morse said. "*Austere* and *Yuriy Ivanov* report that they are ready to take the alien ship under tow."

"Then tell them to begin," Stephen said. "And take all of our ships into cloak."

"Aye, sir."

. . .

Alice couldn't help feeling, as she walked through the alien engineering compartment, as though there was something oddly *familiar* about it. Some aspects of the design—the fusion cores, the power nodes—were almost human, while other elements were very alien. It made her wonder if the virus had had prior contact with humans, although it seemed unlikely. The aliens seemed to have splashed together a hodgepodge of equipment from two or three different races and somehow made it all work together.

"A remarkable piece of work," Doctor Tisane said. He was a tall man, with pale skin and intelligent eyes. "I've never seen anything like it."

"Not since *Warspite*," Doctor Sana Thompson added. "I worked on her back when I was a nipper."

Probably not that young, Alice thought. Sana looked young, but she was definitely older than Alice herself. *It's a good point, though.*

She turned her attention to the rest of the compartment as the two scientists continued arguing about how the aliens had forced the different subsections to work together. It was a mess, the deck covered with pools of lethal golden liquid that seemed to glitter under the UV lights the boffins had brought with them. Alice knew the light should kill whatever traces of the virus remained, but she had her doubts. She'd already had to speak quite sharply to the scientists when they'd started talking about removing their protective suits. There was no point in taking chances. The virus could *not* be allowed a chance to reach *Invincible*.

"I think that half of their computer systems were organic," Sana said, after a moment. "They might have turned the ship into a living creature."

"It certainly reacted like one," Alice said, although she had her doubts. The ship had done nothing that a man sitting in front of a control board couldn't have done. "But we don't know for sure."

"The virus is capable of conveying a great deal of data," Tisane said. "If they used it as...as a computer system, it might have been capable of bridging between two different systems."

"Which creates a weakness," Sana said. "They wouldn't have been able to secure their systems as effectively as they might wish."

"Which explains why the hackers were able to shut some aspects of it down," Tisane added.

"Except the hackers had to get into the ship and find a node first," Alice reminded him, dryly. "It wasn't easy."

"True," Sana agreed. "And I don't see how their data transmission matches ours. Their rates must be quite low."

"Perhaps," Tisane said. "But surely..."

Alice looked up as Parkinson entered the compartment. "Alice. Do you have a moment?"

"I do," Alice said. The two boffins were still arguing over data transmission rates and wondering if the advantages of using the virus as a makeshift computer network outweighed the disadvantages. "What can I do for you?"

"You handled yourself fine during the engagement," Parkinson said. "You did well."

Alice scowled, silently glad her suit would hide the expression. It wasn't really a compliment. She'd gone through commando training, just like any other marine. She wasn't some spook who wouldn't be expected to keep up with the marines, someone who'd surprise her escorts if she *did* keep up with them. She was...

"Thank you, sir," she said, trying to keep her voice even. "It was a cathartic experience."

"I bet it was," Parkinson said. "And I'm afraid the headshrinkers want to talk to you."

"Tell them to go to hell," Alice said. "Sir."

Parkinson snorted. "You know I can't do that," he said. "And you really do need to talk to them."

"I'll go back on the next shuttle," Alice said. The alien ship was under tow. It would be at least five hours before Captain Shields felt they'd put enough distance between themselves and the engagement location. "And then I'll see what I'll tell them."

"The truth, one hopes," Parkinson said. "I can't clear you for active duty until you're ready to go."

I am ready, Alice said, although she knew better than to say it out loud. She'd seen marines who'd suffered serious injuries insisting that they were still capable of active service. She understood them now, better than she wanted to admit. To give up would be a kind of little death. *They don't know if they can trust me.*

"I'll go back on the next shuttle," she said, again. "Until then...have your boffins figured out anything clever?"

"Not really, I'm afraid," Parkinson said. "I left them trying to download the alien computer datafiles."

"And probably trying to decrypt them," Alice said. She was surprised the aliens hadn't destroyed the computer cores—the Royal Navy's officers had strict orders to make sure that no computer core fell into enemy hands—but if the virus itself served as a computer core it was quite likely the hackers would get nowhere. The virus had been devastated during the boarding. The network now had more holes than a piece of cheese. "Have they had any luck?"

"Not so far," Parkinson said. "But their hopes are high."

"And hopefully not misplaced," Alice said. She tapped her helmet in salute. "I'd better stay here until the shuttle is ready."

"See that you do," Parkinson said. He leaned forward. "And like I said, Alice, you did well."

Your approval fills me with shame, Alice thought, wryly. She didn't want or need his approval, certainly not like *that*. She'd done her duty and done it well. *But I know you want to reassure me.*

She watched him go, then turned her attention back to the boffins. Tisane was drawing up a plan to dismantle one of the fusion cores, while Sana had opened an inspection hatch and was examining the components inside. Her suit was dripping with golden liquid, but she was ignoring it. Alice hoped—desperately—that the boffins understood the dangers. It was easy to underestimate an unconventional threat. The concentrated virus didn't have the same impact as a punch in the face.

But it will be a great deal more dangerous in the long run, she thought, numbly. *I'm the only person who survived an encounter with the virus once I was infected.*

"They set up the system to move viral matter around the starship," Sana commented, seemingly unaware of Alice's concern. "I think we have to assume that they *did* use the virus as a makeshift computer system."

"What bad news for the hackers," Tisane said, dryly. "I'll see if it's linked to the fusion cores."

"Make sure you get an engineering crew over to take the core apart," Alice said, firmly. There was no way Tisane could do it alone—and besides, he wasn't expendable. *She* would have preferred to keep the engineering crews and leave the boffin on the mothership, but her superiors disagreed with her. "Don't try to break into the system alone."

"I won't," Tisane said. "It doesn't look to be that different from ours, through."

"Then we won't learn anything useful," Sana called. "At least, not directly."

"We'll learn something about their power curves," Tisane said. "And that will be useful."

And about how we can impede their computer systems, Alice thought. A starship could neither fly nor fight without a working computer network. It had been a long time since spacecraft had flown without computers. *What would happen if we devised a counter-virus and let it run loose?*

She paced the compartment as the boffins continued their work, thinking hard. The boarding action had succeeded, through luck as well as judgement, but they couldn't assume that the next action would be so easy. And it *had* been easy. If the aliens had realised that their ship could be boarded—and that their first line of defence, the virus itself, could be neutralised—they might have taken more drastic action. No, they *would* have taken more drastic action. If they'd blown up the ship, thirty marines would have died for nothing. But if their computer system could be taken down so quickly....

You're here to consult, she told herself, as she activated her recorder. She had to smile, even though she was sure that *consultant* was nothing more than a consolation prize. *So consult.*

She started to speak, outlining her ideas for future analysis. Some of them wouldn't be practical, she was sure, but others *might* be useful. It would be up to the analysts to determine which of them could be turned into workable hardware within the next few weeks—or which would have to be developed on Earth. *Invincible's* machine shop was designed to repair or replace missing components, not produce entirely new hardware from scratch. And yet...

We need a camera flash, she thought. It was a simple idea, although she knew there would be a handful of problems that would need to be overcome. *Attach it to a drone and fly it through the ship's corridors. And keep flashing the UV light so the virus keeps dying...*

"I'd like to call the engineers now," Tisane said, breaking into her thoughts. The scientist sounded remarkably excited. "I think I'm ready to start dismantling the drive."

"That's not your call, not yet," Alice said. She checked her timer. It would be another three hours before the ships were well away from the engagement point. Captain Shields wouldn't want to strip his ship of a third of her engineers before they were clear of any possible threats. "Wait for the captain to make the call."

"But we could do it now," Tisane said. "I could…"

"Don't," Alice said, firmly. She understood the impulse, but she had her orders. "Wait for the engineers."

CHAPTER SIXTEEN

SAMRA WAS DEAD.

Richard looked down at the collection of photographs, feeling an odd surge of guilt that he hadn't seen Samra *die*. He could look back at the records, of course, and pick out the moment when her starfighter had been blown out of space, but it wouldn't be the same. He'd have to go back through the records anyway, just so he could evaluate the survivors and tell them what they'd done right—and wrong—yet...he didn't want to do it. He suspected it would only make him feel worse.

He looked up, silently assessing the pilots as they gathered in the mess room. They looked torn between excitement—and relief for having survived their first *real* engagement—and guilt, for having survived when some of their comrades had died. Samra and her fellow casualties had been popular. Their loss would be felt by their former comrades, none of whom had the experience to understand that they would lose more friends and comrades over the coming weeks and months. Starfighter pilots suffered the worst losses of any branch of the military, at least since space travel had become routine. The British military hadn't suffered so many losses since the Battle of Britain. Even the Troubles hadn't been so costly.

"Take a drink," he ordered, nodding to the decanters on the sideboard. He'd provided the mocktails himself. There was no alcohol, but the taste would ensure no one would be able to tell the difference. He was entirely sure that *someone* would have set up an illicit still somewhere on the ship, yet they were in a war zone. Allowing his pilots to drink was a court-martial offense. "We have a lot to discuss."

He leaned back in his chair and surveyed the young faces. Some of them understood, now. Their faces bore the scars of what they'd learnt. They knew, deep inside, that they were no longer immortal…that they'd never truly been immortal. Others didn't believe it, not yet. They didn't want to believe it. Behind them, the older pilots—Monica and her fellows—kept their faces under tight control. They understood, all too well. The next wake might be for one of them.

It's dangerous to get too close to anyone, Richard thought. Starfighter pilots were given a great deal of leeway—he might well turn a blind eye if two pilots wound up in bed together—but it came at a price. *They never know who might wind up dead tomorrow,*

He stood and poured himself a drink, watching the red liquid splashing into the glass. It looked too thin to be blood, but he couldn't help shuddering at the accidental symbolism anyway. The pilots, too young to appreciate the navy's traditions, might not realise that it *wasn't* intended to be blood. Normally, back home, they would be drinking alcohol and nursing hangovers the following day. *That* couldn't be allowed on the navy's starships, particularly during wartime. He shook his head as he carried his drink back to the front of the compartment. He had to speak, he had to tell them what they needed to know, but the words refused to come. What was he *meant* to tell them?

They don't even have bodies to bury, he told himself. Captain Shields had promised a proper funeral, once they were well clear of the captured ship, but it wouldn't be the same. Everyone would know that the coffins they were launching into space were empty. *They can't even say goodbye.*

He took a long breath, then placed his glass on the stand. "Today, you saw the elephant for the first time," he said, ignoring the fact that Monica and the reservists *had* faced death before. "And it cost the lives of seven of your comrades."

It was hard not to wince at the thought. Seven pilots…that was almost an entire squadron. Thankfully, the losses had been scattered over the five squadrons that had engaged the enemy, but still…it wasn't as if they were going to get any replacements in a hurry. He'd already put out a call for anyone on the carrier who might have experience flying starfighters, but—so far—no one had come forward to volunteer. It was starting to look as though *Invincible* didn't have any spare starfighter pilots. That was an oversight that would need to be corrected when they returned to Earth. It wasn't uncommon for older pilots to transfer into command or engineering tracks when their reflexes started to fail. He'd have to check the personnel files.

"I know how you feel," he added, after a moment. "You are shocked to discover that death can come for any of you, for all of you. You are no longer immune to death. Your comrades died today, but it could easily have been any one of you. This engagement was not fought in the simulator. There will be no resurrections for the dead pilots, not this time. They are gone and they will not be coming back."

He allowed his voice to harden. "Many of you will dwell on their deaths. You will ask yourself, time and time again, if there was anything you could do to stop it, to save them from certain death. And the answer will always be no. There is always an element of chance in starfighter combat. You will face death yourself, time and time again. And, eventually, your time will run out. It already ran out for your comrades.

"I wish I had something more cheerful to tell you. I wish I could say something that would make it all better. But there is nothing. All you can do is remember them, remember how they died, and strive to make sure that their deaths are not in vain. You must learn from what happened to them and apply the knowledge to save your own lives. It will not be long before we engage the enemy again."

He paused and studied them, wondering how the message was sinking in. Some of the pilots looked angry, angry at him for telling them something that they had to consider heartless as hell itself. He didn't really blame them, even though he was talking about the cold realities of life as a starfighter pilot. They didn't want to hear what he had to say. But there was no choice. They *had* to hear him. And they had to take what he said to heart.

"I know you don't want to hear this," he said, putting his thoughts into words. "But you have no choice. You *have* to understand the truth."

There was a long pause. "Stand," he ordered. "And raise your glasses."

He looked at the photos, feeling another stab of guilt. Had he failed the dead? Had there been lessons he could have imparted, lessons that would have saved their lives? He knew he'd done everything he could, but he didn't really believe it. If he'd said something else...what could he have said? He'd done everything he could and...and it hadn't been enough to save their lives. He stood, feeling older than his grandfather. The sense that he'd failed was almost overpowering.

"I ask you to remember Flying Officers Samra Alibis, Christopher Higgins, Luis Cordova, Andrew Gabion, Peter McCray, Elspeth MacDougall and Ted Brannan," Richard said, quietly. He didn't know them as well as he felt he should, now. Samra he'd met—and talked to, privately—and Luis Cordova had been an immigrant from Catalonia, but the others were practically strangers. "They flew beside you. They fought beside you. And they died beside you. The pain of their loss will fade, in time, but I want you to remember them. They died so that you might live."

He paused, again, then lifted his glass to his lips. "Remember them."

The mocktail tasted odd, almost a child's drink. He had to smile, remembering the time he'd gotten in real trouble—as a young man—for drinking below the legal minimum age. He'd been lucky to avoid a trip to a borstal, although—as it had been his first offense—the police had settled for a sharp warning in his record instead. He took another sip, wondering if he should seek out the still after all. But turning up drunk when he was meant to be on duty would probably get him executed. The captain would pitch him out the airlock with his bare hands.

"Remember," he repeated.

He gave them a moment to finish their drinks, then leaned forward. "Does anyone want to say anything?"

There was a long pause. "I liked Samra," Flying Officer Roger Nye confessed. "We went through the Academy together. She was paired up with me more than once. People gave her a hard time because of her skin, but...I never doubted her. She was fun, once you got to know her. I...I was tempted to ask her out. I would have done, if we'd been in different squadrons."

And you never thought about going to Sin City for a weekend, Richard thought, although—if he'd taken someone to Sin City—he wouldn't have bragged about it. Sin City was tamer these days, after the original Sin City had been smashed during the Tadpole attack on Earth, but what happened in Sin City stayed in Sin City. *Or did you go and, afterwards, kept it to yourself?*

"Peter and I were old friends," Flying Officer Stanley Hammond said. "We went through school together, then...we both applied to join the military. Neither of us were expecting to be streamlined into starfighter training, but...the aptitude tests said we'd be good at flying starfighters. And we thought they were right."

He met Richard's eyes. "You were right too, sir," he said. "We thought we were invincible. I always had the impression that we'd die together. And yet, we were wrong. He's dead and I have to carry on, somehow. I have to write to his parents and..."

"I have to write to them first," Richard said. "Make sure your letter goes into storage. It won't be sent until after the family is informed."

He winced. Peter McCray's family would get a letter from him, a letter from the captain and—probably—a letter from McCray's training officer on the moon. Op Minimise would be in full effect to make sure that the family were informed before the media picked up on the death and broadcast McCray's name far and wide. But McCray wouldn't be the only person to die. If a battleship or carrier was taken out, thousands of people would die. The media wouldn't overlook *that*. He still had nightmares about the First and Second Interstellar Wars. It had been all too clear—too clear—that his father could die at any moment...

"Yes, sir," Hammond said. "I understand."

"Elspeth used to joke that she'd been named after the princess," Flying Officer Gavin Patterson commented. "I thought she was joking until I met her parents. They were—they *are*—absurd royalists. Their house was covered with tat from the Royal Wedding, everything from expensive mugs to paintings of the king and his family. They even had a rare painting of Prince Henry. I never understood them."

Richard shrugged. He'd sworn an oath to the king, years ago, but it had been more to the monarchy itself than the person sitting on the throne. He didn't really like—or admire—what he'd heard of Princess Elspeth, although her brother had managed to forge a career for himself that was largely independent of the Royal Family. It was ironic, he supposed, that the man who'd proven himself worthy of the throne had taken himself out of the line of succession. Richard had no doubt he could have followed Prince Henry to the very gates of hell itself.

"They like the Royal Family," he said, finally. "And I hope they understand that their daughter died in the kingdom's service."

He listened as the other pilots shared their stories. Some of them were dramatic, some were funny...a couple were sad, even though Richard had thought they were better not shared for a while. There would be time for a proper wake on Earth, once they were safe from enemy attack...if, indeed, they managed to make it back home. He didn't like their chances if they ran up against the enemy fleet. A knife-range engagement would end with *Invincible* being unceremoniously blown out of space.

We'll just have to keep avoiding them, he told himself. He smiled at the thought. It wasn't going to be easy. Who knew what they'd encounter in the next system? *And when we find out everything we want to know, we can come back with an entire fleet and blow hell out of them.*

"I want you to remember what we said here, now," he said, once the stories were finished. "And remember our fallen comrades. And—also— remember that you are not invincible."

He allowed his eyes to sweep the room. "Dismissed," he said. "Squadrons three and five are to remain on alert. The remainder of you...get some sleep. You'll need it."

"And no hangover tomorrow," Monica added. "If any of you have any illicit alcohol, believe me. You'll regret it when we catch you."

Richard watched them go, then gave her a sharp look. "*Do* they have any illicit alcohol?"

"Not that I know about," Monica said, with an expression that suggested butter wouldn't melt in her mouth. "But you know as well as I do that someone could easily have brought alcohol onto the ship or purchased it from Petty Officer Gordon in Engineering."

"I bloody well hope not," Richard said. Technically, naval officers had no right to privacy—and no expectation of the same—but he was damned if he was searching private lockers without a very good reason. The pilots would be pissed even if the search was technically legal. "And if you find out that someone has alcohol, I expect you to tell me."

Monica lifted her eyebrow. "You don't want to rely on their common sense?"

"They have common sense?" Richard grinned at her, humourlessly. "How long did it take us to develop common sense?"

"Only a year or two," Monica said.

"It's the training," Richard said. "It's designed to make it impossible to actually develop common sense. Probably because someone who *had* common sense would think twice about flying a starfighter into combat."

"You're in a morbid mood," Monica said. She looked pensive, just for a second. "Did their deaths affect you that badly?"

"Not their deaths so much as the remaining pilots," Richard admitted. "They know they're not invulnerable, now. It's going to cost them."

"They'll get over it," Monica said, briskly. She met his eyes, meaningfully. "You got over it, didn't you?"

"I didn't let myself get close to any of my pilots," Richard said. It struck him, suddenly, that Monica was the closest thing he had to a friend on the massive carrier. Starfighter pilots were not encouraged to make friends with anyone outside their compartment. "And I told myself that deaths weren't... important. But now..."

He shook his head. "Did I do alright?"

"I think you laid it on a bit thick," Monica said. "But you told them what you had to tell them, what they had to know. I dare say some of them won't forgive you in a hurry. A couple may even come to hate you."

"As long as they behave themselves, I don't care," Richard said. He'd heard stories of starfighter pilots who'd pranked their commanders, but any one of *his* pilots who thought it was a good idea to prank *him* would wind up wishing he'd never been born. Richard considered himself to be a fairly tolerant man, but there were limits. "How did you learn to cope?"

"I just kept telling myself to carry on," Monica said. She learned forward until her lips were almost brushing his. "Where there's life, Richard, there's hope."

She kissed him, very lightly, then stepped backwards. "I'm due to take command of the next shift," she said. "I'd better get some sleep."

Richard felt his heart begin to race. His body was suddenly insistent on reminding him just how long it had been since he'd slept with *anyone*. He'd hoped to have time to visit Sin City—or a brothel—during his shore leave, but he simply hadn't had time. Instead, he'd just had to make do. He wanted her suddenly, he wanted her so much it hurt. And yet, she was his subordinate. He couldn't sleep with her. There were limits to how far the rules could be bent, even for pilots.

No one would care if we were discreet, he thought. That was true. *But it wouldn't be long before everyone found out the truth.*

He smiled at her, rather wanly. "Go get some rest," he ordered. "We'll go through the records tomorrow."

"I'm sure they'll enjoy it," Monica said. She looked surprisingly flushed. He wondered, suddenly, if she'd expected him to chase her. "I know *I'll* enjoy it."

"You just like rubbing people's noses in their mistakes," Richard charged. "But you're right. It does have to be done."

He winced in pain. They'd have to discuss what mistakes had gotten Samra and the others killed, if they *had* made mistakes. It would be easier for the pilots to accept that their dead comrades had done something stupid, rather than having done everything right and *still* being blown out of space. It simply wasn't fair to do everything right and still lose. But the universe wasn't fair. He'd come to terms with that years ago.

"Yes," Monica agreed. "It does."

CHAPTER SEVENTEEN

"SO TELL ME," STEPHEN SAID. "Precisely *what* are we looking at?"

"A biological computer network, combined with pieces of hardware," Doctor Sana Thompson said. She sat in his ready room, an untouched cup of tea beside her. Doctor Tisane sat next to her, drinking Panda Cola. "It's really quite a brilliant piece of work."

Stephen frowned. The image in front of him was...*odd*. He was no computer expert, but he couldn't help thinking there was something ramshackle about the whole arrangement, as if the person who'd put it together had drawn supplies from a dozen different sources. He hadn't seen anything like it outside the independent asteroid colonies, which *did* purchase obsolete equipment from the Great Powers and refurbish it for practical use. The virus, it seemed, felt much the same way.

"It doesn't look brilliant," he muttered, taking a sip of his tea. The Royal Navy believed in simplicity—and the alien computer network was anything but simple. "Explain it to me, in plain English. Please."

Sana smiled, as if she'd been waiting for the question. "As near as we can tell, they took nine computer cores—from at least three different races—and plugged them into a datanet that used the virus itself as an interface to link the cores together. The bioneural network seems to have had a considerably greater degree of efficiency than ours, although it is hard to be certain as the biological material has degraded quite badly over the last week. *Our* networks would certainly not be able to handle the different cores without a great deal of improvised modification. I wouldn't care to try to take the network into combat."

Stephen frowned. "Nine cores, from three different races?"

"We think so," Sana said. "The cores seem to have been designed by people who had three different ways of looking at the world. Our cores could, at a pinch, be installed on an American or Russian starship, but *these* cores were incompatible with most of their fellows until the virus started linking them together. It's really quite frightening, sir. The virus could presumably do the same to any captured *human* core."

"Presumably," Stephen echoed. The Royal Navy's crews had strict orders to destroy their datacores if there was a reasonable possibility of the cores falling into enemy hands, but anyone who had served in space knew it wasn't always possible. And there was the question mark hanging over *Dezhnev's* fate. "This is starting to sound worse and worse."

Sana took a sip of her tea. "We have been trying to hack the cores, sir, but even our best hackers are having trouble devising translation software. The people who built the cores simply didn't share most of our assumptions about how computer systems should be put together and programmed. It may be a very long time before we manage to draw useful data from them."

"If at all," Doctor Tisane said. "We may find it impossible to relate their datafiles to anything we can use."

"Perhaps," Stephen agreed.

He frowned, again. The Tadpole computers had eventually been cracked—setting off a whole new wave of innovation in the process—but, from the classified reports he'd read, even extracting *visual* data had been a pain in the ass. The Tadpoles had used visual data, just like their human counterparts, but they'd combined it with sensory data humans weren't designed to understand. It had been hard enough to download copies of their starcharts and *they'd* been almost purely visual data. The virus was far more alien than the Tadpoles and, for all he knew, had stored classified data within its bioneural matter. There might be little of value within the captured cores.

The virus was using them to fly the ship, he reminded himself. *They should have* some *data we can use.*

He leaned forward. "Do you believe we can hack the bioneural network, if we managed to capture one intact?"

"I don't believe so, not barring a major advance in biological technology," Sana said. She looked pensive for a long moment. "People have been speculating about bioneural networks for decades, sir, but…they've never produced any workable hardware. The concept of biological starships is light-years beyond us. Even the RockRats concede it will be centuries before we manage to modify ourselves to live in space without technological enhancement, if indeed it is possible at all. The virus may be completely beyond our ability to…hack."

Her face darkened. "It *may* be possible to interface with a cluster of viral cells," she added thoughtfully, "using a neural interface…but I wouldn't care to try. The virus is simply too alien."

"But a cluster of viral cells would be expendable," Doctor Tisane pointed out. "We wouldn't be carrying out the experiment on humans—or alien prisoners."

Stephen shifted, uncomfortably. The Royal Navy had strict regulations governing the care of alien POWs, ordering their captors to ship them back to the xenospecialists as soon as possible. Indeed, alien POWs were almost always treated better than human prisoners. No one knew how an unknown race would react to the mistreatment of their POWs—and no one knew what an unknown race would consider mistreatment. The Tadpole POWs had been treated very well, despite the increasingly hopeless war. But then, it had proven almost impossible to talk to them. One of the darker scenarios his briefing notes had covered had been the prospect of aliens unable to *tell* their captors that they were suffering.

But the virus was…a virus. It might not notice—or care—if humans carried out experiments on viral cells. To it, the infected were little more than skin cells. It might not even notice their deaths. *And*, regardless, it posed a terrible threat. Stephen knew the xenospecialists had been granted wide latitude to do whatever it took to find a vaccine—or, worse, a biological weapon that could be used against the virus. Would anyone care if he ordered Sana to try to design a neural interface that could be used to hack the virus?

"I think that question is probably best decided by the folks back home," he said. The boffins had been bragging about the promise of neural interfaces for the last two hundred years, but—so far—they'd achieved no real success outside the laboratory. The idea of a mind-controlled starfighter was tempting, yet—in the real world—the interface almost always caused significant brain damage. "We can safely leave it in their hands."

Sana looked relieved. Doctor Tisane didn't look anything like so happy. Stephen looked at him. "Doctor, what's your opinion?"

"We have completed our preliminary assessment of the captured ship," Doctor Tisane said, pulling his datapad off his belt. "As you can see"—he brought up a holographic display—"the ship is a curious mishmash of technologies. Their plasma cannons, for example, are inferior to ours..."

"Inferior?" Stephen was surprised. "Really?"

"Yes, Captain," Doctor Tisane said. He sounded annoyed at the interruption. "Their plasma cannons are actually comparable to the early models, the ones we built before the First Interstellar War. We actually noted a pair of them losing containment and exploding well before the starfighters could blast them off the hull. This may be a third or fourth-rate ship, by their standards, but I can't understand why they used such primitive weapons when they certainly have the technology to improve them. If nothing else, they pose a hazard to life and limb."

"True," Stephen agreed.

His face twisted as he thought back to the war. He'd been in his early teens when humanity had discovered it wasn't alone in the universe, but he remembered the stories. The early plasma cannons had been more dangerous to their gunners than the enemy. Even after humanity had reverse-engineered Tadpole weapons, it had proven quite difficult to keep them from overheating and exploding…often doing considerable damage in the process. A starfighter that suffered a containment breach was almost certainly doomed. Only a handful of pilots had managed to eject before it was too late.

"On the other hand, the computer cores and fusion plants are actually more advanced than our own," Doctor Tisane continued. "They don't seem to use their computer cores to their full potential—Sana thinks they prefer to use their bioneural matter for computations—but their fusion plants are another matter. Put crudely, that relatively small ship has more power than a battlecruiser. I'm actually surprised they didn't add more drive nodes. It would give her an upper speed comparable to a destroyer or frigate."

Stephen winced. "Can we duplicate their technology?"

"We can't upgrade *Invincible's* fusion plants, if that's what you're asking," Doctor Tisane said, dryly. "Not *now*, in any case. In the long term, yes; we *can* duplicate their fusion cores and install them in our ships. The technology is relatively simple. We just have to be careful that we don't accidentally cause more problems for ourselves than we solve."

"It would probably be better to redesign the control programming from scratch," Sana put in, mischievously. "Copying *their* programming might lead to an unpleasant surprise."

Stephen looked from one to the other. "Do you think their bigger ships might have higher acceleration curves?"

Doctor Tisane hesitated, noticeably. "I don't know, Captain, and I'm reluctant to make any predictions. We're running up against some pretty hard technological limitations when it comes to making *our* ships faster, not least the need to fit more drive nodes into an ever-expanding hull, but… it's possible they could boost their nodes with the extra power, at least for a short period. And if they've managed to improve their drive systems in a way we cannot anticipate…"

Stephen swallowed a curse. *Invincible* was hardly the fastest thing in space—there was no way a giant carrier could outrun a frigate, let alone a starfighter—but she was extremely fast for her size. The boffins had insisted that she could outfight anything that could catch her and outrun anything that could *outfight* her. Stephen had no doubt that *Invincible* could give a full-sized fleet carrier or battleship a very hard time, even though his ship wouldn't last more than a few minutes if a battleship hove into gunnery range. But if the virus's warships were considerably faster than *Invincible*, the fleet carrier was in deep shit. Being overhauled by a handful of enemy battleships would be utterly disastrous.

No need to panic yet, he reminded himself, dryly. *They didn't manage to run us down back when we were fleeing Alien-1.*

"I get it," he said, softly. "You cannot predict their technological development."

"No, sir," Doctor Tisane said. "There are just too many things about their ship that doesn't make sense. For example, their most advanced computer core was connected to the targeting systems, but the sensor blisters—those that survived—are inferior to our current designs although superior to those mounted by *Formidable* and the other ships that died at New Russia. Tadpole masking fields are unlikely to fool them for long, if at all. Their...ah, their *least* capable computer core was attached to the drive nodes, something that makes absolutely no sense. They *need* to be aware of fluctuations within the drive field."

"Unless the viral bioneural network was capable of handling any problems that might arise," Sana said. "And besides, it isn't like they were using a *truly* primitive system. There's no hint they were having drive problems until we crippled the ship."

"True," Doctor Tisane said. He cleared his throat. "The bottom line, sir, is that they *should* be using some aspects of their stolen technology to improve others. It's like"—he waved his hands in the air—"it's like having fusion cores and power cells, but using gasoline and internal combustion engines at the same time, or advanced computers *and* abacuses working in tandem. They don't seem to realise the potential of their own systems. I have staffers working under me who have *already* devised ways to improve their systems or adapt them to service us. Some of them even believe that we can take their fusion technology and use it to make missiles actually *practical*."

"That would put the cat amongst the politicians," Stephen said, amused. The Next Generation Weapons program had been trying to crack the problem of long-range missiles—and turning missiles into effective weapons—for the last decade, but results had been somewhat mixed. Plasma cannons outmatched missiles every time. Even bomb-pumped lasers were of limited value if they never got near their target. "The missiles would have to be extremely fast, though."

"That's the point, sir," Doctor Tisane said. "They would *be* extremely fast."

Stephen leaned back in his chair. If Doctor Tisane was right—and Stephen had no reason to doubt him—there was going to be another arms race as soon as *Invincible* returned home. It wouldn't even be a bad thing, at least at first. The human race was locked in yet another war for survival. But afterwards...? Who knew what would happen when the war was over?

And the war is not over yet, he reminded himself, sharply. The enemy fleet was massing in Alien-1, but—as far as they knew—it had not yet set course for Falkirk. *It has not even fairly begun.*

"I see," he said. "Do you have any other insights?"

"Not as yet, sir," Doctor Tisane said. "My full report will be with you by tomorrow at the latest. However, we have barely scratched the surface. I would prefer to remain with the alien ship until she can be taken back to Earth."

Stephen considered it, thoughtfully. Getting the captured ship home was a priority, but so was continuing the mission. They *had* to probe the depths of alien space before the war began in earnest, if only so they'd know where to send the fleets. There was no way he could take the alien ship as far as Falkirk, let alone Earth, without incurring intolerable delays. And yet...cracking the mysteries of the alien starship might be the key to winning the war.

"We have no way to know how advanced she is, relative to the remainder of their fleet," he mused. "Do we?"

"No, sir," Doctor Tisane said. "But we can extrapolate from what we find inside her hull."

Stephen met his eyes. "Could you fly her home?"

It was Sana who answered. "No, Captain. The command datanet is a ruined mess and I doubt we could fix the interface links anytime soon. Their system is a little more open than ours, probably because the virus handled the connections between the cores, but I don't think we could replace the damaged or destroyed systems."

"Brilliant," Stephen said, sardonically. Theodore Smith had had it easy. All *he'd* had to do was link *his* captured ship to *Ark Royal*. "I'll detach one of the freighters and a small prize crew. They can take her as far as Falkirk. The fleet there can take her the rest of the way."

Doctor Tisane frowned. "Does that give them a claim on our prize money?"

Stephen resisted the urge to laugh. Commander Newcomb had told him, two days ago, that the main—often the sole—topic of conversation among the crew was precisely how they were going to spend their prize money. The Admiralty would be generous. They hadn't captured a rusty old barge, but a genuine alien starship. The reward money would be divided out by rank and spread out over the entire flotilla, yet even the most junior crewman—or civilian expert assigned to the crew—could look forward to a sizable payday. The Admiralty would be very generous indeed.

And the taxman is forbidden by law to take any of the reward money, Stephen remembered, with a wry smile. *The incentives for taking an alien ship intact are staggering.*

"No," he said. "But we do have to get the ship home to claim our prize."

He felt his smile grow wider. He didn't need the money—his trust fund alone would keep him fed and watered for the rest of his life—but it was the principle of the thing. He'd give the money to charity, perhaps. It had been a long time since Britain's finest had been left to starve in the gutter, but still...there were institutions for retired servicemen that could do with a sizable infusion of cash. Or...he dismissed the thought, curtly. They had to get the ship home before they could claim any of the money.

"I look forward to reading your report," he said. "I'll see you both later."

He watched them go, then brought up the starchart. It was unlikely they'd find anything else in Alien-2. He certainly didn't want to linger. So far, the virus didn't seem to have realised that it had lost a ship, but that would change soon enough. By then, he wanted to be well away from the captured ship's projected course. The virus might not know when the ship had been captured, but it would certainly know *where*. Shaking his head, he keyed his terminal.

"Commander Newcomb, detach one freighter to escort the captured ship back to Falkirk, *after* we transfer its cargo to the rest of the flotilla," he ordered. It was a shame they hadn't thought to bring a mega-freighter—they were so large that the alien ship could have been stowed inside the freighter's hull—but transhipping cargo from one ship to another in deep space was hard enough with a military-designed freighter. "And then inform the flotilla. We will be proceeding to Alien-3 as soon as the alien ship and her escort are underway."

"Yes, sir," Newcomb said.

And hope to hell we find something useful, Stephen thought, as he closed the connection. *We don't know how long we have before the war begins in earnest.*

CHAPTER EIGHTEEN

ALICE PAUSED IN FRONT OF THE HATCH, feeling almost like a naughty girl who had been sent to face the headmaster. It had been something that had happened to her more times than she cared to admit, back when she'd been in boarding school, and only the fact that her father had been a war hero had kept her from being unceremoniously expelled or sent to a borstal for the remainder of her education. She wasn't sure how many of the horror stories about borstals were true—she'd learnt enough, during commando training, to suspect that no one would *survive* the borstals if the stories were true—but she supposed she should be glad she hadn't been sent there. She might not have been considered for officer training.

And yet, half the platoon had spent time in the borstals, she thought sourly. *They learnt how to apply themselves and actually work.*

She stared at the hatch for a long minute, silently cursing herself. She was dawdling and she knew it, something that would have gotten her in trouble during training. It was better to be doing *something*, the sergeants had said, than sitting around waiting to be hit. Even doing the *wrong* something was better than doing nothing. And yet, there wasn't an enemy on the far side...she shook her head crossly. The headshrinker who was on the far side wasn't an enemy, but twenty years of education, training and active service told her otherwise. The headshrinker had her career in the palm of his hand and she knew it. And she hated it. She was—she knew she was—blunt and plain-spoken. It was considered a virtue amongst the marines. But saying the wrong thing could send her career plummeting down in flames.

A low quiver ran through the ship as she picked up speed. Captain Shields had formally announced, five hours ago, that *Invincible* and her dwindling flotilla would pass through the tramline into Alien-3. Alice had been reading yet another report at the time, awaiting her appointment with the headshrinker. The report had been maddeningly uninformative, much to her annoyance. She didn't blame the spooks or xenospecialists for knowing nothing, but she hated it when they refused to admit it. The report read like it had been written by someone who feared they would be fired—out a cannon, perhaps—if they admitted that they'd learnt nothing since they'd written the last report.

And you're woolgathering, Alice told herself, sharply. *Coward.*

The thought spurred her to raise her hand and press the buzzer. She had *never* been a coward, not since she'd been a five-year-old who'd been dared into climbing a rickety tree by her friends. Her mother had been furious—and terrified, Alice saw now—but Alice had been proud of her achievement. She'd felt fear many times in her life, yet she'd carried on regardless. Fear was just another enemy to overcome. But now...she understood bullets snapping past her head, but not verbal warfare. She gritted her teeth as the hatch hissed open, silently inviting her into the cabin. Who knew? Perhaps the headshrinker would be in a reasonable mood.

Sure, she thought. *And maybe the horse will learn to sing.*

Colonel Watson—*Doctor* Watson, she reminded herself—had been given a nicer cabin than *her*, although it wouldn't have been hard to find a nicer cabin than the hot-bunks in Marine Country. The junior crewmen and midshipmen had nicer bunks than the marines. Some of them didn't even have to share! She heard the hatch close behind her as she advanced into the chamber, feeling as if she was moving into enemy territory. Doctor Watson had redesigned the room to make it look like a comfortable place to sit, rest—and chat. She might have been fooled if she hadn't known who and what he was. A headshrinker simply could not be trusted.

At least he cleared you to rejoin the ship, Alice told herself. Her status was still somewhat vague, but at least the marines had started to accept her again. Perhaps she could convince the headshrinker—or Major Parkinson—to reassign her to one of the understrength platoons. It would be hard to be a common bootneck again, after commanding a platoon in her own right, but she could cope. *God knows we need every swinging dick we can get.*

Her lips quirked. There was no way *she* qualified as a swinging dick.

Doctor Watson was sitting in a chair, looking up at her. Alice scanned him with her eyes automatically, checking for threats. He looked at ease, although she knew better than to take that for granted. They weren't going to be exchanging *physical* blows. But then, the Royal Marines still laughed about the burglar who'd broken into a retired marine's house. The bastard hadn't known that the elderly man had been an unarmed combat instructor *and* boxing champion as well as a veteran of quite a few wars...

"Alice," Doctor Watson said. His brisk, no-nonsense approach galvanised and irritated her in equal measure. "Something funny?"

"Just a random thought," Alice lied. A civilian headshrinker would ask her about being a woman—being the lone woman—in the marines. There would be snide insinuations about her feeling inferior to the men, because she lacked a penis. She had no idea what Doctor Watson would say, but she didn't want to find out. "You wanted to see me, doctor."

"Yes," Doctor Watson said. "Take a seat, please."

Alice sat, purposefully choosing the hardest seat in the compartment. Comfort had always struck her as an illusion, something that could be taken away at any moment. She'd learnt that when her father had murdered her mother. And, if she'd had any doubts, she'd lost them when the Tadpoles had bombarded Earth. Millions had perished when death had struck from the skies; millions more had died in the weeks and months that had followed. She knew, beyond a shadow of a doubt, that she'd been very lucky to survive.

"A week ago, you came face to face with the infected," Doctor Watson said. "Again."

"Yes," Alice said, shortly.

The doctor waited for her to continue, then leaned forward. "How did you cope?"

"Professionally," Alice said. She hadn't realised how much she'd missed being a marine until she'd been deputised as a consultant. The thrill of being on a ship that might explode at any moment had never lost its savour, even if outsiders thought it was thoroughly insane. "I did my duty."

"Henry said as much," Doctor Watson said. "He said you did the marines proud."

It took Alice a moment to realise that he was referring to Major Henry Parkinson. She frowned, wondering what her CO and the headshrinker would have found to talk about. Had they served together? Or had *she* been the sole topic of conversation? She wasn't sure she wanted to know. Parkinson knew her well enough to know when she was having problems.

"It may have to be repeated," she said. "What happens when we try to board a bigger ship?"

"It was suggested that the virus controlled the ship directly," Doctor Watson told her. "What do you think about that?"

Alice shrugged. If *she'd* controlled the ship, through computers or some kind of direct brain interface right out of speculative fiction, *she* was sure she would have done a much better job of repelling borders. There were plenty of possibilities, from animating the remote manipulators to simply waiting for the boarders to get comfortable and triggering the self-destruct. Instead, the ship had been crewed by infected aliens and blob-like viral clusters...her blood ran cold as she realised the implications. The virus hadn't developed any automated systems—or robots—because it hadn't *needed* to develop them. It used the infected to handle the jobs humans would entrust to robotic systems. Why not? They were expendable. It reminded her of the terrorist base she'd helped to capture, three years ago, where the bastards had been trying to build a nuclear bomb. They'd used unprotected humans to refine the nuclear material too. The virus was, if anything, even less concerned about its people.

Doctor Watson coughed. "Something you want to share with me?"

"The virus uses its people as…robots," Alice said, and outlined her thoughts. "That's why it didn't put up a more effective defence."

"An interesting thought," Doctor Watson said. "And how do you *feel* about it?"

"Fuck my feelings," Alice said, a little sharper than she'd intended. Her feelings didn't change the world. No amount of wishing for anything would make it real. "The priority is winning."

"True," the doctor agreed. "But *my* priority is getting you back to a healthy state."

And watching how I cope with being the first infected person to survive the experience, Alice thought. She'd read the autopsy reports. The alien bodies had been *riddled* with the virus. It was unclear if they'd ever been anything more than expendable bodies. They'd certainly had no hope of freeing themselves from captivity. *You're not going to put me ahead of anything else.*

"I'm glad to hear it," Alice said. She kept her face impassive. "I've seen worse amongst humans, doctor, humans who don't have the excuse of being alien viruses that need to invade and occupy bodies to survive. If I'd been infected completely, without help, I would be dead…"

She met his eyes. "But the virus doesn't hate us, doctor. It does what it needs to do to survive. The bastards I met on Earth are far worse."

"But they don't have the power to destroy us utterly," Doctor Watson pointed out. "The virus does."

Alice wasn't so sure. She'd seen the settlements—and refugee camps— along the borders of Europe. They'd been creepy places, with women treated as servants and slaves and children raised to hate the people on the other side of the wall. She'd never really understood how they tolerated it, but she supposed they knew no better. A person who was raised in a restrictive culture would find it very hard to shake off if they moved to a far less restrictive environment. And yet, the oppressors were human. They could have made the choice *not* to be assholes. They could have given up and allowed their people to be free. Instead…

She shivered. "Perhaps it does," she said. "But there would be no malice in it."

"I see," Doctor Watson said. "And you consider it to be better than your human opponents?"

Alice suspected she'd been lured into a rhetorical trap, but there was no help for it now. She narrowed her eyes, daring him to challenge her.

"When I signed up, I was warned that I couldn't expect mercy if I ever fell into enemy hands," she said. "I was told that I would be raped and murdered, that my suffering would be filmed and uploaded to the datanet: I was told that there was a very good chance that I wouldn't survive long enough to be rescued. They made it clear that I, as a woman with a mind of her own and a gun of her own, would be singled out for special attention. I resolved to kill myself if there was a serious prospect of being captured. I'd deny them the pleasure of having their way with me."

She allowed her voice to harden. "The virus doesn't make people suffer for the hell of it, doctor. It isn't evil, not in the sense we understand the term. What it *does* is evil, and it has to be stopped, but it doesn't have the option of being good or evil. I don't think it *can* make the choice to be good or evil. It isn't a different culture. It just *is*."

"So you said," Doctor Watson said. "But we have problems dealing with other cultures."

Alice wasn't sure what he was driving at, but she nodded anyway. "That's true," she said, remembering a joint exercise with the Russians. The Russians had been brutal, both to themselves and to their captives. The rumours of mass graves in Central Asia, never officially confirmed, seemed very believable. So did the stories about nightmarish atrocities intended to terrify the locals into submission. "But we can talk to them. We can tell them that what they're doing is wrong. We can even threaten them into changing their ways. But the virus cannot be reasoned with, let alone threatened. We are in a battle for our very survival."

"But you feel the virus isn't evil," Doctor Watson said.

"No," Alice said. "But that doesn't mean that we must *not* fight it."

She met his eyes. "Is there a *point* to this?"

Doctor Watson looked back at her. "One could feel that you are arguing the virus's case. Or that it has influenced you even after you were freed from its control."

Alice felt a hot flash of anger. "It never *had* me under its control," she bit out. "The doctors proved that it never managed to reach into my brain."

"But it might have managed to influence you," Doctor Watson pointed out, coolly. "How do we know it didn't manage to plant commands or suggestions into your brain?"

"It never *reached* my brain." Alice took a moment to place firm controls on her temper. "I do not believe that it managed to influence my thinking in any way."

"There are ways to...*condition* a human being," Doctor Watson reminded her. "And the victims do not *know* they have been conditioned. The conscious mind is completely unaware, even as the conditioning goes to work. They pass lie detector tests because, even at a sub-thought level, they believe themselves to be innocent. And, technically, they *are* innocent."

Alice held his eyes. "I thought there were ways to detect conditioning," she said. "You certainly put me through a hell of a lot of tests."

"You are not...*blatantly*...conditioned," Doctor Watson confirmed. "But how do we know you weren't...influenced?"

"Well," Alice started. "I..."

She took a moment to organise her thoughts. "If I was to say that the Americans built the largest battleships in known space, that *might* be a sign that the CIA or OSS had conditioned me at some point, perhaps when that American pilot was plying me with drinks in the hopes he'd get into my knickers. He was talking about the immense battleship he crewed—all by himself, if you believe him. Or maybe he was bragging about the size of his dick. I don't know. Maybe I *was* conditioned.

"But it is also a point of *fact* that the Americans *have* built the largest battleships in known space, unless the virus has built something larger. It is a fact! And someone who repeats that fact is not a victim of American

177

conditioning, or American alcohol, but merely a reader of *Jane's Fighting Ships*. And what I told you about the virus is a simple fact. We're not talking about a religious cult that wants to wipe out unbelievers, but an alien entity doing what it has to do to survive. It simply isn't capable of recognising us as intelligent entities in our own right."

"You'd think it should be able to realise that we think too," Doctor Watson mused. "It certainly accesses memories, once it has control over the infected victims' brain."

"We *assume* it does," Alice said. She was fairly sure the doctor was right, but she was feeling contrary. "For all we know, it may deduce a great deal about us from simple observation through its senses. And the senses it steals from the victims. We're not talking about forcible assimilation into a mass-mind, doctor."

"Or so we think," Doctor Watson murmured.

Alice leaned back in her chair. "I have an appointment in twenty minutes," she said, although she was grimly aware that Doctor Watson took priority. "Is there anything else I can tell you?"

The doctor shrugged. "Do you have any insights into the alien ship?"

"Nothing I haven't written into my reports," Alice said, bluntly. "It was an odd environment, I will admit, but nothing *too* strange. It wasn't like swimming through a Tadpole starship or walking through a Vesy fortress. They're both *very* alien."

"Nothing too strange," the doctor repeated. "The civvies didn't feel the same way."

"I'm sure they didn't," Alice agreed. The xenospecialists and diplomats might spend half their time in alien environments, learning how to cope with worlds that weren't designed for humans, but hardly anyone else *willingly* chose to travel to alien worlds. Even Vesy, home to a growing cultural and technological enhancement mission, had relatively few travellers. "I think they weren't so focused on actually sweeping the ship before it was too late."

"I'm sure they weren't focused on it too," Doctor Watson agreed. "I wasn't allowed to go over, you see."

"You're too valuable to lose," Alice said. She wouldn't have regretted it if any further meetings were cancelled and she never saw the headshrinker again, but she didn't want him dead. He certainly wasn't as useless as the school counsellor who'd tried to talk to her about her father. She was still surprised she hadn't been expelled for what she'd said to him. "And besides, if someone gets infected, you might be the only one who spots it."

She frowned. Everyone but *her* had had their blood checked twice before they'd been allowed to return to *Invincible*. And *then* they'd been put through a decontamination procedure that had been alarmingly through. But her? She had alien matter in her blood already. Perhaps she should be grateful she'd been allowed to leave the research base after all. The risk of infection was completely beyond calculation.

"I hope that's true," Doctor Watson said. "But none of us know for sure, do we?"

"No," Alice said. "We don't."

CHAPTER NINETEEN

"ALIEN-3," THE *ZAMPOLIT* SAID. "Do we *have* to use their name?"

Captain Pavel Kaminov resisted the urge to shrug. "It isn't a *British* or a Yankee name," he said, instead. "It's a designation laid down by the Alien Contact Treaty that will remain in place until we learn what *they* call it or rename the system ourselves, after the war."

He turned his attention to the display, wishing—again—that the *Rodina* could provide holographic displays to match those he'd seen on *Invincible*. The display in front of him, rapidly filling up as the probes slipped into the alien system, was far in advance of the systems available to the Russians who'd first jumped through the tramlines to explore strange new worlds, but it wasn't cutting-edge tech. Pavel was practical enough to know that weapons and sensors were more important—there, *Yuriy Ivanov* had the best available to the motherland—yet it was frustrating. The classified briefing he'd been given when he'd assumed command had made it clear that Russia simply didn't have the money to keep up everywhere. Some things had to be sacrificed.

The *zampolit* snorted. "What does it say about us that we accept *their* terms?"

"Russia was an equal partner in the discussions," Pavel said, without looking up. It was the official line, but—he suspected—it wasn't true. Russia had been in a weak state when the diplomats met to hash out humanity's response to any further alien threats. Thankfully, the Great Powers hadn't taken advantage of the situation. "And we *will* have the inside track on any star systems discovered on this mission."

He sighed, inwardly, as a blue icon popped into life on the display. He'd been told, time and time again, that a starship captain and his *zampolit* were meant to work as a team...and that the *best* ships and crews had been the ones where the two men worked in harmony. Now, after far too many years in the navy to count, he rather suspected that someone at the academy had been lying to Russia's future commanding officers. He would have blamed the GRU if he'd thought they had the imagination to come up with such a lie. Far too many of the *zampolits* he'd met had been ludicrously unsuited to any position on a starship. He'd been told that some of them had even met their deaths through doing things that any spacer would know were mind-bogglingly stupid.

The sensor officer turned and saluted. "Captain, we're detecting a gas giant and a planet within the habitable zone," he said. "The former appears to have an alien presence."

There goes our finder's fee, Pavel thought, although he wasn't really surprised. The captured alien ship had certainly passed through Alien-3, even if it hadn't come from there. It was unlikely that any species would leave such a valuable world undeveloped. But then, the virus hadn't bothered to continue to expand towards Falkirk. *Maybe we can find a way to attack the world and give the bastards a fright.*

"Route two more probes towards each of the worlds," he said. A gas giant, combined with a habitable world...? This system was prime real estate, as the Yankees would say. "And update *Invincible* on our findings."

He ignored the *zampolit's* snort as more data flowed into the display. *Invincible* was two light-minutes away, lurking near the tramline as her smaller escorts probed the alien system for prospective targets. In theory, Pavel should have asked for permission before launching the probes; in practice, he knew they needed to gather as much information as they could as quickly as possible. Captain Shields would understand. And, if he didn't, he'd just have to put up with it. Pavel was an ally, not a subordinate.

And the zampolit will jump on me if I appear too subservient to my commanding officer, he thought, morbidly. *Mother Russia might have accepted his position, and I may have been ordered to follow his commands, but I cannot be too submissive or my career will be destroyed.*

It wasn't a pleasant thought. He'd read his orders very carefully. If *Dezhnev* was located, he would have to leave the flotilla and carry out his sealed orders. The politicians might assume that he could do it without causing a breach between *Yuriy Ivanov* and the remainder of the ships, but Pavel knew better. They were unlikely to succeed in the first half of their mission without surrendering all chance to complete the *second* half of their mission. Pavel eyed the *zampolit's* back with some irritation. The bastard would probably make it impossible to complete the first half of the mission, let alone the second. And there was nothing Pavel could do about it.

Perhaps I should arrange an accident, Pavel thought. *He's certainly stupid enough to override the safeties on the airlock and walk into space without a suit...*

His attention was diverted from a contemplation of his government's many shortcomings when a handful of red icons blinked into existence on the display. An alarm howled a moment later, warning the crew that the system was inhabited—infected, he supposed—by the alien menace. He snapped out a command as he took his chair, ordering his officers to shut off the alarm. They weren't going to be jumped immediately, not unless the alien sensors and stealth systems were *far* better than he'd assumed. It was unlikely they'd been noticed. *Yuriy Ivanov* was a very small target in a very big system.

"Captain," his sensor officer said as the sound of the alarm died away. "We have two large stations and five small ships orbiting the planet."

Pavel frowned. "What kind of ships?"

The sensor officer hesitated. "Judging by their power output, I'd say they were cruisers," he said, finally. "But it's impossible to be sure."

"Yes," Pavel said, before the *zampolit* could start being unreasonable about the whole affair and say something the sensor officer would regret. "I understand."

He studied the display for a long moment, cursing the alien virus under his breath. He'd read the reports written by the British scientists—and his engineering staff—and noted all the questions they had been unable to answer. If the alien fusion cores were truly as advanced as they claimed, it was quite possible that those cruisers were actually destroyers...but there was no way to be sure. They might also be faster than *Invincible*, faster even than *Yuriy Ivanov* herself. And yet...the only encouraging sign was that the aliens didn't seem to have miniaturised their drive nodes. A cruiser-sized ship designed to overhaul *Yuriy Ivanov* would be nothing but engine. She might catch up with *Yuriy Ivanov*; she wouldn't be able to kill her.

"Direct the probe closer to the ships," he ordered, finally. If they could get a clear look at their hulls, the analysts would finally have detailed sensor records to examine. "And then relay everything we've found to *Invincible*."

"Aye, Captain."

Pavel forced himself to relax as the probes drifted closer to their targets. His family had a long tradition of military service—his father had been in the navy, his grandfather a soldier on the borders of civilisation—but none of them had told him that being in the military was long hours of boredom mixed with moments of sheer terror. He wouldn't have understood, Pavel thought; he'd been so thrilled with the idea of wearing a smart uniform that he hadn't really understood what it *meant*. Service in Russia's military was never easy. It had only been a few decades ago that the knout had been formally banned.

The display updated, time and time again. A small cloudscoop orbited the gas giant, while a handful of asteroid miners moved around a cluster of asteroids. Alien-3 wasn't the *richest* system Pavel had seen, but he couldn't help thinking that there should be more activity surrounding the planets. The virus didn't seem to worry about developing its worlds as extensively as humanity, although it was possible that it thought it had eternity. Mother

Russia's brief flirtation with communism, over two hundred years old, had floundered on human nature. The virus, practically a single entity in billions of bodies, didn't *need* to worry about keeping its people happy, let alone building a capitalistic economy. There was no need to hurry. It certainly didn't have to handle colonists who demanded the trappings of a modern economy even as they fought to tame a whole new world.

And then we lost our first colony world, Pavel reminded himself. New Russia was independent these days, maintaining nothing more than cultural ties to the motherland. *Who knows what will happen if we lose the rest of the settlements?*

The sensor console chimed. He leaned forward. "Report?"

"Captain," the sensor officer said. "There's a whole primitive *settlement* on that world!"

. . .

"It's thoroughly weird," Lieutenant Allen Travers said, as he activated the conference room's projector. The analyst sounded bemused. "As far as we can tell from our probes, there's only one source of high technology—and transmissions—on the planet's surface. The remainder is a primitive society with nothing more advanced than horses and carts. There's nothing comparable to gunpowder, as far as we can tell."

Stephen leaned forward, studying the display. The Russians had taken an immense risk when they'd steered a probe into orbit, yet he had to admit it had paid off. The aliens on the surface were very alien—they looked like absurd crosses between humans and spiders—but they didn't appear to be infected. They seemed to be living normal lives. Or were they? It was impossible to tell. Stephen had no doubt the virus would have infected them, if it could. All the normal calculations about the efficiency of slave labour went out the airlock when the virus was involved.

"Maybe they're holding the world hostage," Commander Newcomb said. "Those stations could easily be bombardment platforms."

185

"They wouldn't need to bother," Major Parkinson pointed out. "They could simply infect the entire population."

"Assuming they can," Stephen mused. He looked at Doctor Nancy Drawn, the ship's chief xenospecialist. "Doctor, can you tell if they're infected? Or if they're somehow immune to being infected?"

"Not from this distance," Nancy said. She had a clipped voice that reminded Stephen of one of his instructors from the Luna Academy. "Captain, we would need bio-samples to examine before we could tell you for sure. The virus does not appear to be making use of the aliens—the new aliens—for anything, as far as we can see, but we might be wrong. We need to get down there."

"That will be tricky," Newcomb observed. "The enemy cruisers alone pose a significant threat."

Stephen was inclined to agree. *Invincible* could take one or two of the alien ships, unless they carried a completely new weapons system, but five of them would pose a serious problem. And they were—he assumed—fast enough to overhaul *Invincible* in a stern chase and bring her under fire. And *that* didn't include the orbiting space stations. They looked like transit hubs, rather than orbital bombardment platforms, but Stephen didn't like their power readings. It looked as if they were designed to defend themselves.

"We *could* get a marine team down to the surface," Major Parkinson said. "The trick would be getting them up again."

Stephen looked at him. "You think you could get a stealth shuttle through the atmosphere without being detected?"

"We've done it before, on Earth," Major Parkinson reminded him. "And it was done under combat conditions too, on Clarke."

"Clarke was hardly covered by an extensive sensor net," Newcomb pointed out, in his role as devil's advocate. "The Indians barely had time to set up their mass drivers. And the planet's weather masked the shuttle as soon as it slipped into the atmosphere."

"We flew a shuttle through the UKADR," Parkinson said. "That was hardly an *undefended* region. And we got away with it."

"You also lost a shuttle the second time you tried it," Newcomb said, dryly. "Yes, I know; the shuttle wasn't actually lost and the pilots weren't actually killed. You were still tracked and, if they'd wanted to kill you, they *would* have killed you."

Stephen held up a hand. "Major, we don't know half as much as we should about the enemy sensor nets," he said. "If we're wrong, if you're picked up by a ground-based detection station, whoever you send on the mission will be dead."

Parkinson nodded. "We understand the risks, Captain," he said, "but my pilots are confident they can slip through the enemy sensor network. They do not appear to have set up a global network. As long as we are careful not to pass too close to the orbiting stations, or the installation on the ground, we should be able to move unnoticed."

"You'd still have the problem of getting off the ground and back home," Newcomb said, slowly. "Are you sure you can make it into orbit without being killed?"

"In theory, we should be able to escape," Parkinson said. "It's basically a question of making a very slow ascent, keeping our power stepped down as much as possible. In practice...it depends on how alert the aliens are. We got away with it on Earth a few times, Captain, but it proved impossible to minimise the risks. There was no way to predict when we'd be detected or what would happen if someone decided to take a closer look at a transient contact."

"And you want to do it," Newcomb said. He shook his head. "It sounds insane."

"It's doable," Parkinson insisted. "Ideally, we'd be landing near an alien town, but well clear of any technological installations. We'd then observe the aliens from a distance before deciding what to do. If we decide they're infected...we might take one of them as a biological sample or merely continue to watch them. It would tell us a great deal about their social structure—and what the virus does to it."

"At the risk of losing whoever we send down," Stephen mused. It wouldn't be the first time he'd sent people under his command into danger, but he couldn't think of any time when the danger had been so...intimate. If the recon team was captured, the best they could hope for was a chance to commit suicide before they were infected and overwhelmed. "Major, Doctor, I want you to ask for volunteers. You are *not* to go yourselves."

Nancy swallowed. "Captain...I wouldn't ask my people to do anything I wouldn't do myself."

Neither would I, Stephen thought. But *he* couldn't go down to the surface. The idea of the starship's commander going on away team missions belonged to bad television programs like Stellar Star, not the real world. *We may never be able to recover whoever goes down.*

"You know too much," he said, bluntly. The virus would learn things Stephen didn't want it to know if it managed to access Nancy's memories. "Your staffers are a far lesser risk."

He ignored her stricken look. "Major, have your pilots refine the plan," he ordered. "I'll review it when they're finished and make my final decision then."

"Aye, Captain," Parkinson said.

"Until then, we will watch the aliens from a safe distance," Stephen added. It was unlikely they'd learn much more from long-range observations, but it *might* yield something useful. "Dismissed."

The compartment emptied rapidly, leaving Stephen alone with his thoughts. He'd sent people into danger before—he reminded himself of that again and again—but this was different. He'd never sent someone into a position where he'd *expected* him to die, let alone an entire recon team. There was a very good chance that the recon team would be trapped, unable to retreat, if they weren't blown out of the air when they tried to leave. Stephen was all too aware of the hard choices admirals and generals had made, during the First Interstellar War, but now...he wondered, grimly, if he had it in him to make the choice. There were good reasons *not* to risk the recon team, volunteers or not. He didn't *have* to send them down the planet.

Yes, we do, he told himself. *We need to know what's really happening on Alien-3.*

He gritted his teeth, feeling—once again—the loneliness of command. The prospect of losing twelve or so of his crew was bad, but the risk had to be balanced against the need to gather more data. There was no way they could land an recon team on Alien-1. If they learnt something new about the virus, something they could turn against it...what if the natives were *immune*? What if their immunity could be duplicated? What if...

Don't be so hasty, he thought, sharply. There was a very real danger of seeing only what he wanted to see. The virus might have infected the alien population years ago. It wasn't as if a society that didn't even have gunpowder could put up any real resistance. The virus might just have hit the planet with a biological bomb and then moved on to bigger targets. *We need to be very careful.*

He didn't want to do it. But he knew, all too well, what the answer had to be.

The intercom bleeped. "Captain," Parkinson said. "The pilots have refined their flight plans as much as possible. They feel the flight is doable. And my entire complement of marines volunteered for the mission."

"Very well," Stephen said, quietly. There was no longer any time for delay. "The mission is authorised. We will launch the shuttle in two hours."

And may God have mercy on us, he thought, as he closed the connection. *If they get one sniff of our presence, the shuttle and her crew are doomed.*

CHAPTER TWENTY

"I MUST HAVE BEEN MAD," Lieutenant Travers bemoaned. "Why did I ever agree to this?"

Alice bit down the urge to make a snide remark about knowing the job was dangerous when he took it. Lieutenant Allen Travers was a naval officer, true, but he was an analyst who specialised in xenobiology rather than someone who expected to be charging into the teeth of enemy fire. Alice was mildly surprised that he'd volunteered to join the mission. He'd had the standard firearms and self-defence training the navy gave to all its personnel, but beyond that he had nothing. The rifle slung over his shoulder looked terrifyingly out of place.

"You'll be fine," she said, trying to channel her school's matron. The senior matron had been a horror, hated and feared in equal measure, but the junior matron had been a solidly reassuring presence to children who had never been away from home before. "We'll be down before you know it."

The interior of the stealth shuttle *was* a little unnerving, she had to admit, even to someone who had been using assault shuttles for most of her adult life. It was cramped, with every last square inch of free space crammed with seats and supplies for twelve marines and five researchers; the bulkheads, formed of a composite that was supposed to make it harder for active sensors to see the shuttle, looked weak, as if they were made of plastic. Alice knew the shuttle wasn't *quite* as fragile as it looked, although she also knew that it wouldn't matter if the aliens detected them. A single HVM or plasma pulse would blow them to atoms before they even knew they were under attack.

But then, an assault shuttle wouldn't be much better, she thought. One of the reasons everyone had dismissed the idea of serious interstellar warfare before First Contact was that transporting an invading army across light-years and landing it on even a *lightly* defended world was a logistical nightmare, although—the cynic in her noted—it hadn't stopped the world's militaries from building formidable spacefaring navies. *Getting down to the surface through a blaze of enemy fire would rely more on luck than judgement.*

She winked at Travers, then pressed her armoured gauntlet against the shuttle's receptor, hooking her suit into the craft's passive sensors. Alien-3 was slowly coming into view, a handful of icons representing the alien stations and starships holding position over the green-blue world. The shuttle's pilot was bringing them in carefully, gliding through a sparse network of sensor pulses that felt a little perfunctory. Alice, who had trained to penetrate places that were far more heavily defended, couldn't help thinking that the virus didn't really care about Alien-3. It wouldn't have taken much effort to construct a sensor network that would have made it far harder for the marines to land without being detected.

We haven't got down yet, she reminded herself. The stealth shuttle was *slow,* compared to even a civilian model. It would be hours before they reached the planet's atmosphere, where the *real* excitement would begin. *Don't count your victories before you actually win them.*

Travers coughed. "How long until we get out of here?"

Alice made a show of checking the timer, although—after more assault landings than she cared to remember—she was all too aware of the passage of time. "Seven hours until we hit atmosphere," she said, calmly. "Consider yourself lucky. You could be on one of the *early* stealth shuttles."

The younger man—it was odd to realise that Travers was actually a year or two younger than her—gave her a sharp look. "What was wrong with *them?*"

Alice grinned. "Oh, they were little more than composite shells," she said, remembering the landing pod she'd seen during training. "They could get down to a planetary surface, true, but they couldn't get up again. There was no way they could get off the ground, let alone climb out of a gravity well. Anyone who was sent down had to wait for pickup. And sometimes their..."

She reminded herself, sharply, that Travers was *not* trained for combat operations. "They were only used in combat once," she said, instead of what she'd intended to say. "And they were quite successful."

Travers sucked in a breath. "They were like colonial dumpsters?"

Alice nodded. Some bright spark—she thought he was British, although she wasn't sure—had hit on the idea of using immense landing pods to land everything a colony would need in one or two craft. The giant dumpsters could be unloaded, then converted into living quarters that would suffice until the colonists built homes for themselves. She'd always considered the concept crude, but she had to admit it was a simple solution to a complex problem. Besides, it was cheap. It would be a long time before even Britannia or Washington built orbital towers of their own. Until then, the colonists were dependent on shuttles to get supplies down to the surface.

"It's the same basic idea," she said. "And it worked, more or less."

She gave him a considering look. "Try and get some sleep," she told him. "It will make the time pass quicker."

Travers looked as if sleep was the *last* thing on his mind, but closed his eyes anyway. Alice watched him for a long moment, grimly aware that he wasn't actually sleeping, then brought up her suit's eReader. There wasn't much else to do on the shuttle, save for sleeping and waiting and she didn't feel like sleep either. She skimmed four chapters of her latest book before finally giving up and closing her eyes. Moments later—it felt like moments, even though her timer insisted that she'd been asleep for six hours—she jerked awake. The shuttle was approaching the atmosphere.

And Travers is snoring like a pro, she thought, as she glanced at him. *Hopefully, he'll stay asleep until we hit the ground.*

She checked his suit's telltales, just to make sure he was fine, then reached out and pushed his visor into place. It had always struck her as a pointless precaution—anything that killed the shuttle while it was in flight would kill everyone onboard before they even knew they were under attack—but it *might* make the difference between life and death. The shuttle's hull was strong, compared to its predecessors, yet there *was* a slight chance it would spring a leak during the landing. She checked, out of habit, the distance between herself and the egress. If the shit really did hit the fan, she'd have to grab a sleeping Travers and run.

I'd have to grab him anyway, she reminded herself. *He isn't checked out on emergency escape procedures either.*

She felt a flicker of sympathy, combined with irritation. She'd leant to dread emergency escape drills too, even though she *knew* the drills were reasonably safe. Landing in the pool was embarrassing, and the taunts from her fellows were merciless, but it beat jumping into interplanetary space and hoping for the best. The odds of survival were poor. Jumping out in a planetary atmosphere wasn't much better. They'd be easy to track as they plummeted towards the ground.

"I need a piss," Corporal Hammersmith called.

"Go in the suit, you stupid bastard," Sergeant Radcliffe snapped. "And if you've disconnected yourself because you wanted a wank, I'll tear your..."

Alice hid her amusement with an effort. The combat suits were supposed to be more uncomfortable for the men than the women, something that had always struck her as curious. She was the only female marine on active service and, as far as she knew, there weren't many other women who were required to wear combat suits. Logically, the suits should have been designed for men, with women as an afterthought. Perhaps someone had been looking to the future, she thought. The toilet system—something else that, for some unaccountable reason, was left out of the recruitment brochures—was technically unisex.

Her lips quirked at the thought. The designer had probably wanted to make *everyone* uncomfortable...

The shuttle shuddered, slightly, as it hit the upper edge of the planetary atmosphere. A faint sound echoed through the hull, a sound that made a shiver run down her spine. The hull was fine, Alice told herself firmly. There was no reason to panic. And yet, she felt helpless. There was nothing she could do to save her life. They were in the hands of the pilots—and the engineers who'd built the shuttle. She gritted her teeth as the craft shook again. Years ago, she'd been told, engineers had been forced to fly the shuttles they'd designed. She doubted it was true—engineers were hardly expendable—but she wanted to believe it. She wanted to know that the designers had every reason to make sure their craft were safe.

You're a marine, she thought. The shuttle shook again, as if it had been slapped by an angry god. *Safe isn't in the job description.*

Travers started awake. "What…what…?"

"We hit the planet's atmosphere," Alice said. She linked into the sensors, long enough to confirm that the shuttle had entered safely and was heading towards the ground. It felt as if they were dropping alarmingly fast, but she knew better. A rapid transit through the atmosphere might leave a heat trail for the aliens to follow. "We'll be down soon."

The shuttle shook again, violently. Travers snapped up his visor and looked around, desperately. Alice opened her mouth to order him to put the visor back down, then changed her mind as Travers threw up. She looked away, granting him what little privacy she could as he emptied his stomach. It wasn't as if she hadn't seen worse. What was a little vomit compared to blood and gore.

"Sorry," Travers stammered, hacking and coughing. "I…"

"Don't worry about it," Alice told him, firmly. The shuttle lurched as it entered the lower atmosphere. She motioned for him to snap his visor back into place. "There isn't a person here who hasn't thrown up once or twice."

But they did it in the landing simulators, she added, silently. The marine recruits wouldn't have survived the first week of training if they got seasick, let alone airsick. Their training included all sorts of tricks to catch recruits who might not be able to keep their stomachs under control, although there were limits. The acceleration simulator eventually made *everyone* throw up. *They didn't do it on deployment.*

She muttered reassuring nonsense to him as the shuttle dropped lower and lower, all the while keeping her eye on the live feed from the sensors. It was local twilight, hopefully making it harder for the natives to spot anything unusual within their skies. Alice had been told that daylight made it easier to spot the landing craft, stealthed or not, while night carried the risk of accidentally being illuminated, but she wasn't sure she bought the logic. The shuttle wasn't lit up like an alien mothership from a low-budget movie.

And besides, for all we know, the natives have eyes that can see in the dark, she thought, morbidly. Her training had included a long section on how aliens had their strengths and weaknesses. The Tadpoles had been *terrible* at fighting on the ground—their infantry tactics had sucked shit through a straw, according to her instructors—but they'd been lethal in space and no one wanted to fight a Tadpole underwater. *They might even have powers we don't understand.*

The ground came up at terrifying speed. She braced herself, a second before the shuttle crashed down to earth. Travers let out a whimper, seconds *after* the craft had hit the ground and stopped. Alice motioned for him to stay where he was as the hatches slammed open, allowing the marines to jump up and race out of the shuttle. Air flowed into the craft, her sensors rapidly assessing that it was safe to breathe. Alice allowed herself a moment of relief. She'd expected viral matter floating in the air. *That* would have forced them to stay in their suits more or less permanently.

But we keep the bloody masks on anyway, she thought. *There's no way to be sure, yet.*

"Clear," Sergeant Radcliffe called. "You may disembark now."

I'm a bloody passenger, Alice thought, as she undid her straps and stood. *And I'm a babysitter too.*

She stepped through the hatch, Travers dogging her heels like an overgrown puppy. It was darkening rapidly outside, the skyline so completely dark that she found herself feeling a little disoriented before she remembered that the natives didn't have anything resembling electric lighting. Britain hadn't been so dark for centuries, even when the planet had been bombarded and power outages—the first in two hundred years—had plagued the entire country. She looked from side to side, silently assessing the landing site. There was no hint that they'd landed anywhere near a native settlement.

Town, she thought, as she walked around the shuttle. *They're native to this world.*

"There's grass here," Travers said. He'd already removed his mask. "Grass and trees and…"

"Grass-analogues," Alice said, curtly. Her sensors insisted the air was safe to breathe, but she was still reluctant to open her suit. "Don't assume it's anything like its earthly counterpart."

She sighed, then removed her helmet. The night air was warm, scented with something that—oddly—reminded her of growing up on the farm. She looked around, reminding herself that she couldn't take anything for granted. Evolution seemed determined to fill all the niches it could, even on worlds that hadn't developed intelligent life. Earthly plants might not do well, if they were introduced to Alien-3. A life-bearing world wasn't always welcoming to food crops from another world.

"So," Travers said. He sounded happier, now they were on the ground. Alice didn't have the heart to tell him they'd probably been safer on the shuttle. "When are we going to meet the aliens?"

"We're going to *watch* the aliens," Alice said. The briefing had made it clear that there was a good chance the alien natives were infected. She shuddered to think of what might have happened to them, over the years. The entire planet might be a deadly trap. "But first, we have to set up camp."

Sergeant Radcliffe banished the specialists back to the shuttle, just in case one of them had the bright idea to ramble off into the countryside, then directed the marines in erecting camouflage netting over the shuttle and setting up basic defences. Alice was relieved to be doing *something* with the marines, even if it wasn't as exciting as boarding an enemy starship. The remote sensors, linked to the shuttle through concealed wires, should hopefully provide warning if the aliens started to move towards them. Alice hoped they'd be enough, although she had her doubts. There was no way they could defend the shuttle against a serious assault—or a KEW, dropped from orbit.

But they'll want to take us alive, so we can be infected, she told herself. She tried not to think about the suicide device concealed in one of her teeth. She'd have to make damn sure she used it before she was infected again or there would be no second escape. She and her platoon would be infected and turned into mindless slaves. *And then we can satisfy their curiosity about how we got here.*

Sergeant Radcliffe reminded them, time and time again, not to use their transmitters unless it was urgent. The boffins might *claim* that the low-power microbursts were undetectable, but no one cared to test that theory in the field. A single transmission might go unnoticed if there were a number of high-power transmitters in the area, yet there were *no* radio stations on Alien-3. Even the alien installation several hundred miles to the south didn't seem to be pumping out more than a handful of signals. Alice had no idea why the virus hadn't bothered to modernise the planet, but it didn't matter. All that mattered, as long as they were on the ground, was staying alive and completing the mission.

"We'll head towards the alien settlement tomorrow morning," Sergeant Radcliffe said, once the shuttle was concealed. They made one last sweep around it, just to be sure the shuttle was well-hidden, then slipped under the netting. "Until then, we'll get some rest."

He detailed a trio of marines to stand watch, with orders to wake the rest of the platoon if anything happened, then directed the remainder to go to sleep. Alice had half-hoped to sleep under the night sky, but she was ordered into the shuttle with two-thirds of the platoon. She wasn't quite a marine any longer, she told herself, even though she wasn't a helpless civvy either. Travers was snoring again, she noted, as she lay down beside him. Two of the other specialists were wide awake. They'd regret it in the morning.

Because we'll be hiking cross-country and praying we don't get spotted, Alice thought, remembering some of her first training exercises. They'd been shown, the hard way, just how easy it was to be spotted and tracked from orbit. The training platoon had read about high-altitude drones—and orbiting stealth satellites—but they hadn't really comprehended what it meant. *And if the aliens see anything out of place, they might send a team to investigate.*

She pushed the thought aside as she closed her eyes and concentrated. They were on an alien world, something that fascinated and terrified her in equal measure, but she needed her beauty sleep. The following day was going to be very busy, even for the people who stayed with the shuttle. She mentally checked a list of things she needed to do, then drew on her training and forced herself to relax.

But, no matter what she did, it felt like hours before she managed to get to sleep.

CHAPTER TWENTY-ONE

THE FOLLOWING DAY DAWNED BRIGHT AND CLEAR, reminding Alice—once again—of happy days on the family farm. She couldn't help feeling wistful as she relieved herself and checked her gear, although the ration bar was a far cry from the meals her grandmother had made when she was a child. The older woman had insisted on growing as much as possible for herself, something that had probably kept her grandchildren healthy during the war and the rationing that had followed afterwards. Alice felt an odd pang as she walked around the concealed shuttle, then met up with the remainder of her party. Travers looked oddly pleased to be finally heading away from the shuttle.

"Remember, avoid all contact with the natives," Sergeant Radcliffe said, curtly. "And, if contact is unavoidable, *don't* let them have a chance to follow us back to the shuttle."

Alice kept her thoughts to herself as the party set out, heading west. Sergeant Radcliffe was right—he'd stated regulations that had been set in stone ever since humanity had realised that it wasn't alone in the universe—but she had her doubts. The aliens presumably knew their planet *far* better than the human intruders. There was a good chance that they could follow the party back to the shuttle, if they realised the party was *there*. And then... Alice didn't know what would happen then, but she doubted it would be good. Even uninfected, the natives might object to the intrusion. And an engagement would certainly draw attention from orbit.

She kept a wary eye on Travers and the others, but—somewhat to her surprise—Travers was holding up fairly well. The xenospecialist was so keen to see the aliens, if only from a safe distance, that he was practically *lunging* forward, even though the marines knew to pace themselves during a long march. There was nothing to be gained by running as though the hounds of hell were after them. Alice smiled to herself, then kept walking. It felt good to finally stretch her legs after being cooped up in the ship. She just wished she felt better about not wearing her suit.

But it would be far more noticeable if the virus was looking down from orbit, Alice thought, as they pressed on. In theory, none of the alien stations or ships were in position to see them; in practice, there was no way to be entirely sure. *We have to be very careful.*

She had to smile as some of the civvies—she had to remind herself that they weren't *really* civvies, even though they weren't marines—started to grumble about how *large* the planet was and how far they had to walk. It made a certain kind of sense, she supposed; Alien-3, or Earth, was tiny on an interstellar scale, but still unimaginably huge compared to a mere human. The spacefarers simply didn't grasp that the thirty miles march across Dartmoor—a requirement that all prospective marines had to meet if they wanted to qualify for active service—might have looked like no distance at all from orbit, but was a very long way indeed for anyone who had to actually walk from one end of the moor to the other. Sergeant Radcliffe glared at any marine who looked as if he would make a smart remark, then offered encouraging advice to the civvies. Alice was impressed at how well he handled them. She doubted *she* would have been so polite.

They're not marines, she thought, wryly. *They're probably not used to what passes for encouragement during a route march.*

They stopped for a brief lunch, hidden under the trees, then resumed the march. Alice kept a wary eye on the local vegetation—she'd seen videos of plants that attacked anything that came near—but saw nothing to worry her. The biochemists claimed that the vegetation was actually safe to eat, if it was fed into a food processor; Alice—and the remainder of the party—was in no hurry to test the theory. If the biochemist was wrong, the results would be disastrous. Their genetic enhancements might not be able to handle a poisonous alien plant.

"It looks a little weird," Travers said. He stepped up beside her, as if they were out for an afternoon stroll. "Have you noticed what's missing?"

Alice tensed. Had she missed something? What had she missed? Sergeant Radcliffe would have chewed her out—respectfully, given that she'd been his superior officer seven months ago—if she'd missed anything, unless he'd missed it too. She looked around carefully, trying to see what *wasn't* there. The plants looked weird—she couldn't help thinking that they looked like purple water lilies combined with trees and bushes—but she'd been in alien environments before. Nothing seemed out of place...

"There are no insects," Travers said. "And that's a little odd."

"Oh," Alice said. "And that means...what?"

"Well, they *could* be scared of us tramping through the undergrowth," Travers said. "Or they might never have evolved on this world, which means that the plants probably use birds to pollinate themselves. Or the insects might have been exterminated by the virus. That would probably have screwed up the local ecology, but something else might have taken their place."

Alice frowned. The researchers hadn't been sure, but they'd speculated that the virus *might* be able to infect animals and insects...that latter, in particular, providing a dangerous infection vector. It had taken centuries for humans to realise that insects spread disease and even now, with vaccines and nanotechnology, they could still be dangerous outside the civilised world. She dreaded to think what would happen if the virus managed to infect a swarm of mosquitoes. It might infect an entire city before countermeasures could be devised and implemented. And what could they do then?

"I hope the virus did kill the insects," she said, finally. "That would be proof, of sorts, that there are limits to its powers."

She pushed the thought out of her head as the team began to approach cultivated lands. The aliens seemed to live in small towns, if the orbital images were to be believed; each town was surrounded by a handful of fields, growing a variety of crops. The aliens themselves worked the fields with surprising efficiency, for a primitive culture, but never seemed to wander too far from their hometown. Alice wasn't sure if that was proof that the aliens were infected or a sign that they simply hadn't been watching for long enough to draw proper conclusions. Someone who took a snapshot of her life when she was sleeping might conclude that *all* she did was sleep...

"We won't go any closer," Sergeant Radcliffe said, as they took up position in a handful of trees near the town. "We'll watch from here."

No one complained, not even Travers, as they settled into place and watched the aliens go in and out of the village. Alice studied them through her binoculars, feeling a shiver running through her entire body as she realised—deep in her bones—that the native aliens were truly alien. Their upper bodies were humanoid, in a manner of speaking; their lower bodies, where their legs should have been, looked like giant spiders. They moved their legs so rapidly, even when they were at rest, that it took Alice several minutes to realise that they walked on eight legs. It didn't look as if they could climb, she thought, but she suspected they could move at terrifying speed. They looked more the military bomb-disposal robots ago than humans.

"Interesting," Travers mused, quietly. "If there is any sexual dimorphism, I can't see it."

"They might all be males," Alice pointed out. *She* was the only woman in the party—and an alien might not be able to tell the difference between her and the men. God knew male and female Tadpoles looked practically identical. *They* could tell the difference, but a human would need to carry out an autopsy to be sure. "The females could be kept inside the town."

"It's possible," Travers agreed. "But farming societies generally needed to put *everyone* to work. Women were needed to tend the fields too, even if they were often allocated different work or put on reduced duty when they were pregnant. Here…I can't see any difference between the sexes. And that means there's something very different about their society."

"They're aliens," Sergeant Radcliffe said, bluntly. "Are they infected?"

Travers shrugged. "I can't tell," he admitted. "Can you?"

Alice said nothing as the wind shifted, blowing an unpleasant scent towards them. She shuddered, remembering tours of duty in the security zone. She honestly couldn't imagine why anyone would choose to live in squalor—or shit—but the locals had seemed used to it. The smarter ones had even started to convert manure into methane, which they used to generate electric power. The aliens she saw in the distance hadn't even gotten that far.

It isn't as if anyone came down from the stars and told them what to do, she thought, morbidly. *The virus may or may not have infected them, but it certainly wasn't interested in showing them a better way to live.*

Another shiver ran down her spine as she studied the aliens. They didn't seem to show any interest in expansion, even though there was plenty of cultivatable land only a mile or two from their village. They didn't even seem to show any interest in *war*. The more she looked at their village, the more she realised it was completely open to attack. They hadn't even built a stockade to give the town—and their women and children—minimal protection. She cursed under her breath as she realised the truth. The town *was* infected. Whatever the natives had been, once upon a time, they weren't any longer. Her skin crawled. She was looking at an entire population that had been infected by the virus.

"They're infected," she said, quietly. "And we have to be very careful."

Travers glanced at her. "How can you be sure?"

"They're not trying to expand—or do anything, beyond bare survival," Alice said. "And that means they *have* to be infected."

Travers looked doubtful, but Sergeant Radcliffe nodded in agreement. There was no such thing as a *pacifist* race, particularly one that had barely learnt to work iron. Every race humanity had encountered was perfectly capable of fighting, even when it had learnt the benefits of cooperation. A race that was incapable of defending itself—against animals, against its own kind, against hostile aliens—wouldn't last long enough to make an impact on the galaxy. Evolution would ensure that it was replaced by something more capable of looking after itself.

And they don't seem to have any pressure to expand, Alice thought, remembering the history lessons she'd taken in school. Population pressure—and demographics—had provoked plenty of wars throughout human history. *They're not only stable, they're stagnant.*

"So," Travers said. "What do we do now?"

"We establish a camp some distance from the town and keep them under observation, while planning our next move," Sergeant Radcliffe said, firmly. "Unless you have any other ideas..."

Travers looked up at him. "Can we get into the village?"

Alice felt her lips twist into a sardonic smile. "Do you want to get infected?"

She resisted the urge to giggle at his crestfallen expression. Stellar Star had faced an enemy—a horde of cyborgs—that had ignored the humans until they posed a threat. Or, if *Stellar Star XVI* was to believed, when they caught sight of Stellar Star's chest. The virus, she suspected, would definitely notice if a human walked into the village—if nothing else, the intruder wouldn't smell right—and take steps. *Violent* steps. Travers had forgotten where he was, she thought. If the aliens saw him, they'd infect him. And then the virus would know precisely where to find the remaining humans.

"No," Travers said, finally. "But if the virus has them—if they've been effectively reduced to nothing more than bodies for the virus—what we learn from their village might be...ah, it might be their only impact on the universe. We can..."

"We can worry about preserving something of their culture later," Sergeant Radcliffe said, firmly. "Right now, we have other problems."

He detailed two of the marines to keep the village under watch, then led the remainder of the party back into the woods. Alice noted, as they walked under the trees, that something else was missing. She'd hunted for mushrooms as a young girl, under strict orders to make sure her grandparents checked her finds before she tried to cook and eat them, but there were no alien children searching the woods for anything comparable. That was definitely odd, particularly in a low-tech society. A single bad winter could ruin them. They needed to look for every food source they could.

And we know the plants are edible, at least for us, she thought. *Surely, the aliens can eat them too.*

She puzzled over it as they headed further into the forest, finally coming to a halt near a hidden cave. Sergeant Radcliffe checked it out, shining his light into every corner, then decided it would make a suitable hiding place. Alice followed him into the cave, keeping a wary eye out for animal droppings or any other signs that the cave was the lair of something dangerous. The old hands had talked about setting up home in a cave, only to discover—too late—that it was inhabited by a family of bears. Alice wasn't sure she believed the story—careless marine recruits rarely passed basic training, let alone went on active service—but she'd taken the lesson to heart. There were dangers that had nothing to do with the enemy, yet could still get someone killed. It was something to bear in mind.

"We need to take one of the aliens alive," Sergeant Radcliffe said, once they were settled. "And check to see if he is truly infected."

Travers looked stunned. "But they'll notice he's gone, won't they?"

"Perhaps," Alice said. The virus didn't seem to give much of a damn about its hosts. It might notice that an infected body had gone missing or it might not. And if it did notice, it might not care. "There is a certain element of risk."

Corporal Hammersmith smirked. "Now I'm afraid that there's going to have to be a certain amount of...*violence*," he quoted, sweetly. "But at least we know it's all in a good cause, don't we?"

"Remind me to beast whoever introduced you to old comedy classics," Sergeant Radcliffe said. He took his datapad off his belt and sketched out a quick map of the town and surrounding area. "We'll keep an eye on them for the next two days and watch for an opportunity to catch one of them alone. Ideally, we want someone quite some distance from the town itself, but it looks as if that isn't going to happen."

Alice nodded. She hadn't seen an alien go further than a mile from the town, even though some of the primitive villages she'd seen on Earth had been so poorly located that their inhabitants had to walk for miles to collect fresh water. A handful of schemes ran through her head to find a way to force the aliens to change their habits, but none of them seemed particularly workable. The virus might take steps to protect its hosts or it might not. It wouldn't see their loss as anything more than losing a skin cell, perhaps even less. Alice was still surprised it hadn't introduced modern technology. Surely, the viral clusters within the alien hosts would find it more comfortable to live in a technological environment.

If we needed proof the virus has an alien mentality, she thought, *we don't need to look any further.*

"And then we grab the alien and bring him here," Hammersmith said. He rubbed his hands together. "And then you guys"—he looked at Travers—"get to go to work."

"Yeah," Travers said. He didn't sound happy. "We'll be experimenting on a POW."

"The virus isn't likely to care," Alice said, although she understood his concerns. "And we are fairly sure they are infected."

She smiled, as reassuringly as she could. The xenospecialists took more care of their alien prisoners than the military or the police took of *human* prisoners. But then, quite apart from the risk of accidentally killing the prisoner, there was always the political dimension. Humans would not be pleased if they discovered that an alien race had dissected a human prisoner. Why would anyone expect an alien race to be any different?

"But we don't have solid proof," Travers countered. "What if we're wrong?"

Alice felt a hot flash of impatience. If they were wrong…well, the nasty part of her mind pointed out that the natives weren't going to start an interstellar war over the matter. How could they? They had nothing more advanced than iron spears…assuming, of course, they had any weapons at all. She found it hard to believe that they could enter an *alliance* with the virus. But without it, there was no way they could do more than wipe out the landing party. They couldn't take the war into space.

"Then we're wrong," she said. "But all the evidence suggests we're right."

"We'll be keeping an eye on them for a while," Sergeant Radcliffe said. "If we're wrong, we'll find out about it well before we commit ourselves."

"Really?" Travers snorted. "I hope you're right. Really I do."

CHAPTER TWENTY-TWO

"WELL," CORPORAL HAMMERSMITH MUTTERED. "Here they come."

Alice nodded, stiffly. Four days of careful surveillance had revealed that the only time that *any* of the aliens was more than a mile from the town was when they sent out small hunting parties, each one armed with bows, arrows and slingshots. They killed a handful of birds and small woodland animals, then carried them back to the town where—presumably—they were eaten. Alice was surprised they didn't hunt more—in human societies, hunters were often regarded as a cut above farmers—but perhaps the virus simply didn't care. It was, she supposed, another piece of proof that the town was about as real as a Potemkin Village. Its inhabitants merely mimicked life as intelligent beings.

And the virus drifts around them, she thought. The mask felt uncomfortable in the heat, but she knew better than to risk taking it off. Breathing in active viral particles would be fatal. *We have to be very careful.*

She watched the aliens walking closer and braced herself. They hadn't been able to learn *that* much about the alien biology from indirect observation—their society seemed *designed* to frustrate observers—but they *had* learnt that the aliens were strong. Alice wasn't entirely surprised—she knew she was a weakling compared to a Roman legionary—yet it added another complication to the operation. The alien weapons weren't a threat to a marine

211

in full armour—even light body armour would stop an arrow—but grabbing one of the aliens and hauling him home might be difficult. *And* they had to render the other two aliens comatose for a while.

"They're nearly within range," Hammersmith muttered. "Go or no go?"

Alice lifted her stun rifle and took aim. "Mark your man," she muttered back, wondering—not for the first time—if she was about to shoot a male, a female or some weird and wonderful alien gender that had never registered on humanity's radar. "Target by the numbers."

"Aye, Captain," Corporal Clive Tartar said.

At least he still thinks I'm a captain, Alice thought. Technically, she still held the rank; practically, at least until she was cleared to return permanently to active service, she had no legal right to give orders. Sergeant Radcliffe had taken a risk when he'd put her in command of the snatch-grab-and-run party, even though the plan had been her idea. *His head will be on the chopping block right next to mine if we fuck this up.*

She smiled, despite herself, as the aliens came closer. The odds of them surviving long enough to be put in front of a court martial board, if they fucked up, were so low that she suspected that even Hammersmith, a brilliant gambler, would have found them impossible to calculate. They could be killed on the spot, they could be chased back to the shuttle, they could be blown out of the sky as they tried to take off…too much could go badly wrong for her to be sanguine about their chances of success. But they had to know what was happening on Alien-3. She was damned if she was letting this chance pass because she was nervous about making a terrible mistake.

"Fire," she ordered.

The stun gun went *click* in her hands, firing a taser bullet towards its target. Alice saw the alien jerk in surprise—being hit by a taser bullet *hurt*, even though they rarely did real damage—a second before the electric pulse triggered, sending the alien falling to the ground in a twitching heap. Alice winced in sympathy, then ran forward. The taser bullet was designed to render a human immobile, at least until the charge ran out, but they'd had to make some guesses about what would be effective on the aliens. She stopped and peered down at her alien, noting that its legs seemed to be trying to wave in all directions, and then hastily secured the alien with duct tape. Up close, she scented something familiar about the alien, something that nagged at the back of her mind. Some instinct warned her never to touch the alien with her bare hands.

"Mine's dead, I think," Tartar said. He prodded the alien carefully. "I'm not sure why."

"Take mine back to camp," Alice ordered. They hadn't seen any aliens checking up on the hunting party, but that might change when the town realised the hunters hadn't come home by nightfall. "I'll take a look at yours."

She bent over the alien and examined the body quickly. It definitely *looked* dead, although she wasn't entirely sure. The taser bullet had lodged in its neck, suggesting that the shock had done something to the alien's brain. She suspected that they'd need an autopsy to find out and she doubted they had the time. Shaking her head, she picked up the body and carried it into the woods. Depending on what happened, they'd either come back to recover the body or leave it to rot.

"Mine's alive, just stunned," Hammersmith told her. "Do we take him too?"

Alice hesitated, then nodded. If the alien was infected, and she hadn't seen anything to convince her that the alien town *wasn't* infected, killing him would be a mercy. But it would be far too revealing. They'd have to make some hard decisions about what to do with the captives, yet they could wait. The first priority was finding out if they were truly infected.

"Let's move," she said, as Hammersmith lifted the alien bodily and slung him over his shoulders. "It's time to go."

She concealed the dead alien in the trees, then followed Hammersmith and Tartar back to the camp. The first captive woke up halfway to the camp and started to struggle, but the duct tape resisted all attempts to remove it. Alice allowed herself a moment of relief. They had stronger restraints, but they were designed for humans. She had no idea if they could be modified to hold an alien without causing serious harm.

They have eight legs, she reminded herself, as they stumbled into the camp. *We'd have to modify the shackles just to hold them properly.*

"Success," she said. "We caught two of the bastards."

Travers shot her a sharp look, then bent down to examine the first alien. "Infected," he said, after he pressed a medical reader into the alien's mouth. "There's enough viral DNA in the mouth alone to guarantee infection with a kiss."

"And to think all *I* ever worried about was cold sores," Hammersmith muttered. "Are these creatures vampires as well?"

"It looks that way," Sergeant Radcliffe said. "But would you really *want* to kiss an alien?"

Travers managed to look both intent on his work and incredibly disapproving. Alice hid her amusement behind her hand. There were no laws against human-alien sexual relationships, even in the most restrictive countries, but she found it hard to believe that anyone would want to try. And even if someone *was* perverse enough to want to try, there was the question of compatibility. The Tadpoles didn't have sex, the Foxes were hermaphrodites...the Cows and Vesy were more like humans, as far as sex was concerned, but Alice found it hard to imagine how a human could have sex with either of them. It would quite likely prove painful to all concerned.

"The blood is also crammed with viral matter," Travers said, after a moment. He didn't look up from his work. "I think we have to assume that everyone in the town has been infected."

"It would seem that way," Alice said, deciding not to point out that the marines had assumed that the town had been infected right from the start. The virus would have spread even if there hadn't been any *deliberate* attempts to infect the entire population. "What else can you tell me about these guys?"

Travers sighed. "Nothing of any real use. I've taken skin scrapings, blood samples and I've got the portable reader trying to break down the DNA, but it will be a good while before we learn anything useful from it. The virus seems to have seeped into just about everything, even the alien's sweat.

There's a small cloud of viral matter surrounding the alien, if my sensors are to be believed. Not enough to infect, I think, but enough to be noticeable."

"How useful," Tartar commented.

"As you were," Sergeant Radcliffe said, sharply.

Travers, lost in his element, didn't notice the exchange. "Internally... well, we won't know anything for sure until we dissect one of them, but my readers suggest they have two hearts and something I think is a combination of lung and stomach. There's also an object in the lower body that I think is an egg—either that or the alien is heavily constipated—yet he doesn't seem to have anything akin to a penis or a vagina. My best guess is that they're either hermaphrodites or one gender lays the eggs and the other fertilises them."

"Or there are three sexes and *this* one is charged with brooding the eggs after they're fertilised and laid," Hammersmith said. "I recall a story with a three-gendered race..."

"It's possible," Travers said, absently. "But I can't see how the egg was inserted into the body. I..."

Alice tensed as an alarm sounded. "That's the sensors we left to watch the town!"

She cursed under her breath. The sensors had been concealed within the woods. They wouldn't have gone active unless they picked up alien activity, let alone risked a transmission that might be detected by orbiting sensors. She activated her helmet, downloading the burst transmission...and swore. Hundreds of aliens—almost the entire population of the town—were coming their way, flowing through the woods as if they were made of water. They were running quickly enough to overrun the campsite within minutes.

"Shit," Sergeant Radcliffe said. "Travers, grab your shit. Tartar, you and your squad get him and his samples back to the shuttle. Go as fast as you can—don't stop for anything. Send an alert signal via laser to the ship as soon as you're clear. Alice, Glen, you're with me."

And we have to slow the bastards down, Alice thought, as Tartar grabbed the readers and hurried Travers out of the cave. *We need to give the others time to break contact.*

215

She scooped up her rifle, silently glad they'd spent so long scoping out the area around the cave. The aliens would *have* to come at them from the front, unless the marines had completely misread their ability to clamber up rocks and trees. It wasn't an ideal situation, but it would have to do. And yet...the hell of it was that the infected aliens might start screaming for help from orbit. A single KEW would be enough to finish off the landing party before they could get out of the blast zone.

So we keep listening for transmissions, she thought. The virus *might* be able to turn itself into a communications and computer system, but she doubted there was enough viral matter in the air to let it send messages to the western installation. Any signal would have to be carried by radio—or hand. *And we take cover if anyone starts sending a signal that looks like targeting instructions.*

She followed Sergeant Radcliffe out of the cave, hastily checking her rifle and ammunition pouches. She had no doubt the three of them could slow the aliens down, at least long enough to let the others escape...as long as their ammunition held out. It wasn't as if they could resupply in a hurry. The machine shops that churned out new bullets were on *Invincible*, lurking somewhere in the icy depths of space. They might as well be a thousand light-years away. She gritted her teeth, recalling stories of desperate last stands during the Age of Unrest. Western troops had always had better weapons and equipment, from pinpoint laser strikes to orbiting weapons platforms, but they'd never had numbers. A unit that ran out of ammunition might well be overrun and put to death.

And while the terrorists might subject me to a fate worse than death, she thought as she tested the suicide device, *the infected aliens will subject me to a fate worse than a fate worse than death.*

The thought made her smile as she took up her pre-planned position, peering down the valley towards the alien town. She could smell the aliens now, she could hear their passage...but she couldn't hear the aliens themselves. She'd expected a howling mob, screaming their outrage at the intrusion and calling on their god to help them as they charged the human position, but—instead—the aliens moved in eerie silence. She leaned forward as they came into view, scrambling up the rocky valley like angry spiders. It was impossible to read any expression on their faces. The virus had even robbed them of their anger.

Sergeant Radcliffe glanced at her. "How did they find us?"

Alice hesitated. "I don't know," she admitted. She didn't blame the sergeant for wanting to know. Sergeant Radcliffe knew better than to place blame in the middle of a firefight. And yet...the marines had been careful, when they'd hurried back to the cave, but it was clear they'd missed *something*. "We didn't see any way they could call for help."

Her mind raced, considering the possibilities. The aliens might have excreted *some* viral matter when they were stunned, warning the other infected that there were enemies in the vicinity. Or they might have sounded the alert at a frequency humans couldn't hear. Or they might have implanted transponders, even though they seemed to exist at a very basic technological level. Or...some form of ESP? It didn't seem likely—every experiment with ESP under controlled conditions had failed or produced results that couldn't be duplicated—but she knew better than to rule out any possibility. They'd done everything right. And yet, they'd clearly failed to keep the aliens from tracking them down.

Maybe they can track their scent, she thought. *They might have better noses than a dog.*

"Get ready," Sergeant Radcliffe ordered. "I'll detonate the mines in ten seconds. Fire on my command."

Alice nodded, switching her rifle to rapid fire. Normally, they would at least have *tried* to communicate with the aliens, to convince them that the human intruders weren't a threat...although she rather suspected that *humans* wouldn't have bought that argument after two aliens were kidnapped and a third killed. Now, it was pointless. The virus couldn't be reasoned with, nor could it be intimidated into surrender. It wasn't even clear that *humans* could surrender. The virus would simply infect anyone stupid enough to give it the chance,.

"Mines detonating...now," Sergeant Radcliffe said.

The ground heaved as the mines exploded, showering the aliens with shrapnel. Alice winced as dozens of aliens were caught in the blast and ripped apart, their bodies disintegrating before they hit the ground. Land mines had been regarded as inhumane weapons for the last three centuries, although the treaties banning their use had been amended, and then discarded completely, as civilisation fought for its survival against enemies who had no qualms about using every weapon in their arsenal to kill as many civilians as possible. The aliens, with no experience of mines, should have hesitated just long enough for the marines to break contact and slip into the forest. A human force, no matter how fanatical, would have stopped in horror at the carnage. But the infected aliens just kept coming.

Alice shuddered as the full implications struck her. *We're going to have to kill them all just to break contact.*

"Fire," Sergeant Radcliffe ordered.

She pulled the trigger, trying not to think about what would happen when the magnetically-propelled bullet hit its target. The alien skull wouldn't offer any resistance at all. The bullet would go through one alien and probably hit several more before it finally ran out of velocity and fell to the ground. She moved from target to target, firing at a rate she hadn't used since basic training. Marines were generally discouraged from using 'spray and pray' tactics, particularly when their logistics chain was weak or non-existent. Now...she saw the aliens take the bullets, lose *more* of their people...and just keep coming anyway. How many aliens had *been* in that town? Their best estimates had suggested the surrounding fields could support five hundred at most. She was starting to suspect that they'd been very wrong.

Unless more aliens are coming from the other villages, she thought. Her rifle bleeped an alert. She was running out of ammunition. *They might have alerted the entire region.*

"We need to pull out," Sergeant Radcliffe said. The valley was bathed in eerie blue blood, but the aliens were still coming. They were trampling over their own bodies in a desperate bid to get to the intruders. "Now, I think."

"I'll cover you," Alice said. She unhooked the grenades from her belt. "Go."

Sergeant Radcliffe hesitated, just for a second. Alice knew what he was thinking. On one hand, he was leaving her in terrible danger; on the other, he *was* the landing party's commander. A dispute over whoever was in charge, if he was killed or captured, would come at the worst possible time. Alice couldn't assume command, technically...

"Hurry," he ordered. "Glen. Come with me."

Hammersmith looked reluctant, but did as he was told. Alice wondered, as she threw the first grenade into the alien mass, just why he didn't want to leave her behind. Maybe she'd made a better impression than she'd thought. Or maybe he just didn't want to leave a woman behind. Alice knew, all too well, that her odds of survival were not good. She threw the second grenade, then aimed the third at the rocks. Hopefully, she could delay the aliens long enough to break contact herself. Getting back to the shuttle would be tricky, but she was sure she could make it.

She sensed something move behind her, a second too late. Something slammed into her back with terrifying force, sending her crashing to the ground. She rolled over, one hand scrabbling for her combat knife...

...And saw an alien looming over her, ready to strike.

CHAPTER TWENTY-THREE

THE SOUND OF THE ALARM BROUGHT STEPHEN out of an uncomfortable sleep. He sat upright, one hand automatically reaching for his jacket even as the second hand reached for the terminal beside his sofa. His Ready Room was nowhere near as comfortable as his cabin, but he'd grown used to sleeping there. It was a few steps closer to the bridge.

"Report," he snapped, as he swung his legs over the side and stood. "What's happening?"

"We just picked up a flash-transmission from the recon team," Commander Newcomb said, calmly. "They successfully captured a pair of aliens—both infected—but they were rumbled shortly afterwards. We must assume that it is only a matter of time until the orbital installations and starships get involved."

Stephen gritted his teeth. They'd run a dozen simulations, looking for ways to punch their way into the low orbitals, but all the simulations agreed that it would be a very close-run thing indeed. *Invincible* and her flotilla *might* be able to take the five cruisers, particularly if they managed to mount a starfighter strike before the cruisers realised they were under attack, yet they had no way to know just how many weapons the virus had crammed into the orbiting stations. They might be completely defenceless. Or, more likely, they were packing enough firepower to give the assault carrier a very hard time.

And they'll notice an incoming mass driver strike, he thought, as he pulled on his jacket and shoes. *There's no guarantee of scoring a hit even if we didn't have to worry about accidentally hitting the planet.*

"Bring the flotilla to battlestations," he ordered, as he hurried for the hatch. "And inform the crews that we will shortly engage the enemy."

"Aye, Captain."

Stephen kept his face impassive as he stepped onto the bridge. The recon team was expendable, technically, but he was damned if he was abandoning them. Someone back home would point out that even *trying* to save them would reveal *Invincible's* presence, yet...Stephen snorted at the absurdity. A REMF might not see it, but anyone with the slightest hint of common sense would ask where the recon team had come from in the first place. It wasn't as if they could transit the tramlines in environmental suits. No, the virus would know that a starship had brought the humans from Falkirk to Alien-3. It would start hunting for the intruder immediately.

He took the command chair and examined the display. The alien starships hadn't brought up their drives—yet—but that didn't make them any less dangerous. They clearly had their weapons and sensors on standby, ready to power up at a moment's notice. It was only a matter of time until they went to full alert. They'd have been told about the recon team's presence *before* Stephen had been warned that the infected natives had engaged the human intruders. The only *good* news, as far as Stephen could tell, was that the aliens didn't have any idea where *Invincible* was lurking. They'd find it impossible to track down the carrier until she entered sensor range.

"Prepare our starfighters for a long-range strike," he ordered, curtly. Ideally, he'd prefer to engage the enemy starships and orbiting stations separately. There was nothing to be gained by allowing the enemy to fall back on their own defences. "And order the mass drivers to stand ready."

He sucked in his breath. Mass drivers had been a terrible shock to the Tadpoles, when they'd encountered *Ark Royal* for the first time. They'd simply never come up with the concept of mass drivers for themselves, while humanity had effectively banned them until the dictates of survival had forced all such constraints to be abandoned. It hadn't taken long for the Tadpoles to devise countermeasures—mass driver projectiles could be taken out by railguns, if they were spotted in time—and Stephen was grimly certain that the virus had countermeasures of its own. But a handful of projectiles would give the virus something else to think about while Stephen was engaging its cruisers. Who knew? Perhaps he'd present the virus with so many problems that it couldn't handle them all.

Don't count on it, he warned himself dryly. *The different clusters of viral matter may as well be individuals, as far as we are concerned.*

"All departments are standing by," Commander Newcomb said. "Squadrons One to Five are ready to launch; Squadron Six is standing by, ready to form CSP as soon as the remaining squadrons have launched."

Stephen nodded. It was unlikely the enemy cruisers carried starfighters of their own, but there was no way to know what the virus might have crammed into the massive orbiting fortresses. The halo of fortresses surrounding Earth, protecting humanity's homeworld, carried ten squadrons of starfighters each, enough mobile firepower to give any intruder a very hard time even without the various national fleets. But they were also fixed in place, defending a single target...Stephen shook his head. They weren't about to challenge Earth's defences. All they *really* had to do was keep the defenders busy until the recon team could make its escape.

"We'll go with Beta-Three," he said, after a moment. "Prepare to drop the cloak."

"Aye, Captain," Lieutenant-Commander David Arthur said.

Stephen felt the tension in the compartment begin to rise. Beta-Three wasn't the most...*adventurous* of their contingency plans, but it still carried the risk of the flotilla being overhauled and destroyed by the enemy cruisers if they made a mistake. Stephen had considered some of the safer options, all too aware that the enemy could respond with extreme force, yet none of them *forced* the enemy to respond. There was so little in Alien-3 that it was easy to imagine the orbiting starships simply ignoring *Invincible* if she stayed well out of range. Or sending one of their ships to Alien-1 to request help. The last thing Stephen wanted was to blunder into a trap and have his ship unceremoniously destroyed.

"Drop the cloak," he ordered. "And bring up full active sensors."

The display brightened as a rapidly-expanding sphere surrounded the central icon. Stephen felt his heart begin to race, even though he'd known it was coming. Any enemy ships or stealthed platforms within that sphere would know that *Invincible* was there, now; they'd know her exact location, her exact course and speed. No platforms appeared on the display, but that proved nothing. The virus, lacking the budgetary restraints that plagued humanity's navies, might have scattered scansats all over the system. Cold logic suggested that the virus wouldn't have bothered, but there was no way to be sure.

They'll know we're here, he thought, as the sphere washed over the planet. It would take long seconds—too long—for him to know if the cruisers had taken the bait. *What will they do?*

He cursed under his breath as the seconds ticked by. A human CO would hesitate before deciding what to do. On one hand, leaving an assault carrier skulking around the system would give the enemy ship plenty of opportunity to smash the system's industry, as little as it was; on the other, sending his cruisers away from the planet would leave the surface open to attack. The virus *had* to be aware of its limitations. Those battlestations couldn't cover the entire planet and the virus *had* to know it. And yet, would it care? The virus might consider the entire planet expendable.

It's a nightmare, he told himself. *How are we supposed to guess what an utterly alien entity will do?*

The sensor display updated. "Captain," Lieutenant Alison Adams said. "The enemy ships are moving out of orbit. They're falling into attack vector."

A least-time course to our current position, Stephen thought. *Invincible* was heading straight for Alien-3, challenging the virus's starships to intercept her before she reached the high orbitals. It was curious, in some ways; he wondered, vaguely, if it was a sign that the orbiting fortresses weren't as heavily armed as he'd supposed. *Or maybe they just want to keep us from getting into bombardment range.*

"Order the mass drivers to commence firing," he said, coolly. "And launch starfighters on my mark."

He studied the display, silently calculating the vectors in his head. The enemy cruisers were already within starfighter range, although Stephen intended to wait for them to converge on their target a little more before he threw his pilots into battle. The enemy ships, perversely, were both too close and too far for his peace of mind, a problem made worse by *Invincible's* headlong charge towards the planet. Stephen's starfighters might not have time to rearm before the enemy ships entered weapons range. *Invincible* was armed to the teeth, but she was no battleship. Stephen didn't want to risk a close-range encounter with an enemy formation that might simply decide to ram his ship.

Not that we have much choice, he thought, as the mass drivers opened fire. Two of the three enemy stations were within range. The third, on the far side of the planet, was effectively out of the engagement for the moment. *We have to keep them busy.*

"Launch starfighters," he ordered. "I say again, launch starfighters."

"Aye, Captain."

• • •

Wing Commander Richard Redbird braced himself as his starfighter rocketed down the launch tube and burst into open space. His display shifted rapidly as the craft's sensors came online, showing the enemy ships and—behind them—the blue-green world that the virus had long since taken for its own. Richard shivered at the thought of landing there, although—he admitted privately—it was unlikely he'd ever be allowed to go down to the surface. The virus might be drifting in the air or lurking within the shadows, just waiting for its visitors to make a mistake. He couldn't help wondering if the recon team would ever be allowed to return to their mothership—or, if they did, if they'd ever be let out of quarantine.

He dismissed the thought as the starfighters formed up around him. Squadron One was at full strength, again, but it had come at a cost. He was all too aware that Squadrons Four and Five were understrength; indeed, he'd seriously considered combining them into a single oversized squadron and to hell with tradition. Only the strong arguments from the squadron commanders, with many appeals to traditions that dated all the way back to the long-gone Fleet Air Arm, had stayed his hand. He still wasn't sure he'd done the right thing. A squadron was supposed to have a life, irrespective of the individual pilots as they came and went, but an understrength squadron was dangerously weak. Losing even a couple of pilots would be disastrous.

And if we were back home, we'd have no trouble requisitioning extra pilots and starfighters, he thought, morbidly. The Royal Navy had been caught short of pilots during the First Interstellar War, but—since then—the navy had always trained more pilots than it needed during peacetime. A reservist could claim a bonus just for keeping his skills sharp. *Out here, we have more starfighters than we have pilots.*

"Prepare to engage," he said, studying the enemy ships on the display. The stealthed probes had told him things he didn't want to know about their size and power curves, but nothing about what sort of weapons might be crammed into their hulls. He had guesses—he would have been astonished if the enemy hulls weren't studded with plasma cannons—yet they wouldn't know for certain until the enemy started firing. "Remember, we're here to kill the bastards!"

"What a relief," Monica said, dryly. "And here I was thinking we were here to ask them for dinner."

Richard had to smile. "On my command, engage with torpedoes," he said, firmly. "I say again; on my command, engage with torpedoes."

He waited for the range to close, grimacing as the enemy ships opened fire. The odds of them actually *hitting* anything at this range were low, but they might get lucky. Besides, they'd *definitely* unnerve his pilots. He didn't need an analyst who was safely out of the firing line to tell him that the enemy ships had a working datanet. The five ships were coordinating their fire in a manner that proved it beyond all doubt.

And that means that launching torpedoes might be a waste of time, he thought. *But we have to* know *before we face a real fleet.*

"Fire," he ordered.

The starfighter jerked as it launched two torpedoes towards its target. Richard yanked his craft to one side a second later, cursing under his breath as a hail of plasma fire shot through his former location with terrifying speed. Another pilot wasn't so lucky, her craft spinning out of control as a plasma bolt scored a direct hit on her fuselage. Richard opened his mouth to scream at her to eject, but it was already too late. The starfighter vanished in a brief, twinkling flash of light. Richard clamped down hard on the stab of grief and guilt that ran through him. There would be time to mourn later. He had work to do.

He watched, grimly, as the torpedoes raced towards their targets. They'd once been the most terrifying weapons in the Royal Navy's arsenal, but ever since plasma weapons had entered widespread use their value had declined. The torpedoes were designed to be hard to hit—their drives were configured to make it difficult to pin down their exact location, as there was no way they could be stealthed or cloaked—but the enemy could simply blanket their rough location with plasma fire until the drive signature vanished. Richard had hoped that one or two torpedoes would make it through the enemy point defence and strike home, yet it looked as if the virus had picked them all off before it was too late. They hadn't even managed to get into bomb-pumped laser range.

"Direct hit," Flight Lieutenant Gabby Rancher gloated. "Scratch one cruiser!"

Richard had to smile, although he knew the engagement was far from over. The enemy cruiser didn't have the layers of ablative armour that protected carriers or battleships, let alone an internal layout designed to minimise the results of a direct hit. The nuclear-tipped torpedo had punched through the hull and detonated inside the ship, blowing it into a cloud of expanding plasma. He felt his smile grow wider, even though he knew they'd have to take the starfighters into knife-range to take out the remaining cruisers. They'd scored one hit without going too close to their targets.

Although we fired twenty-four torpedoes at each cruiser and only scored a single hit, he reminded himself. The boffins had promised that the new penetrator warheads would slip through the enemy defences, but it looked as though they were wrong—again. Something that had performed brilliantly under controlled conditions simply hadn't worked so well on the battlefield. *The day of the torpedoes is over.*

"Close to gunnery range," he ordered, stiffly. "Squadron Four, stand in reserve."

He weaved backwards and forwards as the range closed at terrifying speed, doing his level best to keep his flight path as random as possible. The enemy kept firing, thousands upon thousands of plasma bolts flashing through space and vanishing into the darkness. Richard had to fight down the urge to turn and run as the range closed, jamming his finger down on the trigger as soon as he entered effective range. The plasma pulses tore into the enemy ship, punching through thin layers of armour and wreaking havoc inside the hull. Richard smiled, grimly, as the remainder of the squadron followed him, their guns strafing the giant enemy ship. The cruiser was *definitely* no battleship. It simply couldn't take such a battering and live.

"She's going to blow," Richard said, as he saw the enemy drive compartment start to explode. The hull ruptured a second later, the entire ship shattering into a wave of debris and superheated plasma. "Scatter—*now!*"

He yanked his craft away, for once flying in a straight line as he tried to escape the explosion before it was too late. The risk was small, but it would be embarrassing to be killed by his target's death throes. He wondered, absently, if they'd ever be able to tell who'd struck the fatal blow. They'd all be able to paint a cruiser on their starfighters, but the *true* killer would be in line for a proper reward...he shook his head as they hurried away from the debris cloud, reforming a safe distance from the alien ships. It was unlikely anyone would ever be able to tell who'd killed the enemy ship.

We can all claim a piece of her hull, he thought, although it would bring them nothing beyond bragging rights. The Admiralty wouldn't pay prize money for a cloud of expanding debris, none of which would tell them anything new. *And we can tell lies about how we killed her next time we're in a bar.*

He checked the overall situation, then smiled. Three of the four enemy cruisers had been destroyed, taking three starfighters with them; the fifth was nothing more than a drifting powerless hulk. By any standard, it was a more than satisfactory exchange rate, although—as no one knew how many starships the virus had—it was hard to know *just* how badly they'd hurt the enemy. They might have inflicted a serious blow, limiting the virus's ability to make war, or they might have done nothing more than irritate it.

Hell, he thought. *The virus might not even notice.*

"Return to the barn," he ordered. "We have to rearm and take those stations."

And hope to hell they're not crammed with weapons, he added silently. *Because if they've devoted all that mass to defences, with their entire hull covered in plasma cannons, we're not going to get close enough to land the killing blow.*

CHAPTER TWENTY-FOUR

ALICE WAS CERTAIN, JUST FOR A MOMENT, that she was dead.

The alien reared up, its hands—suddenly looking like claws—ready to plunge down and slice into her body. She was wearing light armour, but she had no illusions about how well it would stand up to a powerful blow. Even if the armour held, even if the alien didn't strike an unprotected part of her body, the impact would weaken her. And she dreaded to think what would happen if the alien tried to infect her instead. The virus would turn her into a mindless slave, again. No, not a slave. A slave could hope to escape. *She* would be nothing more than an automaton.

Her tongue pressed against the suicide device, even as her sweaty hand gripped the knife. It had been a present from a US Marine she'd known, back during a joint exercise that had taken her and her comrades all over the United States; the KA-BAR, he'd sworn, was the best tactical knife in the world. Alice had carried it with her ever since, taking advantage of the policy that allowed Royal Marines to select their own personal weapons. She was sure it would gut the alien, but the creature might kill or infect her even as it died. Alice braced herself, ready to trigger the device. She *had* to blow her brains to bits before the virus had a chance to get into her grey matter.

The alien loomed over her for a long moment, its bulbous eyes peering down at her. Alice stared back at it, feeling uneasy at how the spider-like legs twitched and moved in a manner that bothered her on a very primal level. She was no racist—she'd been tested, carefully, for adverse fear reactions when she came face-to-face with creatures that hadn't been born on Earth—but the alien made her skin crawl. Perhaps it was the presence of the virus, a cloud of viral matter surrounding the alien...she hoped her mask was intact, although she suspected it hardly mattered. Removing a filter mask was hardly rocket science. All the virus would have to do, if it wanted to infect her, was take off the mask. She was morbidly certain that the viral particles would last long enough, even in the open sunlight, to slip into her body and turn her into an...

The alien turned and walked away.

Alice stared, half-convinced she was hallucinating. The alien had had her at its mercy. It could have done *anything* to her. And yet, it had just turned and *left*? She forced herself to sit up, holding the knife firmly in one hand. The remaining aliens were milling around slowly, not paying any attention to her. It looked as if they were probing the area, picking out clues that would lead them back to the shuttle. Alice stood, gingerly, and picked up her rifle. She wanted to point it at the aliens, but a quick check revealed she had only a handful of bullets left. Besides, her instincts warned her that even *pointing* the gun at the aliens might provoke a sharp response. They'd seen enough to *know* that guns were dangerous.

And the virus would know that guns were dangerous too, she thought. The alien charge, right into the teeth of human guns, had shown her just how little the virus cared about its hosts, but still...even from a purely pragmatic point of view, it had been wasteful. The most cold-blooded human in history would hesitate to throw his soldiers into the fire in such a manner, particularly when there were other options. *It might...*

She swallowed, hard, as the answer dawned on her. It wasn't something she wanted to think about, but the conclusion was inescapable. The alien had scented the virus on her. It had *known* she was infected. And it had just walked off and left her to her fate. Alice felt her legs threaten to buckle as fear ran through her. What if...what if she'd been infected—again? There was enough inert viral matter in her body to speed up the process of infection if some *active* matter entered her bloodstream? Her fingers shook as she reached for the medical reader on her belt and pressed it against her fingertip, wincing at the stab of pain as the clipper collected a sample of her blood. She almost collapsed again, this time in relief, when the reader assured her that her blood hadn't changed. But that meant nothing. She really had too much viral matter in her body for anyone's peace of mind.

They said my scent changed, she thought, as she carefully inched back towards the treeline. The aliens didn't seem to be paying any attention to her, but that might change if she did something that was clearly against the virus's interests. *If that means they think I'm one of them, what can we do with it?*

She kept a wary eye on the aliens, ready to draw her gun and start shooting if they turned against her, but they did nothing as she reached the treeline. They didn't seem to be doing anything, save waiting...as if they were robots who lacked a direct datalink to their commander. They weren't even collecting the bodies for a proper burial. Alice took one last look, then turned and ran into the forest as far as she could. The aliens didn't seem inclined to give chase.

They found us somehow, she reminded herself, as she ran. *They had to have some way of tracking us.*

Her mind worked away at the problem, trying to think of a solution. Orbital observation was one possibility, even though they'd been careful to carry out the kidnapping when the orbiting stations and starships weren't in a good position to watch the town. There might be a stealthed recon platform high overhead, although Alice couldn't imagine why the virus would bother. Alien-3 was not an occupied world in any conventional sense. The virus had made resistance not only futile, but impossible. There were no natives to liberate, not now. She tried to imagine the scale of the crime the virus had committed, but she couldn't wrap her head around it. Even the kidnapping program carried out by Nazi Germany, in which children they'd considered to be racially superior had been taken to Germany and raised as Germans—with every last trace of their past lives erased—didn't come close. The virus might not be evil, in any human sense, but it had done something so monstrous that the worst villains of human history were just...*mundane.*

She scowled, forcing her mind to consider something practical. How had they been tracked? Scent? Had one of the aliens released something—a spoor, perhaps—that had allowed their fellows to realise that something had gone wrong? Or maybe the virus had done it. The sensors insisted that there were no free-floating viral particles in the air, but it was possible the sensors were wrong. The particles could have been released while the kidnapped aliens were being taken back to the cave. Or...some form of ESP? She hated to consider the possibility, but it had to be borne in mind. The virus might have more surprises up its sleeves.

And if it could read minds, it would know we're intelligent beings, she thought, although she was fairly sure the virus already knew. It just didn't care. *There's no point in being too paranoid.*

She slowed long enough to listen for pursuit, then checked her blood again. The reader—once again—insisted that nothing had changed. Alice hesitated, wondering if she dared take it for granted. Clearly, there *had* been a massive failure *somewhere.* She would sooner believe that she'd screwed up, even if it cost her whatever was left of her career, than believe the virus had more surprises in store for them. If she *had* been infected—again—did she dare go back to the shuttle? Should she kill herself, now, just to make sure she couldn't betray her comrades? Or...she turned the problem over and over, trying to think of a solution. She thought she was free of infection, but what if she was wrong? Who'd *want* to believe that they were infected?

I have to report back, she told herself, firmly. *If nothing else, they need to hear what I have to say.*

Gritting her teeth, she took her compass from her belt and checked her position. The military was fond of making jokes about officers who tried to navigate—the most dangerous person on the battlefield was a green lieutenant with a map—but she'd grown up hiking in the countryside. Her grandfather had taught her to use a map or navigate by the stars before she'd had her tenth birthday. It wouldn't be hard to find her way back to the stealth shuttle, assuming it hadn't taken off. Sergeant Radcliffe might well assume that Alice was dead. Even if he *didn't*, he'd still have the remainder of the team—and the civvies—to consider. It would be dangerously unwise to hang around for very long.

Alice sighed, then started to walk. The sun seemed to grow hotter as she marched onwards, glancing from side to side to make sure she wasn't being followed. There was no way to be sure, nor was there any way to know what the aliens had learnt from whatever they'd recovered from the cave. She'd been on exercises where they'd camped in the open, without any fear of attack, only to be told—afterwards—just how much their half-cleared campsite had told the enemy about them. A couple of recruits had wondered if it had been a trick of some kind—it wasn't as if the exercise coordinators didn't *know* there were fifteen recruits within the training area—but Alice had believed the officers. There was nothing to gain by cheating. Besides, they'd gone through the campsite in cynical detail. The recruit who'd tossed away the packet of Benson and Hedges had been told, rather sarcastically, that he'd just informed the enemy that they were facing *British* troops. A packet of smokes wouldn't mean anything to the virus, but who knew what *else* might have been recovered?

Let's hope they didn't forget a datapad or a computer in their haste, Alice thought, sweat trickling down her back. The marines had been trained to grab or destroy anything important if they had to break and run, but the civvies hadn't had that sort of training. *If the virus captured a computer intact, who knows what it might find?*

She gritted her teeth in frustration. They would probably never know. Military databases, particularly ones that might fall into enemy hands, were carefully sanitised, but civilian databases were rarely given the same degree of attention. Anything from a starchart to a dictionary file might give the virus an insight into humanity, particularly if it had been one of the programs designed for first contact. Alice hoped—prayed—that the cave had been *completely* stripped, but she had no way to be sure. They'd have to check what had been yanked out of the cave before they took off.

The sun was starting to set by the time she reached the outer line of perimeter sensors. She paused long enough to catch her breath—she hadn't done a forced march since she'd been assigned to *Invincible*, even before she'd been infected—and then pressed her fingers against the scanner. It would give the crew a nasty fright, but she knew better than to walk up to the shuttle without alerting the defenders to her presence. They had to be jumpy. They'd probably shoot her on sight.

It felt like hours before she sensed, more than saw, two men in the treeline. "Keep your hands where we can see them," a voice barked. "And *don't* make any sudden moves."

Alice smiled wryly as Corporal Roger Tindal stepped into view. The marine looked professional, but Alice could tell he was nervous. He was careful not to step into the watching sniper's line of fire. Alice had every faith in the team sniper's ability to shoot a cigar out of her mouth without harming her in the slightest, but she understood Tindal's concern. If she'd been infected, if she was nothing more than a Trojan Horse, Tindal was unlikely to survive the next few minutes. She'd have a clear shot at him before the sniper could put her down.

Particularly if he has to do more than just put a bullet through my brain, she thought, holding herself as still as she could. Some of the boffins had speculated that the virus would be able to keep a body moving, even if the brain was destroyed. Alice suspected that *someone* had watched too many zombie movies for their own good, but she appreciated the warning. It was better to prepare for the worst and hope for the best than allow themselves to believe that the worst wouldn't happen. *The sniper will have orders to make sure this body can never move again.*

"Hold out your bare hand," Tindal said, pulling a reader from his belt. "Now, please."

Alice did as she was told, hoping the sniper wouldn't see it as the start of something violent. It wouldn't be the first time someone had been shot by accident…she kept her face impassive as her blood was sampled again, cursing herself a second later for not realising that showing pain might actually have worked in her favour for once. The virus didn't seem to notice, let alone care, if its host body was hurting. Tindal relaxed, visibly, as the results came back. Alice was relieved too. She hadn't had time to sample her blood for hours.

"Clear," Tindal said. "Welcome back, ah…"

"Thanks," Alice said, dryly. No one seemed to know *quite* how to address her. "Did the rest of the team make it back?"

"Everyone is back—and clear," Tindal assured her. He signalled the sniper, then led her up the rocky path to the shuttle. "We've been preparing defences here."

Alice nodded. She didn't have to be an experienced officer to spot the trenches—or the half-concealed landmines and weapons positions. Sergeant Radcliffe was clearly expecting trouble, lots of it. A couple of civvies— she spotted Travers amongst them—were helping to dig another trench, although Alice wasn't sure they were *really* helping. There was more to preparing a trench—or even a foxhole—than simply digging holes in the ground. But then, the only alternative was leaving them in the shuttle to brood. Better to have them doing something that *might* be useful, she sup-posed. It would keep them from driving themselves insane with worry.

Travers waved to her, cheerfully. "You made it!"

"Barely," Alice said. She decided not to point out that Travers, for all his efforts, had barely managed to dig a hole. It needed to be deeper if it turned out the enemy had modern weapons after all. A single mortar shell would collapse it, along with anyone unfortunate enough to be using it as a hiding place. "Where's the sergeant?"

"Here," Sergeant Radcliffe said, emerging from the shuttle. "What happened?"

"They ignored me," Alice said. It crossed her mind that the aliens might have *deliberately* let her go, in the hopes she would lead them back to the shuttle, but it didn't seem likely. They could simply have followed the remainder of the team. "They just let me go."

Sergeant Radcliffe's eyes narrowed. No one, absolutely no one, would consider a Royal Marine sergeant *stupid*. Alice rather suspected that Sergeant Radcliffe had orders to keep a sharp eye on her, as well as his other duties. If the aliens had let her go, they'd let her go for a reason. She nodded towards the open hatch, signalling that she needed to talk to him in private. He eyed her for a long moment, then nodded curtly. If she'd been infected, if she'd been influenced somehow, he might be putting himself in terrible danger. But he didn't lack courage as well as brains.

Although Jeanette would disagree, Alice thought, remembering all the horrible things her sister had said when Alice had announced her intention of joining the Royal Marines. She'd been worried—Alice had known that, intellectually—but it hadn't been easy to believe when her sister had been openly urging her to join a branch of the military that wasn't so hostile to women. *She thought that anyone who volunteered to go down to a Third World shithole and get shot at was intellectually challenged.*

"So," Sergeant Radcliffe said, once they were alone. He kept his distance from her, one hand ready to drop to his holster. "What happened? Really?"

"I think they smelled me," Alice said. Neither she nor any other human had been able to smell the infection on her, but someone who had been infected by the virus might have a more sensitive sense of smell. The virus needed a way of identifying its own kind in alien bodies. "And then they thought I was infected and just let me go."

"Interesting," Sergeant Radcliffe mused. "Are you sure?"

"No," Alice said, honestly. There was no point in trying to bullshit the sergeant. "I don't know."

"No," Sergeant Radcliffe said. "Go get some rest. The ship's hitting the orbitals, but I don't know when we'll be able to take off. Right now, we're in eyeshot."

"And if we try to take off, we'll be a sitting duck," Alice said. One of the orbiting stations was too close for comfort. It would be hours before they were free to risk heading back to orbit. "Shit."

"Yeah," Sergeant Radcliffe said. "And if they followed us back here, we'll be in even deeper shit."

CHAPTER TWENTY-FIVE

"THIS COULD BE OUR LAST NIGHT," Travers muttered.

Alice fought down the urge to either laugh or tell him to shut the fuck up. If it was a come-on, it was a bloody stupid one. Did he think they'd make love in the cabin, where everyone else could see and hear them, or did he think they'd slip into the undergrowth and probably get attacked and killed by the infected aliens? And if it wasn't a come-on…she snorted, loudly. Travers needed to sleep just as much as *she* did. And he didn't have to worry about an infection gnawing its way towards his brain.

No, he does have to worry, she thought, feeling an odd flicker of sympathy. *He just doesn't know what it's like to be infected.*

"I wanted to do so much," Travers said. She wasn't sure if she was talking to her or to himself. "And I could die here."

"You could also die on the ship," Alice pointed out. "The ship isn't *invincible*"—she smiled at her humourless play on words—"and if she cops a missile or two in the wrong place, she'll be blown to atoms."

She cursed under her breath. The last report from orbit had stated that the carrier was moving into position to attack the orbiting stations, but since then…nothing. One of the wretched stations was still in prime position to detect and take out the shuttle, if it boosted for orbit; another was in a worse position, yet the virus might still get lucky before the shuttle was halfway into space. Alice's imagination, always vivid, showed a plasma pulse hitting the shuttle amidships and blowing them all to atoms. She didn't need to know the exact details to know it would be instantly fatal.

"Sleep," she said. "If you don't, you'll regret it in the morning."

She closed her eyes, drawing on her training. Normally, she could get to sleep within seconds—she'd learnt to take her rest when she could, because one never knew when one would be ordered to muster—but now...she was too unsettled to sleep, despite her long march from the cave to the shuttle. Her body craved rest, yet her mind was too active to allow her to sleep. Was she right? Had the aliens ignored her because she smelled like them? Or had she been infected once again, without her knowledge? Last time, she'd felt terrible as the virus slowly worked its way towards her brain; this time, she felt healthy...just tired. If she went to sleep, she wondered, would she wake up as herself? Or would something alien look out from her eyes?

Damn it, she thought. *I may never feel safe again...*

"Muster," Hammersmith shouted. "Muster now!"

Alice jerked out of her haze, rolling over and snatching up her rifle as she stood. The sergeant was already heading to the hatch, looking reassuringly competent as he snapped his helmet into place. Travers was looking around blearily, blinking rapidly under the shuttle's dim lighting. Alice supposed she should be pleased Travers hadn't slept with a weapon close to hand. He was too dazed to be trusted with anything more dangerous than a piece of plastic cutlery.

She grabbed her own helmet and pulled it on, then hurried out the hatch herself. The moon was slowly rising, bathing the entire scene in a pearly white radiance. She glanced from side to side, giving her helmet a chance to accustom itself to the semi-darkness. Her eyesight was good, thanks to genetic modification, but it was better to rely on night-vision gear. The moonlight, perversely, made it harder for her to see what might be lurking under the treeline.

"We got an alert from one of the sensors," Hammersmith was saying, quietly. "There's a massive alien column heading towards us."

Alice shuddered. Sergeant Radcliffe showed no visible reaction.

"How big?" His voice was very calm, as if he were ordering dinner. "Do we have a rough estimate?"

"Several thousand, at least," Hammersmith said. "The sensors could be having trouble with the alien biology…"

"Or they could have pissed on one of the sensors," Alice said. She'd watched as one of her instructors demonstrated how easy it was to fool the basic sensors. The alarm had started screaming before he'd zipped up his pants, the computers insisting that thousands of insurgents were bearing down on them. "Just because they don't use technology doesn't mean they won't recognise a sensor when they see it. They're not *real* primitives."

"Perhaps," Sergeant Radcliffe said. "But we have to assume the worst."

He started to issue orders, telling the marines to take up their positions in the trenches and then instructing the pilots to prepare for an immediate takeoff. Alice took her place, trying not to think about just how many aliens were about to die. Stopping a mass human wave assault wasn't easy, even when the enemies were utterly inhuman aliens. If they just kept coming, the defenders were eventually going to run out of bullets and get overwhelmed. And then they'd be infected or butchered…

And that doesn't even include the station hanging over our heads, she thought, looking up at the night sky. Was one of the twinkling spots of light the alien station? It was definitely large enough to be seen with the naked eye. *If they get sick of slaughter, they can simply drop a KEW on our heads and kill us.*

She wondered, as she rested her rifle in the firing position, if she should be grateful that she wasn't in command. Sergeant Radcliffe was *not* in a good place. If he kept the recon team on the ground, they would eventually be overwhelmed and killed; if he risked a takeoff, the virus might just cut its losses and blow the shuttle out of the sky. The only thing keeping them alive was the virus's determination to turn them into hosts and who knew how long *that* would last? It might decide to cut its losses after a few thousand host-bodies were slaughtered in a desperate and futile attempt to take the humans alive.

An alert popped up in front of her as the helmet's sensors registered the sound of aliens entering the treeline and making their way towards the shuttle. They were still moving in eerie silence, save for a handful of hoots and hollers that seemed designed to help them coordinate their movements, rather than psyching themselves up for a charge into the teeth of enemy guns. Alice told herself, firmly, that *these* aliens would be better off dead than mindless host-bodies. It wasn't like some of the engagements she'd seen in the Security Zone, where a handful of clerics had pushed their followers to their deaths while they'd waited at the rear...*God*, she'd enjoyed watching those bastards die. Alice wasn't particularly religious, but she had no doubt the fuckers were burning in hell. They'd poisoned minds, then sent them out to die.

A crashing sound echoed through the air, followed rapidly by an explosion as the first mine detonated. She allowed herself to hope, just for a second, that it would deter the aliens, but it barely slowed them down. Two more mines detonated in quick succession, each one killing dozens of aliens and injuring scores more, but they kept coming anyway. Alice cursed out loud as she braced herself, even though part of her wondered if she should be grateful they were pushing so hard. No rational commanding officer would drop KEWs on an enemy force when their own forces were so close that friendly casualties were unavoidable.

But the virus doesn't care, she told herself. *It might drop a KEW on us at any moment and to hell with the number of host-bodies that get taken out too.*

Another alert flashed up in her visor. Sergeant Radcliffe had launched a pair of drones, even though it was technically a breach of orders. Alice was fairly sure that Major Parkinson wouldn't say anything about it. There was no way to dispute that the virus knew where they were, not with thousands of aliens bearing down on them. A screen opened in front of her, showing the live feed from the drones. It looked as if every town within a hundred miles had opened its gates and hurled its population against the invaders. If anything, Hammersmith had underestimated the number of aliens marching to the sound of the guns.

"I think I'm getting a mite depressed," Corporal Tindal commented, dryly.

"Load the mortars," Sergeant Radcliffe ordered, ignoring Tindal. "Fire on my command."

The night sky lit up as the mortar shells crashed down amidst the alien hordes. Alice cursed the virus, once again, as the HE shells exploded, killing dozens of aliens. But there were always more, running towards the trenches. She wondered, grimly, if they should have packed antipersonnel rounds as well as HE, although it was unlikely that Captain Shields would have agreed. Antipersonnel rounds were rarely used in combat outside the Security Zone. They were practically banned everywhere else.

And besides, we don't know what sort of gases will kill them and what will merely make their lives miserable, she thought. *We might make them more determined to kill us than they were even before.*

Alice leaned forward, interested, as Sergeant Radcliffe gave the order to fire a handful of pulsar shells. The boffins had come up with them and fast-tracked production, although—according to the briefing papers—the generals hadn't been too keen on the idea. Testing experimental hardware in the field was not, generally speaking, a good idea...but they had to know if the pulsars worked. Her helmet darkened slightly as the pulsars detonated, blazing the aliens in high-intensity ultraviolet light, but they didn't seem to have any effect. The viral matter floating around the aliens had been killed, she was sure, yet the pulsars couldn't touch the viral clusters inside their host bodies. The results had been disappointing.

"Perhaps we could just drop the shells on their heads," Hammersmith commented. "It might be more effective."

Alice had no time to reply as the first wave of aliens lurched into view. It was a ragged formation, more like a desperate charge than a formal parade, but the aliens kept coming anyway. She depressed the trigger, picking off the first few aliens as she'd done before, yet the oncoming tide was relentless. For every alien she killed, two more sprang up to take their place. She saw blood splashing in all directions as the aliens died. They just kept coming.

A string of explosions shook the ground as more mortar shells crashed down and exploded with staggering force. Alice saw, just for a second, a gap in the enemy formation, but it was gone before she could think of a way to take advantage of it. She checked the live feed from the drones and felt ice tingling around her heart. The reserve alien formations were picking up speed, filling in the holes created by the mortars. No human force could have taken so many casualties and remained in action. It was yet another reminder that the virus considered its host bodies to be utterly expendable.

They're not going to believe this, when we get back home, she thought, as she shot another alien. *They'll think we're making it up.*

"Machine guns, engage," Sergeant Radcliffe said. "Riflemen, pause."

Alice ducked, instinctively, as she heard the *chatter-chatter-chatter* of machine guns—and bullets snapping over her head. The alien line seemed to wilt, just for a second, as the bullets tore through them. She hoped—she prayed—that the machine guns would be enough to stop them in their tracks. It had to be, didn't it? The aliens were practically being torn apart, their bodies disintegrating under the impact of so many bullets. Sergeant Radcliffe and his men were using their machine guns like fire hoses, spraying the alien lines ruthlessly. Each bullet was hitting two or three or more aliens before it finally fell to the ground...

...And yet, the aliens kept coming.

"This is impossible," Tartar said. He sounded as if he was on the verge of hysteria. "How do they keep coming?"

"Focus," Sergeant Radcliffe snapped. They didn't have the numbers to allow even *one* person to leave the trenches. "Concentrate on your job."

Alice understood, better than she cared to admit. Soldiers weren't machines. They could be broken by endless horror and slaughter. They could give up when they realised that, for all their efforts, nothing was really being achieved. But she was damned if she was going to throw down her gun and let the bastards slaughter her. Every host-body she killed was one more native released from enslavement. It wasn't much, but it would have to do.

"You're not going to like this, Boss-Man," Hammersmith said. "We've got movement coming in from all over the place. I think they're sending *zillions* of people to die on our guns."

"...Shit," Sergeant Radcliffe said. "On my mark, we'll go danger-close with the mortars and fall back to the inner trenches."

Alice sucked in her breath. A fighting retreat was nightmarish enough at the best of times. A fighting retreat with a horde of maddened aliens intent on tearing her to shreds—or infecting her with an alien virus—was worse. And detonating HE mortar rounds at danger-close ranges—practically on top of the trenches—might easily turn the engagement into a complete disaster. Mortar shells weren't the most accurate weapons in the world, even under perfect conditions. The engagement was very far from perfect.

"On my mark," Sergeant Radcliffe warned. "Danger-close in ten...nine..."

Alice watched the timer closely. At two seconds, she hurled a grenade at the advancing aliens and ducked into the trench. The ground shook madly a second later, the grenade lost in the far greater explosion as the mortar shells detonated. Dirt cascaded on top of her, a grim reminder that the trench had been dug in a hurry. Thankfully, she told herself as she scrambled up and ran for the inner trenches, it had also been dug by someone who'd known what he was doing. The trench hadn't collapsed with her still inside it.

"Danger-close in ten," Sergeant Radcliffe said, again. "Nine...eight..."

Alice hit the ground, a second before the mortar rounds came down and exploded. The earth heaved under her—she was sure the trench had collapsed now, even if it had survived the earlier explosions—but she forced herself to stand and run anyway. Sergeant Radcliffe and his men opened fire with the machine guns, again, yet this time they were limiting their fire to short bursts. It didn't take a genius to realise that they were running out of ammunition.

And that we have nowhere else to run, Alice thought. The aliens were throwing in attacks from all directions. She'd studied battles where one side let itself get trapped, without a line of retreat, and they rarely ended well for the defenders. There *was* a way out, this time, but it was a trap. *If we head to orbit...*

She keyed her communicator. "What about the ship? Have we heard anything from them?"

"Fuck-all," Sergeant Radcliffe called back. "We don't know what they're doing."

Alice checked the live feed, again. It seemed impossible, but—if anything—the alien numbers seemed to be growing. The forest was littered with the bodies of the dead and they were *still* coming. She wanted to think that the newcomers wouldn't get to the shuttle in time to join the slaughter, but she knew better. Given the speeds the aliens could run—it seemed strange to think of them as natural runners, but they'd win a human marathon with ease—it was quite likely they'd arrive in plenty of time.

"Ah," Hammersmith said. His voice was inhumanly calm. "I've got aircraft lifting off from the alien base. Fast little buggers too. They'll be on top of us in ten minutes."

"Activate the automated defences, but do not clear them to fire until I give the word," Sergeant Radcliffe said, after a moment. He sounded like a man who had come to a grim resolution. "Fire Teams Two and Three, get into the shuttle; pilots, flash-wake the drives."

We could hunker down in the shuttle, Alice thought. The stealth shuttle might be less sturdy than an assault shuttle, but the hull was still impregnable as far as the native aliens were concerned. Sticks and stones would no more break the shuttle's armour than her fists could punch through a battlesuit. But who knew what weapons the incoming aircraft were carrying? *Besides, if the engagement looks hopeless, the virus might just drop a KEW on us anyway.*

She glanced at the sergeant and knew, with complete certainty, what he had in mind. The alien station might be gone—or it might be trading blows with *Invincible* and her starfighters. Either way, their only safety lay in flight. If they could get into orbit before the alien aircraft arrived, or even high enough to make pursuit impossible, they might just be able to escape.

It was a gamble—and if the gamble didn't pay off, they were dead—but what other choice did they have?

"Get the rest of the team into the shuttle now," Sergeant Radcliffe ordered. His tone brooked no contradiction as he snapped out a command, ordering the automatic weapons to engage the enemy. "We take off in one minute."

"Understood, Sarge," Alice said. The shuttle's drives were already whining. She could feel the ground quivering as the drive field powered up. Behind her, the automatic weapons started to fire. "Let's go."

CHAPTER TWENTY-SIX

"SIR, THE MARINES ARE UNABLE TO HOLD the landing zone," Newcomb reported. "They're going to have to take off."

Stephen nodded, grimly. The brief flash-reports from the ground had been horrific. He'd hoped to have time to reduce the enemy station before the marines had to leave, despite the risk of the station dropping KEWs on the marine LZ, but it was clear they'd have to move faster. Their luck might just have run out.

"Order the starfighters to engage the station," Stephen ordered. "They are to concentrate on stripping it of its defences."

"Aye, Captain."

And then we bring the ship into engagement range, Stephen thought. It was possible the starfighters could kill the station by themselves, but he doubted it. The wretched structure appeared to be as tough as a battleship. *And then we take it apart piece by piece.*

•   •   •

"That's a big station," Monica commented, as the starfighters closed in on the orbiting monstrosity. "What do you think it *does*?"

Richard shrugged. The station wasn't a blocky mass of prefabricated components, like the orbital receiving and transhipment stations he'd seen throughout his career, but a single structure, armed to the teeth. Plasma fire was already flashing towards the starfighters, forcing them to scatter into evasive manoeuvres even though there was no way anyone could hope to shoot plasma weapons accurately at extreme range. Any hits would come through luck, rather than judgement.

Not that it would be any relief to anyone who actually gets hit, he thought, coldly. *They'll be dead regardless.*

He was fairly certain the station was nothing more than an orbital battlestation, although he didn't think there was anything on the planet worth protecting. There was no hint the virus considered the natives to be anything other than host-bodies. They certainly didn't have a sizable industrial base in the system...unless, he supposed, they were farming the aliens themselves. There was no reason they couldn't tranship a few thousand natives to another world and put them to work, if they had a sudden manpower shortage. It wasn't as if they had to waste time educating the host-bodies. The virus knew everything it needed to know already.

"It doesn't matter," he said, pushing the macabre thought out of his head. "Concentrate on your job."

"Aye, sir," Monica said.

"Lock torpedoes on target," Richard ordered. "Fire on my command. I say again, fire on my command."

The station's fire grew more accurate as the starfighters slipped closer, zigzagging from side to side to make it harder for the enemy to score a hit. Richard doubted the torpedoes would hit the alien structure—if the virus hadn't realised they were dangerous before they'd taken out one of the cruisers, it certainly did now—but they'd force the virus to concentrate its point defence on the tiny projectiles. His starfighters would have a chance to get closer, for what it was worth. The virus hadn't converted an asteroid into an orbital fortress, if his scanners were to be believed, but it was clear the battlestation was heavily armoured. It was quite likely that the starfighters wouldn't be able to do more than scratch the fortress's paint.

"Launch torpedoes," he snapped. "I say again, launch torpedoes."

There was a fraction of a second's hesitation on the part of the aliens—he thought—and then the virus hastily redirected its fire. Richard smiled to himself, then snapped orders as he gunned the drive, zooming towards his first target. He bottomed out as he neared the station, his guns already opening fire as the targeting computers picked out enemy weapons stations and sensor blisters. They might not be able to take out the station, but they could render it defenceless—and blind. The virus didn't seem to have bothered to invest in a network of stealthed scansats, unlike Earth's defenders. They'd have seen the stealth shuttle, Richard thought, if they had.

"Keep shooting," he ordered, as the last of the torpedoes was blown into vapour. The starfighters were—in theory—underneath the enemy weapons, making it impossible for the virus to bring its plasma cannons to bear on them, but there was no way to be entirely certain the virus couldn't target them anyway. *Invincible's* point defence weapons were designed to close that particular blind spot, if the captain was prepared to take the risk of hammering his own ship's hull. "Don't give them a chance to react."

The station seemed to grow larger as he swung the starfighter past a protruding structure—his scanners suggested it was a docking tube, although it was too large to transfer personnel and too small to tranship cargo—and picked off two more plasma cannons. It looked as though the station's fire was slacking, despite desperate attempts to bring their weapons to bear on the starfighters. The virus, Richard guessed, hadn't expected to be attacked here. It hadn't taken the basic precautions that any human navy would have taken, once it knew a war had broken out. But then, the virus presumably hadn't expected to encounter a major spacefaring race. Its slow expansion towards Falkirk had been marked with a complete lack of concern about what it might discover. There was certainly little chance of picking up radio transmissions from Earth...

"That's the last of their antishipping missile tubes gone," Monica said. "The ship is clear to approach."

Richard nodded. The station had been firing missiles towards *Invincible*, but the range had been so extreme that they'd gone ballistic long before they'd neared the giant carrier. More proof, if he'd wanted it, that the virus hadn't been expecting trouble. The analysts had predicted that the virus could and would manufacture vast numbers of long-range antishipping missiles, assuming it had the technology and inclination to produce them, but they clearly hadn't assigned any to Alien-3. Either that, or they didn't have them. He reminded himself, sharply, not to take it for granted. Even if the virus didn't have long-range missiles, it would rush them into production as soon as it saw them in action.

Which may be a while, Richard thought. *The missiles are so expensive that they're rarely assigned to starships on deep-space missions.*

He shrugged. "Pull back," he ordered. "We don't want to get caught between *Invincible* and her target."

"Aye, sir."

. . .

"The marines are boosting for orbit," Newcomb reported. "There's no sign that they're at risk of being killed."

"Maybe," Stephen said. *Invincible* was gliding steadily into weapons range. The alien station looked harmless, now the starfighters had worked her over, but he knew better than to take that for granted. Besides, he needed to know just how tough the alien armour was. The sensors had suggested that it wasn't anything like the armour protecting his ship. "Tactical, do we have weapons lock?"

"Aye, Captain," Lieutenant-Commander David Arthur said. "Weapons are locked on target."

And they've been locked on target for the last twenty minutes, Stephen thought, wryly. *And you wish I hadn't asked the question.*

"All weapons, fire at will," he ordered. "I say again, fire at will."

"Aye, sir," Arthur said.

Stephen braced himself as *Invincible* opened fire, her massive plasma cannons and mass drivers tearing into the alien structure. The aliens fired back—the virus seemed to be trying to launch missiles from shuttlebays, something Stephen found oddly admirable—but most of their weapons were swept out of space before they managed to get into attack range. Arthur shifted targeting, pounding the alien shuttlebays into scrap. A chain of explosions shook the station, blowing clumps of debris into space. Stephen noted, with a twinge of displeasure, that the alien armour seemed to be holding up very well. Battleships were tough—he'd seen battleships sail into plasma storms without taking serious damage—but the alien station was tougher. It was lucky they'd taken out most of its weapons. He wasn't sure they'd survive a straight battering match.

But they don't use this armour on their ships, he mused. *Could it be an updated version of the old solid-state armour?*

It was an interesting thought. He'd studied *Ark Royal* during his training, paying close attention when his instructors had outlined the strengths and weaknesses of the century-old design. The Royal Navy's Old Lady had been tough, incredibly so, but her acceleration curves had been pathetic even when she'd been on the cutting edge of development. It was no wonder that later designs, concentrating more on speed than armour, had cut protection back to the bare bone. And *they* had been cut to ribbons when they'd encountered a foe armed with plasma weapons.

"Commander Newcomb, detail a pair of shuttles to recover any pieces of alien armour that happen to be intact," he said, as another chunk of debris was thrown into space. "See what the analysts make of it."

"Aye, Captain," Newcomb said. "She's holding up pretty damn well."

Stephen nodded. The interior of the alien station was exposed now—he doubted that any of the virus's host-bodies had survived the holocaust raging through the structure—but it was still trying to fight. The biological computer network must be still intact. It was practically flailing around randomly, yet it was holding up...he grimaced, wondering what it would be like to go toe-to-toe with an alien battleship. If the enemy ship was escorted by starfighters, the fight would be dangerously uneven...

The station came apart, showering debris in all directions. Stephen tensed as chunks of rubble flew towards *Invincible*, a handful targeted and destroyed by the point defence before they could strike the carrier's hull. Other pieces fell towards the planet below, de-orbiting so rapidly that there was nothing the virus could do to stop them. Stephen felt a stab of sympathy for the natives, none of whom had asked to be turned into alien slaves. Too many of them would die when the debris hit the planet's surface. He hoped, grimly, that they'd see it as a relief.

Assuming they can even think for themselves, he thought. The reports, the highly-classified reports, had insisted that all higher brain functions were terminated once the virus had completed its conquest of the victim's body. Stephen supposed that was a relief—at least he'd be dead, instead of trapped helplessly inside his own body as it was controlled by an alien force—but it was still terrifying. *The natives might have been brain-dead right from the start.*

"Target destroyed," Arthur reported. "Station Two is attempting to target us with missiles."

"The point defence can handle them," Stephen said. There was nothing to be gained by engaging the other two orbital fortresses. He'd cleared the way for the marines—and learnt something useful about alien armour—and there was no point in risking the ship just to smash the remaining defences. They were irrelevant to the overall conflict. "Target the structure on the ground and smash it."

"Aye, Captain," Arthur said. A low shudder ran through the ship. "KEW's away, sir."

Stephen nodded. There was probably nothing to be gained by blowing up the surface base either, but it *was* a sitting target...and besides, who knew? It might impede the enemy in some manner. He wanted to believe that there was a native resistance force on the surface, ready to take advantage of the chaos, but he knew it was unlikely. There was no sense that the natives had had any more awareness of how diseases were transmitted than the humans who'd faced the Black Death. They'd been overwhelmed by a threat they couldn't even begin to comprehend, a genuine Outside Context Problem. And there was no hope of recovery.

Poor bastards, he thought. *I wish there was something we could do for them.*

"Captain, the alien aircraft are closing on the shuttle," Arthur said. "I request permission to engage them."

Stephen nodded, curtly. The stealth shuttle wasn't so stealthy when it was boosting through the upper atmosphere. It was a race now, a race to get into orbit before the alien aircraft brought their weapons to bear. A single laser pulse would be enough to do serious damage, even if it didn't blow the shuttle out of the sky. Hell, even an old-style air-to-air missile would be more than enough to bring the marine craft crashing back to the ground. But the marines had an orbital guardian angel. One by one, the enemy craft were picked off and vaporised before they got into firing position.

And so, once again, we learn the importance of keeping command of the high orbitals, Stephen thought. He'd seen the plans for long-term resistance to alien occupation, plans that had been drawn up during the First Interstellar War and hastily revised when the planners had forced themselves to come to terms with the reality of the virus, but none of them had struck him as likely to do more than irritate the occupation force. *As long as the occupiers hold the high ground, KEW strikes can eliminate any resistance force stupid enough to mount a major attack on the surface.*

"All targets destroyed," Arthur confirmed.

"The marines are heading towards us," Newcomb said. "They're requesting permission to dock."

"Have them detailed to the quarantine section," Stephen ordered, as the marine shuttle connected to the datanet and started to upload its records. There was no sense that the craft was under enemy control—the interior sensors were not reporting any trace of the virus—but he had no intention of taking chances. "The marines and the...remainder of the recon team are to stay there until they are cleared."

Until we decide if we dare take the risk of letting them rejoin the crew, he added, in the privacy of his own mind. It was a reality he'd known he'd have to face from the moment they'd realised just *what* the virus did to its hosts. *If they've been infected, somehow, we may have to kill them if they can't be cured.*

He winced at the thought. The marines had known the risks. The entire *crew* knew the risks. Stephen had no doubt that most of them would prefer to die, rather than be turned into mindless puppets; hell, if they were mindless puppets, they would be dead long before their bodies were destroyed. But it wasn't a command he wanted to give, let alone watch as it was carried out. He had no qualms about killing the enemies of Great Britain, let alone the entire human race, yet...he shook his head. He'd give the order, if there was no other choice. He just hoped he'd be able to live with himself afterwards.

"As soon as the marines dock, take us to Point Galahad," he said. "Activate the cloaking device as soon as we are out of immediate sensor range."

"Aye, Captain," Lieutenant Sonia Michelle said. "They won't be able to track us."

Stephen had his doubts. The early reports from the marines had made it clear that they *had* been tracked...somehow. And that meant...what? It was starting to look as though the entire operation had been a waste of time and resources. Taking out the cruisers and the station had been satisfactory, but nothing more. It certainly wasn't a war-winner. Alien-3 was nothing more than an alien transhipment station. They might as well have bombed the handful of depots on Pluto.

He leaned back in his command chair as the marines docked, the drives powering up seconds later. They'd have to go on, sooner rather than later; they'd have to head directly to the next tramline, once they'd broken contact with the alien stations. Sonia was right; the stations *wouldn't* be able to track the flotilla once it was out of immediate range. But there was no way to know if the virus had managed to summon help or not. There was no way to hide the simple fact that a starship *had* managed to sneak into the virus's rear, not now. Stephen had no doubt that a number of very hard questions would be asked, when they returned home. The only upside was that the virus would either have to waste its time detailing starships to hunt *Invincible* down or run the risk of the carrier causing havoc in its rear...

Which it is better placed to judge than ourselves, he thought, coldly. *The virus knows what awaits us in Alien-4. We don't have the slightest idea what to expect.*

He studied the display for a long moment. There was nothing to be gained by remaining in Alien-3, not now. The virus couldn't be allowed a chance to trap them in a useless system—or even to get a starship into position to shadow them until larger, more powerful formations arrived. No, they had to press on and hope for the best. The only other alternative was to reverse course and hope they could slip through Alien-1 and return to Falkirk with their mission unfinished.

"Helm, once we have reached Point Galahad, set course for Tramline Two," he ordered. "Communications, inform the remainder of the flotilla of our intentions and instruct them to accompany us."

"Aye, Captain."

Stephen nodded to himself. They hadn't done badly. The victory would be good for his crew's morale. They'd pulled the virus's beard and got away with it. But...he couldn't allow himself to believe it had been decisive. They'd barely scratched the virus and they knew it. It was easy to imagine his family's political enemies making capital out of the recon team's deployment. If it had been a waste of time—worse, something that had revealed their presence for nothing...

Newcomb caught his eyes. "Captain, I think you should see this," he said. "Something very interesting happened down on the surface. The marines are assessing it now."

Stephen met his eyes. "Interesting?"

"Very interesting," Newcomb confirmed. "You need to see the report now."

CHAPTER TWENTY-SEVEN

"WE'RE DOCKING WITH THE QUARANTINE SECTION," Sergeant Radcliffe said. "I trust you all remember how to behave?"

Alice ignored the groan from behind her. There might be some grumbling—the less said about quarantine procedures, the better—but the marines knew to take them seriously. They all knew what had happened to her, on the alien ship they'd encountered on Alien-1; they all knew that the risk of being infected was inherently unpredictable. It was better to go through the procedure, as unpleasant as it was, than gamble that medical science could save them from being turned into yet another set of host-bodies. Alice was still, as far as she knew, the only person to be freed from alien control.

And it never really got into my brain, she reminded herself. *I wouldn't have survived if it had.*

The hatch clicked open, revealing an airlock tube filled with bright lights. Alice exchanged a glance with Sergeant Radcliffe, then stood and walked into the tube. It was all she could do to keep her eyes open as the light grew brighter. The combination of strong visible light and ultraviolet light was supposed to kill germs and bacteria, including *the* virus, but no one was entirely sure. Anything lurking under her skin was safe from being killed. A second hatch opened up in front of her, closing the moment she stepped through. She gritted her teeth, reminded herself that she'd been through worse, and started to undress. The sense of being watched through hidden cameras grew stronger as she stripped, dumping her uniform and facemask in a basket. They'd probably be fed straight into an incinerator. Naked, she stepped through the third hatch—her skin feeling warm as the lights pulsed brighter—and into the examination chamber. She carefully wrapped the sensor bracelet around her wrist and waited. Two doctors wearing bio-protection suits emerged from the other hatch and walked towards her. Alice absently admired their nerve. If she *was* infected, she could break their necks before anyone outside the chamber could intervene. She wasn't even restrained!

It felt like hours before the examination was finally completed. The doctors took samples of everything, from blood and urine to hair and skin cells, then forced her to drink a collection of vile-tasting medicines before allowing her to walk through the hatch into the waiting chamber. Alice ignored her nakedness as best as possible, feeling oddly exposed as she met the remainder of the recon team. The marines ignored her—she'd bedded down with them before—but the civvies didn't know where to look. She cursed the virus under her breath as she found a robe and pulled it on, then sat down and picked up a datapad. She needed to write a full report while the details were still fresh in her mind. God alone knew how much she'd forget if she waited. The smallest detail, it had been drilled into her head time and time again, might be vitally important.

"We're leaving orbit," Hammersmith commented, as a low quiver ran through the giant carrier. "Where do you think we're going?"

"Off to fuck your mother," Tartar said, sharply. He was rubbing a nasty-looking bruise on his elbow. "I hear she's..."

"As you were," Sergeant Radcliffe said, before a fight could break out. "We'll be on our way to the next target."

Alice nodded in agreement, then bent her head over the datapad. She had to record everything, starting with her puzzlement over how the aliens had tracked the recon team to why she'd simply been allowed to leave after they'd caught her. Cold logic insisted they should have killed her on the spot, but…they'd let her go. She turned the question over and over again in her mind, yet the only answer that made any kind of sense was that the change in her scent had marked her as yet another host-body. It was irrational—and it suggested the virus knew nothing about security—but…she'd taken part in exercises where she'd had to slip onto secure military bases. Wearing the right uniform and looking like you *belonged* could get you a very long way.

Hammersmith caught her eye. "How long are they going to keep us here?"

"Are you *that* desperate for a wank?" Tartar made a rude sound. "Go find a potty and…"

"Shut up, the pair of you," Sergeant Radcliffe ordered. "They'll keep us here until they know we're clean."

"But we *know* we're clean," Hammersmith protested. "Sarge…"

Alice looked up at him. "How would you know?"

The communications console bleeped before Hammersmith could come up with a cutting reply. "Captain Campbell, please go through the hatch into the private compartment."

"I think this is where you're supposed to tell Big Brother that you hate us all and want us to die in a fire," Hammersmith said. "And then they'll vote you out of the house."

"I am not going to dignify that stupid comment with a stupid answer," Alice said, as she stood. Her legs felt stiff, but nothing a little exercise wouldn't cure. She certainly didn't feel as wretched as she'd felt when she'd been infected. Hammersmith might well be right. The virus would be weakening their defences by now if it had managed to infect them. "And I'm shocked—*shocked*—to hear that you watch *Big Brother*."

She stepped into the next compartment and closed the hatch. A holographic projection was waiting for her, wavering faintly in the bright light. Alice wasn't remotely surprised to see Doctor Watson, his hand holding a datapad. She rather suspected that he'd been reading her report as she'd written it, rather than waiting for her to file a cleaned-up version that included all her second and third thoughts. Hammersmith had been more right than he'd known. They were indeed being watched from afar.

"Alice," Doctor Watson said. "Do you think they smelled you...and then let you go?"

"Yes," Alice said. "No other explanation makes sense."

She ran through a handful of others, dismissing them one by one. There was no way in hell a humanoid...well, *human*...could be mistaken for an eight-legged alien. The virus couldn't be *that* unaware of what the host-bodies looked like, could it? And the infected natives had shown every intention of wanting to capture and infect the recon team, but they hadn't tried to infect her. The only answer that made sense was that they thought she was *already* infected and beyond salvation. She had a nasty feeling that she'd been very lucky.

"You may be right," Doctor Watson said. "What do you think we can *do* with the knowledge?"

"Use it," Alice said. "If we could convince the virus we're *all* already infected, it might leave us alone."

"Scent doesn't travel through space," Doctor Watson said. "You're talking about unleashing viral material on a planetary surface."

Alice bit down a comment about just how rank a spacesuit could become after it had been occupied for several hours and leaned forward. "If the virus believes that a marine company has already been infected, that it is already part of its...society, it might let that company run rampant because it can't wrap its head around the concept of someone using its own ID markers against it."

"It might work," Doctor Watson said. "And if you're wrong?"

"Then we're no worse off than we were," Alice said. "But it's worth trying to investigate, is it not?"

• • •

"That's the long and short of it, Captain," Doctor Watson said. "Captain Campbell was spared, for no apparent reason, when she should have been killed or re-infected. I think her theory has a great deal of meat in it."

Stephen frowned. "And what if she's wrong?"

"What if she's still infected?" Commander Newcomb was playing Devil's Advocate. "What if she's been playing us for fools?"

Doctor Watson's lips thinned. "There have been some physical changes between her first deployment to *Invincible* and her second. Most notably, her scent has changed...although most humans are simply not sensitive enough to pick up on it. However, while her body is still playing host to a considerable amount of viral material, it is...well, *dead*. We have monitored her brain activity closely, as well as keeping her under several levels of overt and covert surveillance. If she's infected, she's doing a very good job of hiding it.

"Furthermore, she has had quite a few opportunities to sabotage either the ship or the mission itself. A single unidirectional beacon would have been more than enough to draw an alien fleet to us, would it not? Frankly, Commander, she hasn't done *anything* to arouse suspicion of...well, *anything*. If this was a routine security investigation, with a handful of prospective targets picked out at random, we would have cleared her by now."

Stephen held up a hand. "Can we duplicate her scent?"

"Yes and no," Doctor Watson said. "Drug treatments can be used to produce a scent that, as far as we can tell, is identical to the alien stench. Her words, not mine. I think we can produce the right level of drugs fairly quickly. However, we cannot guarantee that the virus will accept the smell...and there's no way we can duplicate the viral strings used to exchange information. If the virus wants to communicate, or simply run a few basic checks, we're fucked."

"The marines are fucked," Newcomb said. "I'm not a medical professional, doctor, but I do know some history. The people who were vaccinated with cowpox to keep them from getting smallpox...some of them caught cowpox and died, didn't they? What if we accidentally infect our own people with the alien virus?"

"We wouldn't be using viral cells as the base for the scent drugs," Doctor Watson said, calmly. "The marines may smell for a few hours, but they won't be infected."

"And what if the virus realises that the lack of viral cells, even *dead* viral cells, means trouble?" Newcomb scowled. "It strikes me that too many things could go wrong."

Stephen cleared his throat. "So far, this is all theoretical. We don't have any plans to deploy the marines until we find a second target."

"We might be better off testing this under controlled conditions before we test it in the field," Newcomb said. "And I could easily see the marines being reluctant to take the injections."

"It would be neat if they *could* simply walk through the alien lines," Stephen pointed out, seriously. "They might not see our people as threats even after they open fire."

"I doubt it, Captain," Newcomb said. "Surely, they'd recognise that *something* had gone wrong."

"That's the beauty of the whole concept," Doctor Watson said. "They would have to...ah, verify each and every host-body within the area. I don't know how quickly the virus can exchange information between hosts, but it would certainly take it quite some time to isolate the fakes."

"And then it will turn on them," Newcomb said.

"We will keep the idea in reserve," Stephen said, firmly. "Doctor, are the marines infected?"

"Apart from Alice Campbell, whom I would like to keep under observation for the next few hours, I believe our precautions worked," Doctor Watson said. "None of the marines show any trace of viral matter within their bloodstreams—or anywhere else, for that matter—and the medical doctors are prepared to give them a clean bill of health. It looks as though our belief that the virus couldn't become an airborne threat in a planetary environment is largely accurate. Alien-3 has an intact ozone layer, blocking much of the star's ultraviolet output, and they're still having problems. I wouldn't care to spend time in a native village, Captain, but otherwise...I'd say our precautions are good enough."

"But everyone who encounters an infected host will *still* be going into quarantine," Stephen said, firmly. "I will not take chances with the safety of this ship."

"Understood," Doctor Watson said.

Stephen looked down at his desk for a long moment. "Is there anything we can do for the natives?"

"I don't believe so, not now," Doctor Watson said. "I'm not an expert on viruses, let alone *the* virus, but given how aggressive it is I doubt we can improve the human immune system to the point it can fight off infection. Our genetic engineering tools are not up to the job."

"And if we can't do it for humans, we certainly can't do it for the poor bastards down there," Newcomb said. He jabbed a finger at the bulkhead. "Perhaps we should simply put them out of their misery."

Stephen winced. He'd seen some of the contingency plans, ranging from simply quarantining entire planets to literally blowing them into giant asteroid fields. The boffins *claimed* it should be possible to build a planet-cracker—plans to blow up Mercury to make it easier to turn into a source of raw materials had been drifting around for longer than the human race had been in space—but they didn't have to destroy the entire planet to exterminate the entire population. There were plans to do everything from introducing radioactive material that would kill everything, right down to the smallest insects...he shuddered. It was a horrible thought.

And yet, we might have no choice, he thought. *What is this war going to do to us?*

His intercom bleeped. "Captain, this is the bridge," Lieutenant-Commander David Arthur said. "Long-range probes picked up a large enemy force entering the system through Tramline Two. It's on a direct course for the planet."

Stephen felt his blood run cold. "How large?"

"It's impossible to be sure, but we think we're looking at a battleship and a fleet carrier, plus at least seventeen escorts," Arthur said. "I've altered course to avoid contact."

"Good," Stephen said. He keyed his terminal, bringing up the holographic display. There hadn't been much risk of contact, unless the enemy got very lucky, but Arthur was right to minimise the odds as much as possible. The alien fleet was clearly powerful enough to blow his tiny flotilla out of space if it caught a sniff of his presence. "Detail two stealth probes to keep an eye on them, then continue towards the tramline. We'll jump through as planned."

"And hopefully leave that force wasting its time here," Newcomb muttered.

Stephen nodded, although he wasn't sanguine about discovering that the enemy had left the next system undefended. They wouldn't have cut so many ships loose unless they were confident they could hold the next system against attack. Still...it suggested interesting things about what might be waiting in Alien-4. The alien ships wouldn't have headed straight for the planet unless they had some reason to know they were needed. If they'd intended to go to Alien-1, they would have headed straight for the tramline.

"I'll be on the bridge in a minute," he said. "Alert me if anything changes."

He closed the connection, then looked at the doctor. "Start producing the drugs, but do *not* attempt to test them," he ordered. "*No one* is to use them without a clear understanding of the risks involved, such as they are."

"Yes, sir," Doctor Watson said.

Newcomb was looking pensive as the doctor left the compartment. "The timing makes no sense, unless they have a flicker network of their own," he said. "Or the virus really is telepathic after all."

Stephen studied the display, silently calculating transit times in his head. It was impossible to make even an educated guess about what might be lurking on the far side of Alien-4, but...if the virus had sounded the alert as soon as the marines had kidnapped the infected native, and if there was a flicker station along the tramline, it might *just* work out. There was no reason to assume that the virus was telepathic when the orbiting ships had plenty of time to use a perfectly conventional radio signal to summon help. There was certainly no evidence that the virus was telepathic in any sense.

And yet, we fear the unknown, he mused. *Our lack of knowledge blinds us.*

"The timing isn't too bad," he said. The flicker station would probably be hidden quite close to the star. He considered hurling a projectile down the tramline to take the station out, then dismissed the thought. It would be far too revealing. "They still needed nearly seventeen hours to scramble ships into the system. They might have come sooner if they'd been able to call for help instantly."

"Yes, sir," Newcomb said. "But, for all we know, they might have set off at once from the *next* star system."

Stephen had to smile, even though it wasn't really funny. They were poking their way into the unknown, system by system. There was no way to predict what they'd find, no way to be entirely sure where they were going...he shook his head. They'd find out soon enough, he was sure. And then they'd know more about the enigma of alien-held space.

He rose. "Get some rest," he ordered. Newcomb was younger, but he was looking tired. He'd done too much to keep the ship running while Stephen handled the departure from Alien-3. "By my calculations, you haven't had any sleep for the past twenty hours."

"Neither have you, sir," Newcomb said. He wasn't entirely right, but close enough. "And we'll cross the tramline in less than *five* hours."

"I won't be able to sleep," Stephen said. Newcomb was right, he should sleep. But he knew he wouldn't be able to sleep. "Go have a nap. I'll sleep when we cross the tramline."

"Aye, sir," Newcomb said. "Wake me when we cross the tramline."

"Of course," Stephen agreed. The odds of being ambushed were as low as ever, but it was still a constant nagging worry. "Who knows what might be waiting for us there?"

CHAPTER TWENTY-EIGHT

"JUMP COMPLETE, CAPTAIN," the helmsman said. "I…"

Captain Pavel Kaminov tensed as the display bleeped an alarm. "Report," he snapped. They were alone, far too exposed for his comfort. The *zampolit* looked to be on the verge of panic, damn the man. "What is *that*?"

"Energy signatures, Captain," the sensor officer said. "Big ones. This system is heavily industrialised."

Pavel sucked in a breath as the display started to fill with tactical and strategic icons. A large cluster of pulsing energy signatures held station around a super-massive gas giant, a smaller cluster orbited a single life-bearing world; hundreds—no, *thousands*—of spacecraft and starships were making their way between the giant installations and the five tramlines that were clearly visible to his sensors. *Millions* of asteroids were orbiting the star in clouds that suggested they'd once been planets. The sheer *scale* of activity was staggering.

"Holy shit," he muttered.

"It's bigger than Sol," the sensor officer said. "I can't even begin to fathom…"

The timer bleeped. "Captain, we have to jump back," the helmsman warned. "The other ships are waiting for us."

"Take us back," Pavel ordered. He felt cold. To think that Russia had hoped to befriend these aliens. Even without the virus, it was clear that

Russia would have been nothing more than a very junior partner. "And then ready an immediate data dump. They *have* to know what we've found here."

He wasn't sure himself. Earth's industrial output was staggering, although there were so many duplications that the system actually produced *less* material than any outsider observer might guess. But this system was bigger. Had they stumbled across the alien homeworld, the place where the virus had been born and raised? Or was it merely a tiny part of their overall whole? Were there more systems like Alien-1 and Alien-4 just waiting to be found? He didn't want to think about the possible consequences if there were. Humanity and its alien allies might be simply out-produced and smashed flat, then infected. And that would be the end.

The display blanked, then cleared. "Jump completed, Captain," the helmsman said. "I have *Invincible* on my sensors."

"Send them the data," Pavel ordered. "And then...inform Captain Shields that we are awaiting orders."

• • •

"That is one hell of an industrial base," Captain Katy Shaw said, an hour later. The flotilla had entered Alien-4 and immediately cloaked itself. "Just how large *is* it?"

Stephen shared her shock. "The system looks to be at least twice as industrialised as Sol or Tadpole Prime," he said. "If the analysts are correct, it may even be *bigger.*"

He sucked in his breath. They'd gone fishing for salmon and wound up catching a whale. No, a shark. He didn't think there was *anything* big enough to invade the alien system, let alone raid or destroy its facilities. Admiral Weisskopf would certainly be reluctant to take his fleet and invade Alien-4, even if he hadn't had to punch his way through Alien-1. The sheer *size* of the alien facility was terrifying. Stephen couldn't take his eyes off the display. No wonder the aliens had been willing to dispatch so many ships to Alien-3. They'd known Alien-4 was still heavily defended.

"There are a number of ships on the slips," Katy commented. "If we could take them out, we'd set their shipbuilding program back by years."

"We have one assault carrier and a handful of smaller ships," Captain Kaminov growled, acidly. "They have *dozens* of carriers, and battleships, and smaller ships, within range to intercept us. I doubt we could bombard them with mass drivers for long before they caught us and killed us. And that would be the end."

Stephen couldn't disagree with the logic. The shipyard was so blanketed in radio noise—and sensor emissions—that there was no way *Invincible* could get into attack range without being detected. And that would *definitely* be the end. He wondered, morbidly, if he shouldn't order the flotilla to withdraw. What good was the intelligence they'd gathered if they failed to get it home? He had orders to attack targets of opportunity, if he had the chance, but attacking *this* target was suicide. They'd be killed for nothing.

But as long as this structure keeps churning out ships, they can crush us by sheer weight of numbers, he thought, grimly. The probes had revealed far too many ships—modern ships—being put into mass production. If anything, the analysts who'd concluded that the virus's industrial base would be huge had underestimated the case. *We have to find a way to attack it.*

Sure, his own thoughts answered. *And what if we can't? Or if we get killed...*

"We will empty one of the freighters, then send it back home," he said. That, at least, would ensure that Earth knew what it was facing. "And then we will watch the system, looking for an opportunity to strike a blow."

"If there is one," Captain Kaminov pointed out. "They know we're here. They know we could have slipped through the tramline at any moment."

"Yeah," Katy said. "About that...my crews have been studying the tramlines here. Tramline One goes back to Alien-3, of course, but Tramline Four... we think it goes to Alien-1. It matches the gravity patterns we recorded in that system. We might be able to cut several weeks off the way home."

"Except we would still have to get through Alien-1," Kaminov said.

"True," Stephen agreed, with the private thought that they'd be massively outgunned with or without going through Alien-1. "We'll consider that later, I think. For the moment, we remain focused on finding a way to hurt the enemy."

He keyed the display, bringing up the latest reports from the long-range probes. The alien structure was truly immense, larger than anything humanity had ever built. Indeed, it looked as if the virus had shunned the traditional free-floating shipyard slips and chosen to link them altogether into a single massive construction yard. Hundreds of worker bees—or their alien counterparts—buzzed around the structure, performing tasks that wouldn't have been out of place at the Hamilton Yards. It should have been vulnerable, but the sheer size of the defences suggested otherwise. He couldn't help wondering if the virus's nature inclined it towards massive installations, rather than a handful of smaller stations. Perhaps that explained why its starfighter tactics were so limited.

But they're still dangerous, he reminded himself, firmly. *We must not allow ourselves to become complacent.*

"We'll think of something," he said, firmly. "And we'll see what our crews have to suggest."

"I can't think of anything," Kaminov said. "Katy? Jonathon?"

"We could punch one of our ships up to maximum speed and try to ram," Captain Jonathon Linguine suggested. "But they would see us coming, wouldn't they?"

"They'd certainly be well-placed to stop us," Kaminov agreed. "And there's no way we could punch a ship close enough to light-speed to give them no time to react."

"We'll think of something," Stephen repeated. "We'll reconvene once the freighter has been sent on her way. After that, we'll devise a plan."

"Our best bet might be to leave the system now and whistle up some help," Katy said. "I don't see any way to take the shipyard out without getting killed."

Stephen was starting to suspect she was right. The alien installation was far too heavily defended for anyone's peace of mind. But it wasn't in him to give up. There had to be *something* they could do. The virus knew

Invincible was in the sector. Who knew how long it would be before it started to expand the shipyard's defences? God knew it had the resources to make the shipyard completely impregnable.

"Good luck to us all," he said. "Dismissed."

He keyed his intercom, ordering Newcomb to start emptying the freighter, then returned his gaze to the shipyard. It didn't look as if there was *any* way to get close without getting blown out of space...the conclusion, as much as he disliked it, echoed around and around before he finally managed to dismiss it. There had to be a way. But what?

. . .

Alice had seen her fair share of mega-structures before, of course, although she had to admit that the alien shipyard was hellishly impressive. And yet, there was something about it that struck her as fundamentally foolhardy. The aliens had placed all their eggs in one basket, even though that basket was heavily defended. A lifetime of training and experience told her that they'd made a mistake. There would be a weak point. She just had to find it.

She chewed on a pencil as she worked her way through the torrent of data. The captain, for better or worse, had made the intelligence available to every off-duty crewman, no doubt hoping that one of them would come up with a solution. Alice suspected that most of them would fail. They were *starship* crewmen, not marines. They'd see the sheer size of the alien structure—and the massive defences—and back off in horror. Alice, on the other hand, had invaded military bases during her training. She knew there were weak points. The virus, for all of its power, had blind spots. It was just a matter of finding and exploiting them.

Slowly, very slowly, a plan began to form in her mind. It would be risky, very risky, but she saw no alternative. At best, it would cripple or destroy the alien shipyard; at worst, only a handful of lives—all marines—would be risked. Her life too, true. She was damned if she was letting her people, her former subordinates, take the mission without her. She would do whatever it took to ensure she accompanied the marines into battle.

She tapped her wristcom. "Major, this is Alice," she said. "I've had an idea."

"Understood," Major Henry Parkinson said. "Do you want to present it to the captain?"

"Yes, sir," Alice said. She hesitated. She was uneasily aware that there were lingering question marks over her loyalty. It was galling, all the more so because she would have felt the same way if their positions were reversed. "Unless you think he'll take it a little more seriously if it comes from you."

"I'm not in the habit of stealing ideas," Parkinson said, dryly. "And besides, you should get the credit. And the blame."

If the idea fails, I will be dead, Alice thought. *And I will be past caring about who gets the blame.*

"I'll inform the captain," Parkinson told her. "Meet me outside his Ready Room in five minutes."

Alice stood. "Yes, sir. I'm on my way now."

• • •

Stephen felt a flicker of...*something* as Alice Campbell stepped into the compartment, followed by Major Parkinson. It wasn't that she looked intimidating, or so he told himself firmly. There was just no way to be entirely *sure* that she was uninfected. Stephen had no doubts that Alice Campbell was as loyal as they came—she wouldn't have reached her present rank if there had been any doubts at all about either her loyalty or her competence—but he wasn't sure just who was looking out of her blue eyes. Alice Campbell...or a viral cluster that had turned her into a mindless slave? He simply didn't know.

The paranoia alone is going to kill us, he thought, as he motioned for them to sit down. He couldn't help thinking that Alice looked as if she would rather stand. *We'll be shooting ourselves soon enough.*

"Captain," Major Parkinson said. "Thank you for seeing us. Alice"—he stumbled slightly over her name, a reflection of her anomalous position on the ship—"has a plan that may solve the problem of attacking the alien shipyard."

Stephen straightened up. "I see," he said. "Alice?"

Alice leaned forward and tapped the display, bringing up the image of the alien shipyard. Hours of observation had added more and more data to their records, absolutely none of it encouraging. Stephen had the nasty feeling that it would take every ship at Falkirk to punch through the alien defences…and losses, he suspected, would be staggering. Admiral Weisskopf was unlikely to authorise the mission unless things got really desperate. But they were already desperate.

"The enemy defences are…substantial," Alice said, without hesitation. "I believe we can be reasonably sure that they will spot a cloaked ship as it attempts to slip through the sensor network, as well as providing fire solutions to intercept and destroy any mass drive projectiles we might fire at them from a safe distance."

Stephen nodded impatiently. He knew all that already. It had been discussed time and time again.

"They do, however, have one glaring weakness," Alice said. "A handful of very small objects—marines in combat suits, for example—might be able to get through the defences without being detected. Indeed, there is enough debris orbiting the shipyard that they might be mistaken for a few pieces of harmless space rock, if they are detected at all. If we got through the defences, we would be in a position to do a great deal of damage."

"If," Stephen said. "And what if you get caught?"

"We would be killed," Alice said, emotionlessly. "Battlesuits are tough, sir, but they can't stand up to weapons designed to kill starfighters and starships. However, I believe the plan has a reasonable chance of success. We'd certainly have a clear shot at their shipyard and do a great deal of damage."

"Perhaps," Stephen mused. He hadn't considered sending in the marines. "Have you done anything like this before?"

"We did sneak around the Clarke and Hamilton Yards, sir," Alice told him. "The operation was a complete success."

Stephen's eyes narrowed. "How come I have never heard about this before?"

Major Parkinson cleared his throat. "Perhaps I can answer that, sir," he said. "It was decided, at the time, that the outcome would not be commonly advertised. Security procedures were tightened up considerably after the results of the first exercise were finalised and future attempts to penetrate the yards were frustrated. However...it was felt that sharing the data would give our enemies ideas."

"And instead it gave *you* an idea," Stephen said, nodding to Alice. He had to admit it was a neat solution, although it would need some modification. The aliens needed to be distracted to keep them from realising that their shipyard was being infiltrated. "They may not see you coming. But... you would still be taking an immense risk."

"I am aware of the dangers," Alice said. "I volunteer for the mission. And I believe that most of my old platoon will volunteer too."

"We will all volunteer," Major Parkinson said. "We know what is at stake."

"We all do," Stephen said.

He looked at the display, thinking hard. It was risky, but it was also better than anything else he'd been able to devise for himself. And if it failed, he could extract everyone—apart from the marines—and make a run back into Alien-3 or Alien-1. It was worth a try.

"We'll have to distract them," he said, putting his earlier thoughts into words. "Let them think that we are an invading fleet, poking around the edge of their system. They'll come after us and miss you in the confusion."

"As long as you keep the range open," Major Parkinson pointed out. "You'll have problems if they overpower you."

"True," Stephen agreed. *Problems* was understating it. They'd be blown out of space if one of those battleships got into firing range. Even starfighters and smaller ships would be a major headache. They'd just have to do the best they could—and hope. "We can keep the range open as long as necessary."

"Yes, sir," Alice said. "It would keep them moving their defences around.

They'd definitely have trouble keeping track of what they're doing."

And if you're wrong, you'll be dead before you know it, Stephen thought. It was a gamble, like everything else. This time, the marines wouldn't even have the flimsy protection of a stealth shuttle. *And we will never know what happened to you.*

He felt a pang of guilt, which he ruthlessly suppressed. Compared to the prize, compared to the chance to take out the shipyard before it could finish the ships on the slips, the marines were expendable—and they knew it. But he didn't want to send them into a danger he couldn't share...he shook his head, tiredly. He'd just have to get used to making such decisions, time and time again. At least this time there was a very definite prize to be won.

"Major, select a team of volunteers and make sure they are armed and prepared for the mission," he ordered. "I'll brief my senior officers, then make preparations to distract the aliens from seeing you coming from the other direction. You may have to be transferred to one of the destroyers—or *Yuriy Ivanov*—so you can be inserted properly."

He paused. "You'll still be in those suits for hours. Are you sure you can cope?"

"I was in one of those suits for a week, sir," Alice said. "I can't say I enjoyed it, but I survived. A few hours will not be fun, sir, but we will survive."

She smiled, rather wanly. "It can't be as bad as the Conduct After Capture course. That was *terrible.*"

"Yes, it was," Parkinson agreed.

"Very good," Stephen said. He found himself liking Alice. Up close, it was hard to believe that she was infected. Perhaps he was just being paranoid. But it was a kind of paranoia, he told himself firmly, that was entirely justified under the circumstances. "Good luck, both of you."

"Thank you, sir," Alice said. "We won't let you down."

CHAPTER TWENTY-NINE

"THIS PLAN IS UTTER MADNESS," the *zampolit* muttered once again, as they stood outside the airlock hatch. It felt as if he'd made the same complaint several times in a row, ever since they'd been briefed on the British plan. "They're sending us to our deaths."

"Not precisely true," Captain Pavel Kaminov said, keeping his own doubts carefully hidden under a dour mien. The British plan was daring, but not insane. "We should be able to break contact and escape if we're spotted."

"*Should*," the *zampolit* repeated.

Pavel resisted the urge to say something cutting that would probably end up with him in his own brig, awaiting a show trial and unceremonious exile to the *gulag*. Or simply having his throat cut one night. His family connections were strong, after all, and anyone as politically-minded as the wretched *zampolit* would know that the show trial might not be as showy—and the outcome not as preordained—as usual. There was a reasonable chance that the *zampolit*, not Pavel himself, would have the pleasure of watching trees grow in Siberia. But there would be at least one or two people amongst his crew with orders to put the *zampolit's* orders ahead of their legitimate commanding officer, if push came to shove. The *zampolit* might calculate that he had a better chance of surviving if Pavel died in deep space.

"The plan is sound," he said, firmly. "And we will do our part."

He smiled as he contemplated the British plan, even though he was irked *he* hadn't thought of it. Indeed, there was something about it that was almost *Russian*. The British and their allies would normally prefer to use missiles and projectiles, rather than risk lives...even if the lives, technically speaking, were cheaper than ultra-smart long-range missiles. But the technology to glide a missile through the network of sensors—and the haze of electronic noise—surrounding the alien complex simply didn't exist, as far as he knew. His crew hadn't been able to come up with any way to get a missile close enough to guarantee a hit, let alone put the complex out of operation for the foreseeable future. No, the British plan was the only option that offered a reasonable chance of success. He had every intention of doing everything in his power to make it work.

"As you say, Captain," the *zampolit* said.

Pavel kept his irritation hidden behind a blank mask that, he suspected, fooled the political commissioner as little as the man's constant air of superiority fooled him. The man had been smart enough to have the discussion somewhere other than the bridge, at least, but his constant nagging and questioning couldn't be good for morale. Pavel was the ship's commanding officer, yet he had no way of knowing which way his crew would jump if the *zampolit* defied him openly. The *zampolit* was not popular—it had been only a few days ago that he'd confiscated an illicit bootleg of an American pornographic movie and ordered its owners flogged for corruption—but he was powerful. His backers would support him even if they disliked him. They couldn't afford to let a *zampolit's* authority be called into question.

His wristcom bleeped. "Captain," his XO said. "The British shuttle is docking now."

"Very good," Pavel said, as he heard a dull thud on the other side of the airlock. Everything was standardised these days—his airlock could have been switched out for one of *Invincible's* airlocks without difficulty—but it was the first time his ship had played host to a British stealth shuttle. The craft were cumbersome, even if they were hard to detect. And costly as hell. "Open the hatch."

He felt his thoughts darken as the hatch slowly started to hiss open. The stealth shuttles were relatively simple, compared to their bigger brothers, but they were also expensive. Mother Russia had only a handful, all reserved for FSB covert incursions. The navy hadn't been able to scrounge one up for Pavel, even though he'd done his best to argue for a stealth shuttle being assigned to his ship. It was galling to realise that Captain Shields would probably not even have to answer some hard questions if he managed to lose one of the expensive shuttlecraft. It was yet another reminder that Russia, for all of its size, was terrifyingly poor.

The *zampolit* straightened up as the first of the British marines stepped through the hatch. He—no, *she*—looked intimidating, although Pavel wasn't too impressed. He'd grown up with bodyguards who'd fought in Central Asia and the Middle East before they'd been called back to Moscow to join his close-protection detail. He reminded himself, sharply, not to underestimate the Royal Marines. His bodyguards might have claimed that the westerners were more reliant on technology than they should be, that they lacked the simple toughness of Russia's commando forces, but the marines had a long string of victories to their name. And, despite the *zampolit's* sniping, they'd done well on Alien-3. It wasn't as if Mother Russia hadn't had her fair share of covert deployments that had been blown wide open, forcing the commandos to retreat in a hurry.

Pavel smirked, inwardly, as the remainder of the marines followed, each one carrying a heavy-looking box. He hadn't bothered to tell the *zampolit* that the *female* marine had been infected, once upon a time. It would only have upset him. And the simple fact that the *zampolit* hadn't made a fuss about bringing her onto the ship suggested that he hadn't bothered to read the woman's file either. The British had stripped out all the classified information, naturally, but they hadn't concealed her experience during the *last* deployment to Alien-1. Pavel wanted to laugh. If nothing else, he could build a case suggesting that the wretched man had been negligent in his duty. It wouldn't be that hard. And it would give him a shot at the man's neck.

"Welcome aboard," he said, in careful English. It was the common space-faring language these days, something that didn't irritate him as much as it did his older peers. There were definite advantages to having to speak someone else's language during international operations. "I trust you are ready to deploy?"

The woman saluted the Russian flag, then Pavel himself. She ignored the *zampolit*, something that couldn't have done wonders for the man's blood pressure. Pavel found the thought a little amusing. No doubt he'd go read her file now. He just hoped the man wouldn't do anything stupid. Or, for that matter, that his *crew* wouldn't do anything stupid that would cause a diplomatic incident. The British woman was the *only* woman on his ship.

"Alice Campbell, Royal Marines," the woman said. She had a tough, almost masculine voice. Pavel suspected he would have thought her a man if he hadn't seen her. Her file had stated that she was a captain herself, although she hadn't mentioned it. That was standard when there could only be one captain on a starship at any one time. "Thank you for your hospitality, Captain."

"We'll do better on the return journey," Pavel assured her, as he motioned for the marines to head down to their temporary quarters. They weren't much, but they were better than anything they could expect to find on a troop transport. Pavel was *very* glad he hadn't followed his cousins into the Naval Infantry. "There'll be more to drink, for a start."

Alice smiled. "And we'll be happy to drink with you, when we get back."

Pavel keyed his wristcom as the hatch hissed closed behind them. "Mr. XO, take us on our planned course as soon as the shuttle has undocked," he ordered. "And make sure we give any alien ships or structures a wide berth."

"Aye, Captain."

Alice looked at him. "Do you anticipate any trouble in reaching the jump-off point?"

"No," Pavel said. His sensors had picked up more and more alien activity over the past few hours, yet the alien system was still incomprehensibly vast. They could have shaved an hour or two off the journey time if they'd wished, without running any real risk of detection, but he was feeling cautious. Better to be a live paranoid than a dead man. "We should be in position in five hours."

"Just long enough for the carrier to get into position herself," Alice said. "And then we'll see if we can put the cat amongst the pigeons."

"Quite," Pavel said.

He had to admire her nerve. The handful of women in the Russian Navy were all a cut above their male counterparts, and always ready to stab any would-be rapists with a knife, but he'd never met a female *commando* before. The FSB was an equal-opportunity employer, something that never failed to make him smile, yet most of the women it employed were spies rather than fighters. Alice and her men would be doomed if the operation failed. Pavel knew there was nothing he could do to extract them if they were detected before they were in position to do some serious damage.

The hatch hissed open, revealing one of the cargo holds that had been hastily emptied and converted into living quarters. Pavel watched Alice thoughtfully, wondering how she'd react, but she showed no visible reaction as she stepped into the compartment. A handful of ration bars had been placed on a rickety table, a collection of blankets had been placed on the deck, a portable chemical toilet had been placed against the wall...it struck him, suddenly, that a woman—a soldier—who was used to sleeping rough might see the compartment as a five-star hotel. *Pavel* had certainly felt that way when he'd gone home, after summer camp. The camp had been rough, very rough. He hadn't slept so badly since.

"I'll see you after you return," Pavel said. "Good luck."

Alice smiled for the first time. "Thank you, Captain," she said. "And good luck to you too."

The *zampolit* said nothing until they were outside the compartment and heading back to the bridge. "She's an arrogant bitch!"

"She can also snap you in half with both hands tied behind her back," Pavel said, dryly. "Can you name me a commando who wasn't convinced that they were the best of the best, if not the best of the best of the best..."

"Captain," the *zampolit* snapped. "This plan is not wise."

Pavel felt his temper begin to fray. "Then the risks will be borne by the British, and the British alone," he said. *Invincible* and her tiny handful of escorts would be exposed, when they activated their drones, but *Yuriy Ivanov* would be fairly safe. Pavel had already drawn up a private contingency plan for evading contact and slipping back to Falkirk if the remainder of the flotilla was destroyed. "We will have ample opportunity to escape if things go wrong."

The *zampolit* glared at him. "And if we are detected?"

"Then you will have ample opportunity to file a complaint when we get home," Pavel said, dryly. The odds of survival if they were detected by an alien battleship or fleet carrier would be very low indeed. He doubted the *zampolit* was smart enough to know it. "Or would you like to explain to the Kremlin that you refused me permission to cooperate with our allies?"

He smiled, openly. "I'd like those orders in writing, please."

"We will carry out our orders," the *zampolit* said. "But it is my duty to ensure that Russia's interests are upheld."

"Quite," Pavel said.

He allowed himself a moment of regret. If the *zampolit* had been stupid enough to put his orders into writing, Pavel would have had him over a barrel. Moscow would *not* have been pleased with a lowly political officer who dared to rewrite their orders without extremely good cause. He could have made the *zampolit* pay a huge price to have his words carefully removed from the datanet. Just having the man shut up would be more than enough.

"And now we go to start our mission," Pavel said, as the hum of the drives grew louder. "You may as well get some sleep. We won't be doing anything interesting for a good five hours."

The *zampolit* scowled. "Yes, Captain."

• • •

"You know," Monica said. "It strikes me that far too much can go wrong."

Richard gave her a sharp look. They'd spent the last two hours hastily reorganising the starfighter squadrons, once again, and then briefing the pilots on the operational plan. It was relatively simple—or at least *their* section of the plan was relatively simple—but Monica hadn't raised any concerns during the briefing. Richard wasn't sure if he should be relieved or annoyed. Monica had far more status to raise complaints, and have her complaints taken seriously by the other pilots, than someone who had only graduated a few months ago, but it was better to hash such issues out in the open than have them fester in their minds. She might not be the only pilot with concerns about the plan.

"What do you mean?" He glared down at his notes. They'd have only a few hours of sleep, in or out of the sleep machines, before they had to board their craft and wait for the order to launch. "If you have concerns…"

"Just one," Monica said. "What if they don't take the bait?"

Richard looked up at her. "They'll see an immense fleet bearing down on their shipyard," he said. He'd watched as the drones were hastily repro-grammed, then shot into space. "They *have* to take the bait."

"They'll *also* see a fleet that isn't going to be in attack range for several hours," Monica countered, dryly. "What if they decline to panic and merely fall back on the shipyard's fixed defences?"

"Then we're fucked," Richard said, after a moment. No *smart* defender would risk allowing such a large fleet into firing range, not when they had an entire shipyard to defend, but the virus was utterly alien. There was no way to know for sure how it would react when it saw the incoming fleet. "We'd just have to turn and retreat at high speed."

"Which would pretty much tell them that the entire fleet is composed of nothing more than sensor ghosts." Monica cleared her throat, rudely. "But then, when we only deploy four squadrons of starfighters, they're going to know it too."

"Probably," Richard said. It wouldn't be *unusual* for a fleet carrier to keep most of her starfighters in the launch tubes until the range narrowed sharply, trusting in the CSP to deal with any unexpected surprises, but their CSP would be strikingly understrength for a fleet that was supposed to include no less than *ten* fleet carriers. "But they would be foolish to let us close to attack range."

He smiled, grimly. The fleet of sensor ghosts also included three whole squadrons of battleships, each one bristling with mass drivers. They'd be shooting projectiles towards the enemy shipyard as soon as the shit hit the fan and it would only take one hit to do real damage. The closer the fleet was allowed to get to the shipyard, the better their targeting and the greater the chance of scoring a hit...if, of course, the ghostly fleet had been *real*. But could the enemy take the chance that the incoming fleet simply didn't exist?

No human commander would risk letting us close to a range where we could be reasonably sure of scoring a hit, Richard thought. *Their point defence isn't perfect—and mass driver projectiles are tougher than starfighters. But if they call our bluff, we'll have to fall back...*

"I know the logic," Monica said. "But what if you're wrong?"

"Captain Shields is confident that the plan will work," Richard said. He would have been surprised if the captain didn't have his doubts, although he'd done a good job of hiding them during the briefing. "And if it doesn't... at least we tried."

He gave her a droll look. "What's gotten into you?"

"Nothing," Monica said.

Richard felt his face heat as she smirked at him, just for a moment. He hadn't *meant* to say something that could be taken in two different ways, really he hadn't. And yet...he knew Monica was going to find a way to tease him about it, despite the difference in rank. He'd grown to depend on her over the last few months and that made it harder to be strictly professional.

"I just worry about the prospects for success," Monica said, letting him off the hook. "And I know you feel the same way too."

"There's nothing to be gained by doing nothing," Richard said, quoting one of his old tutors at the academy. The man had insisted that it was better to do something, even if it was the wrong thing, than allow the enemy to dictate the pace of events. "And if we fail...we will at least have tried."

He looked up at the holographic image of the alien shipyard. If it could be taken out, if it could be traded for *Invincible* and her entire flotilla… humanity would come out ahead. The shipyard was simply too productive. And yet, if they all died out here, the Royal Navy would never know what had happened to them. Richard had thought himself aware of the dangers, but now he felt ice congealing around his heart. They could all die out here…

Shut up, he told himself, savagely. *We have a war to fight.*

"Get some sleep," he ordered. He'd need Monica to be very well rested when they went into battle. He needed some rest himself. "We'll be launching in five to seven hours."

"Yeah," Monica said. "As long as they take the bait."

CHAPTER THIRTY

"CAPTAIN," NEWCOMB SAID. "The decoys are in position."

Stephen sat upright, rubbing his eyes. He'd ordered himself to get some rest, in his Ready Room, but he hadn't really *slept*. He should have gone to his quarters or used a sleep machine, yet that would have felt like he'd gone too far from the bridge. Getting out of a sleep machine in a hurry was no bed of roses. The last thing he wanted to do was command his ship with a banging headache. *That* would probably have led to disaster.

"Thank you," he said, as he stood. "Do we have an update from the Russians?"

"The last signal stated that they were in position and ready to proceed once they received the final *go* command," Newcomb said. "Should it be sent now?"

Stephen keyed his terminal as his steward entered, carrying a tray of coffee and biscuits. He took the mug with a nod and sipped it gratefully, his eyes flickering over the latest set of updates. Nothing *seemed* to have changed in the last few hours, but he knew it was an illusion. The time-delay—he cursed, once again, the boffins who kept swearing that FTL sensors were a technological impossibility—made it impossible to be *sure* that nothing had changed. It would take an hour for a signal from *Invincible* to reach *Yuriy Ivanov* and another hour, at least, for a reply to be sent back. Who knew what might have happened to *Yuriy Ivanov* in the meantime?

And who knows what might happen to us? Stephen munched a biscuit, wishing—once again—that he could share his doubts with *someone. We might be blown out of space before the marines get into position.*

He pushed the thought aside. "Send the signal," he ordered. "And then prepare to activate the drones."

"Aye, Captain," Newcomb said.

Stephen finished his coffee, mentally running through the plan once again. It was relatively simple. *Invincible*, surrounded by so many decoys that she'd look like the flagship of an invading armada, would blaze towards the enemy shipyard on a course that suggested she'd come through Tramline Four. The aliens, hopefully, would deploy their own ships to intercept her, giving the marines a chance...he shook his head, grimly. This time, at least, he'd be taking himself into danger too. He had every hope of evading the enemy capital ships, but their starfighters were another matter. *Invincible* might find herself in serious trouble if they screwed up the timing.

He pulled on his jacket, then turned and walked through the hatch and onto the bridge. The main display was brightly lit, showing the known and projected positions of hundreds of alien ships...each one capable of giving *his* ship a very hard time. There was no way he could avoid using the decoy drones, even though the virus had seen that trick before. *Invincible* alone simply wouldn't pose any significant threat to the system. The aliens had to see a very real threat boring in towards them at a significant percentage of the speed of light.

And while a human might be stampeded into doing something panicky, the virus might be a little calmer, he mused, as he took his chair. *It doesn't see the loss of thousands of host-bodies as a significant problem.*

"On my command, activate the drones as planned," he ordered. "And then bring up the main drives."

"Aye, Captain," Lieutenant-Commander David Arthur said. "The drones are on standby, ready to move."

"Good," Stephen said.

His lips twitched. If nothing else, the fleet's formation would *look* like an utter nightmare, the sort of thing that no sane spacer would condone for a second. Few commanders were *sanguine* about flying in close formation, not when the capital ships simply couldn't change course in a hurry. The odds of an accidental collision would be a great deal higher if the fleet had to evade a sudden enemy threat. Normally, the armada would be a great deal more dispersed. But now…hopefully, it would look as though he'd fucked up badly. The virus would have a chance to shatter his formation before he could turn and flee. It was just a shame that most of the ships it would think it could intercept and destroy simply didn't exist.

Unless I've outsmarted myself, he thought. *The virus might wonder why I was making such an elementary mistake.*

"Activate the drones," he ordered, after one last look at the timer. The Russians would have around twenty minutes of warning before they saw the aliens start to adjust their formations and—hopefully—set out to offer battle to the ghost fleet. It would be long enough, his operations staff had said. Stephen could only hope they were right. "And take us in."

He felt the seconds crawling by, each one feeling like an hour as the ghost fleet slowly altered course. It had to look *convincing*, of course, and yet part of him wanted to ramp up the drives and present the kind of threat that the virus simply couldn't ignore. But that would make it harder for him to withdraw, when the aliens came after him…at least without abandoning the drones. *That* would start alarm bells ringing all over the system. If the virus realised that it was being conned too early, it might start to wonder why.

And we have no way of deducing how it might react to…well, anything, Stephen thought. By human standards, the virus was insane. Or simply nothing more than an entity that reacted on instinct alone. There was nothing to be gained, surely, by starting a war with a coalition of alien races that might have the technological and biological prowess to defeat the virus at its own game. *If it can access our people's memories, it must know we're intelligent. Why doesn't it talk to us?*

He thought he knew the answer, assuming they *weren't* dealing with an unintelligent life form determined to propagate itself at everyone else's expense. The virus *had* to know that humanity—and every other intelligent race—would react with utter horror to its mere existence. There would be war. The virus hadn't mounted a massive invasion of human space, let alone the other races, but no one really doubted that there would be war. There was no point in trying to co-exist with an entity that turned its victims into host-bodies. One might as well try to co-exist with a race that saw humans as nothing more than food animals.

And if it understands us that well, he mused, *the thought of trying to open a dialogue probably never occurred to it.*

His mind raced. Some of the boffins were entirely certain that the virus wasn't *natural*, that someone had set out to create an ultimate weapon and succeeded all too well. They'd drawn up horrific scenarios, ranging from the virus evolving past whatever restraints had been gene-engineered into its system to an *intentional* leak that should have turned its original creators into an insect hive, with only a handful of people free to think for themselves. Given the horrors that humanity had tried to create during the Age of Unrest—diseases targeted on skin colour, for example—it wasn't unthinkable. And yet, it was utterly insane. There were so few pureblood humans of any ethnic group that a targeted virus would eventually spread to everyone else.

An alarm bleeped. "Captain," Arthur said. "They should see us now."

"Maintain course," Stephen said. The time-delay would shrink as the range closed, but...it was still frustrating. There were too many unanswered questions about the remainder of the system for him to be entirely happy with the situation. "Commander Newcomb, bring the ship to battlestations and launch the CSP."

"Aye, Captain."

Stephen watched, grimly, as the timer rapidly ticked down to zero. The aliens knew...what were they doing? Slowly, surely, a handful of icons started to glide away from the shipyard, heading straight towards the ghost fleet.

He sucked in his breath as the aliens started to launch dozens—no, hundreds—of starfighters, without waiting for the range to close. The virus was sending its pilots to their deaths. There was no way their life-support packs would hold out long enough to let them be recovered before it was too late.

"Realign the point defence," he ordered, quietly. If the virus considered the starfighters expendable, it wouldn't hesitate to order kamikaze attacks. "We have to expect ramming attacks."

"Aye, sir," Arthur said.

"And prepare to alter course on my mark," Stephen added. The starfighters had thrown an unexpected crimp into his plans, one he knew he should have anticipated. If they got close enough to attack, they'd be close enough to punch through the jamming and see that the ghost fleet was nothing more than a handful of decoys and sensor ghosts. "The CSP is to engage the starfighters when they come into range."

"Aye, sir," Newcomb said.

Stephen braced himself as the range closed. The aliens really *had* stuck a knife into his plans, one that was likely to prove disastrous. If they got too close...the CSP had to engage the enemy at extreme range, which would make it harder for the starfighters to rearm before the lighter alien ships entered engagement range themselves. It would be longer before the virus could bring its capital ships to bear, but the lighter ships would be more than enough to deal with *Invincible*. The only thing that might deter them from pressing the offensive was the ghost fleet...

"Mark," he ordered. "Reverse course now."

"Aye, Captain."

. . .

"They're coming in hot and heavy," Richard said. The alien starfighters were overpowering their drives, aiming themselves directly at the ghost fleet rather than preparing to engage the CSP. "We need to wipe as many of them as possible before they get into point defence range."

He smiled, humourlessly. The ghost fleet had many problems, including the simple fact that it had absolutely no point defence. It would be hard for anyone not to smell a rat when the ghost fleet didn't start pumping out plasma fire at incoming starfighters, particularly when it was clear that the starfighters had absolutely no intention of returning home. Worse, perhaps, the handful of *real* starships would be easy to identify. They'd be the ones actually fighting to save themselves from certain destruction.

"Engage at will," he ordered. "I say again, engage at will."

His targeting computers snapped to life, spitting lethal bolts of plasma towards the nearest targets. The aliens weren't just coming in fast, they were coming in straight lines...he blinked in surprise as the enemy starfighters practically impaled themselves on his plasma bolts. He'd expected to kill a few of them, but dozens? Half of his pilots made ace within the first few seconds. Was the virus so desperate to take out the ghost fleet that it was prepared to spend its starfighters so casually? Or did it have something else in mind?

"They must be robots," someone breathed.

"Worse than robots," Monica said, as the alien starfighters returned fire. "They're *hosts*."

"Take them out before they get smarter," Richard snapped. If there was one advantage to the alien formation, it was that they'd have a chance to blow through his pilots and rocket onwards to engage their targets while his starfighters reversed course and gave chase. It wouldn't be a problem, normally, but now it might just work in their favour. The range was already narrowing rapidly. "We don't want them getting any closer."

An alien starfighter shot past his craft—so close he thought he could have seen it with the naked eye—as a new wave of incoming starfighters entered the display. It looked as if the aliens had successfully drawn the CSP out of position, although—as he couldn't help noticing—it was unlikely they realised what they'd done. Unless, of course, they hadn't been fooled by the ghost fleet. They had to assume that the remainder of the human starfighters would be launching within the next few seconds. There was a difference between ensuring the pilots were as fresh as possible before they were shot into battle and leaving them in the tubes long enough to be blown out of space as their carriers came under attack.

But those damn starfighters don't exist, he thought. *And they will figure it out when those fleet carriers don't start launching their ships.*

"Squadrons One and Two, reverse course and cover the drones," he ordered. "Squadrons Three and Four, give the second wave a thrashing."

"Aye, sir," Monica said. "We'll give them a thrashing they won't forget."

Richard nodded as he spun his starfighter around on its axis and gunned the drives. The craft's acceleration curves were high, certainly when compared to a capital ship's, but they weren't fast enough to get them back into engagement range before it was too late. His sensors bleeped, informing him that the jamming was getting stronger in a desperate bid to keep the aliens from informing their comrades that the ghost fleet was nothing more than an illusion, yet there was no guarantee that it would succeed. A starfighter that passed *through* a starship it had tried to ram—and flew out on the other side—would be just as revealing as a single message. Richard and his pilots had a handful of codewords for emergency situations. He didn't dare assume that the aliens would be anything less than well-prepared themselves.

"They're aiming towards the rear of the fleet," he said, watching as the ghost fleet altered course. There was nothing wrong with the enemy tactics, if one accepted both their utter ruthlessness…and the existence of the ghost fleet. Ramming a starship's drive section might not be enough to destroy it, but it would certainly slow it down. Any enemy commander worth his salt would prefer to smash an enemy fleet piecemeal than risk engaging a unified body. "Hit them as hard as you can."

They have to place more value on their capital ships, he told himself, firmly. One of the ghost ships vanished, the nuclear warhead attached to the drone detonating as the alien starfighters pounded the illusionary hull with plasma fire. Hopefully, it would look as though they'd scored a lucky hit. *They won't throw battleships away like starfighters.*

297

And then an alien starfighter came into range and there was no more time for anything, but fighting to the death.

. . .

"They've taken out four of the drones," Lieutenant Alison Adams said. "The nukes detonated on cue."

"Good," Stephen said.

He opened his mouth to ask another question, then thought better of it. There was no point in demanding to know if the nukes had tricked the aliens into thinking they'd taken out a capital ship. Alison couldn't even *begin* to answer the question. A human observer would *want* to believe that he hadn't just expended nearly four entire wings of starfighters for nothing, but the virus had the distinct advantage of not having irate superiors and REMFs who needed to be placated. *It* wouldn't have to answer questions about its conduct, unless they'd grossly misunderstood its true nature. Was it a single entity, or a handful of separate mega-clusters of viral matter, or something so alien that its true nature could not be understood?

"The ghost fleet has completed the redeployment," Newcomb reported. "We're heading away from the target now."

"The rest of their fleet is in pursuit," Alison added. "Their lighter ships will be within firing range in twenty minutes."

"Tactical, engage with mass drivers," Stephen ordered. The odds of hitting a target were low—and the odds of a projectile shooting past its target and striking the shipyard were even lower—but it would keep the enemy focused on the ghost fleet. Hopefully, they wouldn't start to wonder why the entire fleet wasn't pumping out projectiles at a terrifying rate. "Aim for any visible command ships."

"Aye, Captain," Arthur said.

Stephen settled back in his command chair, forcing himself to wait as the battle fell into a brief lull. The alien starfighters didn't *appear* to have realised that the ghost fleet wasn't real, although that was a mixed blessing

298

now. *Invincible* alone could have made a reasonable attempt to outrun the alien fleet, at least until they realised that the assault carrier was *indeed* alone, but that would mean abandoning the drones. And that would be far too revealing.

So will the absence of plasma fire and missile launches, he thought. *Invincible's* crew had battened hundreds of missiles to their hull, ready to launch them into space when the time came, but they couldn't match the ghost fleet's presumed rate of fire. It wouldn't take a genius to start wondering why the human fleet was abandoning its best chance to score a victory—or at least discourage pursuit. *They'll see through the illusion sooner or later.*

"Captain," Newcomb said. "The CSP is requesting permission to return and rearm."

"Granted," Stephen said. The starfighters would be necessary, when the enemy fleet slipped into range. They'd have to mount antishipping strikes to slow the ships down before they had a chance to get too close. "And have them launched again as soon as they are rearmed."

We're going to have to do something about the shortage of pilots on this ship, he added silently, as the range continued to close. *Perhaps if we offer incentives to crewmen who practice flying starfighters...*

He sighed, inwardly. It wouldn't be anything, but a very brief solution. A crewman who spent an hour or two in the simulators each week would be no match for a pilot who spent half his time in the simulators and the other half flying an actual starfighter. But there might be no choice. The Royal Navy hadn't seen fit to assign additional pilots to his ship.

That will have to wait till we get back home, he thought, as the timer bleeped. *It all depends on the marines now.*

A moment later, the alien starships opened fire.

CHAPTER THIRTY-ONE

IF SHE'D BEEN FORCED TO BE HONEST, Alice would have said that she hadn't expected much from the Russians. The Russian commandos she'd met—and worked with—had been used to roughing it, simply because they didn't have the weapons, equipment and technical support she'd taken for granted. She'd expected cabbage soup and a brief nap on a hard metal deck, if she didn't have to fend off invitations from a handful of Russian crewmen who thought a female commando was either glamorous or a fraud. The Russians had a bad reputation, as little as it was deserved.

But instead, she'd been quite happy. The hold might not have been a five-star hotel, but it was more than suitable for the marines. She could have kicked herself for not bringing some MRE's—the Russian ration bars had somehow managed to taste worse than the ones hidden away in storage compartments on *Invincible*—yet it could have been a great deal worse. The promised marathon drinking session was likely to *be* worse, although it would have to wait until they made it back to the ship. If, of course, they *did* make it back to the ship.

She checked her battlesuit carefully, then clambered into the suit and made her slow way towards the airlock. The Russian ship was stealthy, with a cloaking device that should have kept any prowling alien starships unaware of her presence, but she wasn't designed to shoot troops into space. Alice rather suspected that any future mission into viral space, as the boffins

301

were starting to call it, would include a marine transport ship, if the head sheds didn't make the decision to simply blow up any alien world from orbit. Given how hard it was to eradicate the virus, Alice was inclined to agree. The bleeding hearts might call it genocide—and they might have a point— but the genocide had been committed long ago. There was nothing left on Alien-3, save for host-bodies and a swirling reserve of viral matter. It might be better for all concerned if the entire world was scorched back to bedrock.

A mere technological challenge, Alice told herself, as the airlock hissed open. There was a tiny delay as the Russians closed the inner hatch, then the outer hatch opened, revealing outer space in all its glory. *We can cope with it.*

Alice took a step forward, feeling her heart starting to pound as the sheer immensity of outer space battered at her mind, then gingerly thrust herself into the vacuum. The gravity field let go of her a second later. She allowed her suit's sensors to lock onto the nearby stars, providing a precise location check, then waited for the remainder of the marines to join her. It felt like hours before all twenty of her fellows were floating in space, linked together by pinpoint laser beams. She gritted her teeth, all too aware of the risks. On a training exercise, any marine who hit his emergency beacon would be sure to be roundly mocked by his comrades; if, if course, he wasn't unceremoniously ordered to retake the course from the beginning or simply booted out of training altogether. Here, triggering an emergency beacon would bring the aliens down on their heads. They'd have to hope that anyone who lost contact with the remainder of the platoon would be able to wait for pickup, rather than start screaming for help. A panic could—no, would—cost them everything.

They've been out in space before, Alice thought, although there *was* a certain comfort in knowing that you could scream for help if you wanted. *They know the risks.*

She checked the links one final time, then muttered an order. The suits oriented themselves, then triggered the gas jets. Compared to a standard EVA, let alone a starfighter, they were moving with glacial slowness, but—if they were lucky—it was that very slowness that would make them hard to detect. Any mass driver projectile would be coming in a great deal faster. The stealth coating they'd hastily applied to the suits was merely the icing on the cake. Alice sucked in her breath, then told herself to wait. The suit might be claustrophobia-inducing, but it wasn't as if she was short of entertainment. No one would complain if she used her HUD to read, or watch movies, until they entered attack range. It would keep her distracted from the reality of her situation.

As if anything could do that, she thought. She was a tiny person inside a tiny suit, gliding slowly towards the largest structure in known space. Their last set of briefings hadn't been particularly encouraging. Technically, the Hamilton Yards were bigger; practically, the Hamilton Yards weren't a single massive structure. *If we are spotted, we are dead.*

The hour crept by slowly, even when she risked dropping into a semi-hypnotic trance to keep herself from worrying too much. It was impossible to focus on a movie, let alone the book she'd been reading in a bid to catch up before the author brought out the *next* one in his immensely popular series. Alice wasn't too amused with its depiction of boarding school life—she'd endured sadistic teachers without the benefit of learning magic—but it did have its good side. She just hoped the character survived long enough to learn from her constant string of mistakes. *Alice* was sure *she* would have wrapped up the plot by now and gone on to declare herself empress of the magical world.

The timer bleeped, pulling her back to reality. She tensed as the enemy shipyard came into view, visible even to the naked eye. A glowing haze of lights, blazing out into space; it seemed impossible, somehow, that they would not be detected. And yet...and yet...there was no sign that they *had* been detected. Her passive sensors were reporting that the main body of the alien fleet was leaving, heading straight for Tramline Four—and *Invincible*. She shivered, remembering that it had been *her* plan—no matter how many refinements had been added by the captain and his officers—and then told herself to forget it. There was nothing she could do for the carrier now. She had to complete her side of the mission or everything would be for nothing.

She checked the laser links, then examined the alien security network in front of her. It was a complex web, a combination of active sensor pulses and electronic noise that might as well have been a solid fence. No missile or ballistic projectile could have slipped through without being detected and blown out of space by the automated weapons platforms, no matter how carefully it had been programmed. But *she* could see gaps in the defences. She braced herself, hoping that the gas jets would remain undetected, then slipped forward and glided through the first hole. She hardly dared to breathe as she passed close enough to one of the platforms to slap a nuke on it. It was almost a shame she didn't dare waste one of the four tactical nukes she was carrying. The marines followed her. No messages were exchanged as they slipped into the shipyard. They didn't dare risk being detected.

Up close, the structure was almost unimaginably huge. It was a giant spider-web, perhaps one that had been built in zero-gravity. There was little rhyme or reason to its design, as far as she could tell. It looked as if the aliens had slapped shipyard components together at random, with only a handful of concessions to efficiency. The giant vessel slips themselves were at the bottom, allowing the ships to be ejected rapidly once they were completed. She wondered, morbidly, if the aliens produced *everything* on site. A human designer would never have accepted the risk—a shipyard slip was actually the *least* important part of the design—but an alien might have other ideas. Perhaps they'd put efficiency, or their concept of efficiency, ahead of everything else.

And they have good reason to put faith in their defences, she thought. The virus probably didn't even have the concept of independent action, let alone tiny strike teams that could operate without orders from their superiors. *A conventional attack would be immensely costly even if it succeeded.*

She glided towards the nearest structure and landed, neatly, on the metal hull. It was dotted with struts and devices, none of which seemed to be active sensor nodes. She ducked down as the remainder of the marines joined her, linking their suits together physically. There was no point in taking the risk of using laser links here, even though—theoretically—they were completely undetectable. The slightest hint of electromagnetic disruption might give them away.

"I'll hit here," she said, once the suits had compared notes and built up a complete image of the shipyard. "Glen, you're with me. Everyone else, here are your assignments."

She looked down at the metal below her boots, wondering if it was starship-grade armour or something lighter, something they could cut through with their tools. She was tempted to test their theory about using scent to mark them as infected host-bodies—they'd brought the first bottles along, just in case—but it was too great a risk. She had no doubt that the virus would pervade the air inside the shipyard. And, with no natural light within the shipyard, it would be able to spread everywhere. It would notice a handful of host-bodies that weren't responding to its commands and react, somehow. She doubted they'd enjoy its reaction.

"Let's move," she said.

The virus was still redeploying its forces, she noted as they crawled down the structure towards the shipyard slips. Tiny craft—she assumed they were worker bees—were taking up position at the edge of the perimeter, ready to intercept any ballistic projectiles that might happen to come screaming out of the dead night of space. She had to admit that the virus wasn't doing a bad job of preparing for attack, even though all its preparations were focused on the wrong threat. A conventional attack might have been a far bigger disaster than they'd assumed.

Hammersmith touched her back, his suit's systems linking to hers. "Look down there," he said. "My sensors say it's a production node."

Alice was tempted to agree. The virus seemed to be *definitely* producing everything on site. She felt a hot flicker of contempt as they reached the node, then found a convenient place to place the first nuke. If they were right, it would do a great deal of damage; if they were wrong, it would still disrupt operations for weeks or months to come. The virus would have to spend a great deal of time looking for any other surprises the marines might have left behind. She grinned behind her helmet as they slipped down the strut, heading for the shipyard. The battleship taking shape below them, insofar as the term had any meaning in the alien structure, would never leave its slip. It would certainly never have a chance to meet human ships in war. She carefully selected and primed the second nuke as they reached the open hull, placing it neatly within the giant ship. The interior armour might save the ship from complete destruction—up close, she was starting to think that the virus had made faster progress than she'd assumed—but it would still take a long time for them to get the ship online. Hopefully, the war would be over before the battleship could take flight.

Assuming they don't scrap her and start again, she thought, as they started to make their way back up the strut. *We have to hope they don't have many more of these places.*

She shivered at the thought, then froze as she spotted movement making its way *down* the strut. Aliens? Or humans? They looked humanoid, but that proved nothing. Three of the races the virus was known to have overwhelmed were humanoid. She watched, silently confirming that they weren't wearing battlesuits, then led Hammersmith into the nearest hiding place and waited. Normally, she would have jumped any guards they couldn't evade—she'd actually stolen a uniform she'd taken from a guard she'd knocked out and used it to get into a secure area—but she doubted she could make it work on the alien structure. God knew that putting on a suit full of viral matter—*active* viral matter—would be incredibly stupid, even if she *did* smell right. The virus would infect her again and that would be the end.

Hammersmith tapped her arm. Alice followed his gaze and frowned. Two more figures were working their way towards them. A security patrol? Had they been rumbled? Or was it just a coincidence? The aliens didn't look armed, although that proved nothing. Their suits could have enough embedded weapons to fight a small war. She looked at Hammersmith, holding up her fingers to signal to him. They had to move, now. She led the way around the strut, moving from shadow to shadow as they tried to evade contact. The suits were hard to see, in the darkness, but the human eye was attracted to movement. The alien eyes might be the same. She tried to think of a plan as they reached the lower half of the production node and continued to head upwards. Were they being chased?

They rounded a corner—and walked straight into another pair of aliens. Alice didn't hesitate; she lunged forward, her knife already protruding from her suit, and stabbed the lead alien in the chest. The monofilament blade slid through its suit like a knife through butter, suggesting that the aliens *hadn't* been watching for them. Hammersmith killed the second, pushing the body against the metal hull. Thankfully, the aliens were wearing magnetic boots. Alice pushed hers into a convenient hiding place, then led the way around the structure. If they were lucky, they might just be able to find a place to stash the other two nukes before they linked up with the remainder of the marines.

Unless one of them got caught, Alice thought. *She* would have flooded the entire structure with searchers, if she'd discovered aliens poking around her shipyard, but the virus might have different ideas. It might already have infected a captured marine and was waiting patiently for answers. *At least the rest of us would have a chance to escape.*

She allowed herself a moment of relief as they finally reached the RV point and counted heads. She'd brought twenty marines to the party; twenty marines greeted her, their faces hidden behind their helmets. She checked their suit telemetry before she relaxed completely, knowing that the suits would hide any signs of physical distress. Or, for that matter, someone else who might have knocked out a marine and taken their suit for themselves. She had her doubts about the virus's ability to slip a ringer into their party, but she knew better than to assume it couldn't. Thankfully, the marines were alive and well.

"Time to go," she said. The nukes were already counting down to detonation, but—if someone stumbled across them—they'd detonate ahead of time. "Let's move."

She felt uniquely vulnerable as she launched herself back into space, gliding out towards the lurking Russian ship. There were too many worker bees flying around for her peace of mind, even if they were still focusing on threats from the ghost fleet. *Invincible* had planned to hurl projectiles towards the shipyard, but it was starting to look as though they'd either failed to get anything through the enemy ships or that they were being forced to reserve all their weapons for their own defence. She steadfastly refused to think about the other possibilities as she glided out of the shipyard, careful to leave with as much care as they'd entered. The last thing she wanted was to alert the aliens to her presence, particularly now. One solid blow from a hammer would be enough to put a tactical nuke out of commission.

They passed through the outer edge of the defence line without incident, much to her relief. She pulled up the timer as soon as they were clear, watching the remaining seconds ticking away. The aliens would have no idea what had happened—she hoped—but they were about to know they'd been kissed. Her lips curved into a smile as the first nuke detonated, followed rapidly by the others. The shipyard disintegrated in a blaze of light. She felt her smile grow wider as she realised the aliens must have stored dangerous—and explosive—materials within the structure. There was a perfectly good reason most human shipyards were spread out. It kept a disaster in one slip from spreading to the rest.

Success, she gloated. It didn't matter if they were killed now. They'd taken part in an operation that would be remembered as long as the Royal Marines endured. Their names would go down in the record books, along with the marines who'd fought in wars from the very beginning. *Everyone will remember us now.*

She chuckled, alone in the darkness of space, and then turned her attention back to her HUD, reopening her book until they reached the RV point. There was nothing else to do. The mission was over. The mission was over and it had been a complete success. And it had been her idea. She'd like to see anyone try to keep her off the active duty roster now she'd planned and carried out the greatest covert operation since the commando raid on Tehran, back in 2056.

And if they try, she thought, *they won't have a hope. How can they question my loyalty after this?*

CHAPTER THIRTY-TWO

"CAPTAIN, THE ENEMY SHIPS HAVE OPENED FIRE," Lieutenant-Commander David Arthur reported, grimly. "They're firing long-range missiles."

Well, that answers that question, Stephen thought. *We know they have long-range missiles now.*

"Stand by point defence," he ordered. "Prepare to engage."

He cursed under his breath, savagely. The situation had just changed again, changed beyond repair. The ghost fleet would be exposed within minutes, if it hadn't been exposed already by the alien starfighters. The absence of any point defence fire from the drones would be all too revealing. It didn't matter, in the end, what had happened in the alien shipyard, if the plan had succeeded beyond his wildest dreams or failed spectacularly. He had no choice. It was time to run.

"Tactical, disperse the ghost fleet to absorb as many of the incoming missiles as possible," he ordered, coolly. It was unlikely the enemy would be able to retarget their missiles—the time delay between the launchers and the missiles themselves was increasing with every second—but it was well to *try* to maintain the illusion as long as possible. The virus would certainly have a second shot at *Invincible* when it realised that she was the only real capital ship in the ghost fleet. "Helm, ramp up our speed to full emergency power."

"Aye, Captain," Lieutenant-Commander David Arthur said.

"Aye, Captain," Lieutenant Sonia Michelle echoed him. She sounded nervous. Full emergency power would give them their best—their only—chance to put enough distance between themselves and the enemy to slip into cloak and vanish, but it would put a *lot* of wear and tear on the drives. If they lost more than a handful of drive nodes, their speed would fall faster than the government's approval ratings. "Full emergency power, aye."

Stephen nodded as his ship quivered around him. The enemy missiles didn't appear to be any faster than humanity's—it was good to know that he'd trained his crews to face far more dangerous threats—but they didn't *look* as if they were going to lose power and go ballistic before they entered his engagement envelope. He watched the projections as the computers sought to determine which, if any, missiles were targeted on *Invincible* herself. It looked, very much, as if the aliens had decided to try to cripple as many ships as possible, rather than simply blow them out of space. It would give them their best chance at taking one or more of the ships intact.

And then they infect the crews, he thought, as the lines started to converge. Four missiles were aimed at *Invincible*, nowhere near enough to break through her point defences...but it didn't matter. There were enough of them to reveal that *Invincible* alone had point defence, which would draw enemy fire like moths to flame. A long-range battering match might work in Stephen's favour, but—as the range closed—his ship's defences would steadily be ground down to powder. *And then they try to board us.*

"Engage the missiles with point defence as soon as they enter engagement range," he ordered, grimly. On the display, the enemy were launching another wave of starfighters. They *had* to have realised that most of the ghost fleet wasn't real. The absence of a far larger CSP—and antishipping strikes—was a dead giveaway. "We'll have to sacrifice the drones."

He smiled, humourlessly. The beancounters were going to be *pissed*. He'd launched over a hundred expensive drones into space, including some of the most advanced decoy systems in the navy's arsenal. Collectively, they'd probably cost the Royal Navy more than *Invincible* herself. There were probably people back home stupid enough to believe that he could have saved the drones at the cost of his ship, even though he'd never have been able to return the drones to the homeworld. It was the sort of dumb idea that could only come from someone with no experience in the real world. Thankfully, the Admiralty generally insisted that flag officers had to have spent some time on a bridge before they were allowed to direct operations.

Which is probably why we suffered so badly during the First Interstellar War, he thought, sourly. *No one had any real experience of interstellar warfighting because no one had any opportunity to get any experience.*

"Missiles entering engagement range in ten seconds," Arthur said. "Long-range scans indicate that seven missiles have gone ballistic."

"Track them anyway," Stephen ordered. It was unlikely that the burnt-out missiles would pose any threat, but it wouldn't be the first time the virus had surprised him. Admiral Webster's latest generation multistage missiles were *designed* to burn out, or at least to give the *impression* that they'd burnt out, before the next stage activated. The virus was firing at extreme range, but it could have scaled up the concept enough to bring the ghost fleet well within its engagement envelope. "And engage them if they come too close."

"Aye, Captain," Arthur said. "Point defence engaging...now."

Stephen leaned forward as the point defence opened fire, filling space with deadly plasma bolts. Three of the four missiles vanished within the first ten seconds, picked off effortlessly; the fourth missile tried to evade, just for a handful of seconds, before it too was picked off. It would be a long time before anything less than a full salvo of missiles would pose any serious threat to a capital ship, he thought, but that wasn't the problem. The enemy didn't have to punch through his defences on the first try to know they'd stumbled across the human command ship. And if they threw another salvo like that...

He gritted his teeth, torn between grim amusement and growing concern as the enemy missiles expended themselves on the decoy drones. He didn't give a damn about penny-pinching by REMFs who put hardware—expensive hardware, to be fair—ahead of his crew, but every lost drone weakened the illusion still further. He'd had the drones tipped with nuclear warheads, stripping his arsenal to the bone, in hopes of convincing the virus that it actually *had* killed a number of capital ships, yet he doubted that particular illusion would last for long. A human enemy would *want* to believe that it hadn't expended a vast number of very expensive missiles for nothing. The virus might be more sceptical of exaggerated kill claims.

And if we were fighting a human enemy, he thought with a flicker of amusement, *we'd be delighted that we'd caused them to waste so many missiles.*

"Captain, they've taken out forty-seven drones," Lieutenant Alison Adams said. The sensor officer sounded grim. "We've lost a third of the ghost fleet. The remainder probably look more like sensor ghosts now."

"Understood," Stephen said. The jammers were doing their best to confuse the issue, but he'd lost a handful of jammers too. It wouldn't be long before the illusion was completely shattered, if it hadn't been shattered already. "Continue to..."

"Captain, they've launched another spread of missiles," Arthur snapped. He wouldn't have interrupted if it hadn't been urgent. "They're targeted on us!"

Stephen nodded, shortly. The illusion was gone, then. "Reprogram the drones to decoy as many missiles as possible away from us," he ordered. He didn't hold out much hope, but there was no point in trying to preserve the remaining drones. Even if he had time to recover and refurbish them, he was damned if he was slowing down. "And stand by point defence."

"Aye, Captain," Arthur said.

"Their timing is good," Newcomb muttered, through the intercom. "Their starfighters will be on us shortly after the missiles."

Stephen nodded, curtly. It looked as if the *first* salvo—and his mind boggled at the thought of expending so many long-range missiles when the odds of scoring a hit were so low—had been intended to give the enemy a chance to pick out the real ships from the decoys. The idea of any *human* officer signing off on such a strike, unless fuelled by utter desperation, was absurd; the virus, it seemed, had taken the cost in stride. The nasty part of his mind wondered if he shouldn't propose that strategy to the Admiralty anyway, in the hopes of the beancounters having a collective heart attack. They wouldn't be able to interfere with the military's operations any longer…

Except we don't have an infinite supply of money, he reminded himself, dryly. *The economy was already in pretty bad shape before this war came along.*

"Order the CSP to cover us as long as possible," he said. The missiles alone weren't a serious threat—*Invincible* would be able to pick most of them off before they entered their engagement range—but combined with the starfighters they would be able to do a considerable amount of damage. "And warn the damage control teams to focus on the point defence."

"Aye, Captain," Newcomb said. "The damage control teams are being briefed now."

His voice betrayed none of the doubts Stephen knew his XO had to be feeling. There was no way they could rebuild the point defence network, if it took a major beating, in time to save themselves from more missiles. The *third* strike—and he was beyond being shocked at the possibility of a third strike—would be effectively unopposed as it closed to engagement range. And then his armour would be ripped away by nuclear strikes and bomb-pumped lasers.

"Very good," Stephen said. The aliens seemed to be holding their lighter units back, now they'd established that *Invincible* was effectively alone. It made little sense, although he supposed the virus might prefer to expend missiles rather than starships and host-bodies when it had a war on its hands. Even a destroyer took upwards of six months to build…and that assumed that the builders cut as many corners as possible. "We're still putting some distance between ourselves and their capital ships."

The display changed, rapidly. "Captain, the enemy shipyard has exploded," Alison said, as more reports flowed into the datanet. "The marines did it!"

Hah, Stephen thought. He had no idea—yet—if the marines had survived, or if they'd been forced to detonate their tactical nukes to avoid capture and infection, but they'd done a great deal of damage. *It doesn't matter if the virus kills us now. There's no way it can inflict enough damage to make up for the lost shipyard.*

He forced himself to calm down. The shipyard was poorly designed, by human standard, but it was still a vast and heavily-armoured structure. They knew precisely nothing about its interior design, yet the analysts had pointed out that the virus would probably have built a great deal of internal armour into its design. It would be embarrassing if an *accident* caused a chain reaction that blew the entire structure apart. A nuke detonating inside *Invincible's* hull would do a great deal of damage, but it might not be fatal. The shipyard might have been designed along the same lines.

"Check with the long-range probes," he ordered, stiffly. "How much damage did they do?"

"Unclear as yet, but pretty bad," Alison said. "I think they took out most of the shipyard slips, sir, but at this range we have no way to be sure. We'll have to wait for the updates."

And hope we didn't just inflict a great deal of cosmetic damage, Stephen said. He told himself, sharply, not to believe what he *wanted* to believe. He'd studied war throughout the ages. It hadn't been uncommon for advanced missiles and warheads to be expended on fake airfields and decoy ships. Hell, he'd used the drones to lure the enemy fleet out of place and then force the virus to waste hundreds of missiles on expendable targets. *And too many people believed the strike reports because they wanted to believe them.*

"Enemy missiles entering engagement range," Arthur warned. "Point defence going active…now."

Stephen put the enemy shipyard out of his mind as he concentrated on bare survival. The virus had updated its targeting packages, damn it. It must have launched a handful of drones with the first strike, relying on their sensors to pick holes in the illusions and isolate them from the *real* ships. It wasn't a tactic he'd seen before, if only because it was rare for so many long-range missiles to be launched in a single salvo, but he had to admit that it had paid off for the virus. Only seventeen missiles were tricked into expending themselves harmlessly on the drones.

"The ghost fleet is gone," Alison reported. "We lost too many drones to maintain the illusion."

"Switch them back into standard decoy mode," Stephen ordered. "Try to convince them that we're altering course."

He shook his head, grimly, as the missiles closed in on his ship. The virus seemed to be hesitating—its starships were actually *reducing* speed—but it was far too late to recall the missiles, even if it had *wanted* to do anything of the sort. Dozens of missiles died, blinking out of existence as they were struck by plasma fire or railguns; a handful made it through the defences, slamming into his armour or firing bomb-pumped laser beams into his hull. Stephen kept his face impassive, even as his ship writhed in pain and the damage started to mount. The bastards were aiming for his drive sections...

They must have got a very good look at us, he thought. The alien sensor probes might be better than he'd thought. Or the virus had managed to interrogate one of the infected personal on Alien-1 before they'd been recaptured. Or the missing Russians had been forced to talk. *They had a very good idea where to aim their strikes.*

"Drive Nodes Four and Five are down," Sonia reported. "Drive Node Seven is badly damaged and needs to be replaced, urgently. Its power curves could collapse at any moment. We'll have to reduce speed to make repairs."

"Continue on our current course and speed," Stephen ordered. Sonia wasn't *wrong*—they *would* have to reduce speed to make repairs—but if they tried to slow down now they'd be dead before they could complete the work and accelerate again. "Commander Newcomb, have engineering rig up the secondary drive nodes."

"Aye, Captain."

Stephen braced himself as the alien starfighters threw themselves into the attack, ignoring the steadily weakening CSP as they pressed the offensive as hard as possible. A handful of starfighters rammed—one of them missed Drive Node Seven by bare meters—but the others concentrated on weakening his point defence as much as possible. Stephen gave thanks to God that the range was steadily increasing, even though Drive Node Nine was *also* starting to show signs of problems. A *third* salvo of missiles, even at such extreme range, might have smashed through his remaining armour and blown his ship to atoms.

"They're redeploying, sir," Alison said, quietly. "I think they're trying to fan out and protect the shipyard."

Or what's left of it, Stephen thought. A human commander might keep up the chase, in hopes of destroying *Invincible* before she could break contact and flee, but the virus presumably had different ideas. It would need to recover all it could from the remains of the shipyard before it was too late. It would also have a chance to take out the marines before they could link up with the Russians and escape, but there was nothing he could do about it now. The marines were on their own. *We have to concentrate on our own escape.*

A dull rumble ran through his ship as another starfighter rammed into the hull. Alarms sounded, a second later. The bastard had targeted his ship perfectly, Stephen noted. It hadn't done any significant damage, not compared to the missile strikes, but it had weakened part of *Invincible's* armour plating. The next set of strikes would find it easier to inflict major damage to the hull. But, as the enemy steadily redeployed their forces, it was starting to be clear that there wouldn't *be* a major strike. It looked as though the virus wanted to wear *Invincible* down rather than destroy her in a single blow.

They need to know what we know, Stephen thought. It would be true of humans, at least; he was fairly sure that the virus, too, understood the importance of gathering and collating intelligence. *And that means capturing and infecting the entire crew.*

"Redeploy the drones," he ordered, as the alien starfighters started to draw away from his hull. They had an opportunity, a very brief opportunity, to break contact and escape. "I want them programmed to scatter our sensor images as much as possible so we can slip into cloak without being detected."

"Aye, Captain," Alison said.

"Activate them on my command," Stephen added. "Tactical, take us straight into cloak as soon as the drones go active."

"Aye, Captain," Arthur said.

Stephen nodded. It was a gamble, but he was running out of ideas. "Commander Newcomb, recall the starfighters. They are to be rearmed and prepared for immediate launch if we fail to give them the slip."

"Aye, sir," Newcomb said. "They will also have to reorganise their squadrons. They're down to half-strength."

I should have noticed, Stephen thought, glumly. He'd known that starfighters were inherently expendable, certainly when compared to *Invincible* herself, but it still hurt to know he'd lost so many people. They'd died under his command and he didn't even know their names. *And* he didn't have time to look them up, not now. He'd have to write letters to their families, afterwards, and he knew nothing about them. *The survivors won't even get a personalised letter.*

"Captain, the drones are in place," Alison reported. "We're ready to decoy them away."

"Activate the drones," Stephen ordered. "Tactical, take us into cloak."

"Aye, sir."

CHAPTER THIRTY-THREE

"ARE WE GLAD TO SEE YOU," Alice said, as she removed her helmet. "We thought we'd missed the RV point."

Captain Pavel Kaminov inclined his head, politely. "We had problems getting to the RV point ourselves," he said. "You threw a stone into the hornet's nest...that is how you say it, isn't it? They deployed nearly a hundred starships to look for us."

Alice nodded. A British citizen would probably talk about throwing rocks into a wasp's nest, but the principle was the same. She'd done that as a little girl before her grandmother had reproved her for bullying creatures that were much—much—smaller than herself. The wasps had looked nasty, she'd thought at the time, but she'd taken the point. There was nothing honourable about throwing rocks at their nest.

"I'm glad you made it," she said. Her uniform was sweaty—and smelly enough to embarrass her, even though she was used to bedding down with the men. "What now?"

"Now we get out of here," the man behind the captain said. He hadn't bothered to give a name, which was a pretty clear indication that he was the local political officer. The *zampolit*, if she recalled correctly. Her Russian wasn't bad, but it wasn't perfect either. The man certainly looked like a *zampolit*. He had the indefinable aura of a sneak, combined with a prissiness

319

that made her want to slap him. She rather doubted he knew the meaning of the word *fun*. "We risked our ship to pluck you out of space."

"We're already sneaking sun-wards," Captain Kaminov said, calmly. "There's no reason to think we will be detected in the next few hundred hours."

He smiled at Alice, who smiled back. She had to admit he *looked* good, although her sister would probably have thrown up her hands in horror. Captain Kaminov might not be classically handsome, but he had an aura of command—and a great deal of nerve—that she found impossible *not* to admire. He'd certainly taken a considerable risk in bringing his ship to the RV point. Alice's suit had tracked enough alien starships to be fairly sure that the Russians wouldn't have a hope of escape, if they were detected. It was sheer luck the aliens hadn't located the marines.

They might not have realised just how small we actually were, Alice thought. A missile—or a sensor probe—would be considerably larger than a marine, even a marine in an oversized battlesuit. *And they probably didn't recalibrate their sensors to find us.*

"You'd better get a wash," Captain Kaminov said. "And then you are welcome to join me and my officers for a celebration."

"If we get out alive," the *zampolit* grumbled.

"We will," Alice said. She saw the *zampolit's* eyes go wide as she spoke in Russian. It was enough to make her roll her eyes in a manner that would have gotten her in trouble at boarding school. Hadn't the man read her file? She'd been encouraged to learn Russian, as well as French and Chinese. It was useful for combined operations not to have to worry about language barriers. "We have drinking to do."

The *zampolit's* eyes narrowed, but he said nothing as the marines were escorted back to their sleeping quarters. Alice had to smile at his back. Every Russian she'd met had been a heavy drinker, despite frequent anti-drunkenness campaigns by the Russian government. She vaguely recalled one of her briefers speculating that none of the campaigns were ever intended to actually *work*—a drunken population wouldn't be in a fit state to ask questions about who was really responsible for running the state—but she rather doubted the Russian government was that efficient. The Russian military was terrifyingly good—she gave them that much credit—yet the bureaucracy made the British Civil Service look like a paragon of efficiency. She'd heard her grandfather grumbling often enough about the National Farming Program to feel nothing, but contempt for the bureaucrats in Whitehall.

She stripped off the rest of her uniform and stepped into the shower, ignoring her nakedness. Her body felt unpleasantly dirty, as if she'd spent days—rather than hours—in the suit. How long had it been? She closed her eyes as the warm water cascaded over her body, running through the calculations in her head. The hypnotic state made it hard to be sure, but she was fairly certain that they'd been in the suits for nearly thirty hours. They were going to have problems with hypnotic lag for the next few days. She had no doubt that Major Parkinson would force them to overcome it as quickly as possible.

Assuming he's still alive, she thought. She'd seen hundreds of ships heading towards the incoming fleet, the incoming fleet that didn't exist. The virus might have overrun and destroyed *Invincible* by now, with no one on *Yuriy Ivanov* aware of it. *I might be the senior surviving officer in the system by now.*

She finished washing herself quickly, reluctant to spend too long in the shower when her men needed to wash too, and headed back into the next room. Hammersmith was bending over his carryall, his face grim. Alice had no trouble guessing what he'd seen. They'd done a good job of placing the bags against the wall in a manner that suggested they'd just been dumped there, but they'd been careful to note *precisely* where the bags had been. It looked as though someone had taken the opportunity to search the bags while the marines had been on deployment, someone who knew precisely how to minimise the odds of being detected. The *zampolit*? Or one of his men?

Not that it matters, she thought, as she opened her carryall and removed her spare uniform and underwear. They'd been ordered to be careful what they took with them, even though the Russian ship was not hostile territory. *What did they find? Nothing, but Royal Marine-issue underwear and clothes.*

Her lips quirked at the thought as she dressed rapidly. The Russians would have learnt nothing from the carryalls, unless someone had been careless. Very careless. She found it hard to believe that *any* of her people would be so careless. They knew, better than anyone else, the dangers of leaving something behind that an enemy might be able to turn into action-able intelligence. They'd even had their eReaders searched before they'd been permitted to upload them into the suits. Somehow, Alice doubted the *zampolit* had learnt anything useful from his poking and prying. Perhaps he'd be in trouble for wasting his time.

There was a tap on the hatch. Alice glanced around to make sure her team were either relatively decent or out of sight, then opened the compart-ment. A young officer, barely out of his teens, stood there, his eyes drop-ping towards her chest before he brought them up rapidly. Alice snorted, inwardly. He had to have been disappointed. Stellar Star might have an impressive chest size that owed more to cosmetic surgery and computer manipulation than an accident of birth, but *her* breasts had shrunk during basic training. She'd certainly never bothered to have them expanded once she qualified. It was easier to be taken seriously as a woman in the military if one *didn't* look like someone from an absurd porn movie. The Russian might have mistaken her for a *man*.

"Ah…um…Captain Kaminov would like to see you in the conference room," the Russian stammered, finally. His English was oddly-accented. He didn't seem to know what rank he should give her. She couldn't be called *captain*, but she could neither be promoted nor demoted either. "And as many of your men as wish to join you."

"We'll be along in a minute," Alice assured him. She looked back. A handful of her men had lain down to sleep, without even bothering to change out of their clothes, but the remainder looked willing to follow her. As long as she was leading them to the nearest pub, of course. "Just give us a moment."

She gathered her men, those who weren't trying to sleep, and led them down the corridor and up a ladder. *Yuriy Ivanov* didn't seem to have intra-ship cars, something that surprised her even though she knew the Russian starship was an order of magnitude smaller than *Invincible*. She hadn't seen anything like it since she'd served on a destroyer. But the Russians presumably had their reasons. An intership car could turn into a death trap if the ship was heavily damaged. She smiled as she was shown into the conference room, which appeared to have been turned into a drinking parlour. The tables were covered with bottles of clear liquid. Alice guessed, from the smell alone, that it was vodka. A Russian officer was sitting beside the table, strumming an instrument Alice didn't recognise. He was humming a song she'd heard before, in Central Asia. She'd been told it was officially banned.

"Welcome," Captain Kaminov said. The *zampolit* was standing behind him, holding a glass without sipping from it. "We appear to be clear, for the moment."

Alice allowed herself a moment of relief. "How clear are we?"

"Clear enough that we can risk getting drunk," Kaminov said. He held out an injector tab, which she took. "But if we do run into trouble, we will have to sober up in a hurry."

"Ouch," Alice said. She understood the precaution—if the ship was attacked, the command crew would definitely have to sober up in a hurry—but it wasn't something she wanted to use if it could be avoided. She'd used injector tabs herself, back when she'd been a teenager sneaking out to the nearest pub. Throwing up several pints of craft beer was *not* her idea of fun. "Should we be drinking now?"

"Eat, drink and be merry, for tomorrow we may die," Kaminov said. "And besides, we have to celebrate the success of your mission."

Alice sighed, but took the glass he offered her anyway. It was an attitude she'd seen before, during joint operations with the Russians. She'd wondered, at the time, if heavy drinking affected their efficiency, but it seemed the Russians had ways to cope. Besides, half of Kaminov's senior officers were missing. She guessed they were the ship's designated drivers.

Kaminov would probably have some hard questions to answer, if the ship *was* attacked, but he'd taken a string of reasonable precautions. She just hoped his superiors would see it that way.

She took a sip of the vodka—it tasted so strong that she guessed it had been produced onboard ship, rather than transported all the way from Earth—and did her best to answer the captain's questions without giving too much away. Kaminov seemed to think that the shipyard was definitely out of commission, to the point where the virus would find it cheaper to build a whole new shipyard from scratch than try to repair the old one. The *zampolit* was much less impressed and worked hard to pour cold water on the whole idea. They simply didn't know, he said again and again. Alice, who'd seen the nukes go off, had no doubts. The shipyard had been so badly damaged that it would be years before any new ships came off the production line.

"But we still don't know how badly we hurt them," Kaminov mused. He was on his fifth glass, but somehow he still seemed perfectly lucid. "If they have a dozen systems as...industrialised as this one, they will still be able to smash us to rubble."

"There will be a long and hard fight," the *zampolit* said. His face was flushed and his nose had gone red. "But the size of our country will work for us and eventually we will triumph."

Which is pretty much Russian military doctrine, Alice reminded herself. The Russians had always been more...fatalistic than their western counterparts. It gave them an advantage, of sorts. They were used to soaking up immense casualties—and losing vast tracts of land—and continuing the war anyway. *But against the virus, how can their orthodox doctrine hope to stand?*

She felt a chill that had nothing to do with the cold air. The human race was infinitely better prepared to face the virus than the poor natives of Alien-3, but it was still going to be a long and hard fight. The virus was just too powerful to take lightly. She had a sudden vision of hidden redoubts in Siberia or Alaska or other places the virus would find it hard to take root, at least at first. But orbital bombardment would be more than enough to put a stop to any organised resistance. She had no illusions about what would have happened if the Tadpoles had managed to gain control of Earth's high orbitals. The virus would have all of their advantages and more besides.

And the Tadpoles are our allies now, she reminded herself. *They're just as much at risk as ourselves.*

The night—it felt like night, even though her wristcom insisted it was early afternoon—wore on. She drank enough vodka to get a pleasant buzz, silently thanking the genetic engineers for splicing increased alcohol resistance into her genes. They'd done it to protect the marines from other threats, she'd been told, but she rather suspected that keeping her from getting drunk was more useful at the moment. The Russians drank and sang and invited her to join a whole series of party games. Alice was just thankful that the Russians didn't seem to have invented some of the truly awful activities she'd seen during her first leave. Some of them had been disgusting.

"You're not telling me much about yourself," Kaminov said, hours later. Half the Russians and nearly all of the marines had departed to sleep it off. The *zampolit* was sitting in a chair, snoring loudly. Somehow, he managed to keep a glass in his hand. "You must have an interesting story to tell."

Alice shrugged. "There's not that much to tell," she said, shooting a wary glance at the *zampolit*. She wasn't sure he was actually asleep. "I was born in Britain, I grew up, I joined the Royal Marines...what more is there to tell?"

"And you passed one of the hardest commando courses in the world," Kaminov said, seriously. "You're not exactly typical."

"Perhaps not," Alice said. She allowed him to steer her out into the corridor and down to his cabin. "But I haven't joined the SAS either."

Kaminov lifted his eyebrows. "Is that a bad thing?"

Alice shrugged, again. "There were five women in the SAS, before the Troubles," she said, finally. "One of them was killed on active duty, during the Siege of Whitehall. Two others were...ah, *removed* after question marks were raised about how they passed Selection. And the other two retired shortly afterwards. Now...I might get to chance Selection myself, if they are sure they can trust me, but there would be no guarantee of passing."

She winced, inwardly. She'd read all the reports from the Troubles, all the position papers that had made it clear that standards had been allowed to slip for political reasons. She would have been more forgiving, she supposed, if she hadn't gone into combat herself. Lowering standards was a bad idea at the best of times, but it was a complete disaster when a soldier—male or female—was regarded as inherently inferior to his or her fellows because their training hadn't been *quite* so intense. And then someone had been killed. She wondered, morbidly, if any of the senior officers behind the scheme to allow women to join the SAS had ever been punished for their failings. Sir Charles Hanover had been Prime Minister at the time. It was possible.

"And yourself?" Alice turned the question on him. "What about your life?"

Kaminov smiled at her. "I was born to a military family with strong political connections," he said. "There was never any suggestion that I wouldn't go into the military myself. They would have regarded it as outright treason if I hadn't signed up on the day I reached adulthood. I joined the navy and climbed up the ranks until they made me a captain. And that is the whole story."

"Really?" Alice had to smile. She was sure he was leaving out all the interesting details. "And you *just* became a captain?"

"I'm young," Kaminov said. "I haven't even married yet."

"But you have to marry," Alice said. "Don't you?"

"In theory," Kaminov said. He let out a heavy sigh. "It wouldn't matter if I liked men instead of women. I have a duty to the motherland to marry and have children sooner rather than later. I'm surprised they let me put it off for so long."

Alice nodded. She'd heard the stories. Women in Britain were encouraged to have children ahead of anything else, but the Russians made it compulsory. They had no intention of seeing their population drop again. They'd come far too close to demographic disaster.

Kaminov smiled at her, then inclined his head towards the bunk. She knew what he wanted, all right. And she was tempted. It wasn't as if either of them were inclined to boast about their conquests. She wouldn't be putting her career at risk if she slept with him. He was probably in more danger than her. The *zampolit* would probably be annoyed if he realised that Kaminov had spent the night with a British woman. God alone knew what his family would think.

But that's his problem, she told herself, as he leaned forward to kiss her. Right now, her body was reminding her that it had been a very long time since she'd had sex with anyone. It was hard to find a suitable partner who would be discrete. *And if he wants to cope with it, that's his problem too.*

Grinning, she kissed him back. Hard.

CHAPTER THIRTY-FOUR

"WELL," CHIEF ENGINEER THEODORE RUTGERS SAID, two days after they'd broken contact with the alien fleet and sneaked out towards the edge of the star system, "it could have been a great deal worse."

"I believe you," Stephen said, dryly. He'd taken advantage of the down-time to call a full staff meeting in the conference room, rather than speak to his officers individually. "Just how bad *is* it?"

Rutgers tapped his console, bringing up a holographic display. "The enemy starfighters took out around two thirds of our point defence systems, Captain," he said. "We were damn lucky we got away when we did. We're replacing them now, but we don't really have any way to keep them from doing it again—next time. It's a standard tactic and quite effective. The real problem lies in our damaged armour and drive nodes. I have teams repairing or replacing them now, but they won't quite come up to spec. We need a shipyard."

"We wrecked the closest shipyard to us," Newcomb cracked.

Stephen nodded, feeling a flicker of pride. The reports from the probes had made it clear that the enemy shipyard had been smashed beyond repair. If the virus had been human, he was sure it would have been cursing its own failure to run *Invincible* down before she managed to break contact and escape. There was still no way to be *sure* just how much damage they'd truly done to the enemy's war machine, but it was hard to believe that they hadn't inflicted a major blow. Losing that shipyard had to hurt.

And we got the marines back alive, he told himself. *We were lucky the Russians managed to pull them out of the chaos before they could be wiped out by the aliens.*

"It wasn't as if they would have done the repairs for us in any case," Stephen said. "And the rest of the damage?"

Lieutenant-Commander Rebecca Wycliffe, CAG, looked haunted. "We lost twenty-five starfighter pilots in the engagement, bringing our total down to thirty. There is some indication that Flying Officer Falladine managed to eject, but we weren't able to locate her beacon before we retreated and, by now, her suit will have run out of life support. Not that there's any way to be sure. Our squadron rosters were shot to hell. Pilots were flying with whatever wingmen they were able to find before they were recalled to the barn."

Stephen winced. He'd never met Flying Officer Falladine, but if she'd been left to die alone in the inky darkness of space...he pushed the thought aside, savagely. There was no time to mourn, let alone wallow in guilt. He'd write a formal letter to her family later and hope they mourned her properly. He just hoped the aliens hadn't stumbled across her. It wasn't unknown for a lifepod to be mistaken for something more dangerous and swatted out of space before the enemy realised the truth, but the virus had a far worse fate in store for anyone who happened to fall into its hands. Flying Officer Falladine might have wound up as yet another host-body for the virus...

"Do what you can," he ordered, finally.

"Yes, Captain," Rebecca said. She looked pensive. "Wing Commander Redbird is reforming the squadrons now. However, we only have enough starfighter pilots to field two slightly-oversized squadrons. Redbird was suggesting that we conscripted everyone who has ever used a starfighter simulator to man our remaining birds."

Stephen hesitated, considering the matter. It wasn't as if it was a serious problem, unless Wing Commander Redbird wanted someone who was needed urgently elsewhere. In theory, he could operate his ship with thirty men…although he'd better pray he didn't suffer any damage that required a damage control team. *Invincible* had a large crew because it was impossible to anticipate just what demands would be placed on her manpower. Automation could only go so far.

"If he feels they have a chance of surviving their first mission, then he may put in a request for their services," Stephen said. "But I want them cleared with their department heads first. I can't afford to give him any damage control specialists."

"No, sir," Rebecca said. "We do understand."

Stephen looked at Parkinson. "And the marines?"

"In good health, sir," Parkinson said. "I think we've reached the point where we can clear Alice Campbell for a return to active duty. If she was still infected, she would not have allowed us to blow up the alien shipyard."

"I see," Stephen said. "And what does Doctor Watson have to say about that?"

"So far, nothing," Parkinson said. "But I think he will agree."

"If he does, then you have my permission to proceed," Stephen said. "If he raises an objection, however, she can wait until we return home."

Parkinson didn't look pleased, but he nodded. "I've assigned the remainder of the assault force to their bunks for a few hours of sleep, once they had a check-up. The Russians fed them poisonous levels of vodka, but nothing they hadn't already encountered in Plymouth or Colchester. There's no hint that any suits were breached, let alone that any of the marines were infected. I think the operation proceeded without a hitch."

"And we learnt that trying it with missiles wasn't likely to work," Newcomb added.

"Good thing we didn't try," Stephen said.

He took a long breath. "Realistically, we cannot continue with our mission. Do any of you disagree with my assessment?"

There was a pause. "No, sir," Newcomb said. "We took too much of a beating."

"And expended too many of our supplies," Arthur added. "I think we have to concede that we have done as much as we can, for the moment. The next engagement might ruin us."

"We still need to recon the other tramlines," Parkinson pointed out. "We know nothing about what lurks beyond three of the five tramlines in this system."

"No, we don't," Stephen agreed. "But we also have to face facts. We're no longer in fighting trim. The ship needs repairs and the crew, bluntly, needs a rest. It is my intention, therefore, to head directly to Tramline Four, cross into Alien-1 and return to Falkirk."

"Assuming the astrographers are right about Tramline Four leading to Alien-1," Newcomb pointed out. "They might be wrong."

"It's going in the right direction, sir," Arthur said. "And the gravity pulses match…"

"We only made long-range observations," Newcomb reminded him. "If we're wrong, Captain, we could find ourselves lost in space."

"If we're wrong, we simply head back through the star systems we've already explored," Stephen said. He held up a hand before anyone could object. "I understand the issues, but it is my decision. We set off for Tramline Four as soon as we've completed our repairs. Mr. Rutgers?"

"That will be around thirty-six hours," Rutgers said. "We have a clear picture of what we need to do now, sir, so we simply have to run down the schedule and hope for the best."

"Time enough to finish the game and beat the virus too," Newcomb misquoted.

"Drake may not have said that," Parkinson said. "And even if he did, he would have had to wait for the right tides before he took his ship out of harbour and onto the open sea. He might have felt that it was better to keep playing instead of waiting around and doing nothing."

"Perhaps," Stephen said, amused. "We'll leave as planned. Dismissed, gentlemen."

He waited for the room to empty, then sat back in his chair. Parkinson was right, in one sense. They hadn't learned anything like enough about viral space to satisfy their superior officers. But, at the same time, they *had* learnt a great deal *and* they'd dealt a significant blow to the aliens. The virus had been hurt badly. Civilian morale would improve, once they heard what had happened. Who knew? It might even broaden support for the war.

Not as if it would make much of a difference, Stephen thought. *We're fighting for our survival, not for...not for a tiny territorial gain that won't mean anything to the vast majority of the population. It doesn't matter if the population wants to fight or not. The virus wants to fight and that is all that matters.*

He sighed, then stood. There was no time for him to stand around, brooding. He had too much work to do. Traditionally, letters to the families of dead crewmen had to be written as soon as reasonably possible. He didn't want to write them, but he saw no choice. Besides, it would help keep his mind off their situation. He had no doubt that crossing Alien-1 was not going to be easy. The virus would be looking for them.

And if it finds us, we can kiss our asses goodbye, he thought. *It will do everything in its power to keep us from getting home.*

· · ·

"I think we've been here before," Richard said, as he opened Flying Officer Falladine's locker and started to empty the contents into a pair of boxes. "I have that feeling all over again."

"I know," Monica said. "I went out drinking with Helen, you know? It was before I was promoted and...well, you know."

"I know," Richard confirmed. He mentally ticked Helen Falladine's possessions off against a list. Five shipboard uniforms, twelve pairs of underwear, a couple of outfits that had probably been intended for shore leave... surely, she hadn't intended to wear a miniskirt onboard ship. And a selection of chocolate and datachips that would be distributed to the remainder of the squadron. "It doesn't seem like much, does it?"

He finished sweeping the contents into the boxes, then held out the first. "Do you think there's anything here she'd want to be sent back home?"

Monica quirked an eyebrow. "Didn't she say anything in her will?"

"Nothing about her possessions on the ship," Richard confirmed. Flying Officer Falladine had had a will, of course, but most of it related to her savings and a handful of personal possessions that she'd left behind on Earth. The bureaucrats at home would have to handle it, assuming they ever realised that Helen Falladine was dead. The only real section that concerned him was the standard clause transferring her shipboard possessions to her comrades. "No one was named as the primary beneficiary."

Monica smiled, humourlessly. "Does her squadron still exist?"

"I doubt it," Richard said. He dumped the chocolate on the table—they'd eat it during the wake—and put the remaining boxes on the bed. There were a handful of pilots who were near enough in size to their late comrade that they'd probably be willing to take the second-hand clothes. There was nothing like being in the military to appreciate the chance to pick up some extra outfits. "All the old squadrons are gone."

He moved to the next locker, checked the name against the list and opened it. Flying Officer Atkinson had been killed during the desperate flight back to *Invincible* before she cloaked, his death barely noticed in the chaos. *His* will had stipulated that the contents of a particular box, at the bottom of the locker, was to be sealed and returned to his family. He'd been quite clear that he didn't want the box opened, let alone examined. Richard hesitated, feeling as though he was betraying a friend, then opened the box. A black suit and a handful of unmarked datachips lay at the bottom.

Richard blinked. "What is that?"

Monica peered over his shoulder. "A modified VR suit," she said. Her fingers brushed the material, just for a second. "You put one on and you're somewhere—anywhere—else. I'd bet good money that the chips were recorded by his wife. Hugh was married, don't you know."

"He was a little young to get married," Richard commented. "What did he do? Knock someone up?"

"He might have done," Monica said. She smiled, dryly. "Do you want to honour his last request?"

Richard nodded and dropped the suit, datachips and the box into a sealed container. He was damned if he was sharing private material with Atkinson's former comrades, even if there was a very good prospect that they would never get home. He'd grant his subordinate what little privacy he could. It crossed his mind, just for a second, that they could be completely wrong about what was on the chips, but he resisted the urge to plug them into a datapad and see what they contained. He'd bent the rules quite enough over the last few hours.

They went through the remainder of the lockers without incident, collecting quite a haul of material to distribute to the surviving pilots. One of the dead pilots had had a bottle of scotch which Richard confiscated, unsure if it should be returned to the man's house or shared out once the ship reached Earth. The poor bastard would have been in deep shit if Richard had caught him with it, but there was no point in threatening to beast a dead man. He made a mental note not to mention the bottle to anyone. Flying Officer Swenson was dead. He was certainly well beyond punishment.

"You'll have to share it with me, unless you declare it," Monica said. "Or put it in the drinks locker."

"It can be kept until we get home," Richard said. "And then we can all drink it."

"Assuming that there are any of us left," Monica said. "What do we do then?"

Richard met her eyes. "We die, of course. What else can we do?"

• • •

Stephen looked down at his datapad, wishing for a drink. It wasn't something he'd wanted often—he'd seen enough people waste their lives to know *he* didn't want to go that way—but now…he took a sip of his coffee, cursing under his breath. It was never easy to write a letter of condolence, certainly not to the parents of a starfighter pilot he'd never seen. He certainly hadn't known much about her and her file, damn whoever had composed it, was no help. A handful of graduation dates, a couple of testimonials from training officers and very little else...certainly nothing he could use to put together a picture of Flying Officer Falladine's life and times. What had she done, when she wasn't flying starfighters? Had she been the life and soul of the party? Or had she preferred to sit in the ship's library and read eBooks? The file was absolutely no help at all.

No wonder Theodore Smith turned to drink, he thought, crossly. *How many people did he see die when that asteroid exploded?*

"Dear Mr. And Mrs Falladine," he muttered. His letter wouldn't reach the family first, unless so many serving men and women had died in the last few months that the military's bereavement service had collapsed completely. By law, the military was supposed to inform the family first— certainly before the media got hold of the news and started telling every- one—but it hadn't always been possible. "It is with very great regret that I must inform you that..."

He shook his head. That made no sense. The family would already know, wouldn't they? He scribbled a note to himself to check when the ship returned home. The military normally kept very good track of who had and hadn't been informed of a death in the family. He'd have to rely on the bureaucrats to ensure he sent the right letter.

"I had the pleasure of having your daughter under my command during Operation Drake," he mused, after a moment. How the hell was one meant to say *anything* when he didn't know the person in question? It would be a lot easier to write a letter for his XO's family. "I found her to be a brave and determined pilot who embodied the virtues of the military life, a pilot who eventually gave her own life so that others might live..."

And how pleased would I be, he asked himself, *if I got a letter like that about my son?*

He scowled. It had been expected that he would go into the military. The second son of an aristocrat *always* went into the military. He'd known the risks, but he'd also known that there was no way to get out of it. God knew he hadn't really *wanted* to get out of it. It was tradition. The cynics might wonder if the true reason behind the tradition was to kill off the second son before he could start eying the family inheritance with covetous eyes, but Stephen had always seen it as giving something back to the country that had been so good to him. And yet, had Flying Officer Falladine thought the same way? Or had she gone into the military to pay off her debts? Or forge a career? Or…he brought up her file again and skimmed it for clues. There was nothing, just as there had been nothing when he'd looked hours ago. Flying Officer Falladine was nothing more than a blank slate.

And I wouldn't want to know that my son might have died alone, without even the comfort of a quick death, he thought. *But we don't know for sure what really happened to any of the dead pilots. Did she eject—or did she die before she knew she was under attack? Or…*

His intercom bleeped. "Captain," Newcomb said. "The engineering crews have confirmed that we're ready to bring the damaged nodes back online. They think we should be able to return to full power within an hour."

"I'm on my way," Stephen said. He closed the file, promising himself that he'd get back to it as soon as possible. The parents *deserved* a personalised letter, even if it wasn't anything like as detailed as it should be. "Inform Mr. Rutgers that he can start powering up the drive nodes as soon as possible."

"Aye, Captain."

CHAPTER THIRTY-FIVE

"WELL," DOCTOR WATSON SAID. "You've had quite an adventure."

You don't know the half of it, Alice thought. If any of the marines had realised that she'd spent half the night with Captain Kaminov, they hadn't bothered to mention it to their fellows, let alone their superior officers. *It was a good night.*

She smiled at the memory. She'd seen Royal Marines—and Paras and Regiment men from Hereford—who were never short of female company, but it was a great deal harder for a serving female officer to find male companionship. Jeanette might insist that her sister should get married, sooner rather than later, yet Alice knew it wouldn't be easy to find anyone willing to live with her. Most of the men she knew were military officers—and those who weren't were either weak or intimidated by her. It wasn't fair, but it was true. The best she could hope for was a series of one-night stands that wouldn't outlast her leave.

Perhaps they should put that on the recruitment brochures, she thought, wryly. *Join the Royal Marines. See your relationship prospects blown out of the water.*

Her smile grew wider. It wasn't true and she knew it. The men didn't have any real trouble...she told herself, firmly, that she was obsessing, obsessing at the worst possible time. The doctor was watching her, no doubt scanning her face to divine her thoughts. She wondered if he'd deduced what she'd been doing, for a few short hours. *That* might be a problem. She hadn't broken any regulations, technically, but questions might be asked. It wasn't uncommon for soldiers on leave in foreign ports to be picked up by women who were more interested in pumping them for information than merely taking them to bed.

"It was just part of the job," she said, finally. She hoped the doctor hadn't noticed *just* how long she'd delayed answering. "And we completed it successfully."

Doctor Watson gave her a long look. "And how do you feel about that?"

"Pleased," Alice said. "We won. We damaged their war machine—we took out an entire shipyard. If they know what we did, doctor, they're going to have to waste a lot of effort making it impossible for us to do it again. And if they *don't* know what we did, which is possible, they're going to have to waste even more effort sealing up all the holes in their defences."

She felt a surge of vengeful pleasure. She'd made the virus pay for what it had done to her. The coldly logical part of her mind pointed out that the virus probably hadn't drawn a connection between her and the destroyed shipyard—it wasn't as if it would have cared if she'd indulged in a motive rant worthy of a supervillain—but it didn't matter. The infected men and women back home, the ones who were beyond saving, had been avenged. They would never know it…she sighed, inwardly. The hell of it was that the *virus* wouldn't know it either. It would just take the loss in stride.

"And afterwards?" Doctor Watson met her eyes. "Did you have a good time at the party?"

Alice kept her face expressionless. "I've seen worse parties," she said. It was true. She'd drunk herself senseless more than once when she'd been a teenager. The marathon drinking sessions she'd had after she'd qualified as a commando hadn't had quite the same zing. But then, she'd been a little more mature at the time *and* already marked down as a potential officer. "We got very drunk, but otherwise…it was just a party."

"And now you're back here," Doctor Watson said. "How do you *feel*?"

"Like getting back to work," Alice said. She was damned if she was going back to her cabin and sitting around doing nothing, not now. Her original bunk in Marine Country had probably been assigned to someone else, given that space was at a premium, but she could hot-bunk with another marine if necessary. "I just want to get back to it."

"We did a whole set of scans," Doctor Watson said. "The virus within your body remains inert, for better or worse. You seem to be perfectly safe."

"I could have told you that," Alice said, tartly. It was hard to keep her anger from leaking into her voice. "All I had to do was keep my fucking mouth shut."

The doctor nodded, slowly. "That is a point in your favour."

"It's more than *just* a point in my favour," Alice told him. "What the hell does the virus gain from letting us blow up a shipyard? Nothing! It could have taken out the entire flotilla and the loss rate would still be solidly in our favour. What could it *possibly* gain that would be worth the price?"

"We don't know," Doctor Watson said. "But just because we don't know the answer doesn't mean that *it* doesn't have an answer."

Alice sat back, remembering a particularly unpleasant sports mistress she'd had to endure at boarding school. The wretched woman had taken delight in toying with the girls, offering rewards to her favourites while denying them to others...Alice remembered sitting in front of her desk, waiting to hear a denial she already knew was coming. And now Doctor Watson was doing the same. She straightened up, reminding herself that she was no longer a teenager. There was no reason she couldn't file a complaint—or an appeal—if the doctor decided to deny her request to return to active service. Hell, she could demand a court martial if she wished. *That* would create all sorts of problems for the REMFs.

And problems for the marines too, she reminded herself. *It would certainly put the cat amongst the politicians.*

"There's no risk of infection, as far as we can tell," Doctor Watson said. "Or do you feel otherwise?"

Alice felt her lips twitch. Captain Kaminov might be in trouble if his *zampolit* realised he'd spent the night with *her*. She didn't know what rules and regulations the Russians had about foreign affairs—her smile grew wider at the terrible pun—but the *zampolit* might wonder if some viral matter had passed between them during their night of passion. Alice was fairly sure it hadn't, yet there was no way to know for sure. It had been a long time since STDs had been a serious problem. She had no way to prove that something *else* hadn't moved between them.

Perhaps we should have worn condoms, she thought. *But pregnancy wasn't a risk either.*

"I don't believe that there's any risk of infection, at least from me," Alice said, putting the thought aside for later contemplation. Captain Kaminov had known the risks. He could handle his own problems. "And, with all due respect, I wouldn't be here if you weren't fairly sure that the risk was minimised."

"True," Doctor Watson said.

He cleared his throat. "Major Parkinson and I have discussed your case in some detail. It has been generally agreed that you have handled yourself well, although you did spend six months in a secure facility where you had access to...*resources*...that are not available on *Invincible*. Your mental state is fairly good, all things considered; you don't seem like a person who is going to snap and go on a murder spree at any moment. And he would like to have you back."

Alice felt a rush of affection for the older man. Major Parkinson had gone out on a limb for her. He might even have put his career at risk, if his faith in her proved to be unfounded. A weaker man might have temporised, knowing—all too well—that Alice might not be in full control of herself. He knew her well, and he'd watched her during the deployment, but everything he'd seen might be nothing more than the smile on the face of the tiger. She might switch sides at any moment. And, if she did, Alice would bet half her savings that *someone* back home would place the blame squarely on her commanding officer.

There are times when it just doesn't pay to get out of bed, she thought. It hurt, more than she cared to admit. Her *father* had said that, before he'd killed her mother. *And times when people are too busy looking for scapegoats to get anything done.*

"So yes, you are cleared for active duty," Doctor Watson said. He held up a hand before she could say a word. "You will be watched, Alice; you *will* be closely monitored. If we have a reason to worry, something we can actually put our fingers on, you may be removed from active service once again..."

Alice barely heard him. She was going back to active service!

"I understand," she said, when he'd finished. "But the risks are quite low."

She was tempted to give him a hug. Instead, she stood. "I'll go back to Marine Country now," she said. "And thank you for your...assistance."

Doctor Watson stood. "It was little enough," he said. "And we still have to be careful."

Alice nodded. The boffins—and the engineers—had done everything in their power to ensure that the virus couldn't spread through the ship. A combination of enhanced filters and ultraviolet light alone was more than enough to stop the virus in its tracks, although she'd been given to understand that a number of other precautions had been taken. The virus was highly adaptable, and probably wouldn't have any trouble steadily overwhelming their vaccinations, but it didn't seem to be able to cope with their defences. It hadn't even managed to infuse itself into Alien-3.

Not that it matters, she told herself. *It had already overrun the native population and taken control of their world.*

"There will be no infection from me," she said, firmly. "And if I feel ill, I'll let you know."

The hatch hissed open. Major Parkinson was standing on the other side, waiting. Alice straightened up as she stepped through, snapping a salute. The older man looked her up and down for a long moment—she thought, just for a second, that he was going to aim another punch at her—and then nodded, curtly. Alice looked back, waiting for him to speak. Behind her, the hatch hissed closed again. It was a relief to know that the headshrinker was on the far side.

Although he's probably still watching me, Alice thought, with a flicker of irritation. She was used to a complete lack of privacy, but it still grated. *I wonder what he makes of our little stand-off.*

Major Parkinson smiled. "Welcome back, Alice," he said. "Stand at ease."

"Thank you, sir," Alice said. "It's good to be back."

"Said the Lunatics, when they discovered that Earth was no longer their home," Major Parkinson growled. He turned and led the way down the corridor. "You may have the same problem, of course."

Alice nodded, although she knew he couldn't see her. It was unlikely she'd ever be allowed to return to Earth, unless the doctors and boffins found a way to flush the dead or inert viral matter out of her body. It made her wonder precisely *where* she'd be allowed to go, if she reached the end of her enlistment. An asteroid settlement might be able to cope with her—an artificial environment would have no trouble ensuring that any infection was safely contained—but she doubted that many of them would be willing to take the risk. Perhaps she'd spend the rest of her days in a secure medical facility, having doctors poking and prodding at her until she finally cracked. Or maybe she'd see if her father—and his new wife—could find her an isolated mining settlement. The miners would be so glad to have her that they'd overlook any...*irregularities*...in her records.

Major Parkinson said nothing more until they entered Marine Country and walked into his office. Alice took a long breath, feeling as if she'd come home. The smell of sweaty men was weaker than she'd expected—she could *hear* the air filters as they worked to cleanse the atmosphere of anything that *might* be an alien cell—but it was still where she belonged. She took the rickety chair he offered, then accepted a cup of coffee. She knew she wasn't in trouble, or at least she knew she wasn't about to get chewed out by her commander for something that might or might not have been her fault, but she was still relieved to be offered the drink. Major Parkinson wouldn't have offered her anything if he was about to tear her a new asshole.

"I spoke to your subordinates on the mission," Major Parkinson said. "They all agreed that you handled yourself well, in the finest traditions of the service. There are no concerns about you returning to duty from them."

"Thank you, sir," Alice said. It was rare for junior officers, even marines, to be asked for their opinions of their seniors, but her situation was effectively unprecedented. If her subordinates had any doubts, they couldn't be allowed to fester. "Did they have anything *interesting* to say?"

"You will, of course, have to go back on the training roster from today," Major Parkinson said. "You've done well, Alice, but you've lost a great deal of muscle tone. Still within acceptable limits, of course..."

Alice winced, inwardly. She'd worked hard to regain her muscle tone, but...it had simply never crossed her mind that spending several months in bed would weaken her to the point where she had to struggle to go to the toilet on her own. It was *galling* to know that she'd been so weak that she couldn't walk from one end of the asteroid to the other, let alone complete a ten-mile forced march across Dartmoor or the Brecon Beacons. She had been so weak that a mere civilian could probably have overpowered her. There was no way, four months ago, that she'd have completed the entry requirements for commando training. She knew, without false modesty, that she'd come a long way. But she still had a long way to go.

And I will, she told herself, firmly. *I'll qualify if it's the last thing I do.*

"You'll have the next week to qualify," Major Parkinson said, as if he'd peered into her mind and read her thoughts. He might have done the next best thing. An experienced officer was almost always skilled at reading the men under his command. "You'll go into your bunk, with your rank in technical abeyance. Fortunately, you're still receiving the pay for your permanent rank. That could have been a bit of a headache."

"Yes, sir," Alice said. She hadn't been demoted, technically, but it could hardly be denied that she hadn't been carrying out her duties. It was hard to believe that the beancounters would garnish her pay, on the grounds she wasn't on active service, yet she'd met enough sour-faced accountants to believe it. Idiots. It wasn't as if the government's budget would be ruined by paying her salary. "But I'm not allowed to *use* my permanent rank."

"Not yet," Major Parkinson said. His lips twisted. "You'll still have to take orders from the sergeant."

Alice had to smile, even though the sergeant had forgotten more about the military than she'd ever known. "*That's* not going to be easy to explain."

"I'll write some bullshit into the logs," Major Parkinson said. "Captain Shields has signed off on it, in any case, so you're probably in the clear. It will be *me* who will have to provide a written explanation for any irregularities in the roster. Unless the shit really *has* hit the fan, back home. They won't care about you if missiles are crashing down in London and Plymouth has been burnt to the ground."

"No, sir," Alice said. It was easy to forget, sometimes, that they were still deep within viral space. *Invincible* was making her slow way towards the tramline, inching along rather than powering up the drives and running for her life. She took a sip of her coffee, reminding herself that sneaking out might be better than leaving a trail of electronic noise a blind man could follow. "We have to get home first, of course."

"And the paperwork can wait until we do," Major Parkinson said. He grinned, suddenly, as his datapad bleeped. "You'll be pleased to hear that your old comrades are waiting for you in the romper room. I think they want to welcome you back home."

Alice smiled and finished her coffee. "I look forward to it," she said. It wasn't entirely true—she'd been dunked in the duck pond when she'd been promoted to officer rank—but she would welcome almost any kind of hazing, if it meant she got a clean bill of health. "And sir...thank you for having faith in me."

"If I hadn't had faith in you, I would have had you rotated out before we left Earth for the first time," Major Parkinson said. His tone gave nothing away. "I had my doubts about you, just as I had them about everyone who was assigned to my command, but you proved yourself fairly quickly.

Everything that's happened since…it wasn't your fault. You didn't make bad decisions that led to disaster. I won't hold your problems against you."

But you wouldn't let me come back if you thought I couldn't hack it, Alice thought. *And how could I blame you?*

She stood, pushing her doubts aside. "Thank you, sir," she said. "I'll see you on the training deck."

Major Parkinson gave her a toothy smile. "Have fun tonight," he said. "And prepare to have your ass kicked tomorrow."

CHAPTER THIRTY-SIX

"LOCAL SPACE APPEARS CLEAR," the sensor officer said. "A little *too* clear."

Captain Pavel Kaminov held up a hand before the *zampolit* could start snapping at the unfortunate officer. The bastard had been stamping around like a bear with a toothache for the last two days, snapping and snarling at anyone unfortunate enough to earn his ire. Pavel had no idea what had gotten into the man, but he had too many other problems right now to care. Alien-1 was heavily defended. The last thing he wanted was to draw the virus's fleet onto his ship.

"Explain," he ordered. "What do you mean?"

"Long-range sensors show no trace of the alien fleet we saw when we passed through the system two months ago," the sensor officer said. "The orbital industries are still there, sir, but the fleet itself has gone."

The *zampolit* looked up. "Destroyed?"

"Perhaps," Pavel said, although he doubted it. The Yankee officer in command at Falkirk, two transits down the tramline chain, had orders not to attack the virus unless he believed that a full-scale invasion of human space was imminent. It was a great deal more likely that the virus had launched a full-scale attack instead. "Or they might have set out to wage war on us instead."

He turned to his helmsman. "Take us back through the tramline, then update *Invincible*," he said. There was nothing they could do about the missing alien ships. He had no way to know when the ships had departed, let alone if they'd reached Falkirk. "And then set course for the next tramline."

"Aye, sir."

· · ·

"That's confirmed, sir," Lieutenant Alison Adams said, thirty minutes after *Invincible* jumped into the alien system. "The alien fleet we saw has vanished."

"Either that, or they're lying doggo," Newcomb said. He stroked his chin, thoughtfully. "Or they were rerouted to Alien-4 after we went through Alien-3."

Stephen considered it for a long moment. The timing did work out, he supposed, but he doubted it. Alien-4 wasn't the sort of place that would be left undefended, even when there was no reason to believe that a war was about to break out at any second. It was far more likely that the Russians were right, that Admiral Weisskopf was already under attack…or, worse, that the combined fleet had already been destroyed. But there was nothing he could do about that now. They'd just have to wait and see what they found when they reached Falkirk.

"We'll continue on our current course," he said. "And we'll keep our eyes open for trouble."

He settled back into his command chair as *Invincible* inched her way across the hostile system. They'd added *days* to their transit time by coming through the tramline so far from the primary star, something that might come back to bite them now they knew the alien fleet had departed, but there had been no choice. His ship was in no state for an encounter with a flight of alien starfighters, let alone the fleet they'd seen the first time they'd entered the system. Better to take a few extra days to cross the system than be blown out of space.

The hours ticked by remorselessly. More and more data flowed into the passive sensors, each update convincing him that the war had well and truly begun. Alien-1's industrial base, already formidable, seemed to have doubled or tripled in the last two months...he would have liked to believe that the energy signatures were nothing more than decoys, but he didn't dare take it for granted. They had to assume the worst. And *that* meant assuming that there might be shipyards and industrial nodes that had yet to be located. They couldn't be taken out before they were located...

We'll have to get more survey ships up here, Stephen thought. *And then run a sweep through the entirety of alien-held space.*

An alarm sounded. "Captain," Alison said. "Passive sensors are picking up a...ah, something *fuzzy* dead ahead of us. It could be a masking field."

Stephen tensed as a blur appeared on the display. "*Dead* ahead of us?"

"Yes, sir," Alison said. "And it is coming *right* towards us."

Stephen felt his blood run cold. It *could* be a sensor ghost, an artefact of *Invincible's* cloaking device, but he didn't dare believe it. The live feed from the other ships indicated that they were seeing it too and *that* meant that it was more than just a random energy pulse that would be gone within seconds. And yet, if it was an alien ship—or a fleet of ships—how could it have located them? Stephen found it hard to believe that the virus could have pulled off a successful ambush...

Unless they were tracking us as we fled Alien-4, he thought, grimly. *There was so much sensor distortion during the final moments that they might just have managed to stick a cloaked ship on our tail. And then they planned an ambush in Alien-1.*

"Helm, alter course," he ordered, although he was fairly sure it was pointless. The masking field—if it *was* a masking field—was far too close for any hope of evasion. "Tactical, bring the ship to battlestations. Prepare to launch fighters."

"Aye, Captain," Arthur said. "I..."

The display suddenly sparkled with red icons. "Captain," Alison said. "They just dropped the masking field! I'm reading over two hundred small craft!"

They buggered up the timing, Stephen thought, as alarms howled throughout his ship. *If they hadn't launched the invasion, or whatever they did with the missing ships, they would have been able to meet us with battleships and fleet carriers, not gunboats and shuttles.*

His eyes narrowed. The alien tactics didn't make sense. And that meant…that meant that he was missing something. The virus could surely have put together a stronger blocking force if it wished. No, it had made a deliberate decision to use small craft. His sensors were picking up a handful of ships lurking behind the small craft—escort carriers, according to the warbook—but they could have deployed something bigger. Hell, it wouldn't have been difficult to get battleships and fleet carriers from Alien-4 to Alien-1 before *Invincible* crossed the tramline. They were up to something.

"Launch starfighters," he ordered. The alien craft were picking up speed, heading right towards *Invincible.* A handful were already launching missiles—standard missiles—at his ships. "Point defence, stand by to engage."

"Aye, Captain."

. . .

Richard braced himself as the starfighter was catapulted into space, cursing the timing under his breath. He'd had every starfighter pilot under his command in the simulators when the shit hit the fan, trying desperately to smooth the rough edges off before they actually had to follow their new wingmates into battle. He wasn't sure if the older pilots or the new ones, the ones he'd conscripted from the carrier's lower decks, were more of a problem. The latter had less to unlearn, but the former had spent too long in their old squadrons. It was hard to get them to work together as a team.

The alien craft closed rapidly, firing as they came. Richard scowled as his sensors updated, reporting that the alien gunboats carried multiple plasma cannons that were apparently capable of engaging multiple targets at once. They wouldn't have any blind spots, he thought; their main drives had been carefully configured to ensure that their enemies couldn't fly up their rear and blast them out of space before they could alter course. It was rare to see gunboats, certainly outside training exercises, but he had to admit they could be effective in combat. The virus certainly believed they could be useful.

"Engage at will," he ordered. The gunboats were one thing, the shuttles were quite another. Were they crammed with nukes? Or...he swallowed, hard, as he realised the truth. The virus didn't intend to destroy the carrier, it intended to *board* her. "I say again, engage at will."

A gunboat flashed past his starfighter, its weapons firing with a savage intensity that surprised him. Richard blew it away, snapping orders for the first squadron to concentrate on the gunboats while the second took out the shuttles. But there were so many of them...worse, the shuttles were armed too. He saw one of his pilots die because he'd made the mistake of assuming the shuttles were unarmed, giving the enemy crew a clear shot at his hull. There was no time to mourn. Richard killed a shuttle that strayed into his firing arc, then altered course as the remainder of the enemy craft blazed past him and roared towards their target. An alert sounded—enemy starfighters were inbound—but he ignored it. Right now, his priority was the shuttles. The starfighters would have to wait.

"Concentrate on the shuttles," he ordered. They might not be *that* dangerous to the starfighters, not compared to the gunboats, but they were still a major threat. "Don't let them get too close."

He gritted his teeth. *Invincible* was pumping out a hell of a lot of fire—and the shuttles were bigger targets than starfighters—but it was clear that *some* of them were going to make it to her hull. He just hoped they weren't packed to the gunnels with nukes—or antimatter. The boffins had been promising antimatter for decades. It would be just their luck if it had been the virus, rather than humanity or its allies, that had made the fatal breakthrough. A plasma bolt shot past him, coming from the carrier. He cursed, again. *Invincible's* point defence didn't have time to make *entirely* sure of its target before it took the shot. The risk of being killed by his own side was unacceptably high.

It can't be helped, he told himself. The Admiralty would hold an inquest if there was a fatal blue-on-blue, a starfighter blown to atoms by friendly fire, but he already knew what it would say. It had been a tragic accident, one of the tragic accidents that always happened during wartime; there was nothing anyone, even the finest officers in the navy, could do to keep it from happening again. *We'll worry about it later.*

"They're landing on the hull," Monica said. Her voice was grim. "Should we try to blow them off?"

"Yeah," Richard said. The enemy starfighters were getting closer. Worse, the gunboats and the shuttles were sweeping point defence weapons off the carrier's hull. It wouldn't be long before the next waves could land unopposed. "I think we have no choice."

He forced himself to think as he swept along the hull, waiting for the enemy shuttle to come into range. The aliens would have problems opening the airlocks, wouldn't they? Normally, they were designed to be easy to open—at least to allow anyone trapped on the outside into the airlock itself, if not to let them into the rest of the ship—but *Invincible* was on red alert and the airlocks would be sealed. Did they intend to use tactical nukes to blast their way through the armour? It would work if the nukes detonated under the plating, he figured, but it would also vent the compartments directly underneath the blast. *That* would put a crimp in the virus's plans to infect the ship. There was certainly no suggestion that the virus could survive in a vacuum.

Although we can survive for a few minutes in a vacuum, he reminded himself. His instructors had made it clear that it *was* possible, barely. They'd also said that, if emergency supplies were more than a minute away, the pilots might as well spend their last few seconds kissing their ass goodbye instead of trying to find a way to survive. *Maybe the virus can last for a few seconds too.*

A flare of white light caught his attention as the alien shuttle came into view. The craft was holding position above the hull, burning into the armour with a giant plasma torch...Richard stared, unable to help being impressed. The virus had taken a standard mining tool, one that could be found right across the human sphere, and turned it into a weapon. They'd seal the gash in the hull, then send the assault troops into the ship. Richard grinned, then opened fire on the alien shuttle. It exploded in a blinding flash of light.

"They're coming in hot," Monica said. "Sir?"

"Get them off the hull," Richard snapped. He'd assumed the aliens intended to board, but they could cause worse trouble simply by using their plasma torches to melt their way further into the ship. And *then* they could detonate nukes inside the armour. *That* would put *Invincible* out of commission for good. "Hurry!"

• • •

"They're trying to board us?"

"It looks that way," Arthur said. "They're trying to burn through the hull."

"Order the marines to deploy to stop them," Stephen snapped. His mind raced. They'd practiced counter-boarding operations, but never under fire. In hindsight, that might have been a mistake. Half his crew was qualified to operate plasma rifles and cannons, as well as handguns and gaussrifles, yet too many of them would be needed elsewhere. "And order Major Parkinson to draw reinforcements from the beta and delta crews, damage control crewmen excepted."

"Aye, sir," Arthur said.

Stephen swore under his breath as new alerts flashed up in front of him. The damage was mounting rapidly with each shuttle that made it to his hull, even if the wretched craft didn't last long enough to start drilling into the heavy armour. His point defence was already a mess, giving the aliens a clear window they could use to get their shuttles through his defences and onto his hull. The CSP was blowing them off the hull as fast as they could—new alerts appeared, warning him that the armour was starting to take heavy damage—but the enemy starfighters were forcing *his* starfighters to concentrate on defending themselves, rather than shielding *Invincible* from her foes. If the assault continued, it was almost certain that the aliens were going to force their way into his ship.

His fingers touched his console, bringing up a subroutine he'd never expected to have to use outside simulations. And yet, he'd forced himself to consider it as soon as he'd realised the true nature of the alien threat. The virus wasn't a signatory to any treaty that defined the proper and acceptable ways to treat POWs, even if they surrendered as soon as the situation became hopeless. No, there was no way Stephen could *merely* destroy his ship's datacores and render her nothing more than a giant hunk of scrap metal. He had to blow up the entire ship.

The situation isn't that desperate yet, he told himself. The self-destruct system was completely isolated from the remainder of the datanet. It was possible the virus could hack the datanet—the analysts had come up with some terrifying scenarios—but it wouldn't be able to deactivate the self-destruct once it was activated. *We have time to try to push them back out of the hull.*

He gritted his teeth. *Invincible's* bridge was at the very centre of the ship, surrounded by layers of internal armour. It would take time for a determined assault to make its way through the defences, even if the virus moved ahead of its host-bodies, infecting everyone it encountered along the way. Stephen would have plenty of time to trigger the self-destruct if it looked as if the virus was on the verge of winning. And yet, he couldn't help asking himself what would happen if he was wrong. The virus could *not* be allowed to overwhelm and capture his ship.

"Captain, they're on the verge of breaking through," Commander Newcomb reported. "I've had that entire section vented. The marines are taking control of the access hatches."

"Good," Stephen said. He was tempted to order Major Parkinson to swarm the compartment, to be ready to greet the aliens when they forced their way into the section, but he trusted the marine to know what he was doing. "And the reserves?"

"They're drawing weapons and armour now," Newcomb assured him, irritated. "The first squads should be ready in ten minutes."

Another fucking oversight, Stephen thought. He didn't blame his XO for being irritated. Naval crewmen normally carried sidearms during wartime—*Invincible* wasn't the first starship to be boarded by alien forces—but assault rifles and other heavy weapons were normally kept locked up in Marine Country. *Next time, we're going to have to distribute weapons long before the boarding action actually begins.*

A dull quiver ran through his ship. More alerts flashed up in front of him. Stephen studied the warnings for a moment, then dismissed them. Either they cleared the outer hull of enemy shuttles—and wiped out any boarding parties—or they died when the self-destruct was triggered. He'd worry about getting back home if they lasted long enough to drive the aliens away and make it through the tramline. He was starting to think that they'd have to kill every last alien craft to break contact.

"They're entering the ship now," Newcomb said. More alerts flashed up. "And they're pumping polluted atmosphere into the hull."

"Make sure everyone has a mask and a shipsuit," Stephen ordered. Thankfully, as far as anyone could tell, the viral particles couldn't be absorbed through the skin. A mask was enough to keep someone uninfected, as long as it wasn't ripped off. Hopefully, they'd be able to eradicate the virus without having to vent the entire ship. "And tell Major Parkinson..."

He shook his head. "Tell him to proceed as he sees fit," he said. There was nothing to be gained from micromanaging the marines. "And alert the remainder of the crew to be ready to repel boarders."

CHAPTER THIRTY-SEVEN

ALICE HAD NEVER REALLY *LIKED* THE SHIPBOARD armour, although it was better than wearing her BDUs or dress whites. It was heavy enough to make it difficult for her to move, particularly as it lacked the servomotors and exoskeleton of a heavily-armoured battlesuit, but—at the same time—it wasn't armoured *enough* to make up for the lack of manoeuvrability. There was certainly no way she could slip through a Jefferies Tube without getting stuck halfway to her destination, something that would limit her—and the remainder of the squad's—ability to take advantage of their greater knowledge of the ship's interior design. And it was hot, sweaty and thoroughly uncomfortable. She would sooner have worn her body armour over a standard shipsuit, gambling that she could tear off the armour if it became necessary for her to make a hasty escape. But Major Parkinson had ordered them to wear the shipboard armour and she knew better than to argue. The carrier had suddenly become a combat zone.

She hefted her rifle as she stared at the airlock, uneasily aware that an alien boarding party was flowing—perhaps literally—into the carrier. The internal sensors on the far side had practically been *melted* when the aliens had burnt their way into the hull, but enough had survived to show movement heading towards the airlock. Alice was relieved they hadn't been *in* the compartment when the aliens started their attack—they would have been melted along with most of the internal sensors—but she couldn't help finding it a little frustrating. It was impossible to say, with any *real* certainty, just what was happening on the other side of the airlock. The aliens might be preparing to blast their way further into the ship...or they might be stacking tactical nukes into a neat little pile before they hit the detonator. Alice found it hard to believe that the virus hadn't considered the possibility. It certainly didn't want *Invincible* to make it back home after blowing the virus's shipyard to hell.

And if it didn't think of using nukes before now, we certainly showed it the way, she thought, wryly. *It must have worked out what we did to the shipyard now.*

The airlock seemed to bulge, then exploded outwards into a shower of fragments. Alice ducked instinctively, hoping and praying that the pieces of makeshift shrapnel wouldn't hit one or more of her comrades. Holding the enemy was going to be difficult even *before* someone was hurt, forcing her to choose beside abandoning him to the virus or taking the risk of dragging a wounded man down the corridor to the *next* set of defences. She gritted her teeth as a shower of grenades followed, half of them exploding with terrifying force. The remainder showered droplets of sickly yellow liquid everywhere. Concentrated virus, she guessed as alerts flashed up in her HUD. It didn't *look* like an acid attack.

"Here they come," Hammersmith said. "Captain?"

"Fire on my command," Alice said. She hefted her rifle, hoping the aliens would have as much trouble seeing in the darkened compartment as an unenhanced human. "Let them come closer first."

The aliens advanced forward, moving in a pattern that made her think of untried troops who hadn't—yet—learnt to read a battlefield. One group advanced forward, covered by the second group...it wasn't a bad tactic, but in a confined space it could be disastrous. She smiled coldly, one hand unhooking a pair of grenades from her belt as she saw two blobs following the humanoids. The infected aliens would have done a better job if they'd tried to charge the human defenders, rather than give them time to recover from the grenades. There just wasn't enough cover to make standard tactics workable.

She hurled the grenades, aiming at the blobs. "Now," she snapped, as the grenades detonated. "Take them out."

The humanoids stumbled, then started to fall. The follow-up units opened fire a second later, blasting plasma bolts down the corridor...seemingly at random. Alice wasn't sure quite what they thought they were targeting, but it didn't matter. They'd be resuming the offensive soon enough. She silently tried to calculate how many boarders might be coming their way in the next few minutes, but it was impossible to come up with a definite answer. She'd flown in assault shuttles that could carry upwards of a hundred troops and stealth shuttles that were barely large enough to carry a single platoon. Besides, more alerts were popping up in front of her eyes all the time. It looked as if the virus was trying to swarm the defenders.

She ducked, again, as more grenades flew towards her position. The deck shook a moment later, the internal armour directing the blast up and down the corridor. Alice thought fast, then snapped out a series of commands as she threw another pair of grenades back towards the enemy. The marines slipped back, leaving a handful of IEDs in their wake. She heard them explode as the marines reached the second line of defences. There was no way to know what, if anything, they'd hit...but she was sure they'd hit something. She just hoped it would be decisive.

But it won't be, she thought. *We need an edge.*

The aliens kept pushing their way into the carrier, spreading out as their boarding parties started to link up. Alice heard Major Parkinson barking orders as the marines combined with naval reservists to form new barricades, knowing that it was only a matter of time before they'd be spread too thin to keep the aliens from penetrating down towards the most vital areas on the ship. She wondered, as she felt another dull *thud* echoing through the ship, if they might as well press the rest of the crew into service. It wasn't as if they'd have much of a ship left if they didn't.

"They're regrouping, if the internal sensors are to be believed," Major Parkinson said. "And they're still trying to poison us."

"Yes, sir," Alice said. "But at least they're not getting the infection down here."

"The lighting is keeping the virus out, for the moment," Major Parkinson said. He frowned as he studied the display. The virus was systematically wiping out the internal sensors as well as trying to hack the datanet, although that—thankfully—was failing miserably. "But we're going to need to think of something desperate."

Alice nodded. "We could go out on the hull, blow the shuttles and seals off ourselves..."

She checked her squad, quickly. She'd lost two men—and a third *might* have survived long enough to be infected—but they were still ready and able to fight. Perhaps there *had* been some sense in wearing the shipboard armour after all. They could get out onto the hull without changing into shipsuits or battlesuits first. The aliens weren't wearing suits, as far as anyone could tell. They'd have to change themselves if they wanted to wage war in a vacuum.

"Good thinking," Major Parkinson said. His lips twitched into a humourless smile, suggesting he had something else in mind. "But I think I have another idea."

• • •

"They're just not breaking into the encrypted datanet," Arthur said. "But they're still trying."

"As long as they're wasting time," Stephen said. The virus might not be sentient, as humanity understood the term, but it was terrifyingly intelligent. A brute-force approach to cracking the datanet might just work, particularly if the virus had had a chance to practice on another human-designed datacore first. "Cut out the entire section if there's even a *chance* it will hack the network."

He leaned back in his chair, feeling useless. His crew were fighting for their lives, inside and outside the ship, and there was literally nothing he could do about it. There was no point in giving orders, not when his ship's weapons and defences had been worn to a nub. The only thing he could do was wait and see what happened. His fingers twitched over the console, a nagging reminder that he might have to trigger the self-destruct and blow up his own ship before she could fall into enemy hands. Cold logic told him he had time, but—in truth—he didn't really believe it.

His console bleeped. "Captain, this is Parkinson. I want your permission to try something dangerous. And desperate."

Stephen frowned. "What do you have in mind?"

"I think we should test a theory," Parkinson said. He outlined his idea. "And if we're right, we might just be able to really hurt the bastards."

"Do it," Stephen said.

. . .

"This strikes me as silly," Hammersmith said. "Are you sure it is going to work?"

"No," Alice said. She sprayed herself with the aerosol, trying not to think too hard about its contents. Her skin crawled, even though she knew that every last inch of her body was covered in armour. "But do you have a better idea?"

"No," Hammersmith said. "I just feel a little exposed."

Alice nodded in understanding. The remainder of the defenders had retreated back into the interior, leaving her and her squad of volunteers alone. She couldn't help feeling exposed as the attackers advanced towards them, alerts flashing up in front of her eyes as the sensors registered the presence of viral particles in the air. The lighting was still keeping the virus from spreading much further—and hopefully reducing its ability to keep its host-bodies connected—but she knew that wouldn't last. The oncoming force was smashing *Invincible's* internal lighting as well as her internal sensors.

If nothing else, we'll go down in the history books, she thought, in a moment of gallows humour. *Probably under the heading of 'how not to do it.'*

She tensed as the first of the humanoids came into view, weapons at the ready. Every instinct told her to raise her rifle and blow the alien to hell, all the more so as the alien was nothing more than a mindless slave, but she kept her weapon firmly at her side. The alien kept moving, walking right into the aerosol spray. Alice prayed, silently, that the alien would find the smell convincing. If not, they had practically signed their own death warrants. The boarders would have no trouble wiping them out before turning their attention to the rest of the crew.

Sweat trickled down her back as the alien looked at the marines, then continued on down the corridor. A handful of other aliens followed, escorted by a giant blob. Alice felt her stomach churn as she looked at the creature, swallowing hard to keep from being sick inside her helmet. She'd seen horrors, she'd seen the worst that humanity could and did do to its own kind, but *this* was a pulsating alien horror beyond human understanding. It was all she could do to force her legs to move, making her way up the corridor before the boarders could insist on checking their credentials. No one was sure *what* would happen if they failed to make a connection, but Alice was sure that it would end with them being infected. The virus would certainly be suspicious if they failed to communicate when asked.

She tongued her mouthpiece as they slipped back towards the airlock where they'd first engaged the enemy. "We're in," she breathed, hoping that the virus was incapable of detecting the microburst transmission. It wasn't clear if an infected person could send a message, particularly now the virus had adapted itself to infect humans. It certainly seemed to prefer to render its victims effectively comatose until it had taken over their bodies and—presumably—accessed their memories. "We're on our way to the shuttles now."

The sense of being somewhere *alien* grew stronger as they reached the airlock, even though there was nothing *visibly* different apart from a faint haze in the air. She could practically *feel* the virus pulsing beside her, its thoughts passing through the contaminated atmosphere…she told herself, firmly, that she was imagining it. They slipped through the airlock and stepped into the first compartment, where the aliens had melted their way into the ship. A steady stream of yellow liquid was splashing into the section. As she watched, a new blob oozed out of the muck and started to wobble towards the airlock. It was all she could do not to blow it away on sight.

"Get ready," she ordered, as she unhooked a grenade from her belt. The other teams were in position. "Now!"

She hurled the grenade up and into the alien shuttle. There was a tiny pause, just long enough for her to wonder what had gone wrong, then the alien shuttle exploded. The compartment started to vent a moment later, the yellow liquid bubbling furiously as it was sucked off the ground and dragged through the tear in the hull. Alice triggered her magnetic boots as the pull grew stronger, smirking at just how they'd managed to turn the virus's advantages into liabilities. It had pumped poisonous air into the hull, relying on the viral particles to guide their forces through the ship, but now that air was streaming into vacuum. She doubted any of the host-bodies would have time to don suits before it was too late.

Her communicator bleeped. "The entire infected section is venting," Parkinson said, delightedly. "We have the remainder of the ship sealed off."

Alice nodded, resisting the urge to giggle as a blob—already half-frozen—flew past her and out into space. The virus couldn't do *anything* about the scent-spray, not unless it wanted to restrict its options still further. It was going to have to check and recheck every host-body, time and time again… she snickered, helplessly. The delays would mount up until the virus was doing nothing, but making sure it could still tell the difference between a host-body and someone who had sprayed themselves with alien scent. She doubted it would stop the war—she was sure the virus would find other ways to reach its targets—yet it would give humanity time to find new ways to fight back. The virus's days were numbered.

Sure, a pessimistic voice said, at the back of her head. It sounded like her father. *Unless it finds a way to get us first.*

. . .

"We think we have the entire boarding party wiped out now," Major Parkinson said, over the datanet. "I would suggest that we keep the section in vacuum, at least until we have a chance to repair the lighting and take out any remaining traces of the virus."

"See to it," Stephen ordered. *Invincible* was safe, for the moment. The virus's escort carriers had recovered their starfighters and faded back into cloak, as soon as they'd realised the boarding operation had failed. "Can we recall the starfighters?"

"None of the launch tubes were infected," Major Parkinson said. "The boarders never got close to them."

Stephen allowed himself a moment of relief. "We'll do that now," he said. "And...and tell your men I said *well done*."

He closed the connection, then snapped out a set of orders. "Commander Newcomb, recall the starfighters. Tactical, step down the active sensors and take us back into cloak. Helm, alter course. We have to break contact before they come after us again."

"Aye, sir," Sonia said.

Stephen resisted the urge to rub his eyes—or yawn—as everything threatened to catch up with him. In hindsight, he should have gone to his ready room and caught a nap before the shit hit the fan, although he'd had no way to know they'd be ambushed. Now, he'd have to make sure that repair work was well underway before he dared return to his cabin. He whispered a curse as the first set of post-battle reports started to appear. His starboard hull had practically been swept clear of sensor blisters and point defence weapons.

And the rest of the flotilla took a battering too, he thought. Almost all of his remaining ships had taken some damage...he kicked himself, mentally, for not ordering them to scatter before the engagement had truly begun. They had information the human race desperately needed, but it would be useless if they failed to get it home. *It would have been a great deal worse if they hadn't been focusing on us.*

"Tactical, prepare to deploy a decoy drone programmed to mimic our previous course and speed," he ordered, as *Invincible* carefully altered course. If they were lucky, a starship tracking them with passive sensors wouldn't notice the course change. The virus had been very lucky to keep the sensor lock long enough to set up an ambush. "And see if you can get a lock on our shadow."

"Aye, sir," Arthur said. He didn't sound hopeful. The enemy ship wouldn't be radiating much, if anything, or she would have been spotted well before the ambush. And Arthur couldn't bring up *Invincible's* active sensors again without betraying their location to every passive sensor in the system. "The decoy drone is ready to launch."

"Launch," Stephen ordered. It was quite likely that their shadow had fallen back when the ambush had begun. The active sensors hadn't picked up any sign of its presence during the engagement, although they'd had other problems to worry about. "Helm, put some distance between us and the drone, then bring us back on a direct course for Tramline One."

And hope to hell we can get through the next two systems without running into another ambush, he added, mentally. The alien fleet was still out there, somewhere. He would have almost been happier if he'd seen the massive formation bearing down on him. *And that Falkirk hasn't already been blown to rubble.*

"Course laid in, sir," Sonia said.

Stephen put his doubts aside. "Take us out," he ordered. "Best possible speed."

CHAPTER THIRTY-EIGHT

STEPHEN HAD EXPECTED —had planned for, as best as he could— an attack as soon as *Invincible* jumped into the unnamed star system on the far side of Tramline One. The virus's fleet could have been lurking a few light-minutes from the tramline and *Invincible* wouldn't have a hope of spotting it, at least until it was far too late to avoid engagement. It was even possible, although he doubted it, that the alien fleet might have been recalled from Falkirk to intercept *Invincible*. Not knowing, he thought as his ship inched towards the next tramline, was the worst part of being in the navy. There was no way to make any solid plans until they actually had hard information—and they wouldn't have hard information until it was too late to do anything, but fight to the death.

He moved between the bridge, his cabin and the various damaged sections of his ship, inspecting the repairs, comforting the injured and burying the dead. There hadn't been as many deaths as he'd feared, during the brief boarding action, but each and every death felt as if he'd lost a piece of himself. He felt guilty for not knowing the dead men and women, even though he knew he should be grateful. They were just names and faces, not friends and family he would never see again. It was all he could do to speak their names at the brief memorial service, then bury their ashes in space. There was no way the bodies could be returned to Earth.

Which is an absurd level of paranoia, he told himself. Seven of the dead men had requested burial in space—it was practically a naval tradition—but the remainder had asked for their bodies to be returned to their families. Stephen had been prepared to take the risk of freezing the bodies, yet his orders were clear. Any bodies that might—*might*—have had the slightest contact with the virus were to be cremated. *The families will not be pleased.*

He dismissed the thought as he returned to the bridge, just in time for the crossing into Grumpy. The star system remained empty, as far as his sensors could tell, but he didn't need the boffins to tell him that that proved nothing. They'd already been ambushed once and their course was predictable, at least in general terms. Stephen had ordered a handful of course changes, just to make life difficult for anyone trying to follow the tiny flotilla, but they had to use the tramlines. It wouldn't take someone with the genius of Theodore Smith or Alan Cunningham to deduce their eventual destination. But again, there was no way to know how much the virus knew about human space. It might not know that there was a major naval base only two jumps from Alien-1.

And that base didn't exist a year ago, Stephen thought, as he handed the bridge to his XO and returned to his Ready Room. *Falkirk wasn't even accessible until after the First Interstellar War. They might have looked at the system, decided it would make an effective firebreak and didn't even bother to picket it.*

He worked his way through the reports, what few of them there were. The beancounters would probably complain that the paperwork hadn't been filed on time, but Stephen's departmental heads had more important things to do. *Invincible* was badly damaged, something the bureaucrats would never understand. Her engineers needed to repair their ship, not waste their time writing reports. The handful of notes waiting for Stephen's inspection were more than sufficient. He didn't need a detailed report to know that his ship was slowly getting better. And yet, part of him almost missed the reports. Reading them would have been a distraction from fretting over his ship and crew.

No attack materialised as the flotilla crawled across the system, slowly inching towards the second tramline. Stephen caught a few short hours of sleep, then haunted the bridge as his crew watched their sensors for the first sign of an incoming attack. The missing alien fleet nagged at Stephen's mind, demanding answers. Where *were* they? He'd gone through the sensor records from their first pass through Alien-1 personally, hoping to discover that the ships they'd seen in Alien-1 had also been the ships they'd seen in Alien-4, but it was impossible to be sure. The analysts couldn't give a definite answer either. Stephen was unsurprised. They were reluctant to make any predictions about how the virus would respond to a potential threat.

They knew we were slipping up the tramline chain towards Alien-4, Stephen thought. He was mortally certain the virus had flicker technology, although they hadn't managed to locate any flicker installations. The timing only made sense if one assumed the virus could send FTL messages from one star to another. *And they also knew what we'd find there long before we found out for ourselves.*

The intercom bleeped, once. "Captain," Newcomb said. "We are nearing the Falkirk Tramline. All sensors are clear."

Which means they might be lurking on the far side, Stephen said. His imagination was working overtime, offering too many possibilities for his peace of mind. The virus could duplicate its earlier success, if it had managed to keep track of *Invincible*. It might not even realise that Falkirk *was* a human naval base, at least not at first. He found it impossible to believe that the virus was so intent on ambushing *Invincible* that it hadn't noticed a colossal fleet orbiting Falkirk. *Or they might be up to something completely different.*

He stood. "I'm on my way," he said. "Take us across the tramline as soon as we are in position."

"Aye, sir," Newcomb said.

Stephen smiled as he pulled on his jacket and headed for the bridge. Newcomb had argued that they should send the Russians—or one of the other ships—into Falkirk first, just in case there *was* an ambush waiting for them. Stephen would have agreed, under normal circumstances, but

Invincible was badly damaged. They'd lost too many drive nodes for him to be *entirely* confident that he could restart the drive, if something went badly wrong while they were trying to slow the ship. *That* would be a complete disaster. There was no way he could take the risk.

He stepped onto the bridge and took his chair, inspecting the display as the final seconds ticked away. Local space was clear, as far as they could tell. There *should* be a picket from Falkirk somewhere in the system, unless plans had changed after *Invincible* had departed for viral space, but none of their sensors had located the cloaked ship. Stephen hoped that Admiral Weisskopf would have had at least *some* warning of an incoming attack, although it was impossible to be sure. A cunning opponent would have duplicated *Invincible's* course to minimise the risks of detection.

And we know the virus can be cunning, he thought. *It may not think like us, but it is far from stupid.*

"Jump in five seconds," Sonia said. "Four...three..."

Stephen felt his stomach heave as *Invincible* crossed the tramline. It felt, just for a second, as though he'd been punched in the chest. Someone vomited behind him, badly. He didn't look round to see who it was as Newcomb snapped orders, arranging for the stricken officer to be relieved. The remainder of the bridge crew looked pale, gasping for breath, but they were already recovering. They were young, he reminded himself. And the phantom pain rarely lasted more than a few seconds.

He turned his attention to the display as it rebooted. The primary star and a handful of planets blinked into existence, followed by a number of energy signatures. He cursed the light-speed delay under his breath as more and more data flowed into the sensors, reminding himself—again—that almost everything he was seeing was out of date. The planets might be in predictable locations—it wasn't as if the geography of the star system was going to be rearranged on a whim—but any starships and industrial nodes might already have changed position. It was impossible to be sure of anything...

"Set course for Falkirk," he ordered, once the remainder of the flotilla had confirmed their safe arrival. "Communications, prepare to…"

"Captain," Alison said. "I'm picking up multiple energy signatures! There's a battle going on!"

"Red alert," Stephen snapped, as new icons flared into life. "All hands to battlestations! I say again, all hands to battlestations!"

He leaned forward, studying the display. It was hard to be certain—he cursed the time delay, once again—but it looked as through the virus's fleet had passed through the tramline and headed straight for Falkirk. It wasn't a bad tactic, part of his mind noted. Admiral Weisskopf could hardly afford to keep his distance from the aliens when he had to defend the planet and its massive orbital installations. The virus had forced him into an engagement that probably favoured the alien fleet.

The virus can either take out the installations or grind down the combined fleet, Stephen thought. The virus seemed to have a slight edge in ships, although not enough to convince Admiral Weisskopf to break contact and escape. *And it comes out ahead whatever happens.*

He thought, fast. *Invincible* alone wouldn't change the balance of power, even if she'd been in perfect condition. Her full complement of starfighters—and the weapons embedded on her hull—really wouldn't make *that* much difference. And yet, he couldn't afford to simply sneak around the engagement and make his slow way to the tramline. There wasn't a repair yard for several transits towards Earth. Losing a single drive node would leave them stranded in interplanetary space.

"Captain, the Russians are requesting orders," Lieutenant Thomas Morse said. "The other ships are linking into our datanet."

"Order them to remain under cloak," Stephen said. "*Magellan* is to head directly for the tramline and return to the nearest naval base, avoiding all contact with the alien fleet; the freighters are to go into hiding and wait. The remainder of the ships are to escort us."

"They're acknowledging," Morse said. He paused. "Captain Shaw requests permission to remain with the flotilla."

"Denied," Stephen said. *Magellan* was armed, but only a lunatic would take a survey ship into a fleet action. Besides, the Admiralty needed to know what *Invincible* had discovered during her mission. *Magellan* could carry word back to Earth, freeing up the military ships to do what they did best. "*Magellan* is to depart at once."

He took a breath as *Magellan* vanished from the datanet. Captain Shaw would not be pleased—and *someone* would make comments about Lack of Moral Fibre, he was sure—but she had her orders. The Admiralty wouldn't blame her for following them. He smiled, feeling oddly free. They no longer needed to worry about getting word home. Captain Shaw and her crew would have no trouble evading the aliens and returning to Earth.

"Helm, take us towards the alien fleet," he ordered. "Take us right up their blind spot."

"Aye, Captain," Sonia said.

Stephen took a breath. The virus had reacted badly to threats from the rear before—if, of course, the analysts were right. There was a good chance that *Invincible*—and her remaining sensor decoys—would give the virus one hell of a fright if the ship suddenly appeared behind them, weapons at the ready. It would certainly need a few moments to adapt to the new reality. Stephen didn't care if it really was one entity or a cluster of minds linked together by a common purpose. Having to rely on radio and laser transmissions would slow it down enough for Admiral Weisskopf's forces to take the advantage.

I hope, Stephen thought, as he keyed his console. The data was slowly starting to harden up as the range closed. The time-delay would no longer be a factor by the time they actually engaged the enemy. *If they think we're trying to trick them, again, they'll ignore us.*

He toyed with the approach vectors for a long moment, trying to find the best option...but, no matter what he tried, he knew it would be a desperate gamble. The virus would have a chance to retreat—his training rebelled against the thought of *deliberately* leaving a possible escape vector open—yet if it chose to continue the fight instead...Stephen had no illusions about the outcome. They'd be too close to the alien battleships to escape. *Invincible* might win Admiral Weisskopf a few precious moments, but it would come at the cost of her utter destruction. A battleship might survive the maelstrom the virus would unleash long enough to escape; *Invincible*, despite her armour plating, wouldn't stand a chance.

But we may buy the admiral a chance to win the engagement, Stephen thought. It was growing increasingly clear that the two sides were fairly evenly matched. A single shift in the balance of power might be enough to give Admiral Weisskopf a chance to win outright, although it would come at a cost. *He could win the battle and yet discover that it costs him so much that we lose the war.*

"Captain," Arthur said. "We will enter engagement range in seven minutes."

Stephen nodded, curtly. The alien fleet was surrounded by so much electronic noise that he found it hard to believe that they'd spot a cloaked ship, even though they'd brought their active sensors online long ago. They'd be watching the combined fleet, he thought; Admiral Weisskopf was spending missiles like water, combining them with starfighter strikes to force the virus to keep its distance. They wouldn't want a missile to sneak through their defences and slam home, not when it might do real damage. A pair of their fleet carriers already looked as though they'd been through the wars.

"If we reach Point Alpha without being detected, open fire," he ordered. "If they see us, open fire without waiting for orders."

"Aye, sir," Arthur said.

Stephen took a long breath, feeling his heart pounding as the range closed sharply. *Invincible* was designed to fight as well as merely launch starfighters—she was no fleet carrier, unable to risk exchanging blows with a mere cruiser or destroyer—but she'd never been intended to go toe-to-toe with an entire fleet of battleships. The virus might just decide to scratch an itch rather than concentrate on the combined fleet. Not, he supposed, that it mattered. The virus would have every opportunity to blow *Invincible* out of space even if it didn't bother to order its ships to alter course. There was no way to avoid a knife-range engagement now.

"Entering engagement range in two minutes," Arthur said. "All weapons are free, ready to fire; targeting sensors locked, ready to fire."

"Our remaining starfighters are ready to launch," Newcomb added. "They'll do the best they can."

"Good," Stephen said. Seventeen starfighters wouldn't make *that* much of a difference, but he'd take what he could get. "Communications, inform Admiral Weisskopf of our presence as soon as we open fire. Dump a complete copy of our logs and sensor records into the fleet datanet."

Just in case Captain Shaw doesn't make it, he thought, grimly. *We have to hope that one ship gets home if the fleet is ordered to scatter.*

The display flashed red. "They have us," Arthur said. "Firing...now!"

"Launch all starfighters," Stephen snapped. *Invincible's* mass drivers were already pumping projectiles into the alien rear, aiming them right into the blind spot. They'd have drones to cover the gaps in their sensor network—it was quite likely that one of the drones had spotted their approach—but they'd still have problems deploying counterbattery fire. "And activate the decoys!"

"Aye, Captain," Newcomb said. "Starfighters are launching now."

Stephen studied the alien formation carefully, watching for signs of disorganisation. Their smaller ships were already altering course, bringing their point defence weapons to bear on the tidal wave of incoming projectiles; the bigger ships, it seemed, weren't about to allow themselves to be bullied into altering their plans. Stephen hoped they were proceeding on inertia. It would take some time for a *human* to put together a coherent response to an unexpected threat in the rear, particularly when there was still a major enemy fleet in front of them. Stephen leaned forward, silently willing the virus to take the escape vector. It could break contact at any moment if it wished...

"Picking up a signal from *Texas*," Morse said. "Admiral Weisskopf is welcoming us to the party. I'm transferring the data dump now."

"Good," Stephen said.

He gritted his teeth as the battle continued to evolve. The virus wasn't panicking, damn it. It was carefully redirecting a handful of smaller ships towards *Invincible*, forcing Stephen to choose between letting them intercept his mass driver projectiles or redirecting his fire to take them out. The virus was being devious, he had to admit. There was no way Stephen could let an enemy starship into knife-range. The bastard might try to ram, destroying both ships in a single tearing explosion.

"Tactical, engage the smaller ships with our plasma cannons," Stephen ordered. It was unlikely that any of the alien destroyers carried enough armour to survive such a pounding, certainly not long enough to close with *Invincible*. "Continue engaging the bigger ships with mass drivers."

"Aye, sir," Arthur said. The display updated again as the plasma cannons opened fire, the first salvo blowing an enemy frigate into vapour. "Engaging...now."

"Good shot," Stephen said. The virus shouldn't have been surprised. It had seen *Invincible* in action before. "Continue firing."

"Captain," Alison said. She sounded shocked, her voice stumbling over the words as if she didn't believe what she was saying. "I...Captain, one of those ships is *human*. It's *Dezhnev!*"

CHAPTER THIRTY-NINE

"CONFIRM," CAPTAIN PAVEL KAMINOV ORDERED. "That is *Dezhnev?*"

He ignored the *zampolit's* snort as he bent over his console, examining the sensor readings for himself. He'd almost allowed himself to forget his secret orders as the flotilla headed further into enemy space, quietly conceding—at least in the privacy of his own mind—that *Dezhnev* had been captured and taken to an alien facility somewhere far from the combat zone. It wasn't as if a *human* navy would put a captured alien starship in harm's way. The ship would be taken somewhere secret and carefully dissected until it had revealed all of its secrets.

But there was no mistake. It *was Dezhnev*, heading straight towards the tiny flotilla. Pavel had no doubt that the ship was infected. He cursed his superiors and their power games under his breath. Captain Danilovich was a good man—had *been* a good man—but he hadn't known what he was facing until it was too late. Mother Russia had made a terrible mistake in ordering Danilovich to open communications with the virus. Pavel didn't need the GRU's assessment to know that Danilovich hadn't managed to destroy his datacores before the ship was overwhelmed. The simple fact that *Dezhnev* was operating was proof of *that.*

"We have our orders," the *zampolit* hissed. "Carry them out, Captain."

"I will," Pavel said, swallowing his anger. His orders were clear. *Dezhnev* was to be recaptured or unceremoniously destroyed. And yet, he also had orders from Captain Shields to hold position and cover *Invincible*. It was hard to decide what set of orders had priority. *Yuriy Ivanov* would not survive long enough to kill *Dezhnev* if *Invincible* was blown out of space. "Let them come closer to us."

He raised his voice. "Tactical, prepare to target *Dezhnev*. I want her crippled, then destroyed."

"Aye, sir."

"We have our orders," the *zampolit* repeated. "Or do you want to be relieved of command?"

"They're coming right at us," Pavel pointed out. The aliens were swinging more and more smaller ships towards the rear, towards *Invincible* and her three remaining escorts. "There's no need to break formation when they're giving us everything we want."

He kept his face impassive as the enemy formation took shape. *Dezhnev* was a mere destroyer, although her designers had crammed a formidable array of weapons into her armoured hull. There was no way she could stand up to *Yuriy Ivanov* for more than a few seconds. But, with her escorts, she might just be able to survive...Pavel cursed, once again, as the implications dawned on him. He *had* to destroy the ship. The British—or the Americans— might try to board her, convinced they were actually *helping*. Pavel had no illusions about what would happen if the Great Powers discovered the truth. Mother Russia would be shunned for the rest of time.

"Captain, the enemy formation is opening fire," the sensor officer said. "They're targeting the entire flotilla."

And forcing us to worry about defending ourselves as well as covering the carrier, Pavel thought. The virus seemed unsure about the ghost fleet—it presumably suspected the truth, even if it didn't *know*—but there were enough missiles coming towards the flotilla to give the ships a very hard time. *They want to break up our formation.*

"Continue engaging with point defence," he ordered. "And bring our missiles and main guns to bear on *Dezhnev*."

The thought cost him a pang. It wouldn't be the first time the Russian Navy had fired on a ship that had fallen into enemy hands, but *Dezhnev* was no defector. Her captain and crew had followed orders right up until the virus had turned them into host-bodies. They deserved better than to die at Pavel's hands, although they might consider death a mercy. There was no way to be sure if they were still conscious, still aware of what was happening to them. He wasn't sure he wanted to know.

"Weapons locked, Captain," the tactical officer said.

"Fire," Pavel ordered.

• • •

"Captain, *Yuriy Ivanov* has opened fire on *Dezhnev*," Alison reported. "The infected ship is altering course."

"But still coming towards us," Stephen said. He'd feared the worst, when it had become clear that *Dezhnev* was badly overdue, but he'd hoped for the best. It was clear, now, that *Dezhnev* had been infected. She wouldn't have been fighting alongside the alien fleet—and against her fellow humans—unless Captain Danilovich was no longer in control. "Engage her with our main guns if she tries to ram us."

"Aye, Captain," Arthur said.

Stephen gritted his teeth as a dull rumble echoed through his ship. There were so many missiles coming at *Invincible* that it was inevitable that one or more of them would get through his weakened point defence. The virus didn't seem inclined to dispatch starfighters to weaken his defences still further—the enemy starfighters were engaging the combined fleet's starfighters—but it hardly mattered. Alerts flashed up in front of him, confirming that the nuclear strike had taken out a number of point defence nodes. The next salvo would have an easier time of it when they slipped into attack range. His defences were weakening by the minute.

He watched an alien destroyer explode as it strayed too close to his plasma cannons, its escort firing a salvo of missiles before turning away to close on *Daring*. The two destroyers converged rapidly, their weapons tearing into each other before the alien ship made a tiny—but significant—course alteration. Stephen reached for his console, knowing that it was already too late. The alien destroyer rammed its human counterpart and both ships vanished from the display.

Tearing away our point defence, Stephen thought. *Daring* hadn't been *that* formidable, not compared to *Invincible*, but she'd mounted enough point defence to make it harder for the enemy to strike at the carrier. The virus seemed intent on isolating and then destroying *Invincible*, even though it was also engaging the combined fleet. *Does it think we still haven't had a chance to tell everyone what we found?*

Another shudder ran through the ship. "Direct hit, Launch Bay Two," Newcomb reported, grimly. "She'll need a shipyard before we can launch starfighters from the starboard tubes again."

"Understood," Stephen said. The range to the alien battleships was closing rapidly. They seemed unsure what to do—the virus was moving its ships around, but no clear pattern had emerged—yet there was no way to avoid an engagement. "We'll worry about it later."

He studied the display as more missiles roared towards his ship, followed by the enemy's lighter units. *Dezhnev* was hanging back, covered by her new comrades; she seemed more intent on taunting *Yuriy Ivanov* than taking the offensive. Stephen wondered what the aliens were thinking as their ships altered course again, holding the range open. There was nothing to be gained by trying to force *Invincible* to engage them with plasma cannons. It wasn't as if they could run out of plasma!

Unless we lose power, Stephen thought. *But if that happened, we'd be dead anyway.*

The enemy formation lurched, suddenly. Stephen watched as the alien battleships and fleet carriers altered course, slipping onto the escape vector. The combined fleet didn't hesitate to give chase, firing wave after wave of missiles even as the alien starfighters reversed course and raced back to their motherships. Stephen allowed himself a moment of relief, even as the damage continued to mount. His ship would still pass within engagement range of the alien battleships, and she might well be destroyed before she could escape, but the virus had conceded the field. The attack on Falkirk had failed. Stephen had no doubt that the virus would gather reinforcements and try again, but for now the system was safe. Admiral Weisskopf would have plenty of time to repair and rearm his ships before the next engagement began.

"The flag is sending us orders, sir," Morse said. "We're to break off."

"Which may be tricky," Stephen said. *Invincible* had lost too many drive nodes. She couldn't hope to avoid engagement by altering course. "Inform them that we will endeavour to do our best."

He felt his heart sink as the smaller alien ships turned once again, heading straight towards *Invincible*. The matter was about to become academic. The plasma weapons opened fire, blasting two of the alien ships out of space as the range started to close once again, but the remainder of the ships kept coming. Stephen knew, with a cold certainty that chilled him to the bone, that they intended to ram. It would be a poor trade, for him. The virus could replace all the lighter ships well before the Royal Navy could replace *Invincible*.

"Continue firing," he ordered. He opened his mouth to order his crew to abandon ship, then closed it again. The stream of updates from the combined fleet had made it clear that the virus was targeting lifepods. "Try to disable their drives."

"Aye, sir," Arthur said.

Invincible shook, violently. Stephen felt the gravity field flicker, just for a second, as the compensators fought to keep the sudden shift from turning the crew into jelly. The alerts started to blur into a constant liturgy of disaster; two more drive nodes gone, point defence weapons knocked out, a datacore isolated from the datanet, a series of hull breaches that were venting atmosphere into space…it was only a matter of time before *Invincible* was destroyed. He wondered, morbidly, what the Admiralty would say. Had he lived and died in the finest traditions of the Royal Navy? Or had he made a series of tactical errors which had eventually resulted in the destruction of his ship?

"Damage report, all sectors," Newcomb said. "The drive field is failing."

"Understood," Stephen said. They'd be a sitting duck, once the drive field was gone. "Tell engineering…"

"They're closing to ram," Alison said.

"Main power is failing," Arthur said. "Plasma containment chambers are going offline!"

"Reroute emergency power to the plasma cannons," Stephen ordered. It might buy them a few more minutes of life. "And don't let them get close to us!"

"Aye, Captain," Arthur said.

But Stephen knew, all too well, that it was an order his crew wouldn't be able to carry out.

He watched, grimly, as the enemy fleet approached. Admiral Weisskopf had dispatched two wings of starfighters to cover *Invincible*, but it was starting to look as if they weren't going to be able to get there in time to make a difference. His remaining starfighters were harrying the alien ships as best as they could, yet it wasn't enough. He closed his eyes for a long moment, fighting down the urge to just give up. They'd done well—he knew they'd done well—but it wasn't enough.

At least we took out their shipyard, he thought. *It will be a long time before they can resume the offensive…*

• • •

Pavel cursed under his breath as the alien fleet closed on *Invincible*. *Dezhnev* was amongst them, shielded by her fellows…he wondered, savagely, if the aliens were deliberately taunting him. It was hard to believe that the virus *wasn't* mocking them, exposing the infected ship to his fire and then yanking

Dezhnev back before she could be targeted and destroyed. The virus had learnt a great deal from the captured ship, he noted. It had improved its point defence quite significantly over the last few months.

And if they had a chance to copy the datacores, they know everything about the human sphere, Pavel thought. The scale of the disaster was almost beyond comprehension. The virus would know where to find everything from naval bases to shipyards, industrial nodes and population centres. It wouldn't need to waste time surveying the tramlines and feeling their way towards Earth. *Mother Russia cannot allow the truth to come out, not now. It would be the end.*

"Put us between *Invincible* and her foes," he ordered, sharply. The carrier was streaming plasma as well as atmosphere. Cold logic suggested he should alter course and escape—*Yuriy Ivanov* could evade the alien ships if she didn't have to keep station with *Invincible*—but he couldn't abandon the carrier. Besides, it would give him the best chance of finally taking out the infected ship. "Target the incoming ships and fire."

The aliens didn't slow down as they closed on *Invincible*. They didn't even pay much attention to *Yuriy Ivanov*, save for spitting a handful of plasma bolts in her direction as the range closed. The damage started to mount up rapidly. Pavel realised, grimly, that the virus knew precisely where to target its weapons. It might be determined to ram the carrier, just to make sure the carrier was actually destroyed, but it was weakening his ship. *Dezhnev* and her companions might just manage to get into ramming range after all.

The lights dimmed, just for a second. "Direct hit, port drive node," the tactical officer snapped. Another shudder ran through the ship. "Fusion One is offline."

"Offline?" The *zampolit* sounded terrified. "What do you mean, offline?"

"Shift to emergency power mode," Pavel said, strapping himself to his chair. The gravity wouldn't last much longer. Theoretically, *Yuriy Ivanov* could fly and fight on a single power core; practically, he suspected that it wouldn't be long before he lost Fusion Two and found himself trying to power his ship on batteries. "Tactical…"

"Sir, *Dezhnev* is closing to ram *Invincible*," the tactical officer said. "She'll hit the carrier and take her out."

"Good," the *zampolit* said.

Pavel hesitated. *Dezhnev* would be destroyed too, ensuring that all evidence of Russia's misbehaviour would be lost. The other Great Powers might suspect, but they'd have no solid proof. He didn't have to do anything. No one would question the infected ship breaking through the flotilla's defences, such as they were, and slamming into the carrier. *Yuriy Ivanov* had done all she reasonably could...

...But the carrier could be repaired, given time. *Yuriy Ivanov* could be replaced fairly quickly, if the navy thought it was worth building more of her class. *Invincible*, on the other hand, could not. And besides, any questions about Russia's involvement would be buried forever if *Yuriy Ivanov* gave her life to save *Invincible*...

"Move to intercept," Pavel ordered. He ignored the *zampolit's* squawk of horror as the wretched little man realised they were all about to die. "Ramming speed."

"Aye, Captain," the helmsman said. "Intercept in five...four..."

• • •

Yuriy Ivanov slammed into *Dezhnev*, bare seconds before she could strike *Invincible*. Both ships exploded, violently. There were no survivors.

• • •

"Captain, *Yuriy Ivanov* rammed *Dezhnev*," Arthur reported. "Both ships are gone."

Stephen sucked in his breath. "And the remainder of the enemy fleet?"

"Breaking off, on escape vector," Alison said. "They're not even *trying* to engage as they pass."

"I think we won," Newcomb said, quietly.

"Barely," Stephen said. They'd survived through sheer luck—and Captain Kaminov's sacrifice. The Russian had been very reserved, even after the heat of combat had forged the flotilla into a single unit, but he'd given his life for *Invincible*. He promised himself, silently, that the Russians would be remembered. "Shut down the drives and recall the remaining fighters, then hold position. We'll need to beg for help from the fleet base."

"I'm sure they'll send us everything we need," Newcomb said.

"Perhaps," Stephen said. It would take months, even in a shipyard, to restore *Invincible* to fighting trim. Admiral Weisskopf would want to focus on ships that could be repaired fairly quickly first. "They might just give us a tow back to Earth."

"Captain," Morse said. "Admiral Weisskopf is hailing you."

"Put him through," Stephen ordered.

Admiral Weisskopf's dark face appeared in front of him. "Captain," he said. "Thank you for your intervention. Your arrival saved us from a very tight situation indeed."

"You're welcome, sir," Stephen said. The analysts would spend the next few months trying to determine, rather pointlessly in his opinion, if *Invincible's* arrival had been truly decisive or not. Admiral Weisskopf *might* have won the battle on his own. "That said, we do know the virus had other ships at its disposal."

"It would be surprising if it did not," Admiral Weisskopf said. He turned his gaze towards his tactical display. "We may face another attack within hours."

"Yes, sir," Stephen said.

"I'll do what I can for your ship," Admiral Weisskopf said. "But I think the best we *can* do is send you straight home."

"I guessed as much," Stephen said. "Did the captured ship come through?"

"It did," Admiral Weisskopf said. "And there will be a *lot* of prize money when you get back home."

Stephen kept his face impassive. There was enough money in his trust fund to keep him from being *poor*, even if he never worked another day in his life. It had been a shock to discover that some of his fellow cadets at the academy actually had to *work* for a living. He made a mental note to turn down his share of the prize money, even though he was technically entitled to a goodly share. His crew would find a far better use for it.

And I don't want them praying for wounds to be distributed like prize money either, he thought, wryly. The old joke had made a comeback along with prize money itself. *That would be awkward.*

"I'll speak with you again, before you go," Admiral Weisskopf said. "I will probably need to discuss your report with you at some point. I have a feeling it will make interesting reading. And, if we don't have a chance to meet in person, please know that you have my gratitude."

"Thank you, sir," Stephen said. "It was a pleasure."

Admiral Weisskopf's face vanished from the display. "Commander Newcomb," Stephen said. "Begin preparations to return to Earth."

"Aye, sir."

CHAPTER FORTY

THE HOUSE LOOKED AS IF IT HAD COME RIGHT OUT of an urban soap opera, complete with the neatly-trimmed garden, the knee-high wall, metal gate and neighbourhood watch sign hanging from the window. It was the sort of place, Richard thought, that would be very warm and welcoming to any newcomers, as long as they were the *right* sort of people with the *right* sort of attitudes. Any strangers in the area would be quickly noted—he was sure he'd spotted curtains twitching as they'd pulled up outside the house—and anyone who stayed too long might find themselves being asked pointed questions by the police. It was safe enough, but it wasn't the sort of place *he* would have wanted to grow up. There was something faintly sinister about the suburb.

The men go off to work and the women compete amongst themselves, he thought, as he climbed out of the car. The air was fresh and clear. He could hear the sound of schoolchildren playing in the nearby park. *And the children know better than to put a foot out of line.*

"Nice place," Monica said. She stretched, brushing down her dress whites. "But a little too drab for me."

Richard nodded, curtly. The houses were all practically identical. There were no major differences, as far as he could tell, and only a handful of minor ones. It was easy to believe that someone was busy dictating everything from the precise length of the grass to exactly how many kids each couple could have, even though it sounded stupid. Maybe the residents were too scared to express their individuality. Or maybe they were just boring middle-class couples who lacked the money and freedom to make a splash.

He opened the gate and led the way up to the front door, feeling a twinge of nervousness as he noted the black ribbon in the front window. *That* was unique, but no one would have dared complain about it. Someone had died, someone had died serving their country. No one, not even the prissiest social climber in the region, would bitch and moan about remembering the dead. The community would have rallied around the survivors and the local church would probably have already held a remembrance service, even if the dead woman hadn't been a member. It was the right thing to do.

The door opened as he approached, revealing an older dark-skinned woman with penetrating black eyes. Richard felt a pang of sympathy for her, one that had nothing to do with the loss of a child. It couldn't have been easy, growing up in Middle England with dark skin and mixed-race children. She would have found the locals looking sideways at her, at least until she proved herself. It had been nearly two hundred years since the Troubles, but social attitudes died hard. The hell of it was that Mrs Alibis's family had been loyalists for generations.

"Mrs Alibis?" Richard hesitated, unsure what to say. "I was your daughter's commanding officer. I came to pay my respects."

"Aye, you'd better come in," Mrs Alibis said. She stepped aside, inviting them to cross the threshold. "I'm glad someone came."

"Captain Shields may be able to visit later," Richard said. The family would have been visited by the military's bereavement service, but none of the visitors would have known Samra Alibis personally. "However, he has been very busy."

"So I heard," Mrs Alibis said. She led them into a small sitting room. A large picture of Samra, draped in black, rested on the mantelpiece. Beside it, there were a pair of newspaper clippings. One honoured Samra, one honoured Captain Lady Susan Onarina. "Would you like tea? Or coffee?"

"Tea would be lovely," Richard said, as he sat on the sofa and looked around. The room felt a little *too* formal to be real. There was nothing within sight that suggested that the family was anything other than English. "I wanted to express our condolences."

"That would be nice," Mrs Alibis said, as she stepped into the kitchen. There was a hard edge to her voice. "Can you bring her back to life?"

Richard said nothing, honestly unsure how to proceed. Beside him, Monica shifted uncomfortably. He thought he knew what he could have said to a friend's parents or partner, but a grieving mother? What could one say to make the pain go away? Nothing came to mind. Samra had been a much-loved daughter, not a monster. It was unfair to expect her mother to be anything, but saddened about Samra's death.

"She was the life and soul of the party," Monica said, as Mrs Alibis returned with three china cups of tea. "She was a good pilot and we had high hopes for her."

Mrs Alibis's lips thinned. "She wanted to find a place of her own," she said. She jerked a finger towards the wall. "The prats in school always gave her a hard time, just for being a little different. She thought the navy would give her a better chance at life. And it did, until she died."

"She will be remembered," Richard said.

"Maybe," Mrs Alibis said. "My husband is dead. I have no more children. And all I can do is sit here and wait to die. I had hoped..."

She looked down at the carpet, hiding her eyes. "I had hoped...I urged her to get married, but she kept saying no. All those suitable boys...she didn't like them. She wanted to be a captain, she said. Or maybe she'd go to one of the colony worlds, where willing hands are more important than skin colour and anything else. And instead, she's dead."

Richard shifted, awkwardly. "She might well have saved the ship."

"Hah," Mrs Alibis said. "I read the newspaper reports, young man. She died for nothing."

"I wouldn't believe anything written in the newspapers," Richard said, making a mental note to check on what the reporters had actually said. There hadn't been any reporters assigned to *Invincible*, as far as he knew. It was pretty much a guarantee that whoever had written the story didn't have the slightest idea what had really happened. "I was there. She died bravely and well."

Mrs Alibis looked up at him. "Why didn't you die in her place?"

Richard had no answer. No, he *did* have an answer, but it would be no comfort to a grieving mother. Samra had lacked experience. She'd lacked instincts that could only be developed through *real* combat. And while she'd done well in simulations, she had never been truly tested until she'd taken her starfighter into combat for the first time. She had never developed the edge that would have kept her alive.

He found himself unsure what to say, torn between the urge to stay and a growing desire to simply leave. What *could* he say? He would have traded his life for Samra's without a second thought, but that wasn't an option. Perhaps, he admitted privately, he would be less willing to consider it if it *was* an option.

"She died for nothing," Mrs Alibis said. "And all I have to look forward to is dying alone."

"I wish I could offer you something better," Richard said. "But there's nothing we can do."

"I hope it *was* worth it," Mrs Alibis said. "You got the ship home, didn't you?"

"We did," Richard said. He took a breath. "We would have died without her, Mrs Alibis. And that's the truth."

"I hope so," Mrs Alibis said. She cleared her throat, loudly. "Was there anything else?"

"Just this," Richard said. He was surprised at Mrs Alibis's rudeness, but he didn't really blame her. "What do you want to do with her share of the prize money?"

Mrs Alibis blinked. "Prize money?"

"Samra was entitled to a share of the prize money…ah, for something classified," Richard said. He'd been warned not to discuss the captured alien ship with anyone, at least until the Great Powers decided what they wanted to tell the media. "Technically, it should go to you as her next-of-kin and…"

"Oh," Mrs Alibis said. She paused. "Keep it. Give it to the survivors. Or charity. Or pocket it yourself. I don't care. I just don't *want* it."

"Understood," Richard said. "Unclaimed prize money goes to a military charity, normally. I can have the papers sent to you…"

"Do it yourself," Mrs Alibis said. "And now…"

Richard took the hint and stood. "Thank you for seeing us," he said. "And if there's ever anything I can do for you…"

"Unless you can bring back my daughter, I doubt there's anything you can do for me." Mrs Alibis let out a shuddering gasp. "But thank you for coming. I know you meant well."

And that, Richard reflected as they made their way back to the car, sounded more like a curse than anything *reassuring*.

"Three more names to visit," Monica said. "Are you sure you want to go?"

"No," Richard said. "But we owe it to them, don't we?"

• • •

"You'll be pleased to hear that the girls are well," Jeanette Campbell said. Her holographic image paced the compartment. "And my husband is well too."

"I'm glad to hear it," Alice said, dryly. She didn't *dislike* her sister's husband, but she'd never really liked him either. "I'd come down if I could."

"Yeah," Jeanette said. "About that…is there a *reason* you can't come down? Because they had a big ceremony in London for that Russian dude and Captain Shields was there…"

"I had my duties," Alice said. The doctors had advised her not to tell any civvy about the infection. It would only upset people, particularly now the infection was very definitely dead. "I couldn't get permission to go down to the ceremony."

"A shame," Jeanette said. She giggled, but Alice knew her sister well enough to fear she knew the truth. Jeanette was not *stupid*. "And father sends his regards."

"I'm sure he does," Alice said. She shook her head. "Tell him that I still don't want to talk to him."

"You should," Jeanette said. "Particularly if"—she changed the subject, so abruptly that Alice was taken by surprise—"you know they've shut the schools? And started mandatory blood tests practically everywhere? It's pretty bad not being able to go out without having some wanker poke you with a needle and take your blood."

"It could be worse," Alice said. "How are you coping?"

"Well, the girls are wearing through my patience," Jeanette admitted. "Hubby is lucky, of course. His workplace hasn't closed. Pity, that. He'd be able to take care of the girls while I go shopping."

"And get poked with a needle everywhere you go," Alice said. Research had clearly moved on in her absence. The doctors had not only devised a sample kit, they'd put it into mass production. Jeanette—and the rest of the civvies—might bitch and moan about regular blood tests, but better that than the alternative. "Jeanette, if you ever listen to me about anything, take the threat seriously. It's worse than anything you've heard on the news."

Jeanette eyed her for a long moment. "Are you alright? I mean…"

"Sure, couldn't be better," Alice said, quickly. It was actually true. "Just listen to me for once, really. Keep the blood tests going and make sure you're careful."

"I know," Jeanette said. "But it's hard to believe, you know?"

"Yeah," Alice said. "I know."

She sighed. It had been a long time since Britain had been threatened with a disease outbreak that might bring the country to its knees. The combination of genetic engineering and advanced medical treatments had stopped a number of diseases, including the common cold, in their tracks. Even the genetically-engineered diseases hadn't been able to gain a foothold. But now, *the* virus had to be taken seriously. Alice knew, all too well, that even military-grade vaccinations wouldn't do more than slow it down. It could *not* be allowed a foothold on Earth. It would be the beginning of the end.

"I'll speak to you later," she said, softly. "Goodbye."

"Goodbye to you too," Jeanette said. "At least, until we meet again."

Her image vanished. Alice shook her head as she stood. She had orders to meet with Major Parkinson in an hour, just long enough to raise a glass to Captain Kaminov and his men with the rest of the crew. He'd saved their lives. And that meant...

We won't forget him, she promised herself. *And no one else will forget him either.*

• • •

"Well," Duncan said, as he poured two glasses of wine. "Thank God *that's* over."

Stephen scowled at his brother. The formal service had been short—the Russians had been oddly reluctant to participate, even though it was their crew that was being honoured—but *necessary*. He had no intention of allowing Captain Kaminov and his crew to be forgotten, no matter what their superiors thought. Besides, it would hardly be the first time the Royal Navy had honoured a foreign military officer. There was a brotherhood between spacers that transcended simple *politics*. And yet, the moment the service was over, Duncan had insisted on going straight back to his apartment. There had been no time to speak to anyone before they'd left.

He took refuge in crudity, hoping to tweak his brother a little. "And who pissed in your expensive glass of plonk?"

Duncan, Lord Shields, ignored the jibe. "There's quite a bit about the whole affair that doesn't quite make sense," he said. "The Russians insist on assigning *Dezhnev* to Task Force Leinster, then she vanishes somewhere in the trackless wastes of Alien-1. She's declared lost...and the Russians assign another ship, commanded by a very well connected officer, to search for her. And then, when *Dezhnev* pops up again, *Yuriy Ivanov* rams her, destroying both ships."

"And saving my life," Stephen said. "I would not be here today if *Yuriy Ivanov* hadn't rammed *Dezhnev*."

"Oh, I know," Duncan said. He took a sip of his wine. "I'm not ungrateful. But..."

He looked up. "Let me run a scenario past you. The Russians are practically bankrupt. They are spending more than they earn, which is pretty damn bad when we're talking about billions of pounds. In theory, they can make cuts; in practice, any cuts will lead to social unrest, military decline and a slow collapse. They can't depend on us or anyone else for help and even *asking* will be disastrous, if we decide to take advantage of their weakness. And so they decide to make contact with a new and potentially powerful alien race. A risk, perhaps, but one that might pay off."

"Madness," Stephen said. "The virus..."

"They didn't *know* about the virus," Duncan pointed out. "How many of the analysts are still in deep denial over the virus's mere existence? They thought they could forge an under-the-table connection to another race and...well, it blew up in their face."

Stephen frowned. "Do you have any proof?"

"No," Duncan said. "Just a chain of inferences. It could be nothing more than paranoia. But Stephen...things are changing. We have to be careful."

"Yeah," Stephen said. "*How* are they changing?"

"The reports you brought back frightened hell out of a lot of very powerful people," Duncan said. "I wasn't Lord Shields when the Tadpoles showed up, but I remember just how scared we all were after New Russia. The virus alone is an insidious threat, even without a powerful fleet. It came very close to pushing us out of Falkirk. And if what you're saying about their industrial base is accurate, Stephen, we could be out-produced and crushed within the year."

"Perhaps," Stephen said.

"They're talking about amalgamation," Duncan said, as if he hadn't heard Stephen's comment. "The Great Powers and the smaller powers—everyone with any presence in space, basically—are considering a world government, something to tie us all together. They're still working on the specifics, but there's a very good chance it will go through."

Stephen blinked. He'd studied attempts to create a supranational authority, from the League of Nations and the United Nations to the European Union and the Asian Alliance and they'd all ended badly. There was too much room for disagreement and too little trust between the various parties. In the end, they'd all died in war.

"Parliament will *never* go for it," he said. It was hard to believe that the Russians or the Chinese would go for it either. "We're talking about giving up our independence."

"It depends on what the exact terms and conditions are," Duncan said. "But yes, there is a good chance that Parliament *will* go for it."

"...Shit," Stephen said. "Are we really that desperate?"

"You're the one who brought back those reports," Duncan said. "You tell me."

His terminal bleeped. "Excuse me," he said. He stood and walked over to his desk, keying the terminal with one beefy hand. "Yes?"

"My Lord, we just received an emergency message from the Speaker of the House," his secretary said. "Falkirk has fallen. The enemy is at the gates."

Stephen felt his blood run cold. Falkirk was a mere six weeks from Earth. And, if Admiral Weisskopf's fleet had been destroyed, there was nothing standing between Falkirk and Earth for several transits. The virus could infect a dozen colony worlds...or simply keep pushing down the tramline chain towards Earth. It would be weeks before the naval bases could be reinforced. They'd already been stripped of mobile units.

He tried to tell himself that it couldn't be that bad. Admiral Weisskopf could have conducted a fighting retreat, preserving most of his mobile units. But there was no way to *know*.

Duncan met Stephen's eyes. "Yes," he said. "I think we are that desperate."

• • •

End of Book II
The *Invincible* Trilogy Will Conclude in:
The Right of the Line
Coming Soon!

APPENDIX: GLOSSARY OF UK TERMS AND SLANG

[Author's Note: I've tried to define every incident of specifically UK slang (and a handful of military phases/acronyms) in this glossary, but I can't promise to have spotted everything. If you spot something I've missed, please let me know and it will be included.]

Aggro—slang term for aggression or trouble, as in 'I don't want any aggro.'

Beasting/Beasted—military slang for anything from a chewing out by one's commander to outright corporal punishment or hazing. The latter two are now officially banned.

Beat Feet—Run, make a hasty departure.

Binned—SAS slang for a prospective recruit being kicked from the course, then returned to unit (RTU).

Boffin—Scientist

Bootnecks—slang for Royal Marines. Loosely comparable to 'Jarhead.'

Bottle—slang for nerve, as in 'lost his bottle.'

Borstal—a school/prison for young offenders.

Combined Cadet Force (CCF)—school/youth clubs for teenagers who might be interested in joining the military when they become adults.

Compo—British army slang for improvised stews and suchlike made from rations and sauces.

CSP—Combat Space Patrol.

CYA—Cover Your Ass

Donkey Wallopers—slang for the Royal Horse Artillery.

DORA—Defence of the Realm Act.

Fortnight—two weeks. (Hence the terrible pun, courtesy of the *Goon Show*, that Fort Knight cannot possibly last three weeks.)

'Get stuck into'—'start fighting.'

Head Sheds—SAS slang for senior officers.

'I should coco'—'you're damned right.'

Kip—sleep.

Levies—native troops. The Ghurkhas are the last remnants of native troops from British India.

Lorries—trucks.

Mocktail/Mocktails—non-alcoholic cocktails.

MOD—Ministry of Defence. (The UK's Pentagon.)

Order of the Garter—the highest order of chivalry (knighthood) and the third most prestigious honour (inferior only to the Victoria Cross and George Cross) in the United Kingdom. By law, there can be only twenty-four non-royal members of the order at any single time.

Panda Cola—Coke as supplied by the British Army to the troops.

RFA—Royal Fleet Auxiliary

Rumbled—discovered/spotted.

SAS—Special Air Service.

SBS—Special Boat Service

Spotted Dick—a traditional fruity sponge pudding with suet, citrus zest and currants served in thick slices with hot custard. The name always caused a snigger.

Squaddies—slang for British soldiers.

Stag—guard duty.

STUFT—'Ships Taken Up From Trade,' civilian ships requisitioned for government use.

TAB (tab/tabbing)—Tactical Advance to Battle.

Tearaway—boisterous/badly behaved child, normally a teenager.

UKADR—United Kingdom Air Defence Region.

Walt—Poser, i.e. someone who claims to have served in the military and/or a very famous regiment. There's a joke about 22 SAS being the largest regiment in the British Army—it must be, because of all the people who claim to have served in it.

Wanker—Masturbator (jerk-off). Commonly used as an insult.

Wank/Wanking—Masturbating.

Yank/Yankee—Americans

Made in United States
Orlando, FL
01 April 2024

45316115R00232